Praise for *New York Times* and *USA TODAY*
bestselling author

LORI FOSTER

"Foster writes smart, sexy, engaging characters."
—*New York Times* bestselling author Christine Feehan

"Known for her funny, sexy writing."
—*Booklist*

"Foster's latest is pure entertainment and a joy to read."
—*RT Book Reviews* on *Back in Black*

"Foster outwrites most of her peers."
—*Library Journal*

"Intense, edgy and hot. Lori Foster
delivers everything you're looking for in a romance."
—*New York Times* bestselling author Jayne Ann Krentz
on *Hard to Handle*

"Lori Foster delivers the goods."
—*Publishers Weekly*

"Tension, temptation, hot action, and hotter romance—
Lori Foster has it all! *Hard to Handle* is a knockout!"
—*New York Times* bestselling author Elizabeth Lowell

Dear Readers,

I've launched into a new series of über-Alpha hunks. The men are similar to private mercenaries, so they're big, capable, a little dangerous and oh-so-sexy. When it comes to rescuing the innocent, they do what has to be done, however it has to be done. I like to call them my men who "walk the edge of honor."

My novella in the anthology *The Guy Next Door* (available now) got things started by introducing you to characters related to the heroine of *When You Dare*. And stay tuned for the next two books in the series, *Trace of Fever* and *Savor the Danger*, coming soon.

To see more about the books, visit my website at www.LoriFoster.com. And feel free to chat with me on my Facebook fanpage—www.facebook.com/pages/Lori-Foster/233405457965.

I'm very excited about this new series, and I hope you will be, too!

Lori Foster

LORI FOSTER

WHEN YOU DARE

HQN™

Recycling programs
for this product may
not exist in your area.

ISBN-13: 978-0-373-77571-2

WHEN YOU DARE

Copyright © 2011 by Lori Foster

WHEN YOU
DARE

CHAPTER ONE

MIDNIGHT CAME AND went with only the quiet buzz of meager traffic along the beach. An occasional horn blew or tires squealed. Two people exited a bar nearby, laughing too loud before piling into an SUV and steering drunkenly onto the road.

In the shadows of a weed-ridden parking lot at the back of the rundown motel, no one noticed them. Avoiding the glow of the full yellow moon, they stood behind the south wall beneath a broken security lamp.

A lamp Dare Macintosh had broken.

Ocean breezes stirred the air and heightened his senses. While scanning the area and repeatedly peering at the black van he'd rented when first arriving in San Diego, Dare waited. His friend, Trace Rivers, embraced his younger sister with choking emotion.

It had been a long two days filled with frantic preparation, little sleep, less food and loads of pumping adrenaline: the conditions in which Dare operated best.

With the job done, and then some, he desperately wanted something to eat and a place to sleep. Even more than that, he wanted to check on the skinny, abused woman still out cold in the backseat of the van.

"Tell me," Trace said, not to Alani, whom he kept crushed close, but to Dare.

After again glancing at the van, Dare nodded. He'd

found Alani and returned her to Trace as he'd sworn to, but neither man knew yet what she had suffered.

"She was in Tijuana, as you said. Locked in a trailer with some other women in an isolated area."

"Heavily guarded?"

"Yes."

Trace drew a strained breath, and uttered what they both had known: "Human traffickers."

Dare nodded. "Not much in the way of food or drinks. Dirty, airless with the windows screwed shut. They had the women…" He hesitated, knowing how Trace would take it, but he needed to know. "They were leashed, chained to grommets in the floor, with just enough chain to reach a toilet. No sink."

"Fuckers." Overcome with rage, Trace knotted his hand in his sister's hair and squeezed her tighter, protectively.

She didn't complain.

Trace never used coarse language in front of his sister, which meant he was on the ragged edge, barely aware of what he said or did. Dare looked away from them, understanding the lack of control.

He focused on the rented van. "I had to go through several lookouts and a few armed guards to get her out of there."

"Quietly." Trace made it a statement, not a question.

"There wasn't much fuss." Dare always worked in efficient silence; an alarm would have brought more armed guards, possibly too many for him to combat. As much as he wanted to kill them all, he hadn't.

Only those most responsible.

By the time the empty trailer was discovered, Dare was already heading over the border into San Diego—where Trace waited. Over the years he'd built up alliances everywhere, and sometimes worked with the coyotes who made a living taking people back and forth over the border.

Thanks to those contacts, even with the extra cargo slumped in his backseat, no one had stopped him as he went through the border checkpoint. The van had been given only a cursory inspection, his weapons ignored, and the excuse of the women being tired—never mind that one was beaten and haggard, only half-dressed—had satisfied all questions.

Both men were damn good at what they did. But Trace couldn't go after his sister himself as he'd wanted, because the men holding her knew what he looked like. Before he'd have even gotten close to Tijuana, Trace would have been spotted by lookouts.

So Dare had gone—and come back with more than he'd bargained for.

Making a small sound, Alani tucked her face in closer to her brother's shoulder. The siblings shared blond hair and light brown eyes, but that's where the physical similarities ended. Trace was thirty, of an age with Dare, eight years older than his sister. He stood six foot three and weighed over two hundred pounds—all of it muscle.

Next to him, Alani looked tiny and fragile and, presently, wounded. Even since Dare had removed her from the trailer, fresh bruises continued to show on her arms and around her narrow wrists. Because the bastards had planned to sell her, they hadn't harmed her face.

Innocence was a huge commodity, and at twenty-two, having led a sheltered life, Alani gave off a definite vibe of innocence. Blond-haired, blue-eyed women brought the most profit, but he had a feeling that Alani's golden-brown eyes, in contrast to her very fair hair, would have fascinated the sick pricks.

Dare prayed they hadn't raped her, knowing a woman ill-used would bring less, but he left that uncomfortable discussion for Trace.

Hearing a noise like a soft moan, Dare zeroed in on the van with his senses on alert. He'd left the rear door open so he'd hear her if she moved, if she awoke.… But she did no more than readjust.

Three hours had passed since he'd carried her out of that trailer. Worry gnawed at him.

Why didn't she awaken?

"Dare?" His eyes filled with pain, rage and relief, Trace whispered, "Thank you."

Alani gave an audible swallow, and then she, too, said, "Yes, thank you. So much."

Putting a hand on her shoulder, Dare replied without words. He'd known Alani for years, watched her grow up, and felt like a pseudo big brother in many ways. He'd attended her graduation, both from high school and college. He'd been there with Alani and Trace when they buried their parents.

They had become part of his hodgepodge family.

Two days ago human traffickers had snatched Alani outside her hotel while she vacationed near the beach. Tomorrow she would have been sold, and finding her after that might have become impossible.

Right now, what the siblings needed was time alone, and Dare needed to sort things out with his remaining passenger. "I should get going."

Trace followed Dare's attention toward the van, saw the slim, dirty foot that appeared out of the open rear-passenger door, and lifted one eyebrow in an expression of disbelief. "You have a passenger?"

"A small complication, that's all."

"You're serious?"

Dare shrugged. "There were six women in that small trailer, Trace. Four of them were local and scattered as soon as I got them free." He nodded his head toward the van. "That one was drugged, near starved, grimy." And in many ways, even in the cramped confines of the rusty trailer, she'd been separated from the others, kept alone.

For certain, she wasn't the typical woman kidnapped for the growing sex trade.

Trace grew curious in that quiet way of his. "An American...complication?"

"I think so." From what he'd seen of her grubby face, she didn't look foreign. "She hasn't come to yet, so I haven't been able to talk to her."

Alani turned in her brother's arms, and she, too, looked toward the van. "She fought them whenever she came to. She called them names and almost...egged them on." Alani shivered in remembered fear. "It was so horrible. The men slapped her around for being mouthy, but she didn't stop. She just cursed them more."

Dare frowned. The little idiot might have been killed. "Foolhardy."

"I think she was really...angry." As if she couldn't fathom such boldness, Alani took a breath. "Even when they held her down to force more drugs on her, she didn't cry. She...raged."

"Did she speak English?"

Nodding, Alani said, "She sounded American to me. I mean, no accent or anything."

Considering all that, Dare said aloud, "She wasn't there for the same purpose as the rest of you."

"Probably not. Sometimes four or five of them would come in the trailer, but they'd stand around her and I couldn't see what they did. As far as I could tell, they

never really leered at her like…" She bit her lip, shivered again. "Like they did the rest of us. They never seemed to be sizing her up for anything. They just picked on her."

Trace hugged her again. "It's all right. You're safe now."

She nodded, shored up by the courage her brother had given her, and faced Dare. "She was there when we got there, already looking pretty bad. Once, before the men drugged her, she told me her name was Molly."

"Molly what?"

Alani shook her head. "We weren't supposed to talk, so I was afraid to ask her anything."

Trace tucked her back in close and asked over her head, "What are you going to do with her now?"

"No idea." Dare thought of her insubstantial weight when she'd been over his shoulder, of that tangled, light brown hair that had concealed much of her bruised face. "Hopefully someone will pay me for bringing her home."

Without releasing her brother, Alani reached out and punched Dare for the callous comment. He grinned, caught her wrist and kissed her knuckles.

She'd been given a terrible fright, and two days had probably felt like a month, but Alani had spirit. She'd get through this, thank God.

But the other one… How long had they had her? And why? Impatient with thoughts of her, Dare said, "I gotta run."

"Hold up a sec." Trace caught his arm, then dug in his jeans pocket and pulled out a fat envelope.

Pissed, Dare took a step back. "What the hell is that?"

"Expenses. And don't curse in front of Alani."

Hell, just because he usually hired out didn't mean he'd

charge a friend—a brother. He'd have gone after Alani if he'd had to crawl the whole way. "I don't need it."

Solemn, Trace held the envelope out to him. "But I need you to take it."

It hit Dare anew how difficult this was for Trace, not just that his sister had been hurt, but that he hadn't been able to go after her himself.

Dare took the envelope. "Thanks." He leaned in close. "And for future reference, I resolved the issue of you being recognized." There was no one left who knew Trace.

Deep satisfaction glittered in Trace's eyes. He gave a sharp nod. "I should have doubled the amount."

"No." Dare's smile wasn't friendly. "That was all my pleasure."

With no further discussion of money, Trace and Alani said their goodbyes and left the lot in Trace's silver Jag. They'd stay in an upscale hotel for the night and fly home tomorrow. Until then, Trace would keep his sister under very close guard.

Dare stood there, watching them until the purr of the engine faded and their taillights could no longer be seen. Moon shadows surrounded him. Night creatures gave a gentle call.

The peaceful ambiance didn't deceive him.

Hands on his hips, he looked again toward the van.

Now what?

The hospital, with all those questions and a lack of answers?

A hotel room? That would be his preference, but not with a woman on the brink of death.

If she was on the brink of death. Drugs could be a real complication, giving false symptoms and concealing a true state of health. It was possible that if she'd just come to, she'd be okay.

But maybe not.

Dare needed her to drink, to eat. And it wouldn't hurt to get the bugs out of her hair.

Before he even realized it, he strode that way, anxious to look in on her again.

One hand on the top of the open door, the other on the side of the car, Dare leaned in—and found her awake. Enormous, bruised eyes dominated her face.

Before he could register that she'd come around, he got a very dirty foot to the face. Hard.

He jerked back. "Son of a—"

The attack took him by surprise, and even with her meager strength, a heel to the nose hurt like hell. But he didn't want to compound things by overreacting. She'd recovered with a vengeance and most probably a lot of confusion. Though blood trickled from his nose, Dare wasn't disabled in any way.

With no help for it, he leaned into the backseat and, after a very brief struggle, pinned her down with her arms over her head, her legs caught under his.

Those large, slightly unfocused eyes glared at him. They were dark brown, like rich chocolate, and at the moment filled with a wealth of fear and rage.

She didn't scream, thank God, just breathed hard and fast and strained against him.

"You're safe now," Dare told her while trying to control her in a way that wouldn't allow her to hurt herself. "You're in San Diego, not Mexico."

She blinked fast, giving away her nervousness.

Dare sought the right words to reassure her. "I was there to retrieve a friend, one of the girls trapped in the trailer with you. And there you were, too, so…" Lacking a sound business argument for his decision, Dare rolled one shoulder. "So I took you."

She stilled a little, wary, uncertain. Hopeful.

"Your options now are the hospital, hotel or police. Take your pick."

Seconds ticked by. A drop of blood from his nose landed on her chest to mingle with dark bruises, numerous scratches and dirt. She didn't flinch, and short of releasing her, there wasn't much Dare could do about his bleeding nose.

Lifting her head, she looked beyond him, but it was dark, too dark to see and recognize the dubious safety of an American parking lot.

Then, just as suddenly as she'd attacked, she went limp, her head falling back, her muscles weak. Either from her recent exertion or continued terror, Dare felt a fine trembling in her slim body.

Voice quaking, she whispered, "Hotel, please."

Unexpected.

But appreciated. "Wise choice." He waited for theatrics, for that scream that didn't come. Cautious, Dare eyed her. "I can let you go without more violence?"

She gave one jerky nod.

Slowly, he sat up and levered himself out of the van. She didn't move. She didn't look capable of moving.

Stripping off his shirt, he used it to clean the blood from his busted nose.

What to do now? If he went to the front desk to register them, would she try to skip out on him? Dare could see that she wasn't yet herself, didn't have much left of strength or composure. If panic sent her running, she wouldn't get far, and could end up right back in trouble again.

But he couldn't very well traipse her into the motel with him.

For one thing…she reeked.

Not that he held that against her. Thanks to the conditions he'd found her in, personal cleanliness would have been impossible. But to add to that, the space they'd provided her hadn't been much better than a dump. He'd seen rat holes near the moldy mattress they'd supplied her, as well as a variety of bugs crawling around.

For another, she wore only a long T-shirt that didn't quite reach her very dirty, scuffed knees, with another oversized man's button-up shirt over it. The clothes dwarfed her small body, looking absurd. Mud and more caked her bare feet. Her brown hair looked like it had been through a blender.

While he tried to sort out his next move, she slowly sat upright, holding tightly to the back of the seat for balance. She swallowed convulsively. "Do you have anything to drink?"

Without a word, he opened the front passenger door and fetched a bottle of water from the floor. Knowing she was weak, he opened the cap and handed it to her.

He started to caution her about guzzling, but she didn't. She sipped, made a sound of pleasure, sipped again. "Oh, God, that's good. My throat is so dry, I think I could drink a river."

"No problem."

Sitting back against the seat, she closed her eyes, but only for a moment. "What day is it?"

Fascinating. Little by little, she pulled it together, and instead of hysterics, she wanted to make sense of the situation. Dare admired that—because it's what he would have done. "March ninth. Monday."

As if that made her head pound, she pinched the bridge of her nose. "They've…they've had me for nine days?" Lower, more to herself, she said, "I lost track, but…it felt so much longer."

Dare gave a low whistle in surprise. Nine days—and she was still alive? Unheard of. Captured women were not kept around that long, because hanging on to them upped the risk of being caught. "You were in that same trailer the whole time?"

"The whole time." Struggling with emotion, she sipped again, rolled her lips in and turned toward him. "I'm sorry about your nose. I wasn't sure…"

"Don't worry about it." In his line of work, he'd had worse injuries. Already it had stopped bleeding, and probably wouldn't even bruise.

For some reason, his reassurance made her look ready to cry. But she rallied. "I'm still a little woozy. I haven't eaten for days." She touched her hair and flinched. "God knows I need a shower. And a real bed would be like heaven." She took a few more sips, swallowing painfully.

Dare watched her, impressed that she showed great intelligence in not gulping the water, which would probably have made her barf.

She scrubbed at a bruised eye with a small fist, then sighed. "I can't very well be seen like this. Humiliation left me long ago, but it would raise too many questions." She looked at him for a solution.

"I can check us in." With each passing second, he grew confident that she wouldn't skip out. She was more clear-headed, more reasonable than he could have hoped for, given what Alani had told him.

Again she sipped, and Dare knew it was to buy herself some time, to think for a quiet moment.

Holding the bottle tight, she drew a breath. "I have money, Mr.…?"

"Just call me Dare." He didn't share his name, or his

identity, lightly. He still didn't know enough about her to trust her.

After a nod, she stuck out a dirty hand with chipped fingernails. "Molly Alexander."

Ridiculous. But Dare took her very small hand in his. "Molly."

Even though she'd initiated the handshake, his hold must have alarmed her; she drew back after barely touching him. "I have money to reimburse you, Dare. I promise. But obviously...not on me. For reasons I'd sooner go into later, I don't want to involve the police in any of this."

Interesting. What secrets could this skinny bit of a woman be hiding? "Ditto on hospitals?"

"Definitely." She shrunk away at just the thought. "No hospitals."

If she went to the hospital, they'd need a name, and then they'd want to call the police. Why didn't she want them involved?

"You've been drugged." Dare wondered what they'd given her, and if there would be any side effects. "You know, Molly, you could be sick, hurt—"

"No, not hurt."

Her definition of *hurt* differed greatly from his. With a raised brow he eyed several bruises and scrapes on her delicate skin. "Someone hit you. More than once."

Her eyes clouded again, and her voice went gruff. "Yes, and it was the worst experience of my entire life. *But I'll be fine.*"

"Are you convincing me, or yourself?"

"I *will* be. I promise."

Lots of promises, Dare thought. He glanced down at his bloodied, ruined shirt, and tossed it toward an overflowing garbage container in the parking lot. Intending to find a new shirt, he reached around her for his overnight bag.

Gasping, she covered her face and scuttled back into the corner of the seat. But she almost immediately caught herself and sat up again as if in challenge.

Unwilling to press her, Dare paused. "We're on the same side, remember?"

Pained, she closed her eyes and nodded.

Gutsy little thing, he decided. He pulled on the fresh shirt and then waited, arms crossed. If she didn't want to pass out in the van, she'd have to hurry it up and make a decision. Already she looked on the verge of keeling over.

After swaying from what looked like a wave of dizziness, she cleared her throat. "If you could arrange for a room tonight, I'd be really, really grateful."

"I could do that." Her continued formality confounded him. Most women would be babbling and crying for their mommy or daddy, or maybe a husband. Did Molly have a husband, a significant other?

Avoiding his gaze, she rolled her lips in again, took a few deep breaths and then whispered, "One room please, but perhaps with two beds." Tears welled, and she blinked them away before saying in a voice broken by fear, "God's truth, I don't want to be alone right now."

Now THAT SHE WAS safely inside a small but clean motel room, Molly tried to organize her thoughts. In order to keep from collapsing, she had to prioritize her most immediate needs, which were food, clothes, sleep, shower…

One glance down at herself, and she shuddered. Shower first, definitely. Now that she was free, she wasn't about to spend even one more night sleeping in her own filth.

And as hungry as she was, she refused to eat with such dirty hands.

Mustering her flagging courage, she turned to Dare. He was so damn big, and very gruff. Seeing him without his shirt when they were still in the parking lot should have alarmed her; even in the moonlight, she'd detected several scars over his chest, rib cage and shoulders that looked like healed knife and bullet wounds. Even now that he was dressed again, doing no more than settling into the room, he looked powerful, with noticeable strength.

But after being threatened endlessly for nine days by the most corrupt animals imaginable, Molly knew foul intent when she saw it.

Dare wasn't foul. She had the feeling he used his incredible strength to protect, not to inflict pain. Though he hadn't been sent for her, had no promises of payment for his efforts, he'd rescued her rather than leave her behind.

And now, whether he realized it yet or not, he was stuck with her.

She would pay him—once she got his agreement to keep her safe. "Excuse me, please, but if I could impose further…"

"Look." The big man turned away from the twin bed where he'd set a battered leather overnight bag. "Enough with the proper bullshit. You've been through hell, yes?"

Blue eyes, fringed by the thickest lashes, took her measure. The pulling of his black brows drove home just how disgusting her physical state was right now.

Molly nodded. "Absolutely." Hell times ten. Never in her wildest imagination—and as many could attest, her imagination could be pretty wild at times—had she envisioned the awful scenario she'd survived.

But she *had* survived it. And now she had to figure out how to proceed while still protecting herself.

"I don't need you to be formal." He set the bottle of water on the nightstand by her. "I don't need you to put on a good front, either. You're a small woman, probably not weighing more than a buck ten."

Molly glanced down at herself. She'd always weighed one twenty-five, but now…she just didn't know. She *had* lost weight. But that much?

"You're hurt," Dare continued, "and hungry, tired, dehydrated and pretty damn dirty."

Absurdly close to tears again, Molly scowled. "Your point?"

"If you want to fall apart, feel free. I sure as hell won't judge you, and it'll stay between us."

How kind that Dare would offer to keep her confidences for her. "No, thank you." She hadn't survived that hell just to crumple up now. "I'll be fine."

He folded muscled arms over an equally muscled chest. Beard shadow roughened his jaw. His knuckles looked as if they'd recently struck something—or someone.

She sincerely hoped it was one of the pigs who'd treated her so badly.

"Suit yourself," he said. "But I need you to drink that bottle of water, and then another after that. Slowly."

Right. Water would be good—if only her stomach weren't so jumpy.

"And the phony, unaffected act has got to go."

Fresh anger wrung through her already aching muscles. "Look, buster, I'm not going to lose it now, got that?" She chugged a few sips of water and returned the bottle to the small table between the beds. Then she clutched it for support. Her knees wobbled; her voice went husky. "I've held it together this long, and not for you, not for *anyone,* am I going to let those miserable bastards break me down."

One brow lifted in surprise as Dare studied her for long, silent moments, and then he shook his head with annoyance. "Sit down before you fall down."

She didn't take orders well, but this time she gladly sat. It required all her willpower not to sprawl back on the bed and just fade into oblivion. But if she did that, she'd wake just as dirty, and it turned her stomach to even think it.

Dare stopped in front of her. He examined the bottle of water and must have been satisfied—so far. "What do you want to do first?"

"Shower." She *needed* to be clean again. "Oh, God, I want a shower."

"I'll get it started for you." He hesitated. "Can you manage on your own?"

Her heart almost stopped. "Yes, of course."

Still he didn't move away. He crouched down in front of her, and his powerful thighs strained the material of faded denim. Those blue eyes were eerily intense as he studied her face. "You're safe with me, Molly."

"I…I know." She sensed that much. She just didn't have the wherewithal to start asking questions yet. Priorities, priorities.

"If you need help—"

"I'd stay dirty first." She was quite certain about that. No way would she invite a man to bathe her. She shuddered at the thought.

His mouth flattened. "Suit yourself." He straightened and started toward the tiny bathroom. "While you're in there, I'm going to run across the street to grab you something to wear. I'm guessing a size six?"

Something to wear. Like her own personal angel, he would buy her clean clothes to put on after her shower.

God bless the man.

Those blasted tears threatened again, clogging Molly's throat, making her nose feel stuffy. "Yes," she croaked out around a giant lump of emotion. "Anything simple would be...wonderful. Something for my feet, too, please. Size seven. I'm not picky."

She heard the water start, and through the open door she saw Dare set out towels, open the packaged soap, the shampoo and conditioner.

So remarkably considerate.

Her empty stomach cramped and recoiled, but she couldn't think of food just yet. She tried a little more water, knowing he was right, that she had to get some fluids back into her system.

Moving with a silent grace uncommon to a man so large, he came back into the room. "I'll get you a toothbrush, too. Anything else?"

There were so many things she needed that she couldn't fathom a list just yet. Her dry and cracked lips hurt when she licked them. "Something bland to eat?"

"Already thought of that." He paused by the door. "You sure you'll be okay until I get back?"

After what she'd survived, no way would she risk herself in any way. "I'll be very careful. If I get dizzy, I'll shut off the water and just sit in the tub."

Reluctant still, he stood there, and finally agreed with a nod. "Don't put the chain on the door."

As he spoke, he walked over to the desk to retrieve his belongings, including a big black gun and a very lethal-looking knife that folded together. The gun went into a holster at his back, fastened to the waistband of his jeans. He slipped the knife into a pocket, then covered the gun with the hem of his shirt. He treated the weapons as casually as he did his wallet and cell phone, fascinating Molly.

It would make her nervous just to touch either one.

He stopped in front of her again. "If you pass out, I want to be able to get in without breaking anything and causing a scene."

"Okay."

"I won't be gone long," he cautioned. "So don't linger in there."

If he didn't leave soon, she'd be asleep before she could hit the shower. "No, I won't."

Using the edge of a fist, he brought her chin up so that she had to look at him. "You're weaker than you realize."

On the contrary, she was stronger than she'd ever imagined. But his concern was nice, so she only reiterated, "I'll be fine."

Frustration palpable, he ran a hand through short brown hair, nodded once and walked out.

He'd wanted to say more to her, Molly knew. He didn't understand her lack of questions, her acceptance of him as her rescuer. But he didn't push her, and she appreciated his restraint. Right now, all she could manage was the direst of necessities. And thinking that…

It took a lot of effort to drag herself up to her feet again, but she did it. The ragged, torn and stained shirts came over her head and with sublime satisfaction she stuffed them into the garbage can by the desk. Never again would those disgusting scraps of material touch her body.

She'd been denied underwear of any kind, so removing the shirts left her naked. One glance down at herself and Molly saw evidence of her ordeal in places she hadn't considered. She remembered the rough treatment, being jerked, shoved, *hit*... Her breath caught.

No, she was away from there now, and she wouldn't dwell on it.

Anxious for the long-denied comfort of warm water, she stepped into the shower's spray.

Oh, heaven.

Though her every muscle trembled and the most pervasive weakness dragged at her, never had she appreciated a shower more. Lathering the soap into a washcloth, Molly scrubbed all over, determined to wash away the disgust she still felt.

She had to hurry to finish before the last of her strength waned. Already she felt faint, sick to her stomach, her knees quaking.

Lack of sleep provided a perpetual headache that burned behind her eyes and left her hollow.

With her skin now clean, she opened her mouth, filled it with fresh water, swished and spit, then used the cloth to clean her teeth as best she could.

She had to lean against the tiled wall to rest for a minute. Her head pounded with so many impossible problems for the future. But for now, for this moment, she was safe.

Safe. There had been times when she'd thought...when she'd been *sure* that they would kill her. They'd taken great pleasure in taunting her, slapping her, keeping her uncertain and on edge. Sleep had come in only fitful spurts, because sleep left her vulnerable to their intent— whatever their intent had been.

Her hands knotted into fists. Fear curdled with a rage so bright it sustained her. She struggled to fill her lungs with air, to beat down the raw panic that had accompanied her since being abducted.

So much to think about…but for now, she had only to worry about finishing her shower. Then eating.

And then sleeping without the fear of never waking again.

She drew one more breath before picking up the shampoo with a shaking hand. So many tangles knotted her hair that she decided she'd cut it—after it was clean—rather than brush them out. She lathered, rinsed, then lathered again. She refused to look down at the tub to see what had washed out of her hair.

Emptying the entire tiny bottle of conditioner onto her head, she worked it through, rinsed, and then…she had nothing left. No strength. No reserve. She couldn't even dry herself. She barely got a towel around her hair and another around her body.

Stumbling back into the main room, Molly hit the bed hard, snuggled in and literally passed out.

CHAPTER TWO

DARE CAME IN QUIETLY, saw her curled on the bed and frowned. The towel barely covered her, and with her knees pulled up, he would get one hell of a peep show if he moved to the foot of the bed.

Not that he would. In many cases he lacked scruples; it was a hazard of the job. But with women, with *this* woman, he wasn't about to take advantage. Despite her bravado and commonsense reaction to her nightmare, he'd never seen anyone more emotionally fragile.

Besides, the less involvement he had with her, unscrupulous or otherwise, the better. He needed to figure out what had happened to her, and the quickest way to safely remove her from his care.

He'd known she was spent, on the edge, but the fact that she hadn't even pulled the covers over herself proved her level of exhaustion.

More than anything, she probably needed to eat. But should he wake her for that when she also needed sleep?

He wasn't a fucking babysitter, but since he'd personally gotten her out of Mexico, he couldn't very well just dump her somewhere. By rescuing her, he had accepted an implied responsibility.

Trying not to rattle the bags and juggling the food with his other purchases, Dare closed the door and locked it. A glance at the bedside clock showed the time at 1:30 a.m. He'd only been gone a half hour, tops.

Luckily the Walmart across the street stayed open twenty-four hours. He'd found not only clothes for her, but food, too. Dressing and feeding her would go a long way toward resolving her most pressing issues.

With barely a sound, he stowed the drinks in the tiny fridge and put her share of the food into the microwave to keep.

Removing his wallet, change and cell phone from his jeans, he placed them neatly on the desk. Next he took out his knife and the Glock 9mm he carried, and set them beside his other belongings. He stretched out his knotted muscles. Too many hours crawling over rough ground, ducking for cover and demolishing men without enough sleep or food had left him tense and weary.

After pulling a chair out from the round table, he opened the covering on his pancakes and coffee.

He'd taken only one bite when she stirred, sniffed the air and drowsily opened her eyes. Dare turned toward her.

She gave him a deer-caught-in-the-headlights look.

He studied her, a small bundle huddled tight on the bed, face still ravaged and eyes wounded. Never had he seen a woman look so vulnerable.

He swallowed his bite and, sounding as casual as he could under the circumstances, asked, "Hungry?"

She stared back, then struggled up to one elbow. Her expression changed, the wariness hidden beneath that intrepid bravado. "Starved. Literally."

With all the dirt removed, her big eyes dominated her small features. More marks showed on her fair skin, one on her cheekbone and under her left eye, one on her throat, and a darker, angrier bruise on her right shoulder.

Dare thought of men hitting her, manhandling her, and bone-deep disgust ignited. He despised bullies of any kind, but a man who would hurt a woman was at the top of his list of assholes that needed a lesson.

She breathed deeply, her eyes closing and her nostrils flaring. "That smells so good."

Out of his seat already, Dare fetched her food. "Do you want to sit here, or eat in the bed?"

She hesitated, looking down for a moment as if uncertain of her welcome, not wanting to inconvenience him. "Table please, but...I should dress first."

"All right." He set the food on the table and opened the bag of clothes, pulling out a few T-shirts, panties and a pair of pull-on cotton shorts. "You can get more stuff tomorrow if you feel up to it. Something warmer, maybe, and nicer for the plane ride. But for now, I figured this would fit."

She didn't look at the clothes. The arm she leaned on barely supported her, and her breath went choppy with effort.

Voice weak, strained, she said, "I'm sorry, but...I haven't eaten in too long and I'm feeling kind of... faint."

Dare straightened, going on alert. Would she pass out on him?

"If...if you could help me into the bathroom, I'll dress in there."

Shit. He did not want her passing out alone, maybe hitting her head. "Yeah, no problem."

Dare moved to the bed and slipped an arm behind her, then drew her to her feet. She swayed into him, one hand clutching at his shirt and holding on for dear life.

She made no attempt to step away. He didn't ask her to. "What would you like to do?"

"I can't…" She choked, cleared her throat, and her voice was so low he barely heard her when she said, "This is embarrassing, but the shower…" She swallowed. "I think I'm depleted."

Easing her back onto the bed, Dare knew he'd have to be firm to get her agreement. "Okay, Molly, listen up." He kept his tone as impersonal as possible. "This isn't a big deal. I can dress you. I can even feed you."

She rolled in her lips with embarrassment, a habit he'd already noticed.

"It's nothing I haven't done before," he lied.

That brought her dark eyes up to his.

Damn, but her eyes could melt a man's soul. "I'm in the personal protection business. You're not the first woman I've rescued. You're not even in the worst shape." Another lie. Most women he retrieved were found in the first forty-eight hours before too much damage had been done—or they weren't found at all. "Okay?"

Still with her gaze locked on his, she nodded.

"Good girl." He grabbed the clothes from the bag. He wasn't really discomfited by the task, but he'd just as soon get past it.

Taking clothes off a woman, yeah, he had plenty of practice with that.

Dressing the near-dead…not so much.

"Panties first, okay?" He still had no idea what had been done to her, how she might have been tormented or used. If it was sexual in nature, then this would be doubly hard on her. "We'll take this nice and slow, and if at any point you feel panicky, just tell me."

"I won't panic."

He looked up at her. "Yeah, well, I'd just as soon not get kicked in the face again."

For a split second, he thought he saw a slight smile on

her bruised mouth. Then she looked away. "No, I won't do that again."

As Dare knelt down to work her small feet into the legs of the very plain cotton underwear, he noticed more scrapes and bruises. After she ate, he'd dig out the first-aid kit and patch her up.

When he had the panties up to her knees, he took her elbow and pulled her to her feet. "Hold on to my shoulders."

She was so much shorter than him, maybe five-seven to his six-three, that, while he stood upright, holding his shoulders pretty much stretched her out.

He bent to the task and she leaned against him. She was surprisingly…*soft* for someone so thin. And she smelled good now, clean like shampoo and soap and warm, gentle woman.

In a shrill, nervous voice, she asked, "So, who did you rescue? Other than me?"

"A friend. Almost like a sister." Her thighs were trim, firm. He did his best to look away as he dragged the underwear up under the damp towel. His knuckles dragged against her soft bottom, a bottom that wasn't as skinny as he'd thought.

Not that her curves mattered. With her shivering against him, he felt more like a damned doctor than a man who'd been without sex for months. "Now the shirt."

He took the damp towel off her head and tossed it aside. Her hair fell in tangled wet hanks to her bare shoulders. Her neck was long and graceful, her chin stubborn.

And she looked ready to drop with both weakness and degradation. She was not a woman used to needing help, he could tell, especially not with something so personal.

"Feel better being clean?" If he kept her talking, maybe this would be easier for her—and for him.

"You have no idea." Dare pulled the shirt down over her head, and as soon as she popped free, she added, "Do you have any scissors?"

He had to practically lift her arms to get them through the armholes. Because a bra had been well beyond him, he'd bought the shirt big and loose. It fit over the bundled towel she had wrapped around herself. "Why?"

"I was going to cut it."

"It?" He reached beneath the shirt and pulled away the bulky towel. Surprise stilled him for only a moment. Dirt, distress and injury had hidden it, but Molly Alexander had one hell of a rack.

And he felt like a grade-A prick for noticing.

"My hair." Not quite defeated, but close, she sat back on the bed again. Face pale and mouth tight with strain, she kept her shoulders back, her bare knees and ankles squeezed together. "There's no way I'll get the tangles out. And truthfully…I just don't care enough to try."

She was not his problem, Dare reminded himself, and her hair sure as hell didn't matter to him. But damn it, for whatever reason, he didn't want her to give up now, not on anything.

"Let's worry about it tomorrow, okay?" Taking her arm again, he got her upright and helped her step into the shorts. Decently dressed, clean, and marginally rested, she made quite a picture.

Sort of cute, but still very bedraggled and wearied, not to mention abused.

Dare led her to the table. "You sure you don't want to do this in bed?"

A hoarse laugh huffed out. "I've been tied to a disgusting, filthy mattress for nine days, unable to sit up or walk or…anything. Trust me, I'd rather be at the table."

The image sickened him. "Gotcha."

He set juice in front of her. "Try to drink it all, okay? It'll help." Then he opened the microwave and pulled out her still-warm cup of soup.

"I know the pancakes probably smell good, and there's enough for you if you want to give them a go, but I figured it might be too much—"

"It would be." She drank a little of the juice, waited, then drank some more. "It's been so long since I've eaten, I have to take it slow or I know I'll be sick. And I'd rather be beaten than barf again."

"Again?"

Her expression flattened with memories. As if the shock and humiliation still burned her, she didn't look at him as she explained.

"At first they brought me corn tortillas and some kind of strong alcohol. I was afraid of what they'd do if I got drunk, so I wouldn't drink it. But then they gave me the nastiest-looking water, like something out of a mud puddle. I didn't trust that, either, and they tried to insist, but I just…couldn't." Her shoulders hunched a little as she drew into herself. Her voice lowered. "That's when they started…drugging me."

Dare set aside his fork. Hearing even a smidge of what she'd gone through made it near impossible to stay distanced; he wanted to go back and kill people all over again.

"After that, I couldn't seem to resist when they told me to drink it, but I got…sick." Her hands fisted, and her entire small body tightened. "It's not like there was any place for that. I mean, not a bathroom or even a bucket.

I…I soiled part of the small area they'd given me, and tossed up the pills they'd forced down my throat."

Jesus. To imagine being a woman alone, afraid and sick, stuck in such an untenable position—he hid it from her, but it enraged him.

"They stood over me, furious, barking at me in a language I didn't understand, but I got their meaning loud and clear, and I cleaned it up the best I could with the rags they threw at me. After that, they barely fed me. Usually only once a day, but at least the water they brought was cleaner, I guess to avoid a repeat of things."

Motherfuckers.

"But then yesterday and today they brought me nothing at all. I don't know why."

She left out a lot of details, but Dare didn't push her. He couldn't begin to imagine how wretched it'd be to get ill while closed in that hot, airless little trailer. The feeling of helplessness was something he'd never experienced, but he knew it'd be different for a man.

Any woman held captive would be constantly under the fear of more than just physical abuse or neglect. She'd be terrified of rape.

Setting the soup and a spoon in front of her, Dare broached that topic. "They manhandled you a lot."

She said nothing, just tasted her soup, groaned, and tasted it again.

"Molly…if you were hurt…" Idiot. She was so hurt that it pained him to think of it. Dare started over. "That is, if you were hurt in ways that aren't easy for me to see, then a trip to the hospital would be a good idea."

With each bite of soup, she looked more lethargic, as if the nourishment eased a terrible ache and allowed tiredness to take over again.

"Molly?"

"I can't." She took another swallow, but her eyes were getting heavy as color seeped back into her cheeks.

"Can't what?"

Another swallow. The seconds ticked by. "I can't... can't talk about this now, can't give you details, and I can't go to the hospital." She lifted her gaze to his. "Please, if we could talk about it in the morning, I'd be grateful."

Damn it, he didn't want to be responsible for her health. He stood to pace, trying to decide.

"Dare?"

He turned back to her, left eye twitching, jaw tight.

"I wasn't raped. I swear."

Something in him eased. He tried to read the truth in her eyes, but saw only bleak resistance there. He rubbed his bristly jaw. "You would tell me if you were sexually abused?"

"If I had been...I don't know. I don't know how I'd feel." Despite her ordeal, her chin lifted. "But I wasn't."

Dare continued to study her. He could read most people, but this woman had so much emotion in her face, and so many secrets in her eyes, he just wasn't sure.

"That...that isn't what they wanted with me."

Remembering how she'd been separated from the other women, kept unclean, neglected instead of primed...he believed her.

That's what she wanted to talk about tomorrow, he realized. He nodded. "All right."

She started to stand, albeit shakily, and Dare said, "Wait. Let me turn down the bed."

He prepared it for her, much like he would for a child, then came back to her. "Do you need the bathroom first?"

Pale, trembling, she shook her head. "No."

Knowing that decision was likely determined by her

inability to make it there on her own, Dare took the choice away from her. "Of course you do." After all, he'd been pushing fluids on her, and she'd obliged him.

Lifting her up, he carried her into the small tiled room. She weighed next to nothing and felt insubstantial, delicate, in his arms.

He set her down next to the john. "Okay?"

She grabbed the sink and held on. "Yes."

Hardly, but he'd done as much as he could without causing her further embarrassment. "If you need me, I'll be right outside the door. Just let me know when you're finished." He left her to it.

Leaning against the wall beside the door, thinking of what he'd learned, and *what he hadn't,* Dare waited for her. Seconds later he heard her flush and then run water in the sink.

The door opened.

Eyes more closed than open, shuffling along like a zombie, Molly moved past him to the bed. Dare rushed to hold her arm, to steady her and steer her to the sheets.

"Sorry," she mumbled as she literally tumbled to the mattress. "*So* tired."

Worry gnawed on him again. Should he damn her objections and take her to the hospital anyway? Already she looked to be asleep. He knew firsthand how exhaustion, especially when amplified by hunger and dehydration, could weary a body and soul.

Seeing her there, looking peaceful for a change, he made up his mind. A few more hours shouldn't hurt. If she wasn't steadier after sleeping, he'd insist she get checked out by a physician.

Before he thought better of it, Dare smoothed back her hair. It was so thick that it hadn't dried much, but a wet head was the least of her worries.

He pulled the sheet and blanket up to her chin, and heard her sigh. "Rest up, Molly Alexander. In the morning we'll sort things out."

No answer.

For more than a minute, Dare stared down at her, wondering what he was going to do with her. She'd held it together with an admirable iron will and unwavering determination. Despite her horrific ordeal, she'd been reasonable, practical and intelligent.

But it was what she hadn't been that told him even more.

She hadn't been anxious to report to the police, hadn't even looked at his gun or the big knife he carried, and she hadn't wanted to call anyone.

That was a first for Dare. It was his experience that men and women alike, when recovered from a dangerous situation, had someone they wanted to speak to ASAP, someone they wanted to reassure, or have reassure them.

Not Molly.

What a mystery she was.

As efficiently as he could, Dare spread out her hair on the pillow so it'd dry quicker. Valuing order in all aspects of his life, he took time to tidy the room and get rid of the empty food containers.

He put the gun and knife under his pillow. They made a familiar lump that gave him a specific peace of mind needed in his line of work.

After stripping down to his boxers, he neatly folded his clothes and put them away in his duffel bag, kept on the other side of the bed. With one more glance out at the still-quiet parking lot, he drew the heavy shades, putting the room in darkness, and crawled under the blankets. The aged air conditioner hummed and whistled as it sent cool air to swirl around the room; he'd been too many hours without rest.

Within minutes, he fell into a light sleep.

Hours later, a short, guttural sound of panic drew him from a vague dream. He had his gun in his hand and was on his feet before the sound had faded.

HEART PUNCHING, stomach cramping, Molly jerked upright in the bed. Her hands balled into fists and her throat burned from the scream that almost escaped. *Almost.* Someone loomed next to her, someone big.

"Molly?"

She knew that voice. Still tinged with panic, she took quick inventory of her surroundings. The unfamiliar bed didn't crawl with bugs, and the usual stench of unwashed bodies, fear and sickness didn't pervade the air.

Reality crashed back in, and with it shame, mortification and sadness. She gasped, blindly reaching out. "Dare?" Her hand hit something, maybe a hard thigh.

"Yeah, just me." He set something heavy on the nightstand, and then his big body dipped the mattress and his hand touched her shoulder. "Bad dream?"

More like bad memories, but she didn't want to go into that right now. Her breath shuddered in. "Yes. I'm so sorry I woke you."

"You're okay now?"

"I…" What could she say? That she'd never be okay again? *Unacceptable,* because that would mean they'd won, whoever *they* were. "Yes. Now I am." Fear continued to rip through her in agonizing waves. "I'm sorry."

"Enough with the apologies, okay?"

His gruff voice somehow reassured her. She nodded in the darkness, struggling to get her bearings. "I thought…"

"That you were back there again?" Cautiously, a little awkwardly, he drew her against him. "Don't worry about it. It's going to take you a while to shake it off."

Then he put another bottle of water in her hand.

A near-hysterical laugh bubbled up, and she barely repressed it. *Shake it off?* Is that what he would do?

Probably. He was so much stronger, so much more capable than she.

She dutifully drank some water, then handed the bottle back to him. He set it aside, but then pulled her close.

Her cheek met the bare skin of his upper chest and fit neatly against the notch of his shoulder. So much heat emanated from him. He smelled good, too, clean and pure. And he felt even better, like strength, safety.

Her rescuer had nothing in common with the filthy, depraved animals who had imprisoned her, who had likely been hired to…do what with her?

Molly could hear his even, calm heartbeat, and it helped to slow her racing heart. Other than his initial, probably automatic gesture of comfort, Dare didn't touch her. One of his hands rested lightly on her shoulder, unmoving but offering the knowledge that she was no longer alone or in danger.

"Dare?"

"Hmm?"

He seemed perfectly comfortable in their present position, as if he did this sort of thing all the time.

Molly wished she felt the same. Never in her life had she asked for comfort from another person. For her, this was all very awkward, but basic need, the need to survive, drove her now. "Would you mind if I just stayed like this for a few minutes?"

"No problem." As if in affirmation, he coasted his

hand up and down her back, then up again, to tangle in her hair. "At least your hair is mostly dry now."

Another strangling, semi-ironic laugh almost slipped out. "Yeah, I've got that going for me."

He was silent a moment, then said, "I didn't think to ask earlier, but do you need any aspirin or anything?"

Molly shook her head. "I'm not sure what the pills were that they forced me to swallow, but I'd rather not take anything else for a while."

"They were probably some kind of hallucinogen. Or maybe tranqs."

Reminded of how the pills had made her feel, she stiffened, pushed back from him a little to look up at his barely visible face. "I *detest* being out of control."

He went curiously still. "Now?"

"No, when they were doping me." She remembered the lack of control over her sluggish limbs, how her mind dredged up such ridiculous, vague and misty dreams. Everything was surreal, implausible, insubstantial. "I don't drink, and I never, ever took drugs. I've never even smoked pot. And then to have them force me… It was awful. Why would anyone ever drug themselves on purpose?"

He relaxed again. "No idea."

She believed him. Dare was a man who enjoyed being in charge. He wouldn't blunt that ability for the sake of kicks or a quick high.

More to herself than to him, Molly whispered, "I like being *me,* not a loopy version of me."

He said nothing to that.

Needing to talk, to drive away the remnants of that dream, she again looked up at him. "The other women… You said you saved one, but there were others there, too. What happened to them?"

"Four of them were apparently local, because as soon as I freed them and told them it was clear, they took off."

"I hope they're all right."

He shrugged. "They seemed to know right where they wanted to go."

"Those men…" Damn it, she had difficulty finishing thoughts, much less sentences. "They were so cruel, taunting the women, pawing them."

His muscles seemed to bulge. "The blond woman. They pawed her?"

Icy anger sounded in his tone. "Sometimes, but I got the impression she was too valuable to abuse. They said she'd bring a lot of money." Now Molly soothed him, clutching his big shoulder. "She's the one you saved? The one you said is like family?"

"Yes."

She put her cheek against his chest again. "Where is she now?"

His hug was automatic, for them both. "With her brother. Safe."

Safe. Such a strange concept, but Molly now knew that no one was ever really safe. "I'm glad. She's so young." His warmth seeped into her, making her drowsy again. "I tried talking to her, but she was too afraid."

Looking down at her, he asked, "And you weren't?"

"I've never in my life known that kind of fear." The dark and quiet of the small room, the casualness of his touch, made it easier to talk. "Dare, can I tell you something?"

He shifted, almost like he was settling in for something monumental. "Yes."

How to explain it? A prisoner was a prisoner—but she'd been imprisoned differently. "I wasn't like the others."

Rather than question her meaning, he just said, "I know."

Did he? "Those girls were in their late teens or very early twenties, and they were all stunning. They were kept on one side of the trailer, with more opportunity to bathe. They were given clean clothes. Ridiculously revealing clothes, but still... And they had more food, more water. It was almost like the jerks wanted them to look good. Healthy, I mean."

"Yeah, I know."

But Molly frowned at her own words. "I'm not saying they had it any easier than I did. Captivity is captivity, and we were all miserable."

"But?"

She swallowed. "But...I'm thirty years old." She twisted to look up at him. "I know I'm plain. And even if I didn't already know it, I'm not stupid."

She heard something in his tone when he agreed. "No, you're far from stupid."

"They didn't want me to sell, like they did the others."

As if he'd already come to that conclusion himself, he said, "No, they didn't. But then why did they take you? Do you know? Did they say anything?"

They had said plenty, most of it in Spanish. "I've gone over it again and again, and I think... I think someone must have paid them to."

In the quiet security of that small motel room, she counted their breaths, waiting for Dare to react. By small degrees, his muscles again bunched and flexed.

But his hold remained gentle.

When he spoke, he sounded matter-of-fact, as if he believed her without further explanation. "Who?"

Molly squeezed her eyes shut, hating the reality of

what her life had become. "That's the conundrum, isn't it? I have no idea who I can trust anymore."

His hand smoothed over her hair, then cupped the back of her skull. "Do you think you can go back to sleep now?"

Not if she had to sleep alone. Hedging, she asked, "What time is it?"

"Doesn't matter, does it? We're not on a schedule yet."

But she hated to further inconvenience him. He hadn't been paid to come after her. He'd probably rescued her with the thought of dropping her on the other side of the border, someone else's problem to deal with.

Unfortunately, she had no one else right now. "Do you have a flight to catch?"

Before he answered, he urged her back down in the bed. Her head sank into the soft pillow, and the clean sheets, though cheap and scratchy, smelled good. He stayed close as he all but tucked her in.

She should have been alarmed, having a man bending over her, especially a man of Dare's size and obvious strength.

Instead, she felt more at ease than she had since being grabbed and stuffed into the back of an old van right in front of her own apartment building. She doubted the quaint community in southern Ohio would ever again feel boring to her.

Dare smoothed the covers over her shoulders. "When I'm on a mission like this, I can't make plans too far in advance. If anything had gone wrong, if I hadn't been able to get Alani out of there so easily, or if she'd already been moved, then I'd still be tracking her."

"You wouldn't have given up on finding her?"

"Never."

The unwavering conviction in that one word reassured her. Alani was lucky to have someone like Dare caring for her. "How did you know where to look for her?"

He moved to her side, and when Molly thought he'd leave the bed—*leave her*—he instead propped his back against the headboard. After stretching out his long legs, he said, "I've been in this business a long time."

"How long? You can't be much older than me."

"Thirty-two, so I've been at it for more than ten years."

Fascinating. Molly folded a hand under her cheek and got comfortable. "You started young."

With a shrug, he said, "It suits me."

"Adrenaline junkie?" she guessed.

"And a control freak—which means I really understand how you detested being so powerless. I'd have hated it, too."

But he wouldn't have been so helpless against them. Somehow, Molly thought Dare would have found a way to not only escape, but to wipe the cretins out for good.

He took her silence for interest, which was okay because she found him intriguing. And listening to him kept her from stewing over her own awful predicament.

"I'm obsessive about details," he told her. "That's made me reliable enough to cultivate contacts everywhere, but Mexico is the easiest. For a fee, the coyotes can usually give me information I can't uncover otherwise."

"Coyotes? You mean the people who smuggle illegal aliens into the country?"

Dare nodded. "Yeah, but they're also useful when you need help getting back out of Tijuana. It's a sad fact that in many areas human trafficking isn't that much of a secret, so plenty of people are usually in the loop about new acquisitions."

She thought of the young Caucasian girl who'd been held in the trailer with her. "Your friend Alani had very unique coloring."

He nodded. "That made it easier for others to remember her, but not that many got to see her. They were saving her for a big sale, I'm sure."

Wretched, *horrible* men, to plan such a thing for a young girl. She hated them, all of them.

Now that her eyes had adjusted to the darkness, Molly could make out Dare's profile. She remembered that *thunk* right before he'd joined her in the bed. "You have a gun with you."

"On the nightstand," he confirmed. "A Glock 9mm. Does it bother you?"

She shook her head.

When he said, "Good," she realized that he could see her, too.

"May I see it?"

"You've already seen it."

"I mean…hold it."

He made a sound that could have passed for humor. "Hell, no."

Well. Molly didn't know if she should be offended or not. Then she thought of those awful men.… "Have you ever shot anyone?"

With no hesitation, Dare said, "Yes."

Her heart pumped hard. She licked her lips, drew a breath. "Did you…shoot the men who were guarding the trailer?"

He looked at her again. After some consideration, he asked, "Why?"

Her voice sounded more raw than she intended, but Molly was helpless to state things any differently. "They're brutal beasts who take pleasure in hurting women."

"In hurting you," he agreed with quiet sympathy.

Her nose stuffed up. Her throat tightened. "They…"

Oh, God, it was almost impossible to talk. Her voice kept breaking, going higher, weaker. But Dare didn't prompt her, didn't rush her. He just waited in supportive silence.

"They wanted to make me cry. They wanted to make me beg." She sniffed, drew a breath. "Just for sport."

Without a word, as if they knew each other well, he pulled her up against his chest and put his chin to the top of her head. After a few seconds, he said, "You know, Molly, if I could, I'd kill them for you again."

She jerked, then whispered in awe, "Again?"

"Yeah."

Dizziness assailed her. "So you did kill them?"

"Damn right." He looked down at her. "They needed killing."

"Yes, they did." The men were gone; they couldn't hurt her, or anyone else, ever again. As the tension eased out of her, her heavy eyelids sank down, almost closing.

Great relief came from the knowledge that they were gone forever.

Dawn began to creep through the heavy drapes, and for the first time in days, Molly greeted it with hope. "Dare?"

"Yeah?"

She hugged him tight. "Thank you."

CHAPTER THREE

WHILE SIPPING COFFEE and watching her sleep, Dare went over possible scenarios for the day. First on the agenda, he had to decide what to do with Ms. Molly Alexander.

He couldn't just dump her, because she shouldn't be alone right now and didn't seem to have anyone to go to. She refused the police, not that they could be of much help anyway. So, then...what to do with her?

It wasn't like he could keep her.

He wanted to get back home to check on his girls, and thinking that, he lifted his cell phone and put in a call. Chris Chapey, his personal assistant, answered on the third ring.

"Hey, Dare. I want to hear some good news."

Dare rolled his eyes. No matter how he tried, he couldn't get Chris to answer the phone properly. Sure, Chris always checked the caller ID first, so he knew it was Dare, but still... "Alani is with Trace now."

"Fucking-A. *Perfect* news." But then, with more sensitivity: "She's...okay, isn't she?"

"Depends on your definition of *okay,* I guess. But I think she'll recoup. It's for certain that Trace won't let her take another vacation without him—not for a hell of a long time." Or until Alani had a man of her own to keep her safe.

"Can't say as I blame him," Chris said. "I assume that you got through things unscathed?"

He glanced toward Molly, asleep in the bed. A bed they'd shared—*in the platonic sense*. "More or less."

"So, when are you going to be home?"

"Not sure yet. I have a—" Suddenly, as if she'd felt his gaze, Molly's eyes opened. They were puffy from sleeping hard, and a little unfocused—until they locked on his. She again gave him that startled, *caught* look. "A complication."

Showing no reaction to that, Molly rolled to her back a moment and yawned, then pushed back the covers and sat up. She gingerly stretched and winced. Beneath the now-wrinkled clothes, Dare noted once again that although she was thin, she still had an abundance of curves.

How the hell had he ever missed that? Not that he'd been checking her out, but it was a little hard to miss now that he had noticed.

Shoulders slumped, Molly sat on the edge of the bed for a minute, just breathing and maybe taking personal stock of aches and pains. He was willing to bet she had plenty of them.

Finally, with a deep sigh, she stood and padded bare-foot for the bathroom. He noted some definite curves in the back, too, defined beneath the body-hugging shorts and loose T-shirt.

She looked less wobbly today, so the sleep and food must have done the trick.

When she shut the door, Dare realized that Chris was talking to him and he hadn't heard a word.

"I need to go."

Chris snorted. "No being cryptic, boss man. If you're in trouble—"

"I'm not."

"Then what's the complication?"

"Nothing I can't handle." He hoped. "Everything will

be fine." Somehow he'd make that true. "I'll call you later when I finalize my plans."

Molly emerged from the bathroom, her face damp, her thick, tangled hair everywhere. But today, rather than looking like a wreck, her wild hair just looked...freshly tumbled.

She came over to sniff the coffee, lifted a cup in hopeful question, and Dare nodded.

She mouthed a heartfelt, *Thank you*.

In the bright sunlight, her brown eyes looked less wary, but the bruising under and around them had deepened.

Shit.

Dare gave his attention back to Chris. "Give the girls some hugs from me."

"I'm keeping them happy, don't worry."

He never did. He trusted Chris with his life—and his girls. "Later."

Dare closed the phone and eyed Molly. She avoided his gaze, which he found curious. "How do you feel? And don't sugarcoat it."

Her lips curved in the briefest smile. "Glad to be alive and free. But also achy, still a little tired. And *starved*." She peered at the arrangement of food. "Not to impose, but is any of this up for grabs?"

"I've already finished, so help yourself." He watched her sit and open up all three containers, finding scrambled eggs, bacon and toast.

Her eyes widened, then narrowed with hunger. "It's an absolute feast."

"Hardly that." Her mood this morning threw him. He hadn't expected her to be...chipper. Or maybe it was more complacent. Either way, he'd been prepared for the shock to take hold.

Instead, she behaved as if nothing out of the ordinary had happened.

"For me, this is the most delicious-looking food I've seen in far too long, so thank you. And don't worry, I really do have money to repay you for everything. Just keep a tally of it all, if you don't mind. My math skills have always been lacking and…I don't have a notepad or pen." She glanced up at him. "At least, not with me."

Discolorations in blue, purple, green and black marred her skin from her eyes down to her toes, and she spoke as if the cost of a diner breakfast mattered.

"How long have you been up?" She tasted the eggs, tore open a salt and pepper packet, seasoned them, then tasted again. With a roll of her eyes, she said, "Oh, Nirvana."

Dare enjoyed her expression of greedy bliss. "I woke a few hours ago." *Still at your side, with you squeezed up against me.* He'd awakened with women many times, but never a woman like her, never a woman in her situation.

She'd been dead to the world, and still she clung to him so tightly that he had to pry her loose before sliding out of the bed and away from her. After leaving her, he noted the fading of her warmth against his skin, and how her scent still clung to him.

Disturbing.

"What time is it?" She bit into the bacon and chewed with delight.

"Noon."

"Wow. Late for you, I bet." Her gaze flashed up with a hint of humor. "You being such an orderly, organized guy." She emphasized that with a peek around the room. He'd already made his bed, because he hated the clutter of rumpled blankets and really didn't want housekeeping around his stuff.

Dare shrugged. Usually he rose before dawn, but he'd needed the rest, too. Leaning forward, he tried for a note of seriousness. "So, Molly, what do we have on the agenda for the day?"

She paused with another bite of bacon almost to her mouth. Her hand dropped back to the table. "Well, I've been thinking about that."

"While you were in the bathroom for, oh…thirty seconds?" The rest of the time she'd either slept or talked. She hadn't really had time to ponder things.

Her chin lifted. "Actually, since I woke up in your backseat and realized you weren't with the bad guys, I've been considering what to do next."

Amazing. He believed her, though. He hadn't known her long, but he'd already figured out that she was that type of no-nonsense, get-it-together, make-a-plan woman. "Come to any conclusions?" He was dying to know.

"That depends." She fidgeted a moment, then tilted her head at him. "Are you expensive, Dare?"

Now what was she up to? He crossed his arms and sat back. "Very."

"So, that means you're really good?"

His eyes narrowed, and he said again, "Very."

Mulling that over, she nodded acceptance. "I'm not certain what type of work you do, but I know you carry a knife and a pretty big gun, and that you're darned good at getting in and out of dire situations."

All true enough.

"I trust what I know of you, and you *did* rescue me with no incentive other than that it was the right thing to do, so… I was hoping maybe I could hire you?" Very unsure of herself, she ended with a clear question, hoping for his cooperation.

Dare studied her, a little astounded, but also curious.

But again, it proved nearly impossible to know what was in that quick mind of hers. So far just about everything she'd said or done had been unexpected.

"To do what, exactly?" If she thought he was a murderer for hire, he'd just have to set her straight. Yes, he'd killed, but only when necessary to protect an innocent. Never in cold blood. Never for money.

He was as law-abiding as the next guy—when he could abide the law.

Leaning forward in her seat, Molly put her elbows on the table and stared him in the eyes. "Someone wanted me hurt, I'm sure of that. Maybe he even wanted me killed. I need to know who he is, or I'll never be able to relax. Until that person is revealed, I'll need protection." Her gaze dipped over his body, her lips rolled in, and she hurried her attention back to his face.

She let out a ragged breath. "God's truth, Dare, I think you're a man who could protect anything or anyone if you set your mind to it."

Damn right—but he wasn't yet ready to commit himself. There was a lot he didn't know about Molly Alexander. He started with the most obvious. "You said *he*. You think a man set you up?"

Her mouth twisted. "Actually, that was just a figure of speech. I didn't mean to leap to any conclusions. It could be anyone."

No kidding. "Do you have enemies, Molly?"

She laughed with a near-hysterical edge, but she quickly regrouped and picked up some toast. "All things considered, apparently I do."

He couldn't argue that point. The more he'd thought about it, the more her theory made sense. Someone must have wanted her taken, because she wasn't the young helpless innocent usually grabbed.

But he wanted to hear her reasoning. "What makes you so sure you weren't just a random grab gone awry?"

"Besides the obvious unsuitability for the standard— being gorgeous, stacked, younger women?" A new edge showed in her demeanor, a renewed fear and anger. "I wasn't treated the same. Not even close. They leered at the others, saw them as commodities, but they mostly just wanted to taunt me, as if they were allowed liberties with me that were forbidden against the others."

"The bruises on your face," Dare remarked aloud, and he had to tamp down his anger. "A bruised woman doesn't sell for as much."

She shrugged. "They never once struck the other women in the face. In fact, they might have manhandled them a little, but they didn't hit them at all."

"You egged them on." Dare couldn't get over that.

"Did Alani tell you that? Well, it's true, I guess—and it sort of makes me sound nuts, huh?"

"I don't know. Depends on why you did it, I guess."

Her hands curled into fists. "They wanted to break me, and I refused. I was afraid that once I did, once I fell apart, they'd go ahead and kill me. Like maybe that's what they were waiting for."

She'd crumbled the toast, realized it, and brushed her hands before folding them in her lap. "Believe me, I was terrified, but rather than show them that, I showed them the scorn I felt."

Again, she amazed him. She'd sized up the situation and rationalized a way to buy herself some time. "Go on."

"I sometimes overheard them talking. Mostly in Spanish, and my skills are rusty at best, but when one of the guys got really furious with me, another told him that he couldn't kill me. *Yet.*"

Dare said nothing as he absorbed that and considered the possibilities. They'd been waiting for something. But what?

"They followed someone else's instructions."

"Maybe," he agreed. Why else would they have kept her instead of selling her or killing her?

She met his gaze. "And then one of them said that…" She trailed off, distressed, angry.

Anticipating her answer, Dare leaned forward. "What?"

Her brows drew together, and she closed her eyes. "That I had surely learned a lesson."

He dropped back in his chair. Unbelievable. Had someone hired her abductors to torture her with uncertainty, cruel treatment, fear and humiliation? If so, it would have to be someone with a lot of hatred and resentment.

Someone she knew.

But how could one small, average woman incur that much wrath?

"Anyone obvious?" When she didn't reply, he said, "Come on, Molly, you know I'll need some specifics before I can be of any real help to you."

Sighing, she again gave up on the food. "Let's just say it could be anyone from my father and his associates, to my ex-boyfriend, to a disgruntled reader."

Her boyfriend? Then the rest of what she'd said registered. *"Reader?"*

Again she faced him, her shoulders back and her chin up. "I'm a writer."

"Published?"

She blinked before saying, "Well…yeah."

An unspoken *duh* sounded in her words. Dare shook his head. "I've never heard of you."

Something flashed over her features, maybe defensiveness. Had she caught grief for writing?

"You must not read dark, sexy romantic suspense." She tipped her head, not really proud, but maybe...smug. "My fourth book is being made into a movie. There's even talk of Ryan Reynolds playing the lead."

Incredulous, Dare whistled low under his breath. "Son of a bitch. You really can afford me, then?"

She picked up her fork with obvious renewed hunger. "For the breakfast—and with your agreement, a whole lot more."

MOLLY KNEW SHE'D thrown him with the bombshell about her career. But she couldn't hide her identity forever. What he said was true: if she wanted his help, and she did, then he'd have to know everything.

In good time.

The food was so delicious that she devoured it all—or at least what she hadn't destroyed while fretting through her theories. Afterward, she felt fabulous. Well, maybe that was stretching things, but she felt more human than she had in too many days. That hollowness in her gut was now satisfied. She felt stronger, steadier.

Dare had remained silent until she popped the last bite of bacon into her mouth and settled back in her seat with a sigh. "Thank you."

Flinty blue eyes, bright in the sunshine pouring through the window, scrutinized her. "You won't be sick?"

She shook her head. "Nope. I feel fine." And this time, it was true.

"Should I get more? Maybe some cake or pie?"

The courteous offer, in such a mild tone, was at odds with his expression. He looked harder than ever, more capable of deadly force.

She didn't understand him, but she trusted him. "I'm full, but thank you."

Surprising her with his lack of questions, he stood and headed for the door. "I already showered and shaved."

"I slept through that?" Disturbing, but then, she'd been so exhausted.… "I'm usually a very light sleeper."

"Extenuating circumstances," he said. "You can have some privacy for…whatever. I'll be back within the hour."

He shut the door before she could ask him where he was going. She had the distinct feeling that she'd run him off. He was such an independent, skilled person that being around someone like her, someone so damned *needy,* would probably suffocate him.

Determined to withhold further complaints, Molly got up and went to the window to look out.

Usually, whenever she admitted to being a writer, the questions started. *Where do you get your ideas? How long does it take to write a book? How much do you get paid? How did you get started?* She heard them often, sometimes with disdain when people discovered that she wrote for entertainment, not to impress the literary world.

Used to be, people asked her why she hadn't been on *Oprah,* or had her books been made into a movie, as if either was something in her control and easily accomplished. But with the recent movie deal, at least one of those questions had been replaced with another: Can I borrow some money?

Nearly everyone she knew wanted into her pocket. *Friends* she hadn't known she had showed up with great regularity. And when they didn't want money, they wanted an inside edge to meeting a celebrity, to hanging with the "in" crowd.

Molly snorted to herself. She hadn't changed, but everyone now treated her differently.

Pushing open the window, she let in the fresh air. Their room faced the parking lot, and she saw Dare get into his rented van and drive toward Walmart again.

If she looked to the left, she could just see the turbulent ocean as it teased a sandy beach, sending surfers atop waves, and then crashing them down again. People in Windbreakers strolled with their leashed pets. Lovers walked hand in hand.

Molly sighed and decided she could use another shower while Dare was gone. Maybe with enough shampoo and conditioner, she could ease some of the gnarled snags in her hair.

Sometime later, while she still stood under the warm spray, she heard a knock on the bathroom door.

"Molly?"

He'd returned sooner than she'd expected—or she'd lingered longer than she meant to. "Be right out," she called through the door.

"I got you some more clothes, so you don't have to put the same ones on if you want to change."

She chewed her lip. Yesterday he'd seen her in no more than a towel, but she hadn't been capable of presenting herself any differently. Today, feeling stronger, she wanted to be less of an imposition on him.

"Just a second." She stepped out of the shower, wrapped a towel around herself and cracked open the door. "You didn't need to do that."

His gaze dipped from her face to her barely visible right shoulder, and back up again. Handing in the bag, he said, "There's more out here, but this ought to get you started. I stuck the toothbrush and toothpaste in there that I bought yesterday, too."

Biting her lips in a long-standing habit, Molly nodded. "Thanks."

He put a hand on the door, keeping her from closing it. "You sure you're okay?"

Why her heart thundered that way, she couldn't say. She *did* trust him. But now that she wasn't so debilitated, everything seemed…different. More intimate somehow. "Almost like my old self."

His eyes narrowed the smallest bit. "You still look shaky to me."

A little, but that had more to do with talking to a big, powerful man while wearing only a towel than with her past ordeal. "Not at all."

"You're pale."

Odd, since she felt flushed. "My natural coloring?"

He considered her a moment more and must have decided to let it go. "I'll be here if you need anything." He released the door and stepped away.

Breathless with some unidentifiable emotion, Molly closed the door, locked it with an audible click that made her wince, and dropped back against it.

From the moment she'd laid eyes on Dare, she'd been aware of his size, his strong shoulders, bulging biceps and broad chest. For her, his strength equaled safety. He'd proved a capable lifeline when she needed one most.

Now that she could think clearly and those awful shakes had mostly subsided…she saw him as a man.

And what a man.

Why hadn't she noticed before how…how *gorgeous* he was? She was alone in a small hotel room with over six feet of sexiness. Windblown brown hair, piercing blue eyes, quiet control… Her heart continued to thunder.

She'd slept with him last night, curled tight along his side for comfort and security.…

Oh, God.

Heat flooded her face, and she pressed her hands there. On the phone, he'd mentioned "his girls." Did that mean daughters? Or maybe romantic involvements? And who had he been talking to? If he was in a relationship, had she inadvertently trespassed?

"Molly?"

Startled, she jumped away from the door. "Yes?"

"Are you going to finish your shower or not?"

Her eyes widened. Could he see through the damn door? Or was he just so attuned to everything and everyone that he heard her utter stillness in the bathroom?

She cleared her throat. "Yes, getting to it right now." Then she frowned and added, "Turn on the television or something." She didn't want him listening to her every movement.

When she heard the TV turn on—loudly—she rummaged through the bag he'd given her.

Toothbrush and toothpaste! Absurdly excited, she ignored the clothes and went scouting through the rest of the items, finding lotion, nail clippers and an emery board, a razor, and better shampoo and conditioner.

God love the man. How could someone so gruff, so... *deadly,* also be so sensitive?

Thrilled, she climbed back in the shower with much of her stash. Unmindful of wasting water, she cleaned her teeth until her mouth felt fresh again. The shampoo and conditioner had a pleasing scent and went a long way toward making her hair feel less like a rag mop. She even shaved her legs, careful of the scrapes and uglier bruises.

By the time she finished her shower and dried off, her newfound energy had waned. But she wasn't about to put on the new clothes he'd bought until she slathered on the lotion and clipped her ragged nails.

The clothes were similar to what he'd already brought her, just in different colors. Except for the panties; they remained plain white cotton.

Dressed, refreshed but tuckered out, she opened the door and stepped out to find Dare ignoring the blaring television as he stood to the side of the window, peering out. He looked suspicious of something, or someone.

Her heart tripped. Another threat? No—no, it couldn't be.

Molly was about to query him when he said, without looking at her, "All done?"

She didn't want to sit on the bed, so she went to the small table and pulled out a chair. Once again, he'd cleared away their breakfast mess. Dare did have a thing for order and cleanliness.

"I almost feel human again." What did he see outside that window?

"Good." He dropped the curtain and stepped back, then glanced at her. "We're leaving here."

"We are?"

With a nod, he said, "Today. I'll see if I can get us a flight home, and if not, we'll move to another hotel."

A flight home? His home or hers? And then what?

Nothing had been decided. The threat to her existed as strongly as ever. Shaken and again uncertain, she accepted that something must have happened for him to react like this.

Or maybe he'd felt that spark of interest from her... and he wanted no part of it. Remembering his concern for his girls, Molly started to tremble. *Who were they?* Dare didn't notice her reaction as he put in a call to "Chris" and gave instructions that she barely registered.

Was Chris his girlfriend? Or…more? She supposed Chris could be a male friend, or maybe just an employee or colleague.

She should just ask him—but his personal life was no business of hers.

Dare closed the phone, set it on the desk, crossed his arms over his chest and stared at her.

Her mouth went dry…until he said, "I bought the scissors you wanted. But before you use them, I want you to at least try to get the tangles out."

IT ANNOYED DARE, THE way she insisted that she felt fine. Anyone could see that the remnants of her nightmare still dragged at her. He knew from experience that an emotional drain could be as bad as, sometimes worse than, physical exhaustion.

Silent, withdrawn from him, she ruthlessly tugged the wide-toothed comb through her hair. As much as Dare tried to ignore it, he…couldn't.

Shoving away from the window and the beat-up red Ford truck he'd been watching, he stalked to her chair, pulled it from the table so he could get behind her, and said, "Let me have it."

Twisting around to stare up at him, she asked, "What?"

"The comb." He took it from her hand. "You're just yanking through the tangles."

Her eyes widened at him. "Because it'll take all day otherwise."

"You need to learn some patience." Lifting a hank of hair, he started at the bottom and used his fingers to separate the biggest tangles, then eased the comb through, working his way up until that hank of hair was smooth. When he finished, he went on to the next section.

Frozen, too quiet, Molly never objected when the comb snagged and pulled. He needed to get her talking again. Before they left the room, he wanted to know as much about her as he could.

"You mentioned a boyfriend."

"Ex."

That implied a conflict—possibly big enough to account for an abduction and deliberate mistreatment? "Tell me what happened."

She shrugged. "He wanted me to buy him rims for his car. I refused. We argued, and…things just fell apart."

Unable to imagine that, Dare frowned. "Why would he want you to buy him rims?"

One shoulder lifted. "I'd gotten a big check from the movie deal, so I guess he figured I could afford it." She tilted her head around to see him. "He wasn't the only one who thought I should have been bestowing gifts. Actually, just about everyone thought I should *share*."

"I don't know about everyone, but your boyfriend sounds like an ass."

"Ex." Her laughter surprised him. "And I guess he is. But I didn't know that until my career took off. Before that, he was generous and fun. It's not like he's a pauper himself. Adrian owns a bar, and it does pretty good."

With the back of her hair now smooth, Dare moved to her side. "So, just out of the blue, he asked you to buy him things?"

"Sort of."

He watched her profile as he worked through the tangles and saw her chin tighten in memory.

"We were heading home after lunch, and he pulled into this specialty shop, saying he wanted to look at some things. Car stuff bores me, but I went in and waited around while he and a salesman talked for what felt like forever. Then he came over to me and showed me the rims he wanted." She shook her head. "I know nothing about rims, so I just *oohed* and *aahed* over them, you know?"

Dare nodded. "Patronized him."

"Well… Yes, I guess."

Dare didn't fault her for that. "And?"

"He told me he couldn't afford them. So I asked why we were there, then, and he got frustrated with me."

Molly Alexander was an upfront, tell-it-like-it-is kind of woman. Subterfuge would be wasted on her. Imagining it almost made Dare smile. "You weren't picking up on his cues."

"Apparently not." She moved suddenly, saying, "Really, Dare, I could finish this."

He held the comb out of her reach. "You had your chance." He liked to finish what he started. And besides, he was sort of enjoying it.

Resigned, Molly crossed her legs and arms and shrugged.

Prompting her, Dare said, "You argued over the rims? There at the shop?"

"More or less. When he flat out said that I could afford them, and he wanted them, I just laughed. I mean, what do I want with rims? It's not so much that he asked me to buy him things, but how he did it. Just…demanding almost. And then he got furious, causing a big scene."

Dare shook his head.

"It was ridiculous and embarrassing, and when I told him to knock it off, he stormed out."

"Must have been an uncomfortable ride home." Although he figured that in most situations, Molly could hold her own.

She snorted. "I wouldn't know. I took a cab."

"He left without you?"

"He was still railing when I left the store to follow him, so I refused to get in the car until he calmed down. Calming down wasn't his priority, so, yeah, he left me standing there." She let out a long breath. "And for me, that was that. Later, Adrian tried apologizing, but I'm not big on public humiliation."

"Few people are."

"There'd been little things before then, and it all added up. The scene in the car shop was enough for me to realize how his true colors had begun to show once I started making more money with my writing. I made a choice not to be used."

At least she hadn't been in love with him, Dare thought. A woman in love didn't let a few money disagreements, regardless of how unpleasant they might be, end things. "All done."

She ran a hand over her hair, then looked at the small pile of hair on the table, comprised of the knots they'd pulled free and had to remove from the comb.

"Looks like we killed a rat."

He almost smiled—and his cell rang. While he answered the call from Chris, Molly tidied up again, then took the brush he'd bought and went into the bathroom. He heard the blow-dryer turn on with a loud whir. She closed the door to spare him the noise.

"What do you have for me, Chris?"

"Your ticket, plus one, leaving SDM in three hours on a private Beechjet with seating for seven. I know that's quick, but you said ASAP, right? Can you make that okay?"

Chris knew to always lead with the details. "You checked out the pilots?"

"Yup. Squeaky-clean records for both of them."

"Then, yeah, we'll be there."

"One of the pilots gave me his number, so take it down just in case. He said with what you're paying him, he can be flexible."

Dare shook his head. Chris took far too much enjoyment in spending his money. After he'd written down the pilot's name and cell number and stowed the paper in his pocket, Dare decided to clue Chris in. "Just so you know, I'm bringing *plus one* home with me."

Chris fell silent, but it didn't last long. "No shit? A girl?"

"Woman." Dare again looked out at the parking lot. The truck was gone, but he didn't trust it. He sensed they were being watched, and he fucking well didn't like it.

"And you're bringing her *here?*"

Yeah, unheard of. He'd kept his home sacrosanct from his business, but… "It's complicated." Molly was nowhere near ready to travel yet. The long trip back to Kentucky would be grueling for her. But right now, it was the only way he knew to keep her safe until he got things figured out. "She's hiring me to protect her."

"From what?"

Dare dropped the curtain and looked toward the bathroom door. He pictured her in there, worn out but determined to get her hair dried. She was an enigma with a huge problem.

He shook his head, more at himself than for any other reason. "Honestly, Chris, I wish to hell I knew."

CHAPTER FOUR

WHEN MOLLY EMERGED looking like a different woman, Dare did a double take. Her hair was…really nice; not the plain brown he'd assumed but a light brown with red and gold highlights that looked natural instead of salon-created.

Seeing it semi-fixed, soft and curling around her face, altered her appearance drastically, giving her a very feminine edge that was only enhanced by the vulnerability still visible from her bruises and tiredness.

Who knew a woman's hair played such a major role in her looks?

It was, Dare supposed, one of the many secrets to female routines. Not that he had a lot of experience with that, since he'd never been involved with any one woman long enough to dwell on her personal-grooming habits.

With the limited means at hand, Molly's hair was far from polished, hanging loose and shining to just below her shoulders. As Dare stared at her, she tucked one side behind her ear.

To cover his surprise, Dare said, "We're flying out in three hours."

Her eyes flared. "Okay. But…going where, exactly?"

As if he dragged home rescue victims on a regular basis, Dare shrugged. "My place, first. I have a few things I have to do at home. Then I'll accompany you to your place."

Taking his words like a blow, she went to the bed and gingerly sat at the edge. "Oh. Okay."

"I'll be with you."

She tried a smile that fell flat.

"Molly. You have to go back to your place sooner or later, right?"

"Of course I do." She put her shoulders back in telling reaction. "I need to talk with my editor and agent. I have…plants to water." She chewed her lip. "I need my flash drives and my own clothes and…" She shook her head. "Going back will be good."

Had she considered refusing? Dare frowned, then retrieved the first-aid kit from his bag. Given his line of work, he carried a more extensive supply of medicines and bandages than what was found in an average first-aid kit. He dragged a chair over and turned it to face her.

When he sat, he looked at her and saw again that she avoided his gaze. "That's it? Wholehearted acceptance, but no questions?"

She inhaled, expanding that impressive chest so that she filled out the oversized shirt. Her gaze skittered up to meet his. "You don't seem real forthcoming with information, and I don't want to do anything to make you regret your decision to stick with me."

An upfront answer. He should have known where her thoughts had taken her. "You think you've been a big imposition?"

She eyed the first-aid kit warily, but didn't mention it. "If not for me, you'd already be home, right? Instead, you had to deal with me and my problems. I don't like being dependent on anyone, and I really don't like putting you out."

"Since we're flying out today, I was only delayed one night. And if you mean the clothes and food—"

"Well, that and…" Her tongue flicked over her bottom lip with nervousness. "Sleeping with you."

There was that. "You had a nightmare. Don't worry about it."

She glanced up and away. "Logically I know I'm okay now, but at night, in the dark…"

"Yeah." He'd saved women before, but he hadn't slept with them. Hell, he'd had sex with plenty of women without *sleeping* with them.

"Usually," he said, "once I have a woman out of harm's way, she goes immediately to someone else—someone she trusts. Most often it's the person who paid me to get her out in the first place." And if the woman had nightmares, well, she had someone *other than Dare* to get her through it.

Molly nodded. "And with me, you not only haven't been paid, you're sort of stuck with me."

"Not stuck, no." He'd made the decision that she would remain with him. He never allowed others to coerce him, not in any way. "But understand, Molly—*for now,* I'm going to keep you safe. After I figure out the threat and decide how best to resolve it, then we'll come to terms on our agreement."

"Financially, you mean."

What else? He nodded affirmation, but said, "That, and more."

"Such as…?"

He opened the first-aid kit. "If I'm going to be in charge of your safety, you have to follow my directions to the letter. No balking, no arguments."

She licked her lips again—and nodded.

"Good. We'll start with me checking out some of these cuts and scrapes that you have. The last thing you need is an infection." He looked at her. "Give me your arm."

As if only then realizing that she might have cuts, Molly looked at each arm. "I can take care of it."

"I can take care of it better."

"Who says?"

"I say." Hadn't he already proven his capability with her hair?

Dare caught her arm and pulled her forward to reach the injury. Ignoring her protestation, he said, "This'll sting a little." He swiped the cut with the antiseptic and heard her hiss in a breath, but she didn't move and she didn't complain. The cut wasn't deep and didn't need stitches, but he dabbed it with an antibiotic ointment and covered it with a bandage.

The procedure was repeated on a small spot on her other arm, and when he looked down at her legs, her toes curled.

"Dare, really…" He bent to a scrape on her inner thigh, and she said in a rush, "Shouldn't I at least know your last name?"

Her high, shrill voice amused him. It wasn't from fear that she nearly screeched at him. No, it was…something else. But definitely not fear.

"Macintosh."

"Well, surely, Dare Macintosh, you will admit I can reach my own legs!"

She could—but he wanted to do it. Why, he couldn't honestly say, but a small lie would work. "I need to know it's done right, so just hush and sit still."

Molly had sleek, shapely legs and small feet. Her skin, where it wasn't hurt, was smooth and soft. He cupped the back of her knee and lifted her leg to treat what looked like rug burns. Since there'd been no carpeting in the trailer, he assumed the injuries were caused during her abduction. He wanted to know more about that, and would, soon.

He found two more deep scratches on her legs, and a cut on the side of her foot. As he treated her foot, he decided she'd need more than loose sandals to keep it protected.

He sat back. "Anywhere else?"

She rolled in her lips, released them, and gave in, putting a hand to the back of her neck. "I'm not sure, but there might be something here. It stung a little when I was showering." Lifting her hair, she turned to show him.

Dare flinched in rage. Clearly, someone had choked her, given the finger marks on her slender throat. Above the faded bruising, a deep scratch showed.

Under his breath, but not softly enough, Dare whispered, "Fuckers."

She swallowed. "The bruises are left over from when I was first taken. I didn't go along easily."

And so someone had choked her?

"They're almost gone now," she said, as if trying to reassure *him*.

"Not gone enough." He touched her shoulder, and felt her shiver as he turned her a little more so he could better see.

While holding up her hair, she dropped her head forward, and the pose was so innocently provocative, and yet so trusting, that he felt himself stir.

Damn it, it wasn't lust. What she made him feel was something more powerful than that—and more disturbing. He shook it off to concentrate on her injuries.

"How'd you get this scratch?" It looked deep, healed over a little, but still painful.

Her narrow shoulders lifted. "One of them wore an ornate ring."

And the bastard had been manhandling her enough to cut her with it? Yeah, Dare decided, he'd be protecting her—but he decided against sharing solid decisions with her yet. He needed a lot more info, and it'd be best if she thought his compliance hinged on her giving full truths.

In his experience, too many people had secrets that could alter the outcome of an event.

Dare treated the scratch, but didn't bandage it. "Done."

"So…" She turned on the bed again, facing him as he replaced the chair. "You've made plans to leave."

"In a few hours. Soon as we can get packed up, we're out of here."

She nodded, but hesitated. "I, um… Not that it matters in the long run, I guess, but…I feel conspicuous boarding a plane like this." She held out the hem of the big shirt he'd given her. "Do we have time for me to just buy some jeans and maybe…a bra?"

His mouth firmed. Looking at her, he could see the need for the bra, especially with her nipples puckered, pressing against the thin cotton of the shirt.

Yeah, he could make time for that. If she knew they'd be on a chartered plane, away from any crowds, she might not think that shopping was necessary, but it wouldn't hurt for her to get some shoes and socks, too. "We can spare about twenty minutes or so."

"I promise I can find what I need in that time." Hustling now, moving faster than he'd seen her move before this, she gathered up the few things he'd gotten her.

Dare nodded toward his bag on the bed. "Stow it in there."

"What will you do about your weapons?"

"Don't worry about it." Chris had already cleared it with the pilots of the chartered plane.

In no time, they were checked out and leaving the motel. Dare scanned the parking lot but didn't see anyone watching them. Making yet another trip to Walmart, he drove across the street and parked away from other shoppers.

Though she could no doubt afford to shop in a pricey boutique, Molly didn't turn up her nose at the racks. She looked tired, but it didn't slow her down as she located a pair of jeans, three pairs of socks, low boots, a bra, more underwear and a zip-up hooded sweatshirt in under the twenty minutes allotted.

She was a power-shopper—like him.

Impressed, Dare paid for the purchases and started back out to the lot with her.

That's when he spotted the red Ford truck. Handing the bag to Molly, he steered her to the side of the front doors and said, "Stay here until I come back for you. Don't move. Period. Do you understand me?"

"What? Wait." She grabbed for his arm in a flash of panic. "Where are you going?"

Dare scanned the area, deciding on the best advantage. Through his teeth, he said, "Tell me you understand."

She released her death grip on him. "I understand." Fear put a quaver in her voice. "I won't move from this spot."

"Good girl." Keeping his gaze on the truck driver, who hadn't yet noticed them, Dare darted out alongside a driver looking for a parking place. Staying low, uncaring of what others might surmise, he used the parking-lot traffic to conceal him until he could get to the other side of the truck.

Using an SUV for cover, he checked to see that Molly remained near the front doors. The driver of the red truck stepped out. He'd spotted Molly, was looking right at her, and then he started searching for Dare.

The driver, a dark guy with black hair and mirrored sunglasses, held a cell phone in his hand. For backup, or to report to someone?

Darting from car to car, Dare positioned himself behind the unsuspecting driver, and then he stepped out and straightened. Luckily they were far enough away from the front of the store that most of the bustling shoppers wouldn't notice them.

His heart beat slow and steady. His breath remained even; not too fast, not too shallow. He was in his element now, and he would damn well get answers.

Clearing his throat to draw the man's attention, Dare watched as the driver shifted his balance in surprise. Before he could turn, Dare kicked out his supporting knee, but he didn't let him fall. He grabbed his arm in a chicken-wing hold.

The driver cried out in mingled rage, fear and panic.

"Who are you?" Deliberately, Dare torqued the arm a little more. "Answer quick before I snap it."

In Spanish, he muttered, "No one. I was hired, that is all."

"Hired to do what?" And when the guy started to speak, Dare said, "In English, asshole."

"Call when you left the store, so the girl could be retrieved."

Ah. He'd told him to speak in English, and now that the man did, Dare didn't hear an accent. "Who wants her dead?"

"Dead?" He shook his head. "All I know is she escaped when she shouldn't have."

And so someone wanted her back? But *why?* Dare released the man's arm and jerked him around to face him. "Take off the sunglasses."

"Fuck you."

Moving so fast that the guy couldn't brace for it, Dare hit him hard in the gut. The blow stole his wind, collapsing him forward as he wheezed. Dare knocked the sunglasses off his face and, with a hand knotted in his shirtfront, lifted him to his toes.

American, not Mexican. Dare's jaw clenched. When he'd carried Molly out of the trailer, he hadn't left behind any witnesses to recognize him. Someone must have checked in after that, and realized she was gone. Tracking down an American woman rescued from Tijuana would be tough—unless someone had the same level of contacts as Dare. "Who are you supposed to call?"

"I don't know."

"Bullshit." The man briefly tried to struggle, but maintaining his hold on the guy's shirt, Dare drew the knife and pressed it just beneath the bastard's ribs. "You're really blowing my patience, amigo."

Very still now, his eyes wide at how hard that knife pressed into him, the guy spilled his guts. "Whoever had her wants her back. That's all I know, I swear."

Shoving him back against the vehicle, Dare said, "Dial it." Whoever the man was, Dare would talk to him himself. At the very least, he'd let him know the futility of continuing this pursuit.

The shaken driver punched in the numbers and started to hand the phone to Dare.

A ringing sounded over the parking lot.

Stunned, Dare's gaze shot up and locked onto a pay phone near the front entrance to the store…right where he'd left Molly.

Fuck. He leveled the driver with an elbow to the jaw and was already running flat out when he saw someone grab Molly from behind, wrapping an arm around her throat and clamping his other hand over her mouth.

Dare's vision went red.

Charging without making a sound, he closed the distance to Molly. The man holding her tried to drag her toward an idling Charger, but she thrashed and fought, and her captor had a hell of a time keeping control.

People around them watched in horror but offered no assistance.

Dare didn't need any.

Before the fuckers could stuff her in that car, he'd get them. It didn't matter that there were two of them. It wouldn't have mattered if there were four.

He would *not* let them take her again.

At a shout from the driver of the car, her assailant looked up and saw Dare gunning for him. Eyes widening with comprehension of Dare's rage, the man released Molly with a shove and jumped into the already moving black Charger. The car screeched out of the parking lot.

Stumbling into the brick facing of the store, her purchases scattered around her, Molly coughed and gasped for air. Tears rolled down her pale cheeks, more from being choked than weeping.

Bystanders gathered around her. One woman collected Molly's dumped belongings for her and, when she didn't accept them, set them near her feet.

His gaze glued to her, Dare elbowed his way through the crowd and reached out. "Molly."

She launched against him.

Tightening his arms around her, he tucked her face in

close and let her hide from their gaping audience. "I've got you, Molly. It's okay now."

But it wasn't, and they both knew it.

Someone wanted her badly enough to risk grabbing her in the middle of a busy parking lot. The truck driver had been no more than a diversion for him—and he'd fallen for it.

Fury, aimed at himself, made Dare a little more gruff than necessary when he pushed her back to see her face.

"Are you hurt?"

Eyes a little wild, face still white, she shook her head, saying shakily, "No. I don't think so."

But her knees were bleeding, and her hair was again a mess. He'd seen many things in his lifetime, and he'd gained a reputation for his calm, calculated response. Seeing Molly this way left him churning with very unfamiliar feelings.

Cold and precise, he caught Molly's elbow and grabbed up her bags. "Let's go."

He practically dragged her along, but he didn't want to take any more chances. Someone behind them yelled, "I called the cops. They're on the way."

Dare ignored him. Cops would want Molly to stick around answering questions, and that went against what Dare wanted—which was to get her the fuck out of there, away from danger.

No way in hell would he miss their chartered flight.

He opened the door of the rented van, shoved her purchases to the floor, and all but put her in the passenger seat. He even buckled her in—and she didn't protest.

She looked to be in shock, white-faced, shaken and so silent that it hurt him. Damn it, he wasn't a man to act without thinking things through, but now, with her…

The insane pressure built until he couldn't bear it anymore.

Dare cupped her face, leaned in and gave her a hard, fast kiss on the mouth.

That got her focused again. Heat flooded her face, and she inhaled sharply. As she touched shaking fingertips to her mouth, her wide-eyed gaze locked on his.

Still with his hand covering the coolness of her cheek, Dare said, "I'm not going to let them hurt you again, Molly. I swear it."

Two deep breaths expanded her chest. She rolled her lips in, stared a moment more, and then nodded. "Okay. I…" She blinked. "Thank you, Dare."

Her gratitude made him growl, but damn it, he didn't have time to explain something to her that even he still didn't understand. He slammed her door and jogged around to the driver's side. If he didn't hurry, they'd be there when the cops arrived and then he'd lose control of the situation. He needed to focus on protecting her, not dwell on how soft and sweet her mouth felt under his.

Within minutes they were well away from the Walmart and the possibility of police delays.

On the ride to the airstrip where they'd catch the charter plane, Dare questioned her. "Did the guy who grabbed you say anything?"

She held her hands in her lap, her face filled with confusion, maybe as much from his kiss as her near abduction. Dare could still taste her, and that brief touch of her mouth on his had stirred him and left him more determined than ever to keep her safe.

"They said to come along or I'd die." She looked over at him. "But…they probably planned to kill me either way, don't you think? That's why I fought them."

"You did good. You slowed them down."

"I knew you were close by, and I knew that you'd get to me in time."

Her faith struck him even more than that kiss had.

With still-wavering composure, she said, "Thank you, Dare. That's twice now—"

His temper all but snapped. *"Damn it, Molly."*

She jumped, and, feeling like a bully, he moderated his tone.

"I wasn't careful enough," Dare told her. "I didn't think that through. The minute I saw that idiot in the parking lot, I should have counted on a trap. I should have—"

"Stop it." The quietness of her trembling voice added gravity to the command. "You don't have psychic powers, so you couldn't have known."

"No, but I have experience and training."

She reached over and touched his shoulder. "God's truth, Dare, I feel safer with you than I possibly could with anyone else, so please don't get discouraged."

For Christ's sake. She was all but in shock—*again*—and through his ill humor, he'd given her the wrong impression. He drew one breath, then another. "I am not discouraged, Molly. Just the opposite, from here on out I'm going to be a hell of a lot more careful. Got it?"

"Oh. Okay. Thank you. I appreciate that."

Seeing that she was back to being super-proper again, Dare sighed. "Tell me about your family."

"Why?"

"You said it yourself, Molly. It could be anyone doing this to you. You need an outside perspective on things. It's always easiest to start with those closest to you."

Humoring him, she said, "And that'd be my family."

"Right. So tell me everything you can and let me sort out what's important and what isn't."

With a shrug, she pondered things. "Well, like I told you, I ended things with my boyfriend. Actually, he was a fiancé before we separated, but we hadn't yet picked a date to marry or anything."

Fiancé? That nettled him, sent a cold fist tightening in his gut. Why, he didn't want to ponder—except that he couldn't believe Molly had loved Adrian.

Maybe she'd realized that, too, which was why she'd used a good excuse to break things off with him. "Did your family like him?"

"There's only my Dad and Kathi, and my sister, Natalie. My dad's parents are deceased. He was an only child. There are aunts and uncles and all that on my mother's side, but they don't live near us, and I think I've met most of them only a couple of times in my entire life."

Trying to figure out the family dynamics, Dare asked, "So Kathi isn't your mother?"

"Stepmother." Without missing a beat, she said, "My mom threw herself off a bridge—twice—years ago."

Dare did a double take. Molly announced her mother's suicide so casually, it threw him. "I'm sorry."

Antsy, still shaking, Molly stared out the side window. "Dad made Mom miserable. I was twelve the first time she tried to kill herself. She jumped off a bridge, but there was a rescue team doing drills in the river. She didn't know they were there until they fished her out."

"Damn. That had to be rough."

She made a noncommittal sound. "Mom spent some time in the hospital, all the while with my dad harping over her selfishness and her weakness. For a few years after they released her, I thought she'd be okay."

"But she wasn't?"

"No." Molly shook her head, and her voice lowered. "When I was fifteen, Dad cheated on her, and I guess it was too much." She looked at Dare. "When she threw herself off the bridge the next time, she made sure it was a bridge over a highway, not water."

Sorry he'd brought up such painful memories, Dare muttered, "Jesus."

"Yeah." Her hands knotted together, and she stared off at nothing. "Dad never showed much remorse, but he didn't see the other woman again, either. I don't think either of them, my mom or the woman he cheated with, ever meant that much to him."

"Your dad sounds like a real prince."

"He's a selfish, pampered, class-A snob, believe me. He finds fault with everyone or everything."

"Including his daughters?"

"Especially his daughters." She glanced at Dare, her nose wrinkling. "I sometimes wonder how Kathi puts up with him."

Hoping to get her back on track, Dare asked, "Did Kathi like Adrian?"

"She thought he was nice and wished us well. But Kathi is like that. Despite being rich even before she married my dad, who is pretty darned well-to-do, she tends to be very accepting of most people."

Interesting. "So you get along with Kathi?"

Molly shrugged. "We don't have a lot in common, really. She's into social clubs and designer clothes, and she likes decorating, art and museums."

"You said your dad is rich, so you must be used to those things, too."

"No, Dad wanted Natalie and me to make it on our own, to earn our keep, as he put it. We skipped the private schools and travel abroad, and we always had summer jobs. I'm glad he took that attitude, because I wouldn't want to be like him. And I'm not. But now, even though

I've made it on my own, he finds me something of an embarrassment."

With a red haze still crowding in around his vision, Dare knew that he didn't like her father at all, and he wanted to put him at the top of his list of suspects. But he needed to be cold and methodical, not emotional and irrational.

Needing more info, he took a breath, locked his teeth, and asked, "How so?"

"It's funny, really. Well, maybe *ironic* is a better word. See, all of Dad's friends' daughters are active in the community, heading up charitable events and stuff—as they were groomed to do. Some of them even work with Kathi. She's a regular philanthropist. But thanks to how Dad raised us, that world is alien to me. So while the daughters of Dad's peers are being revered in the press for their activism, all I do is mail off a check."

"It's more than most people do." At least he'd distracted her, Dare decided. Her trembling had subsided, and she wasn't so pale.

"Maybe." She gave him a look and then shrugged. "In hindsight, I think Dad feels slighted that his offspring are so dismissed."

"He sounds like an ass."

She smiled and said again, "Maybe," then added, "Most society women live in influential neighborhoods with posh accommodations, but my apartment is pretty simple."

"Simple is good."

"For me, it's less about impressive entertaining and more about being functional so that I can find files and research notes when I need to. I've always been more into comfort than fashion, and when it comes to art, I like movie posters." She gave a mock shudder. "Dad can't stand it that I don't own a single piece of *real* art."

Dare imagined her apartment, and somehow it fit with what he already knew of her.

"Kathi has offered to go shopping with me." Her lip curled. "To *help* me, you know, so that I can better represent my father. She's all about making Dad look good however she can. But usually I stay too busy with deadlines to care about representing anything but my work."

"Kathi sounds a little hoity-toity, but you just sound real."

"Don't get the wrong idea. For the most part, we get along fine. Kathi does enjoy the finer things in life, but unlike my dad, she makes an effort to get along, and better still, she doesn't turn up her nose at genre fiction."

"What you write."

"Kathi actually reads all my work." She managed a half grin, and in a conspiratorial whisper added, "It drives my dad nuts."

"He doesn't read you?"

"God, no." The mere thought had her looking ill.

Huh. "I would think all of your family would read you." He was damn curious himself, and he planned to pick up one of her books at the first opportunity.

"My sister does sometimes, but mostly because...well, she's my sister. You know? It's not really her thing. She's more into political dramas or true crime. And Dad..." Molly gave a mock shudder. "He wouldn't be caught dead with a genre book in his personal library. Especially not one with explicit *sex* in it, and most especially not one of *my* books."

That diverted Dare from his annoyance with her father. "Your books have explicit sex in them?"

She immediately went defensive. "Life has sex in it, and I write about life, about people who face hardships and in the end triumph through it all. Any really good triumph deserves a lasting love, don't you think?"

Before he could answer, she said, "Of course it does. And any lasting love has to have really hot, wonderful sex."

Dare raised a brow. He had no argument against hot sex, with or without love. Again, he brought her back to the point. "How about your sister? You said she reads your books just because you're related. But how do the two of you get along otherwise? Did she like Adrian?"

Molly went quiet for a moment. "My sister... Well, Natalie and I are pretty close. She's only three years younger than me, and through high school and college we hung out together. She's not just my sister but my best friend, too. As my best friend, she doesn't think anyone is good enough for me, but she especially didn't like Adrian. Actually, she pegged him from jump. He *was* a gold digger, a user and a bully."

Dare liked her sister already. "So we can rule out Natalie?"

Molly smirked. "She'd go after anyone who even spoke an unkind word to me."

"Including your father?" Dare was relieved to see the tension leaving her by small degrees. Her inner strength and composure astounded him. There were no tears, no dwelling on what might have happened. She understood the urgency of the situation, but she didn't fall apart over it.

"Dad butts heads with both of us on a regular basis. It's pretty much what our relationship is all about—strife, contempt and strained politeness. If it wasn't for

Kathi, I don't know how often Natalie or I would even see him."

"So Kathi is the glue?"

"Pretty much. She's forever inviting us all over together, hoping against hope that somehow my dad will move beyond his rigid censure of us. I think she's motivated by appearances, mostly. You know, it looks better if Dad's daughters actually like him and enjoy his company." Her smile went flat. "But at least she tries."

Could her father be responsible for her abduction? "You said he's well-to-do."

"Bishop Alexander is an extremely successful businessman. He inherited his father's corporation, which was thriving to begin with, but he's grown it ten times over."

"Meaning he has enough money to arrange and finance your kidnapping?"

The idea stalled her. "Money, means and a cold enough heart. But…" She looked at Dare. "I can't imagine him doing that. We've had our ups and downs, but my dad just isn't the type to dirty himself with something so sordid and illegal."

Dare knew that the most unlikely people often did things that those closest to them could never fathom.

Molly stared down at her hands, struggling with the idea of what had happened. Finally she said, "The thing is, I can't imagine anyone who is the type. Until this happened, I didn't know that anyone disliked me that much."

They were almost to the airstrip, a little ahead of schedule. Dare didn't want her to get upset all over again. "One more question."

"What?"

"If you and your sister are so close, she must know

you're gone, and she must be worried." Molly stiffened a little, but Dare couldn't back down. "So, Molly, tell me. Why didn't you want to call her after you knew you were safe?"

CHAPTER FIVE

MOLLY STARED IN wonder as Dare led her to the small private plane. The wind on the airstrip blew her hair into her face, making her stumble over a step. Dare caught her elbow in a firmer grip and kept her upright.

He had a lot of questions, but she didn't have that many answers.

Luckily he'd received a call that had lasted right until he was ready to drop off the rented van. She thought it might have been Chris again, and the call had left her mired in confusion.

Dare spoke to Chris with familiarity, affection and ease—proof that they shared a definite closeness. Maybe even…intimacy.

If Chris was a girlfriend, then why would Dare have kissed her? He didn't strike her as a user, as a man who would cheat. He was far too protective to be deliberately hurtful to anyone he cared about.

It was possible she was making too much of the kiss. He'd wanted to snap her out of her shock, and…the kiss had certainly done the trick, and then some.

After turning in the van, Dare gave her enough time to go into the ladies' room to change into her new clothes. While there, she'd cleaned the blood off her knees and elbows and tidied her hair. If she thought of how those men had tried to get her, it made her ill.

She never, ever wanted to be at someone else's mercy again. Not like that. She couldn't bear it.

But Dare had saved her, and now, Chris or no Chris, it sounded like he planned to protect her. She drew a calming breath and reminded herself to take it one step at a time. It was the only way she could hold it together.

As soon as she'd emerged in the clothes that mostly fit and were much more comfortable, Dare began hustling her to the plane.

Remembering her mother's death left her aching with fresh hurt. Thinking of her father's disapproval always filled her with burning resentment. And yes, Natalie would be frantic, a fact Molly hated.

But someone had put her through hell, and she had to concentrate on that, and only that. She didn't know who to trust—except for Dare.

He'd kissed her. What did it mean?

When one pilot came out to greet Dare with a healthy dose of deference, Molly realized that Dare must be affluent. How else could he afford to pay for a spur-of-the-moment charter flight from one side of the country to the other?

Or…did he expect her to pay for it? Would this be added to her expenses?

She eyed the spiffy-looking plane anew. Unlike her father, she'd never flown privately before. The plane was small enough to make her extremely nervous.

Until they got aboard.

"Wow."

Distracted, Dare glanced down at her. "What?"

"This is…decadent."

He gave a cursory look around the plane, but just shrugged. "It's comfortable enough. Grab a seat."

There were only seven, but Molly wanted as much

privacy from the two young, *GQ*-looking pilots as possible, so she headed toward the rear of the plane, near the lavatory. The backseats faced forward, so she could see Dare still up front talking to the men, discussing a short layover to refuel and the estimated time of arrival.

At her seat was an entertainment console with a monitor, satellite hookup and a DVD/CD/MP3 player. Still looking around, she made note of the burl wood cabinetry, the butter-soft tan leather seats, plush carpeting and a fully stocked bar.

Dare knew how to travel in style. She only hoped it wouldn't break her bank account. She had no idea what something like this might cost.

He joined her a moment later. "Want a drink?" He indicated the fancy lighted bar she'd already noted.

"No, thank you."

"You sure? Might steady you a little."

"I'm plenty steady, thank you very much." How many times did she have to tell him that she would not fall apart? She couldn't afford to. If she wanted to survive this, she had to keep her nerves steady. Later she could give in to the panicked hysteria that still gnawed on her façade of calm.

Shrugging, Dare sat beside her and fastened his seat belt. "Buckle up."

She scowled at the order but still connected the seat belt around her.

Lifting his armrest and turning in his seat, he leaned forward with his elbows on his knees, his hands hanging loosely. He studied her.

"What?" Just then the pilot started the engines, startling Molly. She grabbed for the armrests. "We're taking off?"

"It'll be easier to get home that way."

She scowled again. "Sarcasm is unnecessary."

He said nothing. Molly cleared her throat. "Where is home, and when will we get there?"

"Kentucky, and it'll be late."

As the plane rolled forward, she sucked in a breath and then swallowed hard.

Dare eyed her. "So, you're one of those women who panics at flying?"

"No." But she was, sort of. That the plane was so small didn't help matters. Rigid from her head to her toes, she repeated, almost by rote, "I'm fine."

"So you keep saying."

He took her hands, and it reminded her of the differences in their sizes. Dare was huge, and she was not. His big rough hands totally engulfed hers, making her feel extra small and delicate.

She didn't quite know what to make of that.

"Molly, look at me."

When she did, she got snared in his bright-blue gaze. He had the most amazing eyes....

"Tell me why you haven't contacted your sister to let her know you're okay."

The pilot announced something over a speaker system, and the plane moved, jarring her heart. She squeezed Dare's hands and when she spoke, her voice was a little too high and squeaky. "Natalie might be a little younger than me, but she's a teacher—meaning she's used to governing with ultimate power."

Dare didn't smile at that small jest. "Yeah, so?"

"So if I had called her, she'd be grilling my dad and Adrian and anyone else she thinks could be responsible. There's no way Natalie *wouldn't* be on the warpath, trust me. If either of them is involved, they might be clued in.

They could hide evidence or, in Adrian's case, maybe even skip town."

Dare looked a little stunned at her reasoning, but damn it, she couldn't take chances.

"Whoever did this to me, I want him to be taken by surprise when he sees me free and unharmed. I want to blow his mind, and then maybe he'll give himself away."

Consternation lowered Dare's brows. "Not a bad plan, really. But you do realize that whoever arranged this must already know that you're free. That's what those thugs at Walmart were about."

"I know. But they don't know when they'll see me, or if the thugs will get me again before it becomes a concern. I can't believe they'll just give up, which means—"

"People are still after you."

"Yes." She shivered and then shivered some more when the plane began lifting. She squeezed Dare's hands as tightly as she could. "Oh, God."

Dare searched her face, looked resigned and…maybe a little expectant. Then he leaned forward and kissed her again.

Molly was so shocked, she leaned away from him—until he pulled his hands free from hers and cupped her face, bringing her back.

His hands holding hers had been startling; his hands gently framing her face were more so.

This kiss wasn't hard and fast. It was warm and easy, slow, lingering and oh-so-distracting. When she didn't retreat again, he turned his head to better fit their mouths together and deepened the kiss.

A rush of heat chased away her icy fear. Her rigid muscles went liquid. Wow.

Molly caught his wrists, but not to pry him away; she

held on for dear life. Being thirty years old, she'd been kissed many times, but never had it felt like...*this*. When she made a small sound, a cross between a moan and a purr, Dare stroked his thumbs over her cheeks.

A second later, he touched his tongue to hers.

Heart pounding and skin burning, Molly forgot about the plane, about unscrupulous dogs who meant her harm. Right now, for this moment, there was only Dare and his warmth and intoxicating scent, his strength and the security of him, the way he tasted and felt and how he touched her.

He smoothed a hand over her face, over her hair and, to her regret, eased away.

Molly got her eyes open, only to find that the blue of his looked incendiary. He glanced down at her mouth, eased his thumb slowly over her bottom lip and, with a frown, settled back into his seat.

She, on the other hand, perched as far forward as her seat belt would allow, still straining toward Dare. With a gasp, she realized how that looked and flopped back. Again, she clamped her hands over the ends of the armrests.

Her heart continued to thunder, and her body burned in select places. She could feel Dare looking at her, and it made her both uncomfortable and more excited. Was he waiting for her to react?

Well, this was not something she could ignore. The first kiss, maybe. But *that* kiss? No way. "Dare?"

He watched her like a hawk watched a mouse, his gaze unflinching, ready and alert, almost as if he expected her to bolt. "Hmm?"

"That's, uh, the *second* time you've kissed me."

His gaze went back to her mouth, his voice deepened. "I can count."

She chewed her lips, saw his eyes narrow and quickly relaxed her mouth again. Rather than ask a direct question about Chris, she said, "You were distracting me, because the flight—"

"No."

No? But of course he was. Wasn't he? She shook her head. There was so much she didn't know about him, but she didn't want to cross the line and become intrusive into his private life. "I don't understand what it means."

His gaze lifted back to hers. "Yes, you do." He looked over her entire body, oh-so-slowly, before coming back to her face. "It bothers you?"

Bother her? She considered his interest, his attention, and…no. It didn't *bother* her, at least not the way he meant. If anything, she felt wonderfully flattered—if he wasn't already involved with someone else. "I just don't understand."

"Hell if I do either." With a wince, he stretched out his long legs as if uncomfortable. "Not once, before you, have I ever come on to a woman I rescued. In every other case it would have been unethical." When he turned his head toward her again, she saw his frustration and knew it was more with himself than with her. "In your case, no one hired me, so that restriction isn't there."

"No, it isn't." He wouldn't be betraying anyone's trust to deliver her home safely, because she was the one hiring him. And she knew without a doubt that if she said no, Dare would respect that.

"But what happened, the hell those bastards put you through…" His gaze searched hers. "What happened just today should be enough to shut me down."

"Why?" Molly really didn't think she wanted him *shut down*.

His expression turned grim. "You haven't exactly been around sterling examples of manhood, Molly."

She'd been held captive by total cretins—who had nothing in common with this remarkable man. Unable to help herself, she put a hand on his muscular forearm. "But don't you see, Dare? That's why you stand out even more. You're very, very different from them."

"I know that." He worked his jaw. "Do you?"

"Yes." She hadn't known him long, but the threatening situation had given him room to prove himself beyond all measure.

"No residual effects, then?" When she just looked at him, not really comprehending, he shook his head. Measuring each word with care, he said, "Sometimes, after a trauma like yours, anything remotely similar can trigger the bad memories, the panic, even hysteria. In your case, a guy getting too close—"

"But you're not just any guy." Molly hoped her smile might reassure him. "You are the guy who got me out of that nightmare. I could never feel about you how I feel about them."

Unconvinced, Dare turned his hand over and waited for her to lace her fingers with his. She did so hesitantly. This was the fastest any relationship had ever moved for her, and the unusual circumstances were such that she didn't entirely trust her own judgment. Not that she questioned Dare or his motives.

But her own?

She didn't want to smother him with her neediness, an emotion normally foreign to her but plenty prevalent right now, no matter how she tried to hide it.

He lifted her hand, stroked her knuckles with his thumb, and while it was the gentlest of gestures, he quickly turned very businesslike.

"We have a lot to get through, Molly. More than you probably realize. Getting the goons off your ass will be the easiest part. Finding out who arranged your abduction—that's going to take some doing. And trust me on this, the truth isn't going to be satisfying. It's a necessity, but it won't make you feel better, and it won't soften the memory."

"How do you know?" More than anything, she looked forward to nailing the ones responsible. She needed some closure on this living nightmare.

"For one thing, it's almost always someone you know, and someone you'd never suspect." He held her hand tighter. "Because it's usually someone you have a relationship with."

Her heart squeezed tight. "But I still have to know."

"Of course you do. And for that reason, I have a million questions I have to ask, and I can guarantee it's not going to be easy for you. Inquisitions seldom are. But it's information I need—"

"It's okay." Molly licked her lips. "If…if this is going to be as hard as you say, then what do you suggest I do?"

His eyes narrowed. "For starters, be one hundred percent honest with me, always."

"All right." She'd never been a deceptive person anyway, and now, more than ever, she knew that honesty over every little detail really mattered.

He unbuckled her seat belt. "I specifically requested no stewardess on the plane to ensure that we were alone."

"You did?" Before she could ask why, he lifted her over to sit in his lap.

He leaned the seat back and arranged her so that they were both comfortable. "You still need to catch up on your sleep. This might be a good time."

With her face against his chest, his scent surrounding her, Molly allowed the lethargy to seep in. She was exhausted, and somehow Dare had known that once she got settled so close to him, giving in to the need for rest would be easier.

After a lusty yawn, she gathered her thoughts. "You said you have questions."

"I do."

His left hand rested loosely at her hip, and his right hand was behind her, keeping her close. Molly felt secure and safe. "So?"

"They'll wait until we're at my place—after we've both slept and eaten."

That worked for her, but… "Well, I have some questions, then."

He tucked in his chin to look down at her, saw that she was serious and relaxed back again. "Shoot."

It was easier like this, without him looking right at her. "You're…attracted to me?"

His short laugh rumbled from his chest beneath her ear. "Definitely." He looked down at her once more. "You had doubts about that?"

"I don't know." She had doubts about Chris, but for the moment, at least, it was easy to push those concerns from her mind. "You're different from other men I've known."

"Not so different. I had to fight off a boner so I could hold you like this without maybe scaring you off."

His plain speaking fascinated her, but she didn't dwell on that. "I'm not scared of you, Dare."

"No," he said slowly, "you aren't, are you? But neither of us yet knows how ready you really are. You're holding it together, so let's don't test the waters too much, okay?"

Honestly, she was so wiped out, and still felt so…raw, she didn't mind that suggestion at all. "The thing is, I don't get it."

"What's not to get?"

"I'm hardly at my best right now. Physically, I mean. I look like—"

"You've been abused for nine days. Yeah, I know." He gave her a little squeeze. "Bruises and fatigue can't camouflage what's there, Molly. You're still an attractive woman. But looks aren't the only draw."

"What else?" He didn't know her well enough to like her personality. Or did he?

"Bravery is something I admire a lot. Intelligence, ingenuity, control, logic. You've got it all in spades, lady, and I think it's sexy as hell."

Even before she'd been taken, her breakup with Adrian and her father's censure had left her struggling for her self-confidence. So many accolades now put her on the verge of being weepy. She didn't feel brave or ingenious. She felt used, duped, angry and, deep down, very scared.

Twisting around a little, she half sat up and looked at Dare. "Those men didn't kiss me."

"No?"

She shook her head. "You don't have to worry about me overreacting to that."

For only an instant, he flashed that crooked grin again. Then something much hotter replaced the humor. "You want another kiss, do you?"

"I really do."

Dare looked at her bruised cheekbone, at another fading mark beneath her eye. "They hit you." His voice roughened; his hands on her tightened in a sign of protectiveness. "And bit you."

Molly drew in a thin breath. She couldn't deny it, but

right now the reality of that seemed further away. "You're not trying to do either."

For the longest time he watched her, trying to gauge her mood, she knew. Molly just waited, anticipation heightened, tension coiling.

He said very softly, with suggestion, "Well, maybe the bite, yeah?"

She blinked, her body clenching with interest as he leaned in, ever so slowly, toward her neck. She felt his hot breath first, then the feather-light press of his mouth, the sensual touch of his damp tongue and, lastly, the light grazing of his sharp teeth along her skin.

Her breath caught loud enough that he paused, but when she didn't pull away, he resumed teasing her, making her toes curl, her stomach flutter. He opened his mouth and treated her to a tantalizing love bite that sent liquid sensation throughout her whole body.

Near her ear, he whispered, "Now, when you think of biting, think of me, okay?"

Caught up in building need, Molly wrapped her hands around the back of his neck and sought his mouth. She actually needed his kiss as much if not more than she needed sleep.

"Easy," he whispered, and then his mouth was on hers, taking and giving, consuming her awareness of everything but him.

Even as his kiss overshadowed her worries, she wondered: *How was this so different?* Before now, she'd thought a kiss was a kiss was a kiss. Some were exciting, some were so-so, but kissing Dare caused a singular effect in her.

In a nanosecond, a kiss from him ratcheted up her need. She wasn't an overly sexual woman at the best of times, and this, most definitely, was not the best of times.

She should have been sleeping as he'd suggested, and instead...

He gave her his tongue, and everything in her tightened with desire.

Molly tried to scoot closer to him, into him. She let her hands wander over his broad, hard shoulders, down over bulging pecs and lower still to his flat abdomen. All over he was solid, hot and powerful.

She got one hand in under his T-shirt, made contact with his sleek skin, up his side to his muscular back...and then she felt it—the telltale rise of an erection beneath her hip.

He pulled his mouth away with a low curse.

"Dare?" She was breathing too hard and fast. "You—"

"I know. Trust me, it's not something I'd miss."

Incredibly, Molly rolled in her lips and tried to figure out the possibilities of the scenario. She glanced over her shoulder toward the cockpit that housed the two pilots. As long as they stayed there, she and Dare had moderate privacy....

Dare gave a gruff laugh. "Forget it. Not happening."

That he'd so easily read her thoughts left her blushing.

He shook his head. "You're something else, you know that?" He kissed her hard and quick before urging her head to his shoulder. "I want you to try and sleep. I need some time to think."

Toes curled and body throbbing, Molly forced herself to relax against him. She hoped he wasn't thinking of how to handle her. She didn't want to be handled. She wasn't sure what she wanted, really. Except maybe more—

Before she could finish that thought, Dare kissed her on the top of the head. "You're more fragile than you realize, Molly Alexander." He caught her chin, turning her face toward him. "Don't push yourself. I want you—that's not going to change. I can't say I won't kiss you, but how far and how fast we go is up to you."

Dear God, did he mean she'd have to…ask?

His mouth tipped in a crooked smile. "You're a big girl, Molly, and you have a lot of backbone. When you're ready, you can tell me."

"But…"

"For my sake, let's give you some time to come to grips with everything. Okay?"

She didn't know herself right now, so maybe he was right. Besides, she didn't have the sexual savvy to insist. "Okay."

She closed her eyes and, with Dare's hand stroking over her back, gradually faded into a deep, untroubled sleep.

EVEN WHEN THE PILOT'S voice broke over the speaker system announcing the weather forecast for their landing, which was thankfully clear and dry, Molly slept.

Hours ago, they had landed to refuel, and she'd slept through it. Dare glanced at his watch. He would have eaten on the plane if he could have without waking her. Now it was well past dinnertime and they still had an hour to drive after they left the airport. A drive-through burger would have to do, because he wasn't stopping, wasn't taking any chances with her at all. He'd feel better about things once he had her secured on his grounds.

While she'd been utterly lax in his arms, he'd studied every inch of her, all the while sorting through what he knew of her, and what he didn't. That she'd survived amazed him. *How* she'd survived was the kicker. She had plenty of backbone, and so much bravado that he couldn't help but admire her.

Seemed he couldn't help wanting her, either.

Though she obviously didn't know it, Molly was a sexy mix of innocence, courage, independence and honesty. The combo hit him on a gut level. It had been a hell of a long time since a woman had really gotten to him. He'd made a point of not letting them.

But with Molly, she got under his skin without even trying.

Maybe that was it—that she wasn't trying. She was just herself, an appealing, wounded woman determined to confront her own personal reality head-on.

Whatever the cause, he had to remember all that she'd suffered so that he didn't rush her into anything.

Beyond that, he didn't want to set himself up, either.

She stirred again, and since the plane would soon be landing, Dare woke her.

"Feel better?"

His voice must have reached her, because she went still but didn't open her eyes. Breathing deep and slow, caught in the enchantment between wakefulness and slumber, she smiled and curled closer.

Warmed by her trust, Dare bent and kissed the bridge of her nose, and then scowled over the impulsive move. He *had* to back off. "Wake up, woman." He jostled her a little. "I'd like to get to my house before midnight."

"Midnight?" Blinking heavy-lidded eyes, she half sat up, took in her surroundings and self-consciously smoothed her hair. "It'll be that late?"

Damn but she looked sweet all sleepy like this. "Depends on how long it takes them to land and let us off the plane. Then we have an hour's drive."

Her stomach rumbled, and she ducked her head. "I've been asleep awhile."

Meaning she was hungry, too? "I want to make good time, but I plan to get some fast food to eat on the fly."

"Sounds good..." Face going pink, she suddenly remembered that she was still in his lap. She eased over into her own seat. "Whatever you want to do is fine."

With a dry tone, Dare teased, "Really?"

Nodding, she fastened her seat belt around her. "I'm sorry I conked out like that." She cast him a sideways look. "You should have woken me or at least told me to get in my own seat."

"I didn't mind." In fact, he'd enjoyed it. But now he needed to stretch his legs and tend to other needs. They only had a few minutes before the plane would begin its landing. "I'll be right back."

He went to the lavatory to relieve himself and freshen up. Cold water on his face did nothing to clarify his jumbled thoughts. Soon he'd have Molly ensconced in his home, where he'd never even brought a woman for dinner, much less invited her to stay.

Running a hand over his face, Dare imagined how it might be with Molly there, how she'd react to his girls and Chris.... "Fuck." Stewing over it in the tiny airplane john wouldn't help, and he wasn't a man who believed in stewing anyway. He was a proactive person. If he didn't like something, he changed it.

With Molly, he'd just have to wait and see.

He returned to find her looking in desperate need herself. "Go ahead. But make it quick, okay?" He waited in the aisle for her as she dashed out of her seat, and while she was gone, he poured her a juice over ice and located some mixed nuts for them both.

She was buckled back in her seat a minute later,

grateful for the juice and snack, and less than half an hour after that, a shuttle dropped them off in the long-term parking area, and Dare, with a close eye on his surroundings, loaded her into his SUV.

What his girls would think of her, he couldn't imagine. He knew damn good and well how Chris would feel, though: territorial and antagonistic. But then that's how Chris usually felt about everything. Dare considered those some of his finer qualities.

CHAPTER SIX

IT WAS NEARING eleven o'clock when Dare pulled down the long drive to his home. Molly had been mostly quiet during the ride, except to thank him for the feast of a hamburger, fries and milk shake.

One thing about Molly: she was still putting the food away. If she always ate like this, she had to have one hell of a fast metabolism to stay so petite. At a little over five and a half feet tall, she had curves aplenty, but in all the right places. Her limbs were slim, and she had a tiny waist. When he'd held her, he knew she weighed next to nothing. She might have lost weight in her nine days of captivity, but it couldn't have been too substantial or she wouldn't have physically recovered so quickly.

So…was she always stacked? Did she maintain that figure even while hiding it from most? She wasn't a flaunter—he knew that right off. With women, you could always tell which ones liked to be front and center, using their bodies to draw attention.

Molly didn't lack confidence, but it had little to do with her figure and a lot to do with her intelligence.

As he neared their destination, she listened to his CD collection and brooded. She was a survivor, so likely she'd put her brain to the task of going over a variety of scenarios in an attempt to be prepared. A futile effort, but Dare wouldn't tell her so.

She was so involved in her own thoughts that Dare knew she didn't realize they were almost home.

By deliberate means, his place was set way back in the woods, hidden by tall evergreens and a variety of hardwoods, with a narrow road that climbed up to the main gate. The way the road twisted and turned in and around trees helped to hide it.

He'd planned it that way.

Headlights shone on the impressive and ornate iron fencing that enclosed the front of his property. The rest of the land, all fifteen acres, was protected with electric fencing. Only the lake offered free access, but that, too, was secured with lights and alarms.

Agog, Molly twisted in her seat to look out each window, taking in the view. "This is where you live? Seriously?"

"Yeah."

She dropped back into her seat. "It's like vacation property."

"Pretty much." Once he reached the security gate, Molly went silent. All movement stopped, and she stared as Dare rolled down a window and punched in a private code that opened the gates. He drove beyond them and they closed again.

She just stared.

In response to her mute amazement, Dare told her, "Be prepared."

She blinked fast as if to refocus. "For what?"

"Chris will come out to meet us. My girls, too."

After moistening dry lips with a quick lick, she said, "I heard you mention them. On the phone, I mean. Back at the motel room."

Her stilted speech amused Dare. "I do love my girls."

She cleared her throat. "Chris, too?"

"Definitely." Knowing she didn't entirely understand, and willing to tease her, Dare said, "Chris will try to intimidate you, so be prepared."

She cleared her throat. "Chris is…?"

"Housekeeper, manager, assistant—pretty much everything."

"Everything?" she asked, her voice high and faint.

Dare couldn't help but grin. "Sure." And then, "Just ask him. He'll tell you how important he is."

Her jaw loosened. *"He* will?" Then, before Dare could reply, "Chris is a guy?" And then with confusion, "You live with another man?"

"Yeah."

"Does…he have a wife? Or maybe a girlfriend?"

"No." Dare knew she was trying to figure out the dynamic. He waited two heartbeats, then said, "Chris is gay."

"Gay?" Mystified, she stared at him. "But you're not…?"

Dare gave her a look. "Are you actually asking me that? Because I thought I'd made my sexual preferences pretty clear already."

"I thought you did, too. But then you kept mentioning Chris and your girls, and I wasn't sure what to think."

"I'm not involved with anyone."

"Good." Her eyes widened when she said that, and she quickly clarified, "I mean…okay." Thoughts visibly churning, she took in the woods and the dirt road that changed to pavement, and then the landscaping as it opened up to his home. She fell back in her seat.

The sight of manicured lawns under bright lights that flickered on with their progress distracted her.

Molly gave up. "Okay, then, since you and Chris don't

have that kind of relationship, why would he want to intimidate me?"

"Suspicion, most likely." And because that explanation didn't suffice, Dare added, "I never bring women here. Hell, I don't bring anyone here. You're a first."

Her interested gaze transferred to him. "You don't?"

Dare shook his head.

"But…why?"

"Policy." He glanced at her, saw her frowning and said, "Don't worry about it, okay?"

Pulling around the circular drive, Dare stopped in front of the pedimented entry. Warm lights poured through the cut glass in the door, the transom and the sidelights, spilling onto the front porch and out onto the paved walkway. The double doors opened and his girls shot out in berserk joy. Each of them had a stuffed toy clamped in her teeth.

Chris came to stand at the top step. He folded his arms over his bare chest and waited.

Eyes widening even more, Molly asked in a whisper, "Is that him?"

Wondering what she'd expected, Dare glanced at Chris. His personal assistant stood there shirtless, sloppy shorts hanging low, feet bare. His shaggy black hair became even more disheveled by a brisk wind.

Shaking his head, Dare accepted that Chris looked nothing like a businessperson and very much like a lake bum. "I think we've kept him up past his bedtime."

"Oh, dear." Casting Dare a sideways glance, she said, "He was waiting up for you?"

"Yeah."

"Is that part of his job description, or just because he was concerned?"

"Most likely, it was curiosity." Dare grinned at her. "Chris and I are best friends. Like brothers, really."

She let out her breath, but asked with accusation, "Did you know what I thought?"

"Maybe." Tamping down his grin, Dare said, "It gave you something to think about besides your kidnapping."

She frowned at him but said nothing more.

"And there are my beautiful girls, Sargeant and Tai'ree, better known as Sargie and Tai."

Eyes rounding, Molly stared as the two Labs bounded toward them.

"Dogs," Molly said, now completely exasperated. "So Chris is a guy, and your *girls* are animals."

"They're members of the family." Impatient to see them, Dare didn't pull on around into the garage. Before he had the SUV in Park, the dogs were at his door, jumping with undiluted joy. They dropped their toys to yap, bark and make other dog noises of pleasure.

For only a moment, Dare was able to take his focus off Molly.

He opened the door and was greeted with sloppy kisses, snuffling and wildly thumping tails.

Laughing, he stroked them both, taking the time to scratch Tai's back just above her tail, which was her favorite spot and never failed to put her into a doggy trance. Sargie immediately did her Chewbacca impersonation, sort of a growling yodel of eagerness, until he rubbed her ears.

"Come on, ladies. I have someone for you to meet." He rounded the car but not in time to open Molly's door for her. After stepping out, she looked at both dogs and gave a huge grin.

"I thought you had daughters. Or…something."

"Something furry," he told her. The dogs eyed Molly, determined she was fair game and charged over to her.

Molly went to one knee—a mistake given that both girls took that as an invitation and immediately knocked her to the ground so they could jump on her, slobber on her and generally give her loads of wet dog affection.

Waiting to see how she'd react, Dare crossed his arms and watched. If she acted like she needed help, or was afraid, of course he'd intervene. But if she was going to stay with him for a spell, and she was, she needed to know how to deal with his dogs.

To his surprise and pleasure, Molly laughed.

"Oh, my God, they're enormous." Catching a collar in each hand, she moved the dogs back enough to sit up again. She opened her arms and embraced them both. "That's the most loving I've had in...forever."

Interesting. Dare pulled Sargie away. "She's seventy pounds. And this beast of a girl—" he retrieved Tai "—is a solid eighty-five. Tai is the older and calmer of the two, but that's not saying much. They both think they're *Lap*radors instead of Labradors. If you're on their level, they'll sit on you. Or at least try to."

"Guess I'll have to remember that—not that I minded, though. It's nice to be so accepted."

Because she wasn't used to it? She'd said many of her readers could count as suspects, too. Family, readers, ex-fiancé... He needed to start making a damned list.

Holding out a hand to her, Dare hauled her to her feet and waited while she dusted off that lush backside.

Both dogs now sat on their haunches, still trembling with energy and excitement but curious about Molly, too.

She offered a hand for them to sniff and then took turns petting them. Tai gave her a soulful look, earning a hug. "I love animals. Dad wanted nothing to do with pets when I was growing up, and my apartment doesn't allow them. I'd actually been thinking of getting my own house just so I could get a dog. Probably not one as big as yours, though."

Dare couldn't imagine not having pets around. They were part of the welcome he got whenever he had time away from work. "House or dog?"

Grinning, she said, "Both—but I was talking about the dogs." She straightened, looked beyond them to his home and shook her head in wonder. "And here I'd thought to impress you with my success. What a joke."

"I am impressed."

"At least enough to let me hire you, knowing I can pay up. But we should probably discuss terms, don't you think?"

"Soon." He released the dogs to retrieve his duffel from the SUV, and then put a hand to the small of Molly's back to get her moving forward. "That's Chris on the porch. He'll stand there and stare all night."

Under her breath, Molly said, "He's as big as you are."

"I'm bigger," Chris announced, "if you know where to look."

"Knock it off, Chris." But Dare was trying not to laugh.

Aghast, Molly whispered, "He heard me?"

"He hears everything," Chris told her. "You might want to remember that."

"Voices carry here," Dare explained in a normal tone, "especially at night. It's the lake that does that."

"There's a lake?"

He could show her that later. Right now he wanted to get her out of the chill night air, get them both settled and eat real food. There was a world of difference in March weather between Kentucky and California. He saw her shivering and wished that he'd thought to buy her a jacket.

"Let's get you inside."

The dogs ran up the steps ahead of them, but then ran back down—and up again.

Dare stopped before Chris. "Molly, meet Chris Chapey, my personal assistant. Chris, this is—"

"The complication. I know." But Chris no sooner said that than he got a good look at Molly in the light. Arrested, he studied her face, saw the injuries, the marks of abuse. "Did Dare drag you here?"

"We're tired, Chris. Can you save the sarcasm for later? After I've eaten, maybe?"

His gaze went over Molly, and his brows came down— proof that Chris abhorred abuse as much as Dare did.

"Not a problem." Still with his attention on Molly, Chris said to Dare, "Just tell me that someone paid for this."

"Oh, yeah."

He nodded with satisfaction. "Glad to hear it."

To break the awkward exchange, Molly cleared her throat. "It's so nice to meet you, Mr. Chapey." She held out a hand. "Molly Alexander. Please call me Molly." Her obvious eagerness to make his acquaintance stymied both men.

Dare watched in amazement as Chris gave in and took her hand. Of course, Molly wasn't just any woman posing as an interloper; she was a woman badly victimized who still had a backbone of steel.

Who could be immune to that?

Molly enfolded Chris's hand in both of hers. "I'm sorry that we've kept you from your bed. I promise that I'm going to try to stay out of your way. I don't want to be a bother."

Given the shape she was in, that took Chris aback. He glanced at Dare in confusion, then said, "Definitely complicated."

Dare leaned against the outer entry wall. "Told you so."

"I get up early," Chris said in an uncharacteristic effort to explain himself. "Crack of dawn to run with the dogs. Otherwise—"

"I totally understand. And again, my apologies for messing up your routine."

"Chris's routine is whatever I say it is."

Chris narrowed his eyes at him. "Does that mean you'll be running the dogs tomorrow?"

"Yeah, it does."

"Great. Then I'll sleep in."

"'Fraid not." Dare half grinned as he told Chris, "I have a long list of things for you to do."

Molly ignored their exchange and, still holding Chris's hand, said, "Mr. Chapey, you're the one who set up the chartered flight, right?"

"It's Chris, and yeah, I make all of Dare's travel arrangements."

"Thank you so much for that. I was dreading a commercial flight after…well, everything."

In case she didn't understand, Chris said, this time slowly, "It's what Dare told me to do."

"I understand that, but you did it so quickly and your choice was terrific. I really do appreciate it."

She was killing Chris with kindness—and Dare loved it.

"Yeah, well, no problem." He gave Dare a "help me" look.

Molly finally freed his hand. "Good grief, I'm keeping you out here talking when you have to be freezing."

"I'm fine—but you have goose bumps."

"It's probably only fifty degrees here, and damp, too." She rubbed her arms. "At least I'm dressed, but you're all but naked."

Chris's brows shot up. "I'm wearing shorts."

"That barely cover you."

He shifted his stance, put off by what sounded like censure. "Is that a complaint?"

Her smile didn't quite answer one way or the other. "It is so beautiful here." She turned a full circle. "And so incredibly quiet."

"Secure, too," Dare told her. Then, tired of the verbal games, he asked Chris, "You reset the alarm codes?"

"Soon as you cleared the gate. And I went grocery shopping for you, too. Fresh food is in the kitchen. After I put your car away, I could cook you something—"

"I'll take care of it." He turned to Molly. "Chris makes a lousy cook."

"Says the master chef."

Molly looked impressed. "You're a master chef?"

"Pure sarcasm." Chris ushered her along and then held the door open for her. "But he is good. At freakin' everything. So get used to it."

Molly stepped inside and went awestruck again. "Holy cow."

Chris paid no attention to her. "Wasn't sure if you needed it or not, but I freshened up the back bedroom upstairs."

"Thanks. I'll get her settled."

"Want me to put your things away?"

Normally, yes, but this time Dare's priority was Molly, not checking messages. "I'll do it."

"Okay, then. I'll be right back." He took the keys from Dare and strolled out to the SUV.

DARE WATCHED MOLLY AS she looked around the central foyer.

"It's a mansion."

"Not really." He was a man of comfort, and, as such, though the house had a lot of amenities, it wasn't fancy enough to be called a mansion.

"I'll get lost in here."

Dare shook his head. "I wouldn't expect someone with your background to be in awe of a house."

She gave him a telling look. "I've known plenty of wealthy people, and they're not at all like you. What I mean is, you don't act like you're rich. You're too nice and normal for that."

"Glad you think so." With a total of forty-five hundred feet of living space, the house was…expansive. But it was divided up in a functional way. To help Molly get acclimated, Dare said, "Think of it as circular. Everything revolves from this spot. Dining hall on the left, library on the right. Straight ahead, up the curving stairs, are a studio and three other bedrooms. You'll have a room up there."

She jerked around to stare at him with clear alarm. "Where do you sleep?"

Indicating beyond the stairs, on the main floor, Dare said, "Master bedroom and bath are on the right, end of the hall is the great room, then the kitchen, morning room, laundry and family room are to the left."

As the dogs moved closer to her, their nails tapped on the marble floor, drawing her attention there. She looked down at them, then up at the recessed ceilings and giant, rustic chandelier. "It's…gorgeous. And enormous."

"Thanks." Dare picked up his duffel and again touched the small of her back, urging her toward the stairs ahead of him. "I'll show you to your room." The dogs started forward in anticipation.

He got her halfway up the stairs before Molly resisted, glancing up at him. "Who else sleeps up there?"

"No one. I have the master suite, and Chris stays in the lake house." Thinking she was worried about privacy, Dare assured her, "You'll pretty much have the whole upstairs to yourself."

Jaw loosening, she turned completely around on the middle of the stairs to face him. The dogs, too, looked at Dare with expectation. "You have another house?"

"A cabin, really, down closer to the lake." He noticed the pink tinge to her cheeks, how her lips parted, the way she tucked her hair behind her ear. "It's small but functional. And Chris values having space he can call his own. Mostly because he's a slob and I'm not."

"Good God, a football team could live in this house and have plenty of space."

Dare couldn't help himself; he leaned forward and kissed her. With her a step above him, it was the perfect fit. "You'll be safe here, Molly, no reason to be concerned. The house is wired for state-of-the-art security. Know that you'll be protected."

She touched her mouth—and continued to look...reluctant. "I wasn't...wasn't worried about that."

"Yeah, you were. But it's understandable. Hell, I'd be more concerned if you weren't. Now, come on." He took the lead, stepping around her and going up the rest of the stairs. The dogs followed him in a rush. "The back bedroom faces the lake. I think you'll like it."

"How could I not? It's all incredible. Very masculine, but somehow posh, too."

"It's relaxed—suitable for dogs and two men." Dare waited at the top of the stairs, watching her.

"I'm sure you guys are very comfortable here, but a woman could be, too." She followed him up. "Who did your decorating?"

Pleased with her, Dare turned toward one of the bedrooms. "I did."

"Oh, that's right." She twisted her mouth. "Chris said you were good at everything."

"Chris is paid to be biased." The dogs forged ahead of him, trying to anticipate his destination.

"But you two are friends, too. You said he's not just an employee."

"We're good friends, have been for years." Over twenty years, actually…but that was a story for another time.

Dare went into the second largest bedroom and set his duffel on a queen-size four-poster bed. It was made up with soft, warm, hand-sewn quilts and luxurious sheets.

The dogs circled the perimeter of the room, trying to watch both Dare and Molly as she looked lost and he unloaded the few clothes and toiletries currently in her possession. It wasn't much, but right now, here with him, she didn't need much.

Attempting to hide her anxiety from him, she patted the dogs and then went to peek into the bathroom.

She would be comfortable here, Dare told himself.

So why was he feeling guilty?

Hands on his hips, he tracked her every movement, trying to gauge her mood, to determine a way to reassure her without crossing boundaries. Hell, he'd already crossed so many lines it shouldn't matter anymore…but it did.

"Go ahead and put your stuff in the drawers, set up

however you want, make yourself at home. The television remotes are on the shelf. There are DVDs in the library if you want to hunt through those. You can bring a bunch up here if you want."

"Thanks."

Damn it, she sounded so lost. "The computer is hooked up to the internet, so feel free to surf, to entertain yourself. But don't check any personal accounts. I don't want you to sign in under your name for anything. It's too easy to track."

"Okay." She showed little interest in the TV or the computer.

More frustrated by the second, Dare narrowed his eyes. "If you need anything else, just ask."

She went over to look out the French doors that opened onto a small deck overlooking the yard below—which led down to the lake. From the deck, she could just see Chris's residence and the dock beyond there, the boathouse, the reflection of the moon off lightly lapping water.

Silence filled the room.

"Molly."

She leaned against the doors and avoided looking at Dare. "I know it's late…"

"Not that late." She'd slept throughout the flight, so she probably wasn't ready to retire yet. Was that what caused her worry? Did she think he'd bring her here and then abandon her? "I don't know about you, but I'm hungry for real food. Why don't you take a few minutes to yourself and then meet me downstairs in the kitchen. I'll get us something to eat."

Tension fell out of her shoulders. "Okay."

She didn't deny being hungry. Again. But Dare was almost positive it was the reprieve from being alone that had relaxed her. Why didn't she just tell him that?

Confounding woman.

"You have time to take a shower if you want."

She inhaled and let out a long breath. "Okay. Thanks."

Dare crossed his arms. "Damn it, Molly, if you have something on your mind—"

She spun around with a false smile. "No, I'm fine. Everything is…fine. Terrific. Go get your food. I'll freshen up and be right down."

He waited, wondering if he should press the issue. She'd been through so much that there had to be awful, residual effects. What did he really know of how a woman reacted to these things? So far, everything he'd expected from her had been off. No hysterics, no uncontrollable sobbing or raging anger.

"Really, Dare. I'm fine. Looking forward to a shower, actually."

Dare didn't believe a word of it, but standing there staring at her wasn't going to help. "Towels are in the bathroom. Come on down when you're finished."

"I hope I don't get lost." She tried a smile that didn't quite make it to her warm brown eyes. Moving to the door by way of encouraging him to leave, she said, "I'll only be a few minutes."

"Take your time." He started out, but the dogs hesitated, whining, looking from Molly to Dare and back again. He rolled his eyes. "She'll join us soon enough. Come on." He patted his thigh, and finally the dogs came to him.

Together, they left, but Dare didn't like it. Surely Molly wanted the privacy of her own bedroom, her own bathroom. It wasn't like he was leaving her alone in a strange place. He'd be right downstairs.

But, damn it, he didn't want to be.

If it hadn't been so inappropriate, he would have dragged Molly down onto the bed and just held her. All night.

As if they felt his mood, Tai and Sargie kept giving him sympathetic glances.

"It's a hell of a thing, isn't it? Trust me, I don't like being confused any more than you do."

The dogs whined in return.

By the time he stowed his duffel in his room and joined Chris in the kitchen, his mood had soured even more. With it well past their bedtime, the dogs went straight for their favorite spot in the attached morning room. They each had a padded bed placed before the wall of windows. Only moonlight shone through, but they flopped down to wallow in it, and they were soon asleep.

Chris handed Dare a cup of coffee, which was always the first order of business. "Is Ms. Apple Dumpling turning in for the night?"

"Taking a shower—and this is no time for you to be an asshole, so lay off of her, will you?" He tasted the coffee and commended Chris with a nod. It had taken him nearly a month to teach Chris the right ratio of freshly ground coffee beans to water to brew time. Now he had it down pat, and it was one luxury Dare missed while out on the road.

"I saw the bruises." Chris leaned back against the counter and folded his arms over his chest. "Someone really put it to her?"

"Several someones."

He acknowledged that, then said, "I hope they aren't still living."

Dare rubbed a hand over his tired eyes. That he killed when necessary wasn't a surprise for Chris, or an emotional burden for Dare. "I took care of them." But now, in hindsight, he wished like hell that he would have kept one of the fuckers around to question.

Chris was curious, but as usual, he wasn't prying. It was yet another reason why he made such an invaluable assistant. "I found Molly in the same holding cell with Alani, but she stood out like a sore thumb." Dare faced his friend. "No way was she there to be sold off, because she was abused too much, way more than the others."

Chris went still. "So why was she there?"

"Fucked if I know. I think someone had her taken. But I have no idea why." Dare frowned. "Yet."

While idly setting out the fresh groceries he'd bought, Chris considered that. "I take it she isn't exactly the norm for that sort of thing?"

"Hell, no."

Chris didn't drink much coffee, which might have been why it took so long for him to get the process of making it right. He took out the orange juice and poured himself a tall glass. "It almost had to be somebody close to her— isn't that what you always say?"

Dare shrugged. "I'm keeping an open mind, and I plan to cover all the bases."

"A few questions come to mind."

"I figured as much." Dare set the half-empty cup aside and went to investigate Chris's food purchases. Skinless chicken and fresh vegetables would be quick and easy to cook. "Let's have it."

"She hired you?"

Dare shrugged again. Molly's offer to pay him for services rendered didn't sit well with him. "I might do this one pro bono. But I haven't told her that yet, so keep it to yourself."

That set Chris back, so it was a few seconds before he asked, "How long is she staying here?"

"Don't know yet." And he didn't want to think about it too much. He preferred to play it by ear, and take it one day at a time. He got out what he'd need to sauté the chicken and steam the vegetables. "Depends on how things go."

"What does that mean?"

He looked up from his chore. "I'm going to take her back to her place, be with her when she sees family and then judge my next step."

"So if things go well and you can wrap it up quick, maybe you won't be bringing her back with you?"

"I didn't say—"

Molly cleared her throat and both men looked up. She'd combed her wet hair straight back and dressed in one of the big shirts—with a bra beneath—and the jeans. Her bare feet poked out from under the denim.

Dare straightened.

Chris stepped around him and held out a chair at the long granite bar. "Coffee or juice?"

Glancing away from Dare's penetrating stare, she said, "Juice would be great. Thank you." She visually explored the island gourmet kitchen with stone countertops and lots of stainless steel. It opened into a family room and the morning room, where they ate breakfast. "Every room is more amazing than the next."

Dare said nothing. The second she'd entered, he again felt her tension.

The dogs came to investigate, sniffed her feet and dropped down beside her. Hell, Dare thought, even they felt protective, so why would he expect himself to be any different?

Maybe because he knew it wasn't just protectiveness that he felt.

"I'll have food ready in twenty minutes."

"Sounds great. What can I do to help?"

"You can tell me why your readers could be suspects. And then we'll go from there."

CHAPTER SEVEN

"READERS?" CHRIS DID a double take. What the hell did he mean by *readers?* Molly wrote? Like...*what?*

"She's an author," Dare told him as he began preparing the food. "One of her books is being made into a movie with Ryan Reynolds as the lead."

Chris's jaw loosened. Why did Dare just keep dropping bombshells on him? He'd already found her interesting, in part because Dare had brought her here, which was an aberration of the major kind.

But this was something altogether different.

"You're shittin' me."

"Nice language, asshole."

Chris waved that off. It wasn't like Dare was any better. Hell, neither of them was used to having a female around the place—not counting Tai and Sargie, who didn't care what language they heard as long as they got treats and plenty of attention.

As a genuine movie buff, Chris felt suitably impressed. But then, he'd already been impressed with her before that. Somehow, Molly didn't fit his vision of the creative sort. She wasn't...glamorous enough. And she seemed far too grounded, instead of artistic.

But hell, she'd just been rescued from kidnappers who had battered her pretty badly. Maybe under better circumstances she had more savoir faire.

As he considered it, he realized that Molly didn't fit

any stereotype familiar to him. Most people in her situation would be either demanding of attention or withdrawn and fearful. Not Molly. Perhaps she was different with Dare, in private.

But in his presence, she wasn't intrusive, needy or whiney. In fact, she tried hard not to inconvenience them in any way.

Chris shook his head. He knew Dare expected him to resent female intrusion, and before Molly, he would have. He protected his position, and he always had Dare's back.

With Molly, there was no threat—not of the type he'd always guarded against.

If anything, he fell in line with Dare, sharing the need to keep her safe and help her feel secure.

"Ryan is a possible lead," Molly corrected. "We're waiting for confirmation...." She looked oddly chagrined, then downcast. "Well, actually, it might have already been confirmed or denied, but I haven't had access to a phone or computer or anything."

"Soon," Dare told her.

"God, this sucks. I have no idea what's going on with my career. But I was so focused on..."

"Surviving?" Chris supplied.

"Well, yeah. I was surviving, and so caught up in... in just holding it together that I..." She trailed off with a groan.

"You're a trouper," Chris told her in a grand understatement.

"I hope my editor or agent hasn't been trying to get hold of me. What would they think? We were right in the middle of negotiations on this thing before I... I..."

Chris set the juice before her and pulled up a chair. He took her hand, so small and female, and wished he could have helped Dare destroy the ones who had done this to her. "Getting snatched by thugs is so damned inconvenient, isn't it?"

She choked on a laugh and nodded with exaggeration. "More so than I ever could have imagined."

Dare shot him a look of warning, which almost made Chris roll his eyes. He had to be the least threatening guy Ms. Molly was likely to come into contact with.

Even if he wasn't gay, he'd have no sexual interest in her. Dare had already staked a claim. End of story.

But was he supposed to ignore the fact that she was a famous writer? No, of course not. "How long did they have you, Molly?"

"Dare helped me to figure out that it was nine days."

Good God. Nine days of unending fear, pain, despair… Nine days of hell.

Overwhelmed with emotions he'd seldom felt, Chris gently squeezed her hand. "Well, then, I take back my earlier thoughts. You actually look incredible, all things considered."

She snorted at that and, pulling her hand away, smoothed her hair behind her ears in a female show of insecurity. "Yeah, if looking like death warmed over appeals to you."

He helped her tuck away a wayward strand. "Actually, you only look wounded, which sometimes appeals to the big protective male."

"Chris…"

He laughed at Dare. "What I really meant was that I thought there were two types of writers, the glamorous ones who donned feather boas and dripped diamonds, and the harried ones who lived in a fantasyland."

"I'm far from glamorous, and I'm only harried when

I'm in the middle of a book. And when that happens, I can forget I have hair, much less how to groom it."

Before Chris could ask for more details, Dare said, "We'll be going to your place soon. You can get updated on everything important then."

"Soon as in…like, when?"

"Depends. Probably in a couple of days." He put the thinly sliced chicken into a hot skillet with spices. "You said you live north of Cincinnati, right?"

Molly toyed with her glass of orange juice. "It's a small community, but nice. My apartment building is pretty old and quaint, but it's comfortable for me."

"Good security?" Dare asked.

"Not really. I mean, compared to this fortress, it's just a plain old building. We have floodlights in the parking lot, and the halls are well lit. But we don't have any hired guards or anything."

"Is the front door kept locked?"

"Well…no."

Chris shared a look with Dare. Most people were never forced to face danger in daily living. But as Dare's personal assistant, he knew only too well the peril that could invade a person's life, especially a woman.

It made him ill to think of Molly alone and susceptible to danger.

"It's not that bad," she told both men, recognizing their expressions of concern. "The locks on each apartment are sturdy, and we all have dead bolts, too."

Only a small part of Dare's attention was on the food. "You said the building is old. Do the windows lock?"

"I guess most of them do."

When Dare turned toward her in exasperation, she rushed to explain.

"I'm on the upper floor, so I never worried about it as much as the people on the ground floor might."

"It's two stories? Do you have a fire escape?"

"Yes and yes."

Chris always enjoyed seeing Dare in analytical mode. You could almost hear the gears turning as he figured things out in his mind.

"You need windows with secure locks."

"Trust me, when I finally get my life back together, I'm going to be the most lock-happy woman you've ever met." Wrapping her arms around herself, she shuddered. "I don't know if I'm ever going to feel totally safe again."

Dismissing that, probably because he was intent on ensuring her safety, Dare asked, "Busy area? Much traffic out front?"

"Not really, no. In fact, it's really quiet. That's…that's how those men were able to grab me without anyone noticing. It's a neighborhood of older people." She breathed a little faster, a little more shallowly. "And it's not that I'm oblivious to my surroundings, honest. I…I saw the old, rusty white van when I went out to the mailbox. But it just never occurred to me… I mean, why would I think that anyone wanted to grab me? It wasn't the middle of the night, and I don't live in the slums."

Dare and Chris waited as she sorted the details out in her mind.

"I did wonder why it was just sitting there. Then, when I dropped my mail into the box, and I was ready to head back in, suddenly…" She faded off, staring at nothing in particular, sort of vacant and lost.

"Molly."

Face pale, she lifted her gaze to Dare.

"They're gone now, remember?"

Slowly, by small degrees, she gathered herself and nodded. "You killed them."

"Yeah."

Chris listened to the exchange in amazement. Dare had admitted that to her? He'd told her that he killed them?

Un-fucking-believable.

Letting out a shuddering breath, she relaxed again. "Where I live, older cars aren't uncommon, but usually they're sedans or compacts, not vans." She shook her head. "Other than early evening, when the old folks sit on their porches, there aren't a lot of people outside to pay much attention to what's going on."

Molly was about the most fragile woman Chris had ever met, but she also put up one hell of a good front. And she had a very likable disposition that excluded any self-pity at all.

She was shaken, but she wasn't damaged. Hoping his curiosity wouldn't upset her, Chris asked, "How'd they get you all the way to Mexico?"

"I don't really know. They…someone held me down, and another guy gave me a shot of something. I fought to stay alert, but there wasn't anything I could do. I passed out. I came to a few times, but before I could get my bearings, they'd stick me with another needle, keeping me drugged. When I finally came around, we were driving again, but in a different car. Everything was different. It was so hot, and I felt sick. Then they dragged me into that awful little shack." She swallowed hard. "It didn't take me long to figure out that I was in Mexico. But I never found out why."

Deliberately removing Molly from those memories, Dare went back to cooking and told Chris, "Get her address and find the easiest way to travel there."

Chris heard the edge in Dare's tone and knew he was affected by Molly's unrelenting manner, too. "Right."

"I'd prefer to drive if I can go up and back in one day, overnight at the most. If that's not possible, then charter another flight."

Anxious to help her in any way that he could, Chris went straight to the computer area. "Nothing commercial, right?"

"Not until I know what's going on."

"Another private flight? Is that much precaution really necessary?"

"Yes." Dare left no room for argument. "It is."

Molly fretted. "But we have to finish discussing our—" she glanced at Chris "—terms." And then, in a lower voice, and with a frown, "Dare, I'm not sure I want to pay for two chartered flights."

Chris choked on a laugh, saw her face and sucked it up. "Why don't you give me the address while you and Dare hash that out?"

Begrudgingly, she shared her address but then turned on Dare. "We need to talk about this."

"You already hired me, and you already agreed to do things my way." He turned the chicken as if he didn't have a single concern. "It's too late to change your mind now."

She tucked in her chin. "Dare, I do not have unlimited funds. The way an author is paid… Well, it's sometimes feast or famine. I'm not saying I'm poor, because I'm not. I'm very comfortable financially. But I need to check my accounts and see when my next big check is due."

"Don't worry about it right now." And then to Chris, "What's taking you so long?"

Never before had Chris seen Dare disconcerted by

a woman. Usually his word was law, period. Intriguing stuff—not that he'd dare say so.

Chris turned his attention to the computer and typed in the address Molly had given him. "Hmm. It's not far at all." He skipped past Dare and glanced back at Molly. "Are you up for a four-hour drive?"

Looking mulish, voice low, she said, "Whatever Dare wants is fine by me."

Such a loaded statement, full of possible sexual innuendo.

Knowing Dare was already poised to verbally shut him down, Chris quickly held up a hand. He wasn't about to say anything that might make Molly uncomfortable.

He got back to business and finished checking a map. "It's looking good. A fairly straight shot. Morning soon enough for me to finalize things?"

"What's to finalize?" Molly asked. "You have the route right there."

"Dare likes details. Lots and lots of details. He'll want me to include where to stop to eat, and if eating isn't necessary, then possible locations for a bathroom break. Any construction in the area. Any landmarks that he'll pass that might be conducive to sabotage—"

Dare interrupted to say, "Morning is soon enough."

"You taking your SUV or a rental?"

"Mine is fine."

"Got it." Chris couldn't help but give in to a grin. It wasn't that Dare showed much emotion; on the surface, he was the same cool cucumber. But Chris knew him better than that.

Probably better than anyone.

Sure, Dare and Trace were close. Alani, too. But as Dare's personal assistant, Chris was involved in every aspect of Dare's life. That gave him insights that the others wouldn't be privy to.

And right now, he knew the biggest source of his boss's temperament was a bad case of lust. Given the little lady had just gotten through an extended spell of abuse, with a very uncertain future ahead, Dare was too noble to act on that lust. Even though, Chris observed, Molly seemed to have her own wealth of feelings for Dare. It was there in the way she watched him, her body language when he was near.

But that could be gratitude as much as anything, which Dare had to realize, too. Dare had saved her, had slain her dragons, and he was now protecting her.

There was more than enough room for misconstrued emotions—on both ends.

Poor Dare, to find himself in such a complex romantic situation. It was going to be interesting to see how things rolled out.

Chris turned around on the desk stool. "Did you want me to clean up after you're done in here?"

"I can do it," Molly volunteered.

"Morning is soon enough for that, too." Dare checked the veggies with a fork and decided they were steamed enough.

Since Chris didn't care much for cleaning—immaculate conditions were Dare's forte—he finished off his juice and put the glass in the dishwasher. "I left messages on your desk in the library, but did you maybe want them on your bedroom desk instead?"

"That'd be fine."

"Some of them were from Trace. I think he's hoping to somehow help with your..." He started to say *complication,* but when he glanced at Molly, he decided to censor the usual mockery and instead nodded toward her with his head. "With her."

"I'll touch base with Trace tomorrow, but he should really just concentrate on Alani right now."

"True," Chris said. "I'll put an updated calendar in your room, too, although the next few weeks are pretty clear—"

"Dare?"

They both looked at Molly.

Chris noted her unease.

Dare must've, too, given how he gave her his full attention. "What is it?"

Hesitation had her fidgeting, but in the next breath she straightened her shoulders. "You said you don't want me signing in to any of my online accounts."

"No, I don't." He served up the meal on two plates. "We don't yet know who wanted you taken, and I don't know how smart or connected that person might be, but someone with a little computer experience could trail you here through your online activity."

"I don't think I know anyone with those types of skills."

"You didn't think you knew anyone who would have you shanghaied to Mexico, either, right?"

Expression tight, she said, "Which is why I'm happy to defer to your expertise."

Chris stared at her with new respect. A lot of people quailed under Dare's intense manner, but the way Molly said that was patronizing as hell.

No quailing for her.

"The thing is," Molly continued, "I need something more respectable to wear, especially if we're going to be four hours on the road. And it's not a complaint, but it's downright cold here in Kentucky, and in Ohio, too. I'll need some warmer things."

Dare looked over her casual clothes and agreed. "I suppose you do."

"I think she looks comfortable," Chris said. "Sort of sloppy-cute."

"That's because you have the fashion sense of a goat."

Glad that he'd led Dare into that one, Chris said, "So you *don't* think she's cute?"

"Excuse me?" Molly looked at each of them with clear censure. "Do you think we could use your account to do some online shopping? I know my credit-card numbers and can charge it to myself but have it delivered here overnight. I don't need much, because once we get to my apartment, I can grab my own things."

"Shouldn't be a problem," Chris said before Dare could. "I'll take care of it for you."

"Oh, no." Opposed to that idea, she shook her head. "You were ready to go to bed. Really, I can do it."

But Chris was already back on the computer. "Do you have a favorite place to shop and an idea of what you want? We can get it done right now."

Dare didn't hide his exasperation. "I wanted to talk to her about her disgruntled readers."

"I multitask, as you know. Once she tells me what she wants, I can take care of most of it." He went back to the computer. "Where do you shop?"

Deflated and probably overwhelmed, Molly gave in and told him.

Dare set her plate and a tall glass of water in front of her. "Eat up. And be sure to stay hydrated." Ever so briefly, he touched her cheek. "I know you feel better, but you aren't fully recovered yet."

She smiled, then inhaled the fragrance of real food. "It smells fantastic."

"Told you he was a good cook," Chris said, amused by that telling exchange. "Okay, got it. Where to first? Slacks, tops, dresses or jeans? I'd put an outfit together for you, but as Dare already told you, I'm a fashion disaster. So, what are you thinking?"

Molly gave him direction in between eating.

Dare kept nudging the water at her until she drank half the glass.

Pulling up certain brands she'd suggested, Chris found that she was very easy to please. With little fanfare she chose dark designer jeans, black ankle boots, a simple white blouse and a thick charcoal pullover sweater with a self-tie belt.

"Here's a nice corduroy blazer that'd go with it. What do you think?"

"That'll work, but get it a size larger so it'll fit over the sweater. Maybe a scarf, too?"

"Not a problem." When he was ready to check her out, she came over and, leaning around him, typed in her credit-card numbers.

"To stay on the safe side, I'll have it delivered to our post-office box in town. But don't worry. I can go pick it up as soon as it arrives."

"You make an amazing assistant."

Dare gave a rude sound over that. "He's a pain in the ass, but I tolerate him."

Grinning, Chris turned on the stool toward him. "I'd like to say that you'd be lost without me, but that would be a lie. However, I know for a fact that I make your life more comfortable."

Lifting his glass, Dare saluted him. "Yeah, I'll give you that one."

Chris accepted his due with a nod. To Molly, he said, "Dare has many areas of expertise, only one of them being organization and a certain finesse at details. But I excel at comfort—my own and others'."

Molly smiled. "Comfort is high on my list of priorities, too. It's one reason I'm a writer. I can write from my own home, in my jammies, drinking hot cocoa and listening to the music of my choice."

"A dream job. If only I had the talent to write…"

"But you don't, so you're stuck with me." Dare focused on Molly. "Tell me why you think a reader could be responsible for your abduction."

She waved off his question. "I didn't really mean that. I was just being snarky."

They both waited for an explanation of that.

She pushed away her mostly empty plate. "Well, the thing is, my last book garnered a lot of controversy. There was a vocal group of readers who really…" She looked from Dare to Chris, and shrugged. "They were really pissed off with a certain twist in the plot."

"How do you know?" Chris asked.

"Trust me, readers make sure you know when you've let them down."

Chris noticed that she didn't look overly hurt by that.

"They reach authors through online reviews, emails, written letters. And that's a good thing, just not so fun when there's so much of the negative stuff."

Dare sat back in his seat. "How'd the book do with all that reader disgruntlement?"

"Great, actually." In an effort to explain to them, she leaned forward, elbows on the stone bar. "With every book, there are good reviews and bad reviews, rants and raves, readers who love it and readers who hate it, and a whole bunch of reactions that are in between those extremes. You know the old saying where you can't please all the people all the time. The same goes for reviewers and readers."

Dare didn't look convinced. "So it wasn't a big deal?"

"Well, it was a big deal to me, at least in some ways. Given the level of anger over it, I'm sure I lost some longstanding readers. No matter what, I hate to disappoint anyone, but I especially hate to let down loyal readers who've been reading me from the beginning."

"Bummer," Chris said.

"But…" She lifted her shoulders. "I also gained new readers and expanded my audience. Truth is, if I had it to do over again, I'd do it exactly the same way, because I *have* to write a story the way it wants to be written, not the way readers want me to. That's how my muse works. If I fought that natural process, I'd probably never get a book done, and I probably wouldn't be as successful."

Still not entirely sure he understood, Chris told her, "Good for you."

"The level of anger you mentioned," Dare said, bringing the conversation back around to possible suspects. "Give me an example."

A little embarrassed now, she glanced away. "There were threats, with people wanting to beat me up, people wishing terrible things would happen to me. But most of it was posted online for all the world to see, so I can't imagine that anyone was serious. They were just letting off steam. In a way, it's really a compliment."

Chris stared at her. "How the hell do you figure *that?*"

"If the reader wasn't so invested in my characters, it wouldn't matter enough to get angry over it. Right?"

"If you say so." Dare left his seat and headed for the computer. "Where can I find this stuff on the Net?"

Aghast, she said, "You're going to look at it right now?"

"Why not?"

"Well…" Again she looked at both men. "Okay, call me vain, but I don't really want you to see all the bad stuff said about me or my books."

Chris couldn't help but grin. "Think we'll get the wrong impression?"

"Of course you will." She left her seat to rush after Dare. "Seriously. There's no point—"

They both stopped next to Chris. Dare touched her chin, lifting her face up and silencing her at the same time. "You promised to trust me and to do as I said."

"Sure. But you don't know anything about this industry."

"No, but I understand you, and you're worried that I'll feel sorry for you."

She drew back, surprised.

Chris wasn't. In most instances, Dare was damned astute. But in this case, things were pretty obvious. Molly didn't want sympathy after the ordeal she'd suffered, so of course she wouldn't want it over a few internet slights.

"Look," Chris said, "if you said it's routine to get slammed on occasion, I buy it. What section of the entertainment industry doesn't get hammered on a regular basis? And besides, you have a book being made into a friggin' movie. How awesome is that? You're a star, and regardless of what a few reviews might say—"

"Over three hundred reviews."

Dare lifted both brows. "Seriously?"

Chris blew it off. "Whatever. You're still a resounding success." Rather than drag out the suspense for her, he turned back to the computer. An internet search of her name brought up plenty of hits. "Bingo. Found some sites."

Molly went rigid. "Fine, you two want to see all the gory details, go ahead. But you can do it without me. I'm going to bed."

She was almost through the kitchen doorway when Dare said, "Molly?"

Shoulders still stiff, she paused. "What?"

"If you need anything during the night, my room is across the hall, next to the great room." He stared at her back. "Anything at all."

"Thanks." And with that squeaky reply, Ms. Molly Alexander fled the room.

CHAPTER EIGHT

MOLLY LAY IN THE BED well past 2:00 a.m., trying to go to sleep and failing. At one point she got up and opened the French doors to look out at the beckoning lake. She loved water, being near it, on it or just listening to it.

With the night so quiet, she could hear the water lapping gently at the shoreline. Crickets sang, leaves rustled and the world seemed at peace.

Yet a strange turbulence boiled inside her. Fear, anxiety, insecurity and a sort of conspicuous yearning all left her too unsettled to sleep.

As she went back to the bed and burrowed under the soft, warm quilts, she promised herself that tomorrow she would investigate the area. This time of year the air was crisp and everything newly green. Maybe Dare had a boat and they could go out for a ride.

She wanted—*needed*—to find some perspective, to grasp some normalcy, even if short-lived.

Once they returned to her home, what would happen? If Dare found nothing amiss, would he be…done? Would he consider it safe for her to remain there while he looked for the culprits alone?

Shudders went over her, as much from the chill breeze blowing in as deep-boned fear.

Finally, with her thoughts churning and an expanding uneasiness creeping in, she pushed the quilts aside and left the bed. She tried turning on the lights, but that just made her feel foolish. Pacing, she tried to figure out what to do, how to get settled—but being alone in the room kept her skin crawling.

That awful hysteria built until she bolted from the room and, barefoot, rushed down the curving stairs. She held tightly to the railing so that she wouldn't fall, and was grateful for the bright moonlight pouring through the windows, as well as for the tiny, glowing green security lights on monitors and alarms.

She wanted to go to Dare's room, but what would she say? *I'm scared?* No, never.

Instead, she veered into the kitchen and decided on a glass of juice to help her calm down. And maybe she could find a cookie or two. A small snack—that's all she needed.

Remembering where Chris had gotten the glasses before, she went to the cabinet. The tile floor froze her feet and, maybe because of that, she trembled. Badly. Deep breathing didn't really help.

She found a thick mug and decided it would do; no reason to keep rummaging around, breaching Dare's privacy. After her snack she'd sneak back to the room and stay there.

She had just opened the refrigerator when she heard movement from behind her.

Pure, illogical terror imploded. As she turned with a silent scream stuck in her throat, the mug dropped from her hand and broke into large chunks. Every sound seemed amplified, echoing again and again inside her thoughts.

Vision closing in on her, she stared straight ahead—and saw Tai, the older of Dare's two dogs, sitting on her haunches, staring back at Molly. Beside her, Sargie waited for any sign of welcome.

Oh, dear God.

The haze faded—and mortification leached in.

Going weak, Molly sank down onto her knees. With tears stinging her eyes, she stared at the dogs. "You girls scared me half to death."

Her whisper must have sounded like an invitation, because both dogs surged forward.

"No," Molly hissed, holding up her hands and trying to see past the tears that kept welling. Though the broken glass from the mug hadn't splintered too much, she didn't want to take any chances. "Stay. Please." She'd die if either of Dare's pets got cut because of her ridiculous reaction.

The overhead lights came on, blinding Molly.

She shielded her eyes and found Dare standing there in the doorway. Hair rumpled and eyes heavy with sleep, he took her measure, looking at her there on the floor and then at the broken mug near her. His gaze came back to lock on hers.

He wore only boxers, and he had his big bare feet braced apart.

Molly's heart launched into a wild, frantic rhythm. "I'm sorry," she whispered.

He released her from the snare of his bright blue eyes and instead called the dogs over to him. He petted them both. "You girls want to go out?"

When both dogs enthusiastically agreed, Dare said to Molly, "Don't move. I'll be right back."

There was no emotion in his tone, no censure or surprise or...anything. She didn't know what to make of that.

He strode past her across the kitchen and into the family room to a back door. Frozen, humiliation chok-

ing her, Molly stayed right there on the floor. She wasn't
sure she could move.

When he returned, she heard herself say, "Go back to
bed, please," when that was the very last thing she wanted
him to do. "I'll clean this up and—"

"Shush, Molly."

That was the gentlest tone she'd ever heard from him,
and it made even more tears well up and spill over. Molly
pressed her fists to her damp eyes, trying to stop the flow
of emotion, but all that did was choke her up more.

She was not a weak woman. She was not a woman
who sat in the middle of a kitchen floor all but begging
for…what? Comfort? Company? She hated it, and at that
moment, she hated herself.

Still with her eyes covered, she sensed Dare's movement near her, heard the clink of glass, then the closing
of a cabinet.

Seconds later she knew he was near, though only the
heat of his body touched hers.

"Did you hurt yourself?"

His impassive tone left her grateful; any real sympathy
from him and she'd be bawling like a baby.

Unable to look at him, she shook her head. "I…I didn't
mean to drop it. The dogs startled me." But that wasn't
true. "I forgot you had dogs. I just wanted a snack."

"You wanted not to be alone." He took her wrists and
pulled her hands down, placed them on his shoulders, and
then, before she could even assimilate what he planned,
he scooped her up into his arms.

She didn't mean to, but she wrapped her arms tight
around him and buried her tear-damp face against his
neck. He strode off, maybe taking her back to her room,
and she couldn't find a single word to say.

But it wasn't her room they entered. It was his.

As he lowered her to sit on the side of his mattress, she had no choice but to stop hiding. Dare pulled up a quilt from the bottom of the bed and wrapped it around her. "You'll be warmer in a minute." He rubbed her arms through the quilt to help hurry things along.

She hadn't realized she was so cold, not until he mentioned it, and then she felt every chill, every shiver that racked her spine.

Furious at herself for the pathetic display, she swiped at the tears on her cheeks. "I feel so stupid."

Again he caught her wrists, stilling her movements. "Don't. There's no reason." He went through a doorway in his room and came back with a handful of tissues that he pressed into her hand. "Stay here. I'm going to let the girls back in, and then I'll be right back."

When she said nothing, he tipped up her chin, giving her no choice but to meet his direct gaze. His thumb brushed her cheek, smoothing away a tear. "I want to find you sitting right here when I return. Understood?"

The softness of his tone kept it from sounding like an order. Appreciating his calm manner, Molly nodded.

He wasn't gone long, but Molly used those few minutes to try to gather herself. She blew her nose, wiped away the tears and took several deep breaths.

Hoping for a distraction, she studied Dare's room, starting with the incredible, multilevel tray ceiling. The room wasn't square but instead had one wall of windows that extended out in a semicircle. The curtains were open, and through the floor-to-ceiling windows, Molly saw a million stars shining.

Heavy, masculine furniture included the bed set but also an upholstered couch and chair in a sitting area. An interior door led to his master bath. Curiosity got her off the bed, and she peeked into that sumptuous room. It, too, had a wall of windows that jutted out. They surrounded a large, sunken Jacuzzi tub. The entire bathroom was tiled for a spa-like feel.

Given her father's wealth, she wasn't unfamiliar with luxury. But in Dare's home, he mixed it with a kind of functionality that was both cozy and comfortable. She could spend days just admiring the various rooms in his home, Molly thought as she cleared away the last of the tears, tossed her sodden tissues in a waste can and then headed back to her seat on the king-size bed.

Emotionally spent, she touched the indent in Dare's pillow, proof of where he'd been before she'd so rudely awakened him.

She heard the dogs' nails on the floor as they charged across the kitchen tiles, skittered to a turn and entered the room a few steps ahead of Dare.

Dare stopped in the doorway to scrutinize her, but the dogs headed straight for the bed.

When they jumped up onto the mattress, Dare made no move to stop them, leading Molly to believe that the dogs slept wherever they pleased.

She liked that about Dare. He was an orderly man, very particular about cleanliness, but a little dog fur didn't put him off. There was something very appealing about that down-to-earth quality, especially in a man with his ability.

Tai circled once, then dropped down at the foot of the bed and closed her eyes with a lusty sigh. Sargie tried to get her whole body into Molly's lap and ended up half sitting on Molly's thighs. Giving a watery, choked laugh, Molly hugged the dog tight and buried her face in her ruff.

Silence filled the room. The bed dipped when Dare sat beside her, but he said nothing. He didn't press her, didn't hold her. He simply sat there beside her, his shoulder touching hers, his nearness calming her and, at the same time, filling her with new, different sensations.

Molly knew she couldn't continue this way. When she stopped squeezing Sargie, the dog thumped her tail twice and snuffled Molly's neck with her nose. But when she didn't get a reaction, she crawled off her lap, over Dare, and flopped down next to Tai.

Awareness of Dare beside her, mostly undressed, expanded by the heartbeat. Molly glanced at him. His muscled, hairy thigh was right next to hers, pinning down the quilt he'd wrapped around her. She licked her lips, inhaled deeply and breathed in his hot masculine scent.

It was already familiar, comforting, enticing.

Her gaze skimmed up to his throat, his shoulders. He had the most remarkable chest, wide, strong, sculpted with obvious strength. Even relaxed, his abs remained defined. And a very sexy trail of dark brown hair led from his navel down into his snug boxers.

Beneath the soft cotton material she saw the bulge of his sex.

"Want me to lose the boxers for you?"

She jerked her gaze up to his. His slow smile showed more satisfaction than humor.

For Molly, one thought overshadowed the rest. "This should be awkward, but it's not."

"No."

"I mean, the crying and being stupid and weak is awkward, but being here with you is just…nice."

The smile faded, and his eyes warmed. "You feel better now?"

"Yes." And she did. That thrumming panic was no longer a part of her, leaving her at a loss. "I don't know what happened. I swear I felt fine earlier today."

"I know." He put a hand on her thigh, over the quilt. "But trust me, that sense of well-being is ephemeral at best. After your ordeal, you can't expect it to last. Not this soon. You need to cut yourself some slack. We'll get there eventually, I promise."

We? Did he mean that?

No, how could he? Dare barely knew her, and what he did know was shaded by extreme circumstance, not the routine, day-in-and-day-out parts of her life; not the mundane parts that made up the real her.

All in all, her mostly solitary life of research and writing equated to a very boring existence. Her life revolved around her desk, in her apartment, in a quiet town in Ohio.

Nothing exciting about that.

Even the few book signings and speaking appearances she did were low-key, attended by die-hard fans only.

With this one exception, she was not a woman who gained real enemies, or got kidnapped or abused, and she was definitely not a woman who crumpled under stress.

What would Dare think of the real Molly Alexander? When she wasn't so needy, would he still be drawn to her? Or was it his heroic nature that made her seem appealing to him now?

Soon, when she returned to her normal routine, he would continue on with rescuing those in need, facing off with danger, and making a mint in the bargain. He was a high-stakes player…and she was the girl next door.

Dare squeezed her thigh. "Molly?"

"Oh, sorry." She shook herself. This was no time to go meandering off mentally. "I was just… I'm better now. Thank you."

"I'm glad to hear it. But the next time you feel that

edginess coming on, don't wait until it's full-blown, okay? Just come to me. Let me help."

Whatever tomorrow might bring, or next week or next month, she needed to get through tonight first. "Fine. I accept that I need time." She *would* regain herself. Somehow, she would.

"That's a start." His hand stilled on her thigh. "What about tonight?"

"It's almost over." She tried to sound accepting instead of wretched. "But for what remains, may I sleep with you?"

"Yeah." He turned a little toward her. "I'd like that."

Relief robbed her spine of strength. Until he agreed, she hadn't realized how tense she felt. "Thank you."

"You don't mind sharing with two hounds? Because the girls look settled in for the rest of the night." He reached over to pat the dogs. "They usually favor the kitchen, but they sense you're upset, I think, and they want to stay close."

Somehow, Dare always took the most bizarre situations and made them feel…normal. Did nothing disconcert him?

"I don't mind." Given how being alone had thrown her, the more the merrier.

"Good." He stood and reached out a hand to her. Molly let him pull her to her feet, and then she waited as he turned to the covers. "You won't need this," he said, and he took the quilt from her and tossed it to the foot of the bed, half over Tai, who didn't stir.

Molly wore one of the big T-shirts and her panties, nothing else, but Dare paid no attention to that.

"In you go."

Trying to be discreet, she crawled into the bed and then scooted over as Dare got in next to her. He turned out the bedside lamp, reached an arm around her and pulled her in close. Her head fit nicely into the space between his hard shoulder and his chest. Already his warmth penetrated her. She felt the prickly hair on his legs and the softer chest hair against her cheek.

She felt…at peace.

The soft kiss to her temple offered so much comfort. "Okay?"

Molly nodded. "I guess if this was somehow…sexual, it'd be different. But I know it's not, and that makes it—"

"Let's try for a little more sleep before the sun comes up and the birds start singing. But Molly?"

Her heart pounded so hard, it was a wonder he didn't mention it. "Yes?"

"If you need to, wake me."

She'd try her best not to do that, but all she said was "Okay. Thank you."

In that dark, quiet room, she could hear the dogs breathing, the wind outside the doors leading to a deck and the settling of an unfamiliar house.

Odd, but it felt more like home than anyplace she'd ever been.

HAIR STILL DAMP FROM his shower, carrying his shoes in one hand and his belt in the other, Dare came down the steps and across the hall. He paused by his bedroom door, heard nothing from inside and knew Molly still slept.

Sneaking out on her had been easy. Even when he'd gathered up the clothes he'd need and had ushered out the dogs, she hadn't stirred. The sight of her there, crowded onto his side of the bed, her dark hair spilling out over the pillows, had moved him in unfamiliar ways.

He thought again of what she'd said, how holding her in his bed hadn't been sexual.

For her.

For him, it equated to a true test of his control. All night he'd felt her warm breath on his skin, felt the softness of her thigh, her hair, her scent. Awareness of her body against his, separated only by a cotton T-shirt, had tortured him.

He wanted her. Bad. It had been all kinds of sexual for him.

Determined to do the right thing, Dare turned away from the bedroom door and went into the kitchen.

Looking like death, wearing only lounge pants and a wrinkled oversize white T-shirt, Chris slumped at the table, eating cereal. Both dogs sat at the ready near his feet, hoping for a bite.

Dare helped himself to coffee. "I'm surprised to see you up already."

Chris rolled a shoulder. "I wasn't sure if you were serious about running the dogs or not."

"Already done."

Chris eyed him. "Then you could have fed them, too."

"I did—they just like your cereal. I told you not to start that or you'd regret it."

Lip curling in a sneer, Chris mimicked Dare's words, then gave each dog a piece of cereal. "You know, I detest that super-efficient, do-it-all, know-it-all attitude of yours."

Dare saluted him with his cup. Right now, he wished he knew a little more—about Molly.

As if reading his mind, Chris asked, "Did Molly get any sleep at all last night?"

"Enough." He helped himself to the coffee. "But she's in my bed, so stay out of my room."

Eyes widening, Chris froze with the spoon halfway to his mouth.

"Try to keep it quiet down here, and let her sleep as long as she needs to." Dare met his gaze. "And shut up."

Dropping the spoon back into the bowl, Chris held up his hands and tried to look innocent. "I wasn't going to say a single word."

"Yeah, you were." Dare threaded the thick leather belt into his jeans. It looked to be a nice day ahead, so he'd only need his light jacket.

"Okay, I was," Chris admitted as he scratched his bristly chin. "I mean, you slept with her."

"Exactly. We slept."

"Ah…" He looked confused. "So it's not…?"

"No, it's not, and that's all the explanation you're getting, so let it go." Dare joined him at the table. "I'm taking off for most of the day. Without her."

"Huh."

"I did my own research last night. Her dad is on a golf outing only a few hours from here."

Chris's brows shot up and he said again, "Huh."

He didn't question Dare's intel, knowing his personal resources were vast and accurate.

"Don't tell her what I'm doing."

"Easy enough." Folding his arms over his chest, Chris said, "Because I don't know what the hell you're doing."

Since he wasn't sure himself, Dare ignored that. "Just say I'm out on business—which will be true enough. I'll get back as soon as I can."

Rocking the chair back on two legs, Chris considered

everything and came to his own conclusions. "You don't trust dear old dad, and you don't want Molly walking into a booby trap."

"Emotional or otherwise." Dare set his coffee aside and bent to pull on his shoes. "I went ahead and called Trace last night, too."

"Is he joining you?"

"No." Dare shook his head. "I don't need him to, and like I said, he needs to be there for Alani. But he did some additional checking for me."

"And?"

"No one has reported Molly missing. Not her dad, not her stepmom and not the sister that she trusts so much."

"But she was gone nine days!" The legs of Chris's chair hit the floor. "And she doesn't seem the type who disappears without a word."

"No, she doesn't, does she?"

Indignant on Molly's behalf, Chris scowled. "That's fucked up."

"Maybe." Dare straightened again. "I don't know what it means. Yet. But I want to get a sense of things before I take her back there."

"You didn't want me to map out the trip?"

"Already did it." Before Molly had come to him last night, he'd had his own issues trying to sleep. He'd filled the restless hours with plans on her behalf.

After she'd joined him, his thoughts had been diverted from wanting to protect her, to just…wanting her.

"Will you confront her dad?"

"Not sure yet." Dare wasn't the type to back himself into a corner by stating his intentions prematurely. "I'm playing it by ear for now."

"Dare." Chris leaned forward and folded his arms on

the table. "Whatever is waiting for her back home, she eventually has to go back. You know that."

"Yeah. And I'll be with her." No way in hell would he let her out of his sight until he could assess the risk. "I don't like surprises, so I'm going to scope things out first. Do a little surveillance. That sort of thing."

Chris looked toward the kitchen doorway. "I hope she sleeps the day away. I suck as a babysitter."

"Just keep her safe. Don't let her off the grounds, but maybe she'd like to check out the lake, explore the woods a little." Dare stood and fished his keys from his pocket. "Make sure she drinks plenty of fluids, too. Whatever she likes. Order it if we don't have it. And I want her to eat. She has to build up her—"

Exasperated, Chris pushed out of his chair to interrupt Dare's laundry list of instructions. "I was kidding about babysitting, Dare. I can handle it. Just go. The sooner you leave, the sooner you'll be back, and the sooner I can give up guard duty."

Dare slapped him on the shoulder. Once again he appreciated having Chris around. Too many times over the years, trusted friends had been few and far between. "I'll keep you posted."

Dare went to the dogs and told them both that he'd be back soon. They were smart, and they understood the difference between an extended trip that involved his duffel bag, and one that'd last only a few hours. They followed him to the door but showed no signs of anxiety.

"You girls keep Molly company, okay?" To Sargie he said, "And no shenanigans. I don't want you to wear her out." As Dare went out the door, he realized he was already missing her, and it pissed him off.

Hopefully, once he secured her safety, he could take her to his bed with no intention of sleeping. Once he had her, then he'd be able to get her out of his system. He'd have to.

There was no room for a romantic relationship in his line of work—and he was a long way from retiring.

CHAPTER NINE

DARE SAT IN HIS SUV, waiting. Impatient, but unwavering. He'd done many stakeouts, but this one was different. This time he wasn't watching for the victim or planning to trail a suspect. This time, he wanted information only.

And he'd get what he wanted. Already he'd discovered things, and he didn't like any of it. Now he needed more. He needed a clearer picture of the circumstances.

Molly's father could supply that.

Trace had been invaluable in doing a quick rundown on Bishop Alexander. A more thorough analysis would follow; in fact, Trace was working on that right now. He would scour Bishop's past, dig into his present and even take apart future plans to get as much intelligence as possible. Very shortly, Dare would know more about Bishop Alexander than he knew of himself.

Dare grinned, glad that he'd have an opportunity to return Trace's money to him. Accepting financial compensation from his friend hadn't felt right, especially when the job involved Alani. Years of hard work, wise investments and good sense had already amassed him a small fortune. He didn't need Trace's money. He didn't really need anyone's money. More often than not, he continued to accept assignments to keep his edge and to feed his need for excitement.

Money had little to do with it these days. Thanks to

Trace's incomparable investigative skills, Dare now had the excuse to pay him back in full.

Dare considered the information Trace had already supplied. By all accounts, Molly's father felt omnipotent to all the "lesser" people around him, including his daughters and his wife. Other than some shady business dealings, he didn't even try to conceal his transgressions. Because he hadn't done a very good job of building a bond with a longstanding assistant, it had been easy to glean info.

Some people had no idea how to cover their tracks.

One kernel of data led to another, public records gave clues to private information—and now Dare had enough to accomplish his task today.

Beneath the shade of an ornamental tree that blocked some of the bright sunshine, Dare had watched Bishop drive up in a shiny black Mercedes. The older man had emerged in *GQ* golf duds, a cell phone to his ear and a shiny platinum ring glinting on his finger.

Bishop had paid little enough attention to the valet as the young man took his keys to park the car. Dare heard him laugh, saw him lift a hand to hail other men and then join a small group of distinguished-looking friends or colleagues.

Bishop Alexander did not act like a man with a missing daughter.

That had been hours ago. Sooner or later, he had to come back out. Dare checked his watch and considered what his next move would be. Should he confront Bishop here, in front of the others?

How dare the man play golf anyway? Wasn't he worried about Molly? Or was it just that he had business responsibilities? Dare well knew the value of cultivating connections; could this be Bishop's purpose today?

Maybe he was putting on a good front to hide the personal troubles in his own family.

The emotional involvement of this assignment was different for Dare. Usually he hunted for the truth with detached resolve. He did a good job because that's what he was paid to do.

Now, for Molly, he wanted to ferret out the truth because keeping her safe mattered to him personally.

Last night… God almighty, he'd wanted her. He still wanted her. Being away from her hadn't changed that.

But last night she'd needed something altogether different from him. She hadn't even noticed his boner, or the heat pouring off him. She'd held on to him like a lifeline, and…he'd liked it. He liked her.

It didn't matter how hard the circumstances might be on him; until Molly got through this, until she regained some control over her life, he would continue to do what he could for her. If that meant holding her every damn night, then so be it.

He would damn well keep his hands to himself.

Until she was ready.

Dare was thinking of her eventual readiness when Bishop finally emerged from the club. Though he'd been out in the sun for hours, his well-groomed, silver-tipped hair looked like it had just been styled. Aviator sunglasses hid his eyes, but not his smile as he chatted up another, taller man. They laughed together, and Bishop clapped the other fellow on the shoulder as a farewell. The friend veered off in a different direction, leaving Bishop alone, waiting on the valet.

Fuck it.

Before the valet noticed him, Dare got out of his car and looked over the roof. "Bishop Alexander?"

Molly's father looked up.

Predatory anticipation filled Dare. "Got a minute?"

Taking off his glasses, Bishop stared toward Dare. "Do I know you?"

Dare didn't move from his relaxed position outside the driver's side of his SUV. "We haven't formally met, but your daughter has told me about you."

Bishop went still, but only for a second. A calculated expression reshaped his features, and he slunk closer with caution. "Which daughter would that be?"

Of course the bastard felt safe. They were in front of an exclusive club where only members were allowed. Bishop wouldn't realize that Dare went where he wanted, when he wanted. Getting past the gate had been child's play for a man of his means.

For Bishop, his money and social influence were his strength. But Dare didn't give a shit about any of that.

"The daughter who's been missing."

In an instant, Bishop's jaw firmed, and he surged forward with the confidence of a man used to power and prestige. "What do you know of that?"

So he realized Molly had been missing. Interesting. "I found Molly, and I thought you might be interested in the…details."

That did it. After waving off the approaching valet, Bishop moved to confront Dare. Voice lowered and infused with suspicion, he said, "I don't know what this is about, but if you think to blackmail me, I can tell you that it won't work. You won't get a single cent from me."

It took all of Dare's resolve not to plant his fist in Bishop's face. Feigning a boredom he didn't feel, Dare said, "Does that mean you're not curious about where she was, or how she got there?"

On uncertain ground, Bishop flexed his fingers while trying to gauge his opponent. Finally, after smoothing his already smooth hair, he tweaked the collar of his golf shirt and played blasé. "I assumed she was off on another research trip."

"Yeah?" Arms relaxed, stance negligent, Dare smiled. "And you thought I'd blackmail you over that?"

"What else?" All decorum fled as he said, "Thanks to her absurd vocation, Molly gets herself into preposterous situations."

"Like what? Being kidnapped?"

"Kidnapped?" For only a moment, Bishop rocked back in shock before realizing how loudly he'd spoken. Appalled at himself, he again looked around to ensure no one had overheard him.

"That's right. Taken against her will." Enunciating slowly, Dare said, "Abducted."

"But…" He blustered in disbelief. "That's absurd."

Dare shook his head. "It's a fact."

Not missing a beat, Bishop asked, "But she's safe now?"

Did the man care? Or was he pondering his own position in things? "She's safe."

After letting out a breath, trying to shush Dare with his own example, Bishop said, "Look, this has nothing to do with me."

"You're her father."

"An irrefutable fact." Bishop sounded pained by the relationship. "But you'd have to understand my daughter. She is not conventional. She is not circumspect. It's a fault I have lamented for years."

Dare said nothing—which prompted Bishop to say a lot.

"Just what the hell do you want from me? You certainly can't expect me to take charge of Molly's every misfortune."

Being kidnapped was a misfortune? "You're a real asshole, aren't you, Bishop?" Dare didn't bother being circumspect, which prompted Bishop to another quick survey of their surroundings. "Do you have any idea where your daughter was?"

"Since I didn't know of any of this, how could I?"

"Do you even care?"

Bishop flattened his mouth—and refused to reply.

Deep down, rage simmered in Dare, but he didn't show it. "You know, I have to ask myself—why would a father be so indifferent to his daughter's well-being—unless he was the one who had arranged her *misfortune*."

Jaw going slack and face coloring, Bishop blinked in an effort to reconcile himself with the accusation. "You're serious, aren't you?" And then with new heat: "What the hell are you talking about? Do you know who I am? Do you know my standing in society?"

Hmm. He *had* looked genuinely surprised by it all.

Dare decided to press him. Coming out from around the SUV door, he closed the distance to Molly's father. At around five feet, nine inches, Bishop stood damn near a half foot shorter than Dare. He was lean, toned, but he lacked any real strength.

Physically, he was half the man Dare was. In character, he was a worm.

"So, Bishop," Dare said, "it would surprise you to learn that your daughter was snatched out front of her apartment building?"

"That's ridiculous. Who would want Molly?"

God almighty, Dare wanted to hit him. One good pop to the nose, that's all. Bishop wouldn't be so smug or condescending with his own blood splattered over his face. "And I guess you didn't know that she was taken to Tijuana, held captive, starved, tormented and threatened?"

"I don't believe you," Bishop blustered. The earlier hot color leached from his face. He said again, "I don't believe you."

"She was taken, all right."

Even while shaking his head in denial, Bishop muttered, "But...*why?*"

"That's what I want to know."

Perplexed, Bishop looked down in thought, then glared at Dare. "This is hard to accept. And what do you have to do with it, anyway?"

"Not a damn thing, except that I'm the one who found her."

With even more suspicion, Bishop asked, "In Tijuana?"

"Yes." Keeping it vague, Dare gave a bare-bones assessment. "I was there for unrelated reasons, and I saw her. Her condition was not good."

"What do you mean?" And in accusation: "You said she was okay."

"She's alive, and she's healing." Physically. Emotionally... Dare just didn't know. "But she was poorly treated."

The seconds ticked by; Bishop swallowed. "Raped?"

"She says not." The rapid-fire questions felt more devious than frantic.

"Who had her?"

"People who deal in white slavery."

Bishop blanched in horror. "Dear God. White slavery? But surely... Where is she now?" He looked around aghast as if expecting her to suddenly appear. "She's not with you, is she?"

"I told you, she's safe. I have her well away from here."
Away from you.

"I see." Though he tried to hide it, Bishop's evident relief couldn't be missed.

It wasn't relief for his daughter's safety—the bastard.

"Well." Bishop tugged at his tailored shirt. "I'm pleased to hear that she's all right."

"I didn't say that."

Disregarding Dare's statement, Bishop forged on. "She obviously can't come back home."

"Home?" Dare inquired.

"To Ohio."

His eyes narrowed. "To where you live, you mean?"

As if justified, Bishop said, "There would be a ghastly scandal. The media would have a field day if they got wind of this, and knowing Molly, she won't even attempt to keep it quiet."

"You would expect her to?"

His chin shot up. "For the sake of her family, and to protect our good name, of course that's what I expect."

"She didn't ask to be taken, you know."

"Maybe not in so many words." Bishop curled his lip in disdain and distaste. "But still…"

Wishing he could demolish the smaller man, Dare asked, "What do you mean by that?"

"She's my daughter. Of course I care about her well-being. But odds are she brought this on herself."

"Are you fucking kidding me?" Dare had seen some hideous people in his time, but Molly's father beat them all.

"With that filth she writes and the way she—"

As Dare stiffened in fury, Bishop trailed off.

Through his teeth, Dare gritted out, "It is not her fault."

"This is absurd." Bishop dismissed the topic with a shake of his head. "I'm not going to continue this conversation with you. I don't even know your name."

Straightening to his full height, Dare glared down at him. "But I know yours, Bishop. And if I find out you had anything to do with Molly's abduction, I'll damn well take you apart, piece by piece."

His mouth fell open in disbelief. "You're *threatening* me?"

Bishop obviously couldn't believe such a notion.

"I'm explaining the facts to you."

Umbrage stiffened the older man's spine. "I don't have to listen to this."

As he turned away, Dare said, "Fact number one is that Molly *is* coming home."

That stalled Bishop in his tracks.

"She needs to know who did this to her. And so do I. The best way to find that out is to confront people."

"That's outrageous! Good God, man, you don't *brag* about it when you've been defiled. You show some common decency and you *cover it up*."

"Fact number two," Dare said, speaking over Bishop's protestations, "is that Molly isn't going to hide anything—but you are."

He bristled at the order. "I don't know what you're talking about. What is it you think I need to hide?"

"That we've met, that you know Molly is safe with me and that I'm hunting for the one responsible. You aren't going to say a word about this to anyone. No one is to know about Molly, not until she or I tell them."

Bishop narrowed his eyes and pointed a finger at Dare's chest. "You do not dictate to me."

"Yeah, I do." Dare stepped closer until that rigid finger touched him. Bishop jerked his hand away and retreated, but Dare didn't allow that.

He caught Molly's father by the front of his shirt. "Because, Bishop, fact number three is that you don't want to be on my bad side. I can destroy you. I *will* destroy you if you cross me on this."

Squirming to get free, Bishop feigned courage that he didn't possess. "You don't know who you're talking to. I am not a man you can bully."

"That's a claim I can put to you, Bishop." Dare knew the slow show of his teeth looked like pure evil. "I have contacts in businesses that you can't even imagine. I have friends in high places, and better friends in low places. No matter what you do or where you crawl away to, I have ways of getting to you. Cross me, and I *will* obliterate you, Bishop, socially, financially and personally."

Teeth gritted, Bishop tried to knock Dare's hand away, but couldn't. "Just who the hell are you?"

"I'm the person who knows all about you." He dragged him closer, up onto his tiptoes until their noses almost touched. "I know about your summer house, and your apartment in the city. I have access to your various accounts, a detailed record of your worth and a list of all your business acquaintances."

Breathless, fearful, Bishop whispered, "You're bluffing."

"I don't waste time bluffing." Digging up info on Bishop Alexander had been insanely easy for Trace. "I know you're cheating on your wife *and* on your girlfriend. You're considering an offer to sell part of your company, without telling any of the shareholders. You have a dental appointment in two days, and you just bet two grand on the outcome of your golf game."

Bishop went pale, gasping like a fish out of water. "How…?"

"Even better, you don't know jack shit about me, do you? Where I live, how I get my info, when I'll be back… or if you'll see me when I do return." After that ominous threat, Dare released him with a small shove. "I don't like you, Bishop. You're a shitty father, a cheating husband and an unscrupulous businessman."

"I…I…"

Dare shook his head. "Save your breath. I don't care about your excuses or justifications. Just know this—I want answers, and they better be truthful."

"But…" With a fleeting look around, Bishop appealed to Dare. "We can't stay here. People are starting to take notice of us."

Like he gave a shit? Being around Bishop soured his stomach and quadrupled his sympathy for Molly.

"Believe me, I don't want to extend this visit any longer than I have to." In fact, he was damned anxious to start the drive back to see Molly. He'd wasted a good portion of the day waiting for Bishop to finish his game, and he still had a little more surveillance to do. Hell, by the time he finished, it'd be late, much later than he'd first intended.

He glanced at his watch. Was Molly lonely? Worried? Without him there, would she have another episode of near panic? He'd have to check in with Chris.… *No.*

Never before had he been a person to fret, and he damn well wasn't going to start now. Molly was a strong woman, and she was in good hands with Chris. If anything had happened, Chris would have called.

The glare he put on Bishop had the man swallowing hard. "This will take less than five minutes," Dare told him, "as long as you're straight with me. If not…well, then, we can be here all fucking day."

"Fine." Trying to regain his aplomb, Bishop rested a hip on the hood of Dare's SUV and attempted a cavalier pose. "Let's get this over with, then."

That Bishop kept trying to take charge should have sent Dare's temper to the breaking point; instead it reinforced just how obnoxious and pretentious the man was.

How the hell did Molly stand him? Had she gained her incredible willpower through necessity, from dealing with such a cold, uncaring father? Dare thought of her mother's suicide, and how Molly's life must've been after that loss.

Molly's choices had been to be strong, or take the same path as one of her parents. She'd chosen strength.

And damn, he admired her as much as he wanted her.

"You had questions?" Bishop prompted.

Shaking off his distraction, Dare said, "Molly's boyfriend. What do you know of him?"

"Who?" Looking genuinely perplexed, Bishop asked, "Do you mean Adrian?"

Unwilling to give Bishop any guidance, Dare didn't reply.

His silence impelled Bishop to continue. "They're not together anymore, which is a shame, but to my knowledge that's the last man she dated." Bishop pretended to give it some thought.

Dare wasn't fooled. "You're pushing your luck."

"I don't know that much about him. He seemed pleasant enough. Successful." Bishop shrugged. "He owns property, his own business."

"He owns a bar, but he's hocked up to his eyebrows—and you'd know that, too, Bishop. No way in hell would you have let your daughter date anyone without doing a background check. You're too protective of your own interests to risk letting anyone seedy in the door."

Provoked, Bishop snapped, "If you already knew, then why are you bothering me?"

"Judging your honesty—and so far you're failing."

Taking that as a threat, Bishop rushed to say, "Fine. He was a graspy little worm who no doubt dated Molly for *my* money. But I wasn't worried."

"Because even Molly won't see a dime?"

In his own defense, Bishop said, "She does well enough for herself."

But she hadn't always. When she was a little girl with hopes and dreams, all she'd had was Bishop, and it broke Dare's fucking heart. "You're talking about the writing career that you scorn?"

"I did not raise her to indulge in vulgar means of entertainment."

From what Dare could tell, Bishop hadn't really raised her at all. "Like whoring, cheating and gambling, you mean?" Those were Bishop's sins, and they had not been passed on to the daughter.

Umbrage darkened Bishop's complexion. "Are we through here?"

Dare shook his head. "Tell me about Natalie."

"What do you want to know?"

That Bishop didn't even make a pretense of trying to protect his youngest daughter didn't surprise Dare. The man would guard his own interests first and foremost. "Where is she?"

"At this moment? I have no idea. She teaches, so she's likely home by now. Probably grading papers or some related tedious task." He caught Dare's impatience and rushed on to say, "If you're asking me where she lives, then you'll find her in an apartment complex not far from Molly. The two of them have always been thick as thieves. For as long as I can remember, if one of them lied, the other one swore to it."

If they had lied, Dare would bet it was to protect one another. "And your wife?"

Bishop shrugged. "At this particular moment, Mrs. Alexander would be presenting a grant to the Historical Society in Cincinnati." He waved a hand. "She's very into her little clubs and charitable affairs."

So far, Bishop was the sole unscrupulous family member. Not that Dare was done digging. "When did you realize that Molly was missing?"

"When you trapped me here. Before that, I had no idea. My daughter and I don't keep track of each other's social calendars."

"Bullshit. You knew."

"I knew she was out of touch. I knew she was likely annoyed at me and therefore not returning her stepmother's calls. But she travels without alerting me, and she's always been independent."

Because she'd had no choice. "Didn't Natalie notice?"

Bishop looked at his nails. "Natalie did call me, concerned, but I had nothing to tell her, and neither did Kathi. I haven't heard from her since, so I assume she came to the same conclusion that I did, that Molly was off on business with her book contracts."

"Or the movie deal?"

Blank-faced, Bishop asked, "What movie deal?"

Huh. So he really didn't know about that. Dare had already determined that the man was a lousy liar; if he'd known, he couldn't have hidden it.

"I'll be in touch, Bishop." Dare wasn't about to

share Molly's news. If she wanted him to know, she'd tell him herself. "When Molly calls you, you fucking well better answer. I don't care what you have going on. Understood?"

"Does this mean we're done?"

"For now, yes." Dare smiled again. "Don't forget what I told you, Bishop. This never happened. Tell a single soul, and you'll regret it." Stepping around his SUV, Dare opened the driver's door and started to get inside.

For a second or two, Bishop stood there, unsure what to do. Finally he hissed low, "Why the hell are you even involved in all of this?"

And Dare couldn't resist. He knew it was a mistake, knew he was acting out of character, that if he was truly in control he'd stick with the plan and drive away.

But he couldn't.

Slowly he closed the door and came back toward Bishop.

Sensing that he'd erred, Bishop tried to backpedal, but he wasn't fast enough. Dare grabbed him by the front of his shirt.

The older man screeched when Dare slammed him up against the hood of his car. "You try my patience, Bishop. That's a very dangerous thing to do. Don't let it happen again."

With that warning, Dare shoved Bishop from him, forcing him to stumble before he gathered his composure and staggered away, taking his temper out on the valet who had yet to retrieve his car.

Dare had learned more than enough, for now. He got in the SUV, put it in gear and drove out of the club's lot. Rage continued to simmer inside him, making him clench his jaw and lock his teeth. He wanted to see Molly. He wanted to hold her and tell her how sorry he was for her lot in life.

Just as he cleared the gates, his cell phone rang.

Thinking it might be Chris with news of Molly, he snapped the phone open on the first ring. "Yeah?"

In a tone far too grim, Trace said, "I have some info you'll want to see."

Damn. Dare glanced at the time on the console. "I was just heading home." And for once, seeing his girls took second place. He wanted to check on Molly. And more. But the way Trace had worded that, Dare knew he had some photos. "They're important?"

"You'll want to see them ASAP, yeah. I can upload them to you, or I can meet you somewhere along I-75."

"Let's meet. I'd like to get your take on things anyway." Knowing Trace, the photos would be telling. Anything that'd make it easier for Dare to ensure Molly's safety was a priority. "Say in forty minutes?"

"That'll work."

After they agreed on a restaurant that catered to truckers, Dare asked, "How's Alani?"

"Throwing herself into her work. I wanted her to take some time off, to chill with me, but she said that'd be the worst thing to do."

Dare grinned. Thanks to Trace's financial backing and business influence, Alani owned an interior-design business, so she could easily set her hours to be as busy or as idle as she wanted. "You hoped to hover over her and instead she's out and about with strangers."

Voice going lower, Trace growled, "She's remodeling for some asshole businessman."

Given what Alani had just been through, Dare understood his friend's need to shelter her. But while Alani might look delicate with her fair hair and slim build, she had the same strength of character as her brother. "I suppose you already started a background check on him?"

"First thing I did—against Alani's protests. So far he's come out clean enough. He's a financier. His family is old money, and I don't like him."

"Because he's rich?" Dare laughed. "Hate to break it to you, but most would consider us rich, too."

"We worked our asses off for our money."

True, but not really the point. "Alani has always had every advantage, and she's still grounded." Being eight years older than Alani, Trace had ensured that she wanted for nothing, and yet she remained sweet and unspoiled.

And if it was old money Trace objected to, well, hell, Molly's father was well pedigreed, but she was the least overindulged person he knew.

Trace sighed. "Plain and simple, I don't like him, okay? I don't know him, but I still don't like him."

"Right now, you're not going to like anyone who's around her." Odds were it'd take Trace longer to recuperate from the ordeal than it would Alani, because Trace also had guilt working on him. "But she's only remodeling for this guy, right? It's not a personal relationship."

"You know what Alani looks like. Do you really think the guy—who's single, damn him—will want to keep it strictly business?"

Trace had a point. The combo of fair hair and golden-brown eyes was remarkable on Trace; on Alani, coupled with her figure and sweet sex appeal, most guys wouldn't be able to resist hitting on her. "Want me to talk to him?"

"God, no. Alani would pulverize us both. I'll keep an eye on the situation."

Dare grinned again. "If you need backup, let me know."

After disconnecting the call, Dare let his thoughts meander back to Molly. It was odd that she affected him so profoundly. Not once, ever, had he gotten emotionally involved with a woman. He enjoyed socializing and sex, but that's where it had always ended.

With his career choice, anything more was absurd, because he knew, deep down to the marrow of his bones, a relationship would never work. Not only did he spend too much time away, but the job made secrecy necessary. Add to that the level of danger often involved, and it wouldn't make sense to let a woman get too close.

Before Molly, that reality had set fine with him.

Now...now he found himself wondering about impossible things. He found himself thinking longer term. He wasn't the kind of man who could commit to a lifetime, but a month? Two months? The idea of having her around, getting his fill of her, tantalized him.

But she'd need time to recover from her trauma, and he had no idea how long that might take, or how long she'd tolerate his intrusion into her life.

If he was able to nail her father for the sin of her abduction, where would that leave them? Once Molly knew the culprit, she could get on with her life without fear of another threat—and she'd no longer need Dare around.

Driving down the highway by rote, his reflexes on autopilot, Dare let himself examine every possible scenario. He was damned good at what he did, and he had a hell of a lot of resources at hand. Through the years, he and Trace had built up contacts in the government, the military and within all the highest-profile businesses.

Bishop Alexander thought he possessed power; in truth, he had no idea what real power could do.

No matter how Dare looked at it, his time with Molly would be short-lived. Yes, she was a complication to his life, but now…now he rather liked the way she complicated things.

Somehow he'd have to figure out a way to solve her dilemma and still give himself the time he needed to indulge his every carnal urge.

And with Molly, the carnal urges were plenty.

CHAPTER TEN

CHRIS TRIED TO DO all his chores, but at every moment he was aware of Molly. She'd awakened disoriented, confused that Dare had left and a little hurt even, but determined to hide that reaction behind calm acceptance.

Both he and Dare had told Molly to make herself at home, and to an extent she did. But she remained cautious, trying her best to be inconspicuous, when such a thing wasn't possible.

She didn't like to rock the boat or draw unnecessary attention to herself.

Chris snorted. All the woman had to do was breathe to draw attention. True, she wasn't a classic beauty with her average brown hair and dark brown eyes. She didn't flirt, and what figure she had she managed to disguise.

Most of the time, anyway.

But there was something about her, an aura of sensuality that he knew had Dare on high alert. Her gentle smile and sedate manner emphasized that natural sex appeal. Chris had already noticed how she looked him in the eyes when she talked to him, how she listened intently when he talked, how she protested too much attention, and her effort to be unassuming.

All very admirable qualities.

Maybe it was the little things, too, like how she bit her lips, the way she lowered her lashes, the movement of her hands while she spoke, and her gratitude and graciousness about everything. One would never know the awfulness of what she'd recently gone through. She wasn't clingy or needy or even all that shaken.

At least, not with him.

But she had slept with Dare, *in the platonic sense,* so she must still be feeling the effects of her ordeal.

Since he'd never before considered Dare to be a coddler of any kind, it was a pretty incredible setup.

Chris couldn't help but wonder how long the nonphysical aspect of their bond would last.

So far today, she'd done her utmost to stay out of his way. In fact, other than watching her on the monitors whenever possible while she was outside, he'd barely seen her since she'd eaten breakfast.

For hours she'd strolled around the grounds. She'd stayed within the fenced perimeter, but that encompassed a lot of woods and rugged land. Molly Alexander wasn't a princess or she wouldn't have hiked and communed with nature for so long.

She'd also walked along the shore, skipping rocks, examining leaves, testing the chill in the water with her toes. She appeared to like the outdoors as much as Dare did.

Late March had brought an uncharacteristic warm spell, with daytime temps hitting in the low- to mid-sixties. Combined with the bright sunshine, it felt more like early summer than spring. Chris could understand why she'd wanted to get some fresh air. But most women would have been bored in no time.

Not Molly.

She played with the dogs by throwing their Frisbee and then racing them down the hill a few times, laughing all the way. When Sargie knocked her down, Chris waited for her to complain, to push the dog away and scold her.

Instead she sat there in the dirt and leaves and smiled.

She appeared to love the dogs, which meant that Dare was a goner for sure, whether he knew it yet or not.

At one point late in the day, Molly came in to find a brush for the dogs, then went back out to sit peacefully on the dock, grooming first Sargie and then Tai. The girls loved to be brushed and gladly allowed the attention. Most importantly, Dare wasn't around, so Chris knew this wasn't a female ploy to get on his good side through his precious girls.

Nope, Molly was just being Molly, genuine and honest and straightforward, and that was powerful enough to level any guy.

Off and on, Chris checked on her, but Molly stayed there on the dock for a long time, just taking in the serenity of nature.

Chris understood her awe, because he'd done the same many times. The way the setting sun cast long red ribbons across the surface of the lake could mesmerize him still. Little by little, the sun sank lower behind the western hills in a blazing crimson display that slowly faded to golden, then gray, until everything turned dim and chilly.

Because he'd been keeping tabs on her, Chris wasn't surprised when she poked her head around the door to the library.

"Chris?"

"Hmm?" One of his last chores for the day was refilling the paper trays to the many printers throughout the house. He looked up and found her windblown, rosy-cheeked and looking quite adorable again. "Had enough fresh air?"

Her smile charmed him. "I had no idea that being on a lake was so…"

"Relaxing?"

She nodded. "The sounds and smells and the incredible quiet… It sort of saps all the tension away."

Meaning she'd been tense? Well, of course she had. Dare had left her alone in strange surroundings when she was still battered and uncertain of her safety. Chris understood Dare's motives, but did Molly? And even if she did, would that make it any easier?

Chris stored the remainder of the paper in a drawer and started toward her. "I'm glad you enjoyed it."

She hugged her arms around herself. "After the sun set, it started to get pretty chilly out there. I'd love a nice soak to warm up again." She bit her lip. "Would it be okay if I used the tub? I mean, the Jacuzzi tub in Dare's room? Or would he prefer that I didn't—"

"Of course you can." Dare would love for her to make use of his tub. If he called, Chris just might tell him about it. That thought forced him to bite back a grin. "Do you know where everything is? Towels, soap…?"

"Dare already showed me." She hesitated. "Is there anything you wanted me to do to help out around here? I could do that first. I wouldn't mind pitching in—"

"I've got it covered." He shooed her on her way. "Go, relax, enjoy. When you're done, you really should get something to eat, though." If he didn't keep her fed and well hydrated, Dare would have his head.

"I will, thanks." She took off, again with the dogs trailing her.

A few minutes later, Chris heard the hum of the Jacuzzi tub in Dare's room. If Dare were here, he'd go nuts thinking of her in there, all wet and relaxed among swirling bubbles.

Chris shook his head before making the rounds, checking the monitors first, then checking Dare's messages both on the phone and on the computer. One of his duties was to sort out the emails, answering what he could and flagging those that required a personal reply.

Over an hour later, just when he was starting to worry that she'd fallen asleep in the tub, the jets turned off. Chris paused, listening, forgetting what he was doing for the moment. A glance at the clock showed it was after 8:00 p.m.

Now that she'd finished with her bath, she'd be at loose ends again, and, for all his many talents, he had no idea what to do with her. He hoped like hell that Dare would make it home soon.

Not ten minutes later she poked her head into the kitchen, where he busied himself by taking inventory of groceries and cleaning supplies that he'd need to pick up tomorrow. Dare had a cleaning crew that came in once a month to really get things spic-and-span, but between those highly supervised visits, everyday tidying fell to Chris.

Tai and Sargie remained Molly's shadows, bemusing Chris. Usually, when Dare wasn't around, the girls stuck close to him. They'd never met a person they didn't love, but they seemed especially taken with Molly.

Her damp, pinned-up hair left little wisps curling around her ears and nape and showed off sharp cheekbones, a refined jaw and an innate elegance. It also emphasized the marks of mistreatment that remained on her soft skin. He couldn't forget, even for a second, how badly she'd been abused.

Straightening to face her, Chris asked, "Enjoy your bath?"

"Yes, thank you. I might have to invest in one of those tubs. It was heavenly." She moseyed over to a chair but didn't sit. The dogs followed her, so she knelt down to pet them both and ended up with Sargie knocking her to her butt.

Molly just laughed and let Sargie crawl across her lap.

"Do you think Dare will mind that I borrowed his hoodie?" She pulled together the unzipped front of the sweatshirt. "I was a little chilled after that hot bath, but I don't really have too many clothes yet."

"Of course he wouldn't mind." Chris cursed himself for not thinking of that himself. The house was kept on the cool side to accommodate two men, but naturally a woman might find it uncomfortable.

"I didn't get in his closet or anything. It was on a hook in his room."

"It's fine, Molly." They had to get the woman some more clothes. Hopefully what she ordered would arrive tomorrow, and then Dare could take her to her place to gather her own, familiar belongings. "Hungry?"

She gave it some thought before nodding. "A little. Is it okay if I roust up something myself? I won't make a mess."

"I'm not worried about that." Did he really come off as such a bastard? Hell, he was the sloppy one. Dare was the one who wanted everything immaculate. "What sounds good to you?"

"Do you have peanut butter and jelly?"

That surprised him. "Sure. But don't you want something more? Forget Dare's insults. I really can cook, I promise."

She shook her head and wiggled out from under Sargie. Because Tai wasn't as aggressive, she took a moment to give her some attention, too, then went around the kitchen gathering what she needed. "I missed the simple snacks, you know? Bowl of cereal, peanut butter and jelly, ice cream. I always keep that kind of stuff around my place because I'm not a big fast-food person at all, and I usually don't see the point in cooking for one person."

"Dare isn't into fast food, either. I have to twist his arm to get pizza on occasion." Chris glanced at the clock. "He should be home soon." God willing.

"You don't have to babysit me, you know?" She glanced toward him with a quirky smile. "I know you have your own place, and without Dare here, you probably would have been there already, right?"

True. While Dare was away, he could complete his work and have the rest of the time to himself. But he didn't want her to know that. "I had some chores to do."

Her expression said she didn't believe him. "You've been keeping an eye on me all day."

Had she seen the viewers mounted around the property? "What makes you think so?"

"I don't know. I just felt it."

Ah. Something else she and Dare had in common—keen awareness. "Actually, I keep an eye on everything, including the property, and you just happened to be in the scene."

"Did you expect trouble?"

"Nope. At least, not any more than any other day. Dare is nothing if not cautious."

She said nothing to that, but Chris knew she'd just stored away that knowledge. After she finished preparing her snack, she put away the utensils and food and said, "Would it be okay if I used a computer?"

"Uh…" Dare didn't want her on any of her accounts, but how was he supposed to police that?

In dramatic fashion, she crossed her heart. "I won't break any rules, I promise. My accounts are off-limits. It's just that while I was out walking earlier, I had an idea for my WIP and I wanted to get it down while it's fresh in my mind."

"WIP?"

"Work in progress. I haven't been able to write for a while, and not writing makes me...antsy."

Being held captive probably made her antsy, too, but he got her point. "Hey, have at it. I just refilled all the printers, so feel free to print off whatever you write."

"Actually, if you have a flash drive or something that I could pay you for, that would work better. Then if I want to change things later, I can."

Fascinated by her writing process, Chris said, "I'm sure I have some extras stored in the library." She trailed him as he started out of the room. "You can use the computer in the room Dare gave you." But maybe she didn't want to be alone there, so he quickly added, "Or the one in his room, or the library... Doesn't matter, really."

"I'll use the one upstairs." She wrinkled her nose. "I like a lot of privacy when I write."

Was that a hint for him not to try looking over her shoulder? Bummer. It'd be cool to watch a writer at work.

Chris located a flash drive in the library desk and handed it to her. "There you go."

"Thanks." She juggled her glass of milk and the plate with the sandwich and pushed the flash drive into the sweatshirt pocket. Then she gave Chris a direct look. "And since I'll be occupied, you really don't need to hang around—that is, unless you want to. But don't change your plans on my account, okay? I really, really detest being a bother."

Telling her that she wasn't a bother wouldn't have made a difference to how she felt about it. So instead, Chris asked, "You're going to stay in the house for the rest of the night?"

Molly hesitated. "Do I need to?"

"No." God, he hoped she wasn't planning another jaunt around the perimeter. "You're safe enough anywhere on the grounds right around the house, under the security lights, but I'd rather know what you're doing, and where you'll be." *Just in case*.

Her shoulder lifted. "If it's okay, I might go down to the dock again later. The change of scenery jogs my muse, and the fresh air keeps me alert. Will that be a problem?"

Since the dock was closer to his place, and monitored, Chris was relieved. "That's fine. Just be careful, okay?" And then to tease her, "We wouldn't want you to fall in."

As he started out of the room, the dogs followed, making Chris pause with a laugh. "I guess they're ready to turn in for the night, so now they're coming with me." He eyed Molly. "You don't mind being alone?"

She shook her head. "I usually am."

And for whatever reason, that damn near broke Chris's heart.

THROWING HERSELF into her work, Molly spent two hours on the computer and managed to write the entire scene before her muse took a rest and reality sank back in. The house was so quiet, and when she looked at the clock, she saw it was almost 10:00 p.m.

She saved her file and stored the flash drive with the few belongings she owned. Earlier, she had carried her dishes back down to the kitchen and stowed them in the dishwasher. The silence of the big house hadn't really sunk in then; she'd been too anxious to get back to her story.

Now, however, she heard every unfamiliar noise.

Arms wrapped around herself, she walked over to the French doors to look out. Her head started to ache, so she freed her hair from the haphazard topknot fastened with paper clamps she'd found on the desk. Of course two men with short hair didn't have any hair clips or bobby pins just lying around.

She shook her hair free, rubbed her temples a little. And still the tension continued squeezing in.

Earlier, the walk had helped. Then the hot bath. And then writing. But now…

Surely Dare would come back tonight…right?

She looked at the bed and shuddered at the thought of trying to sleep there, alone, with only her turbulent memories.

Regardless of how Dare had told her to come to him, it wasn't fair to impose on him that way.

But…she didn't want to sleep alone with her nightmares, and she had no one else.

Pacing the room, she took note of all the shadows cast from the glow of the computer monitor and the full moon outside. She took note of the silence, the chill, how the walls closed in.

She fought it, but anxiety tightened around her, smothering, insidious, consuming.

She drew a deep breath, then another—and knew she had to move now, before she lost control.

Swiping the quilt off the bottom of the bed, she went down the stairs, through the house and out the back door. Immediately, a million stars shone down on her, twinkling bright around a fat opalescent moon.

This time she filled her lungs with the brisk night air—and the freedom of it calmed her.

Dare would return tonight, and if he didn't, she'd stay outside. Out here, she didn't feel trapped or small or helpless. Having the wide-open skies over her was nothing like that cramped, airless room where they'd kept her chained up like an unwanted mutt, breathing the scents of fear and desperation and filth.

Where they had taken pleasure in tormenting her.

Hurting her.

But not too much, not enough to really injure her. They'd been waiting for something, she knew it.

But what?

When she stepped off the porch and onto the path, ambient security lights flickered on to show the way to the dock. She could hear the lake washing up to the rocky shoreline. She heard the teasing rustle of leaves, the songs of crickets and other night creatures.

She didn't know what else might be out there with her, but she wasn't afraid. Not anymore, not of this. Not of everyday, normal life. To the contrary, she'd never again take it for granted.

Off to the left of the path was the quaint white cottage where Chris lived. The large, front windows were shielded by drawn curtains, but light shone through, letting her know that Chris hadn't yet gone to bed. Of course, he probably wouldn't until Dare returned, because he felt responsible for her.

Dare did, too.

She wanted to be responsible for herself again.

Leaves blew over the path, crunched under her feet. The chill breeze cut through her, but she embraced it. She was alive, and after thinking she might die in that sweltering-hot, squalid little hellhole, being cold reminded her that she hadn't let them win.

She'd held on—and then Dare had saved her.

The dock squeaked and rocked as she walked out onto it. The light didn't reach this far, and she felt safely concealed in shadows provided by the high walls of the boathouse to her right. She moved close to it, letting it block some of the wind.

The moon painted a glow over the rippling surface of the lake, so beautiful that it engrossed her and further eased her angst. Molly sank down on the hard wooden planks with her knees drawn up close to her chest and wrapped the quilt tight around her.

How long she sat there, she wasn't sure. Her thoughts drifted over the present and the future. She thought of Dare, of what he'd done for her, but more importantly, of who he was. Not many men could ever be like him. No other man would affect her this way.

Without even meaning to, she drew comparisons to Adrian, and felt like a fool. Now that she knew Dare, Adrian seemed less than insubstantial in every way. He didn't have the strength of character or conviction that was such a part of Dare. He didn't possess even a fraction of Dare's honor and courage.

And in no way did he possess the same sex appeal. Around Dare, she could not ignore her own sexuality—as she'd often done with Adrian.

She couldn't discount the incredible circumstances, because they had happened; they served as an impetus for everything that followed. But what she felt didn't depend on what she'd suffered, or how Dare had saved her.

If she'd met him back in Ohio, maybe while on a book tour, she still would have recognized him as an amazing man. She had to believe that.

When she heard the sound of a car approaching high up on the road, she turned to see the headlights veer into the drive.

She knew it was Dare, and relief left her boneless. She considered going up to greet him but…she wasn't ready yet.

Sitting there on the dock beneath the wide-open skies, snuggled into the quilt, feeling safe and serene kept her captivated. It enabled her to think objectively.

More comparisons presented themselves as she thought of her abductors and how Dare helped her to put the ugliness into perspective.

The men had hurt her, but Dare eased the pain.

They had taunted her; Dare reassured her.

They belittled her, and Dare showed her respect.

He served as the antithesis to all the harsh, ugly memories. Through him, she could counter the remaining abhorrence and lingering fears.

He soothed her fear, and her soul—even while inflaming her senses. She wanted him, not just his comfort, but so much more. Sleeping beside him made her feel safe, but it wasn't enough, not when his nearness heated her blood and sharpened her desire almost painfully.

Tonight, she'd make her feelings known to him.

If he came to her.

Not for a second did she doubt that Dare would know right where to find her, if he wanted to. But he could be tired; he could want to shower and sleep.… *No.*

Their time together had been brief, but she already knew him, and she knew he would seek her out first thing. And so she waited for him.

Like glittering diamonds, starlight reflected off every ripple in the surface of the lake. The lulling sound of gentle waves rolling up to the shoreline had eased her tension earlier, but now they amped up her awareness, heightening her senses. Molly concentrated on the feel of the cold air blowing off the lake and into her heated face.

And she listened for Dare.

Her heart began to pound, and her skin tingled. Somewhere out toward the middle of the lake, a fish jumped. To her left, in a small cove between this dock and the one situated in front of Chris's cabin, a frog croaked.

When she felt Dare's approach, Molly closed her eyes. The dock shimmered with his every footstep.

"Molly."

At the sound of his deep, soft voice, her starving lungs reminded her to draw breath. In an agony of anticipation, she tipped her head around and, sounding more breathless than she intended, said, "Hi."

He came to crouch down beside her. "I didn't want to startle you."

"I heard you pull up."

He reached out to touch her hair. "Chris went on to bed."

She twisted, saw that the lights had gone out in the cabin, and nodded. "I think he was waiting for you." She hugged her arms around her knees. "I hate that he feels responsible for me."

Dare hesitated, saying nothing, and then he eased down to sit beside her. He, too, stared out at the lake. After a time, he spoke softly, saying, "You're in a precarious situation. Any man would worry for you. But the fact is, Chris is paid to do as I tell him, and I told him to keep an eye on you."

It amused her how both Chris and Dare constantly tried to make light of their protective instincts. "Maybe, but it was more than that." She rested her chin on a knee.

"He's one of the good guys, and I know that." She peeked over at Dare. "I know the difference."

Brushing the backs of his fingers along her cheek, Dare said, "You're chilled."

Molly shook her head. "It's beautiful here."

His hand eased under her hair to cup around the nape of her neck. "I think so, too." He tugged her a little closer to him, sharing his body heat. "We both worry for you, Molly. No woman should have to go through what you did, and it's understandable to have some difficulty with it. All Chris wants, all *we* want, is to make sure you're okay."

Closing her eyes, Molly bit her lip and tried to decide how to speak her mind. His thumb brushed over her skin, inciting her and doing so much to obliterate clear thought.

"I like your hands, Dare."

He went still, cautious. "My hands?"

"Before...before what happened, I never paid that much attention to the differences in a man's hands." She reached out and found his other hand, cradling it in both of hers. "They're so much bigger, so much stronger than mine."

"True."

Her throat felt tight. "And they can do a lot of damage without a lot of effort." Palm to palm, she compared their hands—but there was no real comparison. He was large and strong and capable, more than able to defend himself from harm. But she had been utterly helpless.

Dare laced his fingers with hers. "They can also protect."

"I know." She looked up at him. That silvery, magic moonlight limned his features, emphasizing the sharp lines of his face and making his dark blue eyes fathomless, sexy and so appealing. "That's the difference I see now, with you. Not the possibility of inflicted pain, but the compassion. The care. I look at your hands, and I think of how you touch me, and how it makes me feel."

"Molly." As if pained by her words, he touched his forehead to hers.

"You've given me a whole new perspective, right when I needed it most. If you hadn't shown up that day—"

"Shh." His hold grew tighter. "I did, and that's all that matters."

Needing him to understand, Molly shook her head. "Every day got a little worse, and I got a little weaker. I don't know how much more I would have suffered. I don't know if I'd even be alive right now if it wasn't for you."

His hand shook as he smoothed her hair behind her ear. "I'm damned glad I was there."

He couldn't promise that nothing bad would ever happen to her again, because they both knew he wouldn't always be around. And it wasn't his responsibility to protect her, anyway. It was hers—and it was time she took control of her life, starting with recovery from her fear.

"Those men…they hurt me on purpose."

"I know." He kissed her forehead.

"Sometimes, especially when I'm alone, I can't help thinking, remembering, what it was like."

"Molly…"

She drew a slow breath. "It hurt, but the fear was worse than the pain. One of them would do something, and the others would like it, and they'd join in, and I wouldn't know…" She swallowed. "I had no idea how far it'd go."

"I wish I could kill them again for you."

She fisted her hand in his flannel shirt. "Knowing that

the other women were watching, and that they knew how afraid and helpless I was, made it worse."

"You hated being defenseless. Most people do."

"I thought I would fear all men after that. But I opened my eyes and saw you that first time—"

"And kicked me in the nose."

She couldn't really laugh right now, though she smiled with him. "Right after that, as soon as you spoke to me, I felt so damn safe and so grateful.…" The tears burned her eyes, but she blinked them away. This wasn't a time for crying. It was a time for healing.

Dare tipped up her chin. "You've been incredibly brave and smart, and I admire you a lot, Molly. I hope you know that."

He admired her. Great. It was nice—but she wanted more. She *needed* more. "Would you do something for me, Dare?" Before he could speak, Molly carried his hand to her breast.

His body went very still. Seconds ticked by.

Sounding hoarse, Dare whispered, "Tell me what you want."

The feel of his broad, strong hand against her left her quaking inside—in a good way. The tremble sounded in her tone as she tried to explain. "I want to be whole again. I want to be *me,* the person I was before I was taken to Tijuana."

Dare said nothing. Molly felt his hesitation, his indecision. God love the man, he didn't want to take advantage of her.

"I know what I want, Dare." She covered his hand with her own, pressed him closer. "I want to replace the bad memories with new ones. Better ones."

His hand curved around her, but he said nothing.

Watching his face, Molly whispered, "I want to do that now, with you."

CHAPTER ELEVEN

LITTLE BY LITTLE, Dare relaxed until his hand curved around her breast, cuddling her. Molly could hear the acceleration of his breathing, the increased heat from his body.

With his voice going low and harsh, but his touch gentle, Dare asked, "They put their hands on you?"

Recalling the total humiliation, the nausea and fear, she nodded and said brokenly, "Yes."

"Here?" When Dare's thumb found her nipple, they both drew in sharp breaths.

"Yes." Oh, God, she couldn't think when he touched her. "They did…but not like that."

The maddening stroke of his thumb continued. "More to hurt you?"

Words were beyond her, so Molly nodded again.

With small kisses to her temple, her cheek, the bridge of her nose, Dare nudged her face up until he could feather light, teasing pecks to her open mouth. When she made a sound of excitement, he nibbled on her bottom lip, licked her upper lip—and finally sealed his mouth over hers in a consuming, tongue-twining kiss.

All the while, his hand played with her breast. Molly wore a T-shirt and the sweatshirt, and still the touch of his hand on her was unbearably intoxicating.

Clasping a hand around the back of Dare's neck, she tried to kiss him harder, deeper.

He lifted away, but not far. "If I'm going to do this—"

"You are." She needed him so badly that she'd insist if she had to.

Dare smiled. "Then I want to do it right."

She had no idea what he meant by that.

His eyes glittered at her in the darkness before she saw his resolve. "Tell me if you feel any panic at all."

"I won't. Not with you."

He freed her from the quilt and spread it out behind her.

Cold air washed over her, but she wasn't chilled. Far from it.

Easing her down to her back, Dare stretched out beside her. Even with the quilt as a cushion, the wooden boards of the dock should have been uncomfortable to her back. But at the moment, all Molly felt was Dare, breathing so close to her, touching her so carefully. She stared up at a velvet blanket of stars and the fat, glowing moon, and she knew the truth.

She was fast falling in love with a man who wanted her almost as much as he pitied her.

For now, it just didn't matter. She needed this, she needed *him*, too much to care about anything else.

DARE LOOKED DOWN AT Molly, so trusting and so vulnerable in ways she didn't even know. He'd made a vow to himself, but how could he have known that she'd offer herself like this?

All during his drive home, he'd thought of Molly's life thus far. Her mother had died too young, and her father was a world-class bastard. Growing up under Bishop Alexander's rule would have been a trial of endurance; that man could make anyone's life hell.

Now, thanks to the photos Trace had shared, Dare knew that Bishop had the affiliations necessary to continue making Molly's life miserable. He held close associations with a number of shady characters, but two in particular were of interest to Dare.

The grainy shots had been of Bishop and his wife at a formal party, chatting up well-dressed couples. But Trace had recognized a few faces: Ed Warwick and Mark Sagan. Trace had gone one further and done a preliminary dig on the relationship background between the men.

During a political fundraiser years back, Bishop had aligned himself with Ed Warwick, a retired military man who'd taken a post as an immigration official. On the surface, the two had only associated in their combined effort to financially back a senator. Later, when Warwick was accused of accepting bribes to clear the way to citizenship for ineligible aliens, Bishop broke ties, and Warwick hired Mark Sagan, a highly paid, very elite lawyer to represent him.

Amazingly enough, Sagan was known as a white separatist. Many despicable deeds had been attributed to him, but without proof. Sagan was the kind of man that Dare detested: polished and suave on the outside, bloodthirsty on the inside. Throughout his law career, Sagan had acquainted himself with numerous criminals who always managed to skirt the law.

Shortly after Warwick hired Sagan to represent him, one witness died in a hit-and-run, and two others changed their stories. Warwick wasn't cleared, but lack of evidence made it impossible to prosecute. Bishop and Warwick had celebrated a subdued reunion, and since then, they'd been involved in many joint efforts with Sagan.

It was clear to Dare that Molly's father had contacts

he could have easily used to set up her kidnapping, and with Sagan, he had access to the muscle to see it done.

The facts didn't lie: Bishop had the associations and the means.

But what would be the motive?

As Dare smoothed back Molly's hair, he couldn't think of a single reason why her father would want to cause her so much physical harm. And without a reason that would lead him to some hard evidence, he couldn't officially accuse the man.

That meant that the worst—*not knowing*—was still ahead of her.

How could he ever turn her loose without knowing she'd be safe? And how could he, in good conscience, accept her intimate offer when she needed him so badly for protection?

Dare made up his mind, and it already tortured him. He'd give Molly what she needed, but he wasn't going to have sex with her.

Not yet.

Finding her on the dock, half-frozen and with so much need, worked miracles toward shoring up his sometimes-misplaced honor. She needed to know that her life could still be the same, and that the nightmare would eventually fade into a dark but manageable memory.

"Are you cold?" She kept trying to crawl into him, clutching at him to keep him near, pressing herself close.

"No." Her nails dug into his upper arm. "Dare, I want—"

"Shh. It's all right." He unzipped the oversize hoodie and slipped his hand inside. "Just relax for me."

The second he touched her breast through the thin T-shirt, she tensed—and a soft moan escaped her parted lips.

The sound was sweet and desperate, proof that she'd been thinking about this, about him, for a while now.

"You're in a bad way, aren't you?"

She nodded, licked her lips. "I need you, yes."

Because they had touched her, hurt her, abused her.

He had to remember that this was to eradicate ugly memories. He had to remember all that she'd suffered.

Seeing the bruise on her cheek, Dare bent to brush his mouth over it. "They hit you…here?"

She said nothing, but her breath hitched.

"And here?" Skimming his mouth along her throat, he gently touched each mark, occasionally licking over a fading bruise or putting a soft love bite over angry fingerprints. It was so dark out that he worked by memory—not that he'd ever forget a single mark on her delicate skin.

"My…my ribs," she whispered by way of encouragement, making Dare smile.

Overcome with tenderness, rigid with lust, he pulled the T-shirt up. "Right here," he whispered, knowing that his jaw brushed her breast as he pressed openmouthed kisses to her ribs.

"Dare." She tunneled her fingers into his hair and arched up a little.

Her tight hold on his hair stung a little and showed her level of urgency. Knowing she was ready, Dare turned to see her breasts. Thanks to the cold and her excitement, her nipples were puckered tight.

God. Holding her shoulders, he bent to lick first one nipple, then the other, before closing his mouth around her.

Her drawn-out groan echoed over the lake. Her knees

came up and she started to turn toward him. Dare held her down and tried to slow her response a little.

This was for her—but he wouldn't deny himself the pleasure of her body in the process.

She grabbed his wrist and pushed his hand down to her belly.

Dare paused. His chest tightened with painful possibilities. Repeatedly Molly had told him that she wasn't raped. But had they—

"They didn't," she said as if reading his mind. "They threatened, and, yes, they sometimes touched me…in ways they shouldn't have. But…but that's not why…"

He laid his hand over the soft, womanly rise of her belly. "You're a woman, and you want me?"

"Yes."

He kissed her nipple again. "Already?" And then, a little more desperately, "Are you sure, Molly? We have all night. There's no rush.…"

"Don't make me wait, Dare." She shifted and squirmed. "Please."

Amazing. Still unsure, but unwilling to push her, Dare cupped his hand between her legs, touched her lightly along the seam of her jeans.

Her reaction was swift and strong.

He sat up in a rush and had to move aside her hands so he could unsnap and unzip the jeans. Once he had them opened, he paused. Hell, it was March in Kentucky. The breeze tonight was downright frigid.

He glanced up at his house. Not that far away, and a hell of a lot more comfortable for her…

"Dare?"

She clutched at him, confused and anxious, and he whispered, "Fuck it." He dragged her jeans and panties down to her knees, exposing her sex. Everything was in shadows, and the moonlight that had felt so bright moments before didn't give him the light he wanted now.

He wouldn't take her, but he wanted to see her, damn it, all of her.

But of course he remembered, so maybe it was better that he couldn't see; bruises, scratches—injuries that went deeper than the marks on her skin and flesh.

Aching for what she'd endured, Dare lowered his head and put a gentle, barely there kiss to her ribs, her abdomen, her flat belly. "I don't want to hurt you, Molly."

Eyes huge and dark, she stared up at him. "Then don't stop."

He smiled to reassure her, but his heart was breaking and his body burned. "I won't." He wouldn't stop, because she needed this too much, but he would go easy. He would use ultimate care with her.

Resting on his elbow beside her, close enough to share his body heat, Dare cupped each breast in turn, enjoying their heavy weight, the sensitivity of her taut nipples. Slowly, he stroked his hand down to her belly and finally cupped it between her legs again, this time over her naked sex. Exhibiting uncommon patience, he lightly teased the soft pubic hair. "Can you open your legs for me, Molly?"

He needed her to be a willing participant every step of the way. He needed to know that she was with him, not held captive in bad memories.

On a sharp inhalation, she turned her face away, and her knees parted.

"Nice." The cool air now felt good to him, he was so damn hot. "Look at me, Molly."

When she did, Dare leaned over to kiss her again, touching his mouth to hers, easing her into the kiss to help relax her. At the same time, he explored her with his fingertips, finding her flesh sleek and hot and already damp.

Dare thought of sinking into her, of making her his in every way, and his body tightened, hardened. Carefully, he opened her, stroked over her, slipped his fingers slightly inside her.

She felt so perfect that, without meaning to, Dare pressed his erection against her hip.

Holding on to his shoulders, kissing him with hunger, Molly moved against him and with him.

Damn, but she wouldn't let him go slow.

He left her mouth to kiss a trail down her throat to her collarbone and down to her breasts. She had beautiful, full, firm breasts. How the hell she kept them from being a focal point, he didn't know.

He wished he knew the color of her nipples, but as he took her into his mouth again, he knew the texture and taste.

Perfect.

The air was cold, but their combined body heat, scented by lust, wafted around them both. As he sucked on her left nipple, Dare pressed his middle finger into her.

She clenched hard, cried out and lifted her hips.

Moving to the other nipple, Dare licked her, closed his teeth gently around her and tugged until she groaned raggedly, and then he suckled. He felt her slick moisture on his finger, and worked a second into her, stretching her, filling her. As she cried out again, already on the ragged edge, he brought his thumb up to her distended clitoris. Teasing over it, manipulating, he found a rhythm that pushed her.

Within minutes she was lost, her head back, her eyes

closed as she cried out long and loud with a hard release.

Dare raised up to look at her, drawing in a shuddering breath, feeling so connected to her and caring so much about her.

Fuck, but it scared him.

Shaken, he watched her as the sensations faded and she went utterly limp, and very silent.

Did she expect him to move over her now, to take her on a damn dock in the cold of the night? Or was she dreading the possibility?

Trying to find the right words, Dare gathered her close and held her to his chest. She sighed against him, her pants still down, her shirt still up.

What the hell was he doing?

Stroking her hair back from her face, he kissed her forehead and hugged her again.

Somewhere behind them, a light came on. Molly flinched in reaction, and Dare, going on the alert, moved to shield her with his body.

He waited, poised to react.

From the front door of his cabin, sounding chagrined, Chris called out, "The dogs are barking." He cleared his throat loud enough for even the fish to hear. "I guess they heard something."

With no threat imminent, Dare relaxed, cursed and then muttered, "I'll kill him."

Chris laughed at that. "Voices do carry."

"Shut up, Chris."

"Just letting you know that the girls refused to stay inside."

Just then, Tai and Sargie came charging across the yard and onto the dock. Dare groaned, looked down at Molly and saw she was snickering.

And that made him grin, too.

He pulled her T-shirt down and closed the hoodie around her. "Britches up, woman. We need to go to the house."

He stood and then moved in front of her to ward off the enthusiastic dogs. They were thrilled to see Dare, and doubly thrilled to think it wasn't yet time for bed.

Aware of Molly moving behind him, of her silence, Dare petted the dogs and waited.

She touched his shoulder. "Dare?" She sounded horribly uncertain and more than a little embarrassed.

Dare faced her, bent to kiss the bridge of her nose and asked, "Ready to go?"

She held the quilt in her arms. "Yes, but…what about you?"

He put an arm around her. No reason to tell her that he'd intended to suffer in silence. Not now. "I'm fine. Tired, actually." He urged her along the dock toward the house. "Time to call it a night."

"But I wouldn't mind—"

He had to interrupt her. If she offered herself again, no way in hell would he be able to resist. "My girls aren't used to overnight guests." Circling them with every third step, the dogs showed their excitement. Dare laughed. "Definitely not used to women sharing my bed. And they have no respect for privacy."

Molly went silent, and it bothered Dare. What did she think? Was she feeling rejected?

Bending to her ear, he said, "The lake amplifies everything, even a whisper, remember? Whatever we say, Chris will hear."

"Oh, my God." She stopped dead in her tracks. "That's what he meant…"

"Don't worry about it." Dare's arm around her back

propelled her along the path. "But we might want to hold all conversation until we're inside, okay?"

She looked toward Chris's cabin. He'd turned the lights back out, but Dare was willing to bet that Chris was inside laughing his ass off.

Molly put her palms to her cheeks. "Was I…loud?"

She spoke so low that Dare barely heard the question. He hugged her into his side. "You were, *are,* beautiful, and Chris is just a dumbass. Don't give him another thought."

He opened the back door to the house, and they both stepped inside. Dark except for a low light over the sink, it was even more difficult to see in here. Dare drew her up against his body and put his chin to the top of her head. "Are you hungry?"

She shook her head.

"Still cold?"

"I'm fine."

Of course. She was always *fine.* "Then let's turn in, okay? Together."

She perked up, until Dare shook his head. "To sleep, Molly. I like having you next to me, but we're not going to have sex tonight." He used the side of his fist under her chin to lift her face. "Not because I don't want you. You know I do." He nudged his erection against her and saw her lips part.

So damned sweet and honest.

Dare opened his hand on her face and cradled her cheek. He couldn't resist kissing her one more time. She leaned into him, languid and warm and ready.

When he lifted his head, her eyes slowly opened, and as she refocused she looked down at Tai and Sargie sitting beside him. The dogs started thumping their tails.

"No," Dare said, reading her thoughts. "Not because

of the dogs, either." He loved his girls, but if they were the only thing keeping him from her, he'd put them on the other side of his bedroom door for an hour or so and not feel even a smidge of guilt about it.

Her exasperation sounded in a small huff. "Okay, then why?"

Might as well be honest with her—to a degree. "Because I think we need to go slow. I think *you* need to go slow."

She licked her lips, bit them and cleared her throat. "You told me to tell you when I was ready."

Yeah, he had, but he hadn't expected her to be ready so quickly.

"Soon," he promised her. He led her out of the kitchen and toward his room. "There are a few more things we need to clear up first."

He could feel her consternation—and maybe a little annoyance.

"Like what?"

Like whether or not her father was enough of a monster to arrange for her kidnapping, and the abuse she'd suffered. But he knew from experience that bedtime was no time to dwell on upsetting possibilities. Whether Molly felt "fine" right now or not, she still had a lot of adjustment ahead of her.

"Let's save that big discussion for tomorrow, all right?" Relieving her of the quilt, Dare eyed her clothes and asked, "Are you sleeping in all that?"

"No." She stripped down to the T-shirt and panties and crawled into his bed.

Just like she belonged there. And maybe…maybe she did.

The dogs jumped up onto the bed after her, circled,

found a spot and dropped. They, too, acted as though she'd always been a part of their lives.

As Dare went into the bathroom to wash up and brush his teeth, he thought of what he'd learned about her father. He saw again those incriminating photos and felt the animosity Bishop Alexander had revealed toward his oldest daughter.

After he'd finished up and returned to the bedroom, he found Molly resting on her side, her hands beneath her cheek, her eyes watchful as she took in his every step.

Tomorrow, on the way back to her apartment, Dare would tell her what he'd uncovered so far. He hoped like hell she was as strong as she seemed, because she'd need that strength to come to grips with reality.

"I'm cold," Molly said. "Are you ready to come to bed?"

"Yeah." Dare undressed down to his boxers and got in beside her. After he turned out the light, he automatically reached for her, and she automatically curled into his side.

If someone hadn't tried to harm her, and if that someone wasn't still a vital threat, life would be pretty damned sweet.

AFTER A REFRESHING sleep, Molly woke before dawn. Dare had one big arm around her waist, one leg trapping both of hers. His chest hair tickled her nose, and she loved it. He was always so warm, so secure.

But she'd awakened with a fabulous idea in her mind, and she needed to write. It amazed her that, with very little time for recovery, her muse was back in full force. But then, it had always been that way for her. Writing was her escape, her entertainment, her catharsis for whatever bothered her. Through storytelling, she could set aside worries and instead immerse herself in someone else's problems—problems that she could and did fix.

Trying not to awaken Dare, Molly scooted out from under his hold. Right before she left the bed, his hand snagged her wrist.

"What's wrong?"

Oh, crud. She hadn't meant to disturb him. "Nothing," she whispered. "Go back to sleep."

Instead he sat up and looked at the clock, then ran a hand through his hair. "It's only five-thirty."

"I know." Now feeling foolish and very conspicuous, Molly tried to explain. "I wrote a few pages yesterday. I sort of stopped at a good spot, and I wanted to get back to it."

"Where?"

"Where...am I in my book?" No way was she going to start trying to synopsize for him.

"No." He scratched his chest. "Where did you write?"

Why did that matter? Molly shrugged. "In the room you let me use. Upstairs." Since she'd yet to sleep there, she couldn't very well call it *her* room.

In the dim, gray light, Molly watched him stretching. The bed shifted as he rolled to his feet. Then he walked off, and a second later the bathroom light came on. He pulled the door shut, but he wasn't gone long.

Molly heard the toilet flush, then heard water splash in the sink. When he returned, he left the door open so that the light spilled into the bedroom.

God help her, but Dare looked delicious in the morning with his whiskers and his rumpled hair.

And his body mostly bare.

So much strength showed in his physique, without him

being muscle-bound. Tall, strong, gorgeous… How was she supposed to resist that?

He went to a drawer and pulled out sweats.

Molly stopped staring and jumped out of the bed. That made the dogs attentive, too. "Dare, what are you doing?"

"I'm usually up by six anyway." He sat to pull on white socks and running shoes. "It's a good time to jog with the dogs."

When they heard that, both dogs stood, ears perked, in preparation to following him.

Glancing out the window, Molly saw the darkness. The whistling of wind sounded cold. And he'd still be sleeping if she hadn't awakened him. "You're going jogging *now?*"

"Yeah." He stood and pulled on a hooded sweatshirt. "I'll wait for my coffee until I get back, but help yourself if you want it now. Otherwise, Chris will be over soon, and he'll get it ready."

The dogs looked from Molly to Dare—and excitedly went to Dare.

She trotted after all three of them as they started out of the room. "How long will you be gone?"

"An hour or so. Maybe longer." He turned, and she almost ran into him. Dare caught her shoulders. "After that, I'll be downstairs working out for a little while."

Who crawled out of bed before dawn, ran and then worked out—without coffee? "You're kidding."

He bent and kissed her hard and fast. Sargie barked, reminding them both that she had need of a grassy spot outside.

"Take your time writing today. I don't have any plans until the afternoon." And with that, he turned and started down the hall.

Molly stared after him. Plans? What plans did he have? And what did that have to do with her?

Unless…he planned to take her home.

The idea was both tantalizing and frightening. She probably had a dozen important calls to return; she could only imagine what her editor and her agent thought about her disappearing in the middle of negotiations. But going home meant she was that much closer to ending her association with Dare.

Was he anxious to get rid of her? And if so, did it have anything to do with her botched seduction effort last night?

She dredged up every word she'd said, and even though she tried to reassure herself, one fact come slamming back into her brain: Dare had been generous, but not interested enough to take what she had so freely offered.

CHAPTER TWELVE

LONG AFTER THE FRONT door had closed behind Dare, Molly stood there in the dim hall trying to understand him. Finally she decided that caffeine would help, so after snagging jeans and the all-purpose hoodie, she went into the kitchen and got the coffee started.

As it brewed, she went back to the room to clean her teeth and wash her face. Her hair was a mess, and she tried smoothing it with Dare's comb, but she had no way of styling it. Blah. She looked terrible, and there was no way around it.

She found a rubber band in the library desk drawer where she'd seen the office supplies, and she pulled her hair back into a high ponytail. That at least kept it out of her face and gave the semblance of order.

It wasn't until after her third cup of coffee that it really hit her: *she looked like hell.*

Yes, of course she'd *known* it; she wasn't obtuse about her own appearance. But in light of more important issues, she hadn't really thought about it. She had so much on her mind, and so many adjustments, including the bombardment of feelings toward Dare....

Oh, God, she'd come on to him all hot and heavy while looking her absolute worst. If he had been a more average guy, it might not have been so bad. But Dare was gorgeous, the most physically fit man she'd ever seen, and she looked like...well, a haggard victim.

Groaning, Molly sat back in the desk chair where she'd been trying to work. The scene that she'd been polishing blurred in front of her. Not only was her hair frazzled and unkempt, but she had zip for makeup, and the physical mistreatment she'd suffered still showed in the hollowness of her eyes and the marks on her skin.

She looked as wretched as a woman could look, so why had she thought that Dare would want her? Her come-on had probably been embarrassing and uncomfortable for him. Sure, he'd had an erection, but after all, he was a guy, so that didn't really mean anything. Physical arousal did not equal personal interest—which Dare had proven last night.

He'd been kind, telling her that he wanted her and that he only wanted to wait until she was truly ready.

How much more ready could she have been? She'd all but begged him to have sex with her.

And instead he'd given her an orgasm, then taken her to bed and slept with her held tight against him all night.

What guy did that?

Every male she'd ever known had made sex the number-one priority. It hadn't taken seduction or even encouragement—a look was more than enough to get things rolling along. She couldn't imagine any other man she'd dated ever turning down an offer for sex, not if he was attracted to the woman—and sometimes even if he wasn't.

Even though she accepted that Adrian had never really loved her, he'd wanted her. Or maybe not her specifically, but he had wanted sex. For certain, he'd never turned her down; in fact, when she'd been uninterested from illness or stress, or when she'd just been too busy, he'd still tried to insist.

She'd accepted that as a natural way for men.

Did Dare hold back because he wanted to be rid of her, even though they didn't yet know the one responsible for her abduction? Maybe, to his mind, sex would complicate things and in some way obligate him.

Too many unanswered questions made Molly's head ache.

When she heard Chris in the kitchen, she saved her file and went downstairs, hoping for some insight into Dare's personality.

Chris stood at the sink, staring out the kitchen window. Dressed in worn jeans and a faded sweatshirt with running shoes, he looked comfortable and handsome. She imagined he got plenty of attention wherever he went.

As she came through the doorway, Chris glanced over his shoulder at her, and his expression warmed. "Hey."

"Good morning."

"Thanks for making the coffee." He looked her over, but then turned to stare out the window again.

What was that about? Molly looked down at herself but saw nothing amiss. "I almost drank it all, too, so maybe you shouldn't thank me."

Holding up a mug, he showed her that he'd already gotten his, and he had another pot brewing for Dare. "Dare likes it stronger." Leaning against the counter, he nodded toward the window and said, "Did you see this?"

"What?"

"The sun rising over the lake." He beckoned her forward. "Come here. I think you'll like this." And then, more to himself than her, "Somehow coffee tastes better with such an amazing background."

Intrigued, Molly walked over to the window, too. She

bumped shoulders with Chris as she peered out, and her creative soul soaked in the sight.

"Wow. It's beautiful." From this distance, higher up the sloping landscape, she could see through the trees to the dock and boathouse, and beyond. Wisps of fog, mysterious and magical, floated up from the glassy surface of the calm lake. In select, glistening places, the sunshine cut through and reflected back on itself. "It's almost breathtaking."

Chris looked down at her. "Inspiring, huh?"

"I'll say."

"Looks like it's going to be a gorgeous day." He headed to the bar with a bowl of cold cereal. "Soon as I'm done with my breakfast, I'll be driving into town to pick up your new clothes."

Reluctantly, Molly turned away from the scenery. "They're in?"

"Got an email confirming delivery." His gaze never wavered from her, and when he realized he was staring, he asked abruptly, "Cereal?"

"Oh, sure." Not understanding him, Molly went for a bowl and spoon.

"Dare will cook something hardier when he's done downstairs, but don't hold your breath. He's beating the heavy bag pretty hard today." Expression enigmatic, Chris said, "Can't imagine what has him so worked up."

"Cereal is fine." Molly frowned as she joined him at the bar. Trying to sound cavalier, she said, "You say Dare's worked up?"

Chris blinked at her. "You couldn't tell?"

"I barely saw him this morning. Within minutes of being awake, he was dressed and off jogging."

"Mmm." Chris coughed. "Well, all I can say is that

Dare often takes out his frustrations in the basement. It's always best to leave him to it."

Was Dare annoyed with her and exerting energy because of it? Trying to sidle in on that possibility, Molly said, "I think we might be going back to my place today."

"Yeah, he told me." Chris shoveled in a heaping spoonful of cereal.

Molly went blank. "He told you?"

Chris nodded.

Affronted, Molly sat back in her chair. So, Dare had shared his intentions with Chris, but not with her? "When?"

"Last night, before he joined you down on the dock." Catching on to her mood, he explained, "He told me so that I could pack for him and get the travel plans all set up."

She felt cantankerous enough to say, "You shoot up I-75—not much to plan, is there?"

"Unless you're Dare. Remember what I told you? He likes to arrange for every possibility. I've made note of gas stations, restaurants and…motels."

"Motels?" Molly paused with a spoonful of cereal almost to her mouth. That made no sense to her.

Teasing, Chris said, "It's a four-hour drive, five if you stop to eat. You really never know when you might need a…room."

Oh, for heaven's sake. "Why would we…" And suddenly she caught on: Chris was referring to what he'd heard last night. *From her.*

Aghast, Molly threw a piece of wet cereal at him, hitting him dead center in the chest. The cereal bounced off onto the table but left a spot of milk on his sweatshirt.

Not even trying to hide his laughter, Chris snatched

up the cereal and popped it into his mouth. "I'm all done here." He rose from his seat. "If you see Dare, tell him I'll be back within an hour."

With heat still throbbing in her face, Molly tried to play off her embarrassment. "Where are the dogs?"

"Downstairs with Dare." Chris walked toward her, paused to give her shoulder a squeeze and then whistled as he snatched up keys and left the kitchen.

Dare had warned her about Chris, but he hadn't mentioned how much the man liked to tease, and his lack of propriety.

At a loss as to how to proceed, Molly took her time finishing her cereal. She didn't even know herself anymore. Not only had Chris reminded her of last night, but she'd just behaved like a child by throwing her food at him.

Propping her head on her fist, she wished she at least had the dogs for company. She'd gotten used to their constant shadowing. But it made sense that now that Dare was around they wanted to be with him. She could see how much he loved Tai and Sargie, and how much they loved him.

It would help her to sort things out if she knew more about Dare. Things like how much time he actually spent away with his work. And more details about his work would be nice, too. He obviously did very well for himself, given his property and his ease in spending money. Did his career choice often involve killing monstrous bad guys? Or had her situation been somehow unique?

Given the oddity of his work, when did he last have a steady girlfriend? Was a steady girlfriend even possible?

Molly wanted to know about his family, other friends he might have, preferences and dislikes and...*everything*.

She didn't have Chris or the dogs to keep her company, but when the noise in the basement continued, she decided she'd do well to stay busy.

After clearing away the breakfast mess, she dragged herself back upstairs to write. This time her attempts at that distraction didn't last beyond a half hour. Her muse wouldn't cooperate anymore.

She tried going out the French doors for some fresh air, but instead she ended up staring at the dock and… remembering. Her skin tingled and warmed, and her body felt tight.

Sometimes a steamy shower helped kick-start her muse. She spent almost half an hour under the hot spray, and even washed her hair again, adding extra conditioner. Afterward, her hair was fluffier and her skin glowed, but overall the effort was wasted.

As Molly stared in the mirror, she couldn't help but pay attention to the bruising that colored her skin. The once-purple marks were already fading to a sickly yellow and pale green.

Her stomach twisted in that now-familiar way, wrenched by remembered fear and choking uncertainty. Those men had hurt her so much, not just physically, but her pride and her spirit. Never in her life had she been so scared, and so despondent. Never had she thought anything so awful could happen to her.

Now she knew, and her life would never be the same.

If it hadn't been for Dare, she might be there still. Or she could have even been killed, and no one would have ever known what happened to her.

But he had saved her. In a no-nonsense way, he'd reassured her, cared for her, protected her.

And last night he had touched her, giving her new memories to focus on.

The ugliness of captivity faded as she thought about Dare and how he'd made her feel. She almost felt it again, just remembering.

Her pale, marred skin now had a becoming flush. Thanks to Dare and what he'd done, she looked better, but she couldn't lie to herself.

She was still an average thirty-year-old woman, and nothing would change that.

To hell with it, Molly decided. She'd never been vain, and she wasn't going to start now. She liked herself, and she was satisfied with her looks. No, she wasn't glamorous or flashy. She would never turn heads. But neither would anyone call her a troll, even with a few discolored bruises.

With new resolve, she went back downstairs and stood right outside the basement door. Dare worked for her, she reminded herself. In the end, she would be paying him an indeterminate yet surely hefty fee. That meant she was due a few answers, whether she had a romantic involvement with him or not.

As soon as she opened the door, she could hear a steady punching sound accompanied by loud, hard music. At least she had one curiosity satisfied; Dare liked hard rock, just as she did. Surely music wouldn't be the only thing they had in common.

Her heart pounded in time to the beat. Putting her shoulders back, Molly descended the steps.

EVEN BEFORE SHE showed herself, Dare sensed Molly's approach. So did the dogs. They jumped up, and the tail-wagging began.

Few people had ever encroached into his private

workout territory, but oddly, he didn't mind that she was here. In fact, he'd been thinking about her, wondering how her writing was going, and if she'd eaten.

Worrying for anyone, especially a woman for whom he'd accepted responsibility, was new to Dare. He'd always been able to separate the liability of the job with emotional attachment.

But with Molly, every damn thing seemed different, and very personal.

When he felt her burning gaze on his back, he paused and looked toward her. As a man who always noted the smallest details, he realized right off that she'd taken extra care with her appearance. To impress him?

His eyes narrowed at that thought. If the woman understood how much restraint it took to resist her, she wouldn't be so comfortable with him.

As their gazes locked, Molly tried for a smile that didn't quite reach her eyes. Holding back, she stayed a good distance from him, as if unsure of her welcome.

That bugged him.

Picking up a towel and wiping sweat from his face, Dare turned toward her. "You look nice, Molly."

Color tinged her cheeks. "Thank you." And then, in a rush, "There's really not much I can do. I mean, not without makeup and styling products for my hair—"

"You look damned good without it." He liked it that she didn't spend hours in the bathroom primping. Or maybe she did under normal circumstances. He couldn't know.

He had to remember that in many ways, Molly was still a stranger to him.

What he did know about her counted for a lot, though.

She'd dealt rationally with her ordeal, forfeiting the expected hysterics as much from bone-deep pride as a commonsense need to survive. In a crisis, Molly would be a help, not a hindrance. Under pressure, she kept her wits about her.

Most of all, he knew that she was a fighter. And damn, but he admired that. Too much.

"So." Aware of how she stared at his naked, sweaty chest—and lower—Dare studied her stiff posture. He sounded gruff when he asked, "Did you need something?"

"No." She looked around the gym area. "Not really."

Other than filling the basement with fitness gear, he'd never bothered to do anything with it. He had plenty of living space upstairs, and he sure as hell didn't need fancy surroundings to stay in shape and break a sweat.

In organized fashion, mats covered the concrete floor, and equipment hung from hooks in the walls. A refrigerator stocked with cold water sat along the back wall, and adjacent to that was a treadmill, an elliptical machine, a bench and weights, and other assorted exercise apparatus. He had a generous, tiled corner shower and a cabinet filled with towels.

Picking up the stereo remote, Dare turned down the music. Molly had come to him for some reason, but she was being shy about speaking her mind. "Everything's okay?"

She nodded as she continued to look around.

Not that there was all that much to see. Other than when it was cleaned and sanitized, no one ventured down here but him.

Leaving the towel to drape around his neck, Dare went for a water bottle. Since Molly stayed silent, he supposed it was up to him to figure out the reason behind her visit. "Get much writing done?"

Her gaze came back to him.

Then went over him. Slowly.

She drew in a shaky breath.

Ah. She still wanted him. Good thing, too, since he didn't know how much longer he'd be able to wait.

Maybe he should have taken her last night. That thought had driven him to a hard jog, and then a pounding workout. Not that the exertion had worked to relieve his need. Not enough.

He burned with wanting her. It was insane, unaccountable, but Ms. Molly Alexander pushed all his buttons. Even now, covered in sweat, he could take her. He saw it in her eyes and in the way she held herself. It was a unique type of hell, having to resist her.

But never in his life had he abused anyone's trust, and he wasn't going to start now. They would both live with the need until the time was right. Waiting just meant that when he did finally have her, there'd be no holding back.

She had to be ready, because he intended to keep her naked and in the bed for hours.

Affected by her intimate look, Dare dropped his head to stare at his feet in consternation. Molly couldn't hide her feelings worth a damn, which meant her physical attraction to him was more than obvious—and it pushed him.

He'd just spent a long time trying to work off the sexual tension, but knowing how much she wanted him brought it all right back.

Watching her, Dare swigged the water, set the bottle aside and took a few steps closer. "I'm sweaty."

She looked from his bare feet to his hips to his chest, bit her lips and said, "You look powerful, like an ancient warrior."

That sentiment surprised a short laugh out of him. "If

you say so." Trying to put her at ease, he added, "I like to wear as little as possible when I'm working out. Gives me more freedom of movement."

"I see." She glanced down at his gym shorts, and then away. "How often do you do this?"

"This?"

"Work out for so long."

Hadn't been long enough to alleviate his knotted muscles, but he saw no point in telling her that. Instead, he rolled a shoulder. "Whenever I can." He thought to add, "It's important for me to stay in shape."

Her gaze latched on to his again. "Because of what you do?"

"Yeah." And because of what he might have to do. In his line of work, chasing down a target was as likely as a direct physical confrontation. And in more than one instance, he'd had to combat multiple adversaries.

He always won.

Molly crossed her arms under her breasts. "I, um, I saw you hitting that punching bag."

"A heavy bag." Dare flexed his hands inside the fingerless gloves. His muscles burned, and so did his libido. "I use it to practice strikes and kicks." He knew how to debilitate, or even kill, with a single blow.

"You're really good, aren't you?"

He was, but she hadn't come down here to compliment him, and they both knew it. "I have to be good at my job, Molly. And that includes being able to defend myself, and others."

"Like you defended me?"

He'd killed for her. Remembering that, thinking of how she'd looked when he found her, added a strain to his tone. "I do what I have to do."

"Have you killed many people?"

Narrowing his eyes, Dare stared at her, trying to figure out where she was going with this. But for once, she hid her thoughts from him.

Would she be disgusted with the truth? Could she handle the reality of what he did? "Let's just say that I've killed on more than one occasion and let it go at that." Waiting for her reaction, he walked over to the bench and sat down to unlace his gloves.

"It's easy for you?"

"Not easy, no. Just accepted." Hoping she'd understand, Dare said, "It's important for me to have that capability, and to know that I won't hesitate to go there—when it's necessary."

"Why?"

She didn't look frightened or disgusted, just very interested. Dare rested his forearms over his knees and studied her. "Knowing that I can go the distance, that I can do whatever has to be done to finish a job, makes me a better fighter because I can engage in a calm, calculated way, without fear." And usually without anger. But then he thought of the incident in the Walmart parking lot, and how blindly furious he'd been when those men had tried to take her.

Without meaning to, without even trying, Molly fucked with his performance, demolishing years of skill and training.

She was dangerous, and he wanted her too much to care.

"It must be nice," she said, surprising him with her acceptance of the darker side of his life. "To not be afraid, I mean."

There it was, the reason for his restraint with her. For the rest of her life, Molly would remember what she'd suffered, and she would fear things that she hadn't, until recently, known were possible. "You're a nice woman, Molly. I wouldn't want you to change."

"I think you're nice, too."

If vipers could be considered nice.

It was important to him that she understood one crucial aspect of his ability. "I can kill with my bare hands. Knowing that makes me more effective in a fight because having that ability usually lets me end things without deadly force."

"You don't kill unless you have to."

Or when he knew the world would be safer without someone left alive. But that was a point he could make later—if they had a later.

Dare held her gaze. "Does that satisfy your curiosity?"

It sure as hell didn't satisfy his.

"About your work, yes." She kept her distance. "But I'd like to know more about you. How you got your start, the things you enjoy, the day-to-day stuff."

Too much curiosity would be dangerous. "You want the bare bones of my life?"

Measuring her words with care, she said, "I want whatever you'll share with me."

His mouth twitched. It was a little late for her to worry about seeming nosy, but he still appreciated her good manners. "When I was seventeen, I joined the service."

"But that'd mean you were a minor. Is that allowed?"

Dare shrugged. "With parental consent, yeah."

She looked appalled that anyone had agreed to his enlistment.

"It was a good decision, Molly, one of the best things I ever did. Everyone realized right off that I had a knack for defense and for following through." He pulled off the gloves. "If that meant killing someone intent on harming me or others, then that's what I did."

She said nothing to that. Dare set the gloves aside and braced his hands on the bench. "But, Molly, understand that I detest bullies and needless violence. I would never harm an innocent or watch someone else cause harm. Whenever possible, I avoid all physical conflicts. I have no problem at all walking away from a fight—when walking away is an option."

"You killed those men in Mexico."

"Yeah." She hadn't said it as an accusation, but as confirmation. "But, Molly?"

She looked at him with big, dark eyes.

"That was before I saw what they'd done to you. You aren't responsible for any of that."

She bit her lips and nodded. "I'm sure you did what needed to be done."

Dare felt strangled by her trust. His fingers curved around the bench, gripping it hard. "They had taken Alani."

"I know." She sounded far too gentle, and far too understanding. "You told me that she's like a sister to you."

Shit. He didn't want to explain emotional entanglements. But he still heard himself say, "She and Trace are more like family than my real family is."

She thought for a second, then asked, "Do you see your parents often?"

Dare shook his head and relaxed a little. He could talk about this, about his parents, without the sentiment. "Dad died in a small-plane crash years ago. Mom is remarried and living in Michigan. I visit with her a couple of times a year."

"You're not close?"

"Not really, not since Dad died." He shrugged. "We get along fine, mostly because we don't see each other real often." He waited for her to dig into that, and he had no idea what he'd tell her.

How could he make her understand that he'd always been a loner? His mother hadn't been the same since the plane crash, not that she'd ever been real clingy before that. But maybe it had nothing to do with his mother. He loved her, but he had no need to be in constant contact with her. She seemed to feel the same.

Molly bypassed his expected questions to ask, "Any siblings?"

This felt like an interrogation, but all things being equal, he supposed he owed her some info. "No. A step-brother from Mom's second marriage. He's a doctor. Nice enough guy." And Dare had nothing in common with him.

"Does your mother know what you do?"

Hell, no. Only a handful of people were trusted enough to know the full truth. "She knows I hire out as a defense and security specialist. The nitty-gritty details aren't up for public consumption."

"Even with your mother?"

Leveling a look on her, Dare emphasized, "With no one."

"Oh." Molly retreated emotionally. "Sorry."

Damn it. Dare felt her withdrawal, and it pissed him off. It wasn't her fault that he'd already told her more than most knew. Only Chris and Trace were privy to the private particulars of his work, but for some reason, talking with Molly was far too easy.

If he wasn't careful, he'd find himself spilling his guts—and he knew that wouldn't be smart, or prudent. "Forget about it."

"I didn't mean to pry."

"Yeah, you did. But it's okay. We might as well get this over with."

She winced.

Because he was watching her so closely, Dare saw her uneasiness, and it bothered him. She'd been through enough without him badgering her. Gently, he asked, "Anything else you want to know, Molly?"

Her bravery waned, but she finally asked, "Do you travel a lot with your work?"

"These days, not as far and not as often. Trace says I'm semiretired. Only when a really important case comes along do I get involved." Only when he felt he was truly needed, or if it became personal, as it had with Alani.

Neither of them would ever say that it was a good thing that Alani had been taken. But at the same time, if she hadn't been…what would have happened to Molly? If not for Alani, Dare wouldn't have been there, and Molly would have had no one to get her out of that hellhole, and no one to protect her even if she had managed to escape.

As if they shared that thought, their gazes locked and held. Dare felt the growing sexual tension between them.

Molly's lips parted; Dare's control slipped.

Knowing he was a goner, he took a step toward her—and his cell phone rang. Brought back to his senses, Dare stopped dead in his tracks.

Sad, and maybe a little lost, Molly gave a halfhearted smile. "Do you need privacy for that call?"

Oh, no, he wouldn't let her slip away that easily. "No. Stay put." He waited until she leaned back against the wall, then added, "I'll only be a second."

CHAPTER THIRTEEN

DARE HATED THE interruption, but since most calls went through the house phone, where Chris could vet them, any call on his cell was personal and therefore important.

With one last lingering look at Molly, he walked over to retrieve his phone from atop the refrigerator. After a quick glance at the number to identify his caller, he flipped the phone open. "Yeah?"

Without preamble, Trace said, "Would you be willing to do me a favor?"

"Depends." Dare looked at Molly. For Trace, he usually gave blind agreement, knowing that his friend only asked when necessary. But now he had someone else's welfare to consider. For now at least, ensuring Molly's safety was his number-one priority. "What's up?"

Frustration sounded in Trace's tone. "Alani is insisting on meeting your…complication."

Dare's mouth twitched at how Trace put that. Molly was a complication, all right, in more ways than he'd figured on. But maybe he should stop referring to her as such, considering how she'd gotten under his skin. "Why?"

"Hell if I know. I hate to ask, Dare. God knows you've done enough. But I think it might be good for her to talk to another woman who's been through the same thing."

Watching Molly wander over to the heavy bag to give

it a tentative push, Dare said, "It wasn't the same. I told you that."

"And I told Alani. But she's pressing me for a meeting anyway."

Molly tried smacking the heavy bag, and, with an expression of pain, she cradled her hand and frowned.

The personalities of the two women couldn't be more disparate; one was a commonsense survivor, the other a very lovable princess. "Want to tell me why?"

It wasn't easy for Trace to admit that he needed help with his sister. "She's having trouble adjusting, Dare. I'm worried about her."

"Hang on." Dare lowered the phone, which gained Molly's attention. When she looked toward him, he said, "Alani wants to meet with you."

Surprise flashed over her features. "Me? But why?"

"You were both taken, both held against your will. Knowing Alani, she's probably worried about you still, and she maybe just wants to connect with someone who'll understand what she's been through." Already knowing what her answer would be, Dare waited.

"Is she okay?"

That was debatable, but Dare said only, "She's safe and healthy, and still coping."

"Well, sure. I mean, of course she is." Hands together, brows down in worry, Molly nodded. "I'd be happy to meet her if she thinks that will help. But when?"

Dare went back to the phone. "No problem, Trace. When were you thinking?"

"Let me talk to Alani, and I'll get back to you. We'll work it out."

"Give me a call when you know."

"Will do. And Dare, thank you."

They hung up, and Dare dropped the phone down onto

his gloves. He watched Molly, saw her put her hand to her stomach as if to calm an unsteady belly. Did the idea of meeting with Alani distress her? Would it be an ugly reminder to her of how she had been separated and treated differently from the others?

"I feel so bad for her." She looked up at Dare. "She's young, isn't she?"

Molly's capacity for compassion amazed Dare. "She's twenty-two."

Appearing distressed, Molly shook her head. "Thank God she has you, Dare. I'm not sure anyone else could have gotten her out of there."

Dare stepped over closer to the heavy bag. "Molly?"

She jerked her attention back to him. "Hmm?"

"How are you feeling?"

She waved that off. "I'm fine."

Something was going on in that quick mind of hers— but what? Molly hadn't come downstairs just to talk to him about his work or his social life. She wanted, *needed,* something.

For now, Dare let her keep her distance. Besides, he was sweaty as hell and still edgy with lust. He figured he could work himself into the ground, and the second he saw Molly again it wouldn't matter one iota.

"You know," he said to her, "you always say you're fine, about everything."

As if to keep from chickening out, she rushed into speech. "Actually, I wanted to talk to you."

His senses prickled. "We *were* talking."

"I know, but there's something else I wanted to know."

"Yeah?" What more could there be? She had the basics of his history. If she wanted a body count, she could forget it. He didn't dwell on the men he'd killed, but he didn't celebrate them, either.

Her teeth caught her bottom lip. She shifted her stance. "Last night…"

Awareness sharpening, Dare took a step closer. "Last night?"

She half turned away, then jerked around to face him again. Hands out, face scrunched, she said, "I'd sort of forgotten how *bad* I look."

Objection to that snapped down his brows. The second she'd come downstairs, he'd lost his battle with lust. Every muscle in his body burned, but not from exercise; it was sexual need that made him rigid.

And she thought she looked bad enough to discourage him? Dare put his fists on his hips and stared at her hard. "Come again?"

Her expression showed torment and determination. "I know the bruises and other marks are bad enough, but it's worse than that. I don't wear a lot of makeup, but like most women I have my own routine, and the fact that I've missed it shows. On top of being worn-down, my hair is the worst ever." Self-consciously, she shoved a hand into the unruly tresses. "I look like…like a hag."

Dare's jaw tightened. "Not even close."

But it was as if she didn't hear him. "You had kissed me…before, I mean…so I assumed that…"

A constriction started in his chest. "I already told you why I kissed you."

She shook her head as if dumbfounded by his reaction. "I know, but all things considered, it still seems like it was just to distract me, and to…help me." Gesturing, she added, "You're a guy, and guys don't always do or say things that they mean."

She dared to group him in with the assholes she'd

known? Did she compare him to that dipshit ex-fiancé of hers?

Son of a bitch.

He hadn't figured on that; if anything, he thought he'd be too different from other men.

Fighting himself was hard enough; fighting her, too, was damn near impossible.

Staring into her eyes, Dare held her gaze. "I want you, Molly. Never doubt that."

This time her hand went over her heart, and Dare saw a pulse beat wildly in her throat.

"I know you said you did, but—"

"Still holds true." He took a step closer, but then stopped himself. If he touched her, he'd lose it for sure. "After last night, more than ever."

Shoulders slumping, Molly shook her head. "I don't understand you at all. Everything you did last night—"

"Yeah." God, he would remember that for the rest of his life. No way would he let her deny what they'd done. "I got you off, and you liked it."

She blinked fast in mixed embarrassment and confusion. "But then you stopped!" Her dark eyes were huge and filled with accusation. "If it's not because I'm ugly right now, well, then, tell me why you stopped. Make me understand."

Ugly? Jesus, is that what she thought? Here he was, doing his damndest to be noble, and she thought she wasn't appealing enough?

Through his teeth, Dare said, "You want me to spell it out for you?"

Uncertainly, she nodded.

"Fine." Let her deal with the truth. "If all I wanted was a fuck, trust me, Molly, you damn well would have been fucked."

Her mouth fell open.

Dare turned, pounded the heavy bag three more times, but it didn't help. Knuckles aching, he dropped his hands. How the hell could he make her understand what he hadn't yet figured out for himself?

Voice strained, he said, "I like you, Molly."

He heard her inhale.

Over his shoulder, gaze sharp and temper primed, he looked at her. "I care about you."

"You do?"

In two long strides, he closed the distance between them. She backed up, but then bumped into the wall.

"Tonight." Because he couldn't stop himself, Dare flattened his hands on the wall to either side of her head. He leaned closer, loomed over her without letting his body touch hers.

"Tonight?" she whispered.

At five-seven, she was considerably shorter than him, small, delicate, vulnerable. And he was wild for her. He wanted to carry her to the ground, pin her down with his body and take his fill.

Breathing hard, Dare bent and put his mouth to hers. He didn't touch her in any other way. He didn't dare tempt himself that much; he couldn't go there, not right now.

The kiss was warm and firm, and though Molly didn't realize it yet, it was possessive as hell. A line had just been crossed, and he didn't give a damn. She'd asked for it, so she'd get it, and then they could deal with her reaction together.

When she moaned and touched her hands to his chest, he straightened and took a quick step back. "Tonight, Molly. If you still feel the same tonight, then I'm done objecting."

"Tonight?"

Was she having second thoughts? "Make damn sure you know what you want before then, because I'm not a man who's good with half measures." He caught her chin, determined to make her understand. "Once we're in that bed together, we're going to be there for a few hours, maybe all damn night. And trust me, Molly, before we're done, you'll know there's not a damn thing about you that I find unappealing."

Her lips trembled; she covered his hand with her own. "All right." She drew in a slow, shivering breath and started to reach for him again.

And Chris yelled down the stairs, "Is Molly down there? I can't find her."

Molly jumped back as if she'd been caught doing something naughty. Her reaction was amusing, but Dare was a long way from humor. "Chris was gone?"

She nodded. "He went into town to get my stuff."

Dare studied her flushed face, and then he noted how her nipples had tightened beneath her sweatshirt. Without taking his gaze off her breasts, he yelled up to Chris, "She'll be right there."

"Ooookay," Chris said, and they both heard the basement door close.

Chris was giving them privacy, but Dare didn't want it. Not here, not like this. But now that he'd told Molly how he felt, the barriers seemed very insubstantial. If he didn't get some space, he'd end up taking her on the cold concrete floor.

"I need to shower," he told her, "and then I'll be right up." As dismissals went, that was pretty clear.

"Oh. Right." Keeping her back to the wall, Molly sidled toward the stairs. "I'll just be up there. With Chris."

Dare couldn't take his gaze off her. "Give me twenty minutes."

She continued to retreat. "Twenty minutes."

Obviously he'd thrown her for a loop. Seemed fair to Dare, given how she'd turned him inside out.

His jaw flexed. "Get going, Molly, before I change my mind."

She turned and hustled up the stairs, fascinating Dare with that taut behind and the bouncing of her full breasts. He stood there transfixed, watching her until she reached the top of the stairs and disappeared from his sight.

Damn, but she was something. Pure. Honest.

A great contradiction to the life he'd built for himself, a life of precision, deception and detection.

Being around Molly felt good.

Today he'd make her confront her life back home, and, God willing, tonight she'd still want him.

KATHI BERRY-ALEXANDER finished giving directions to one of the well-mannered household staff before she started down the hallway of the mansion she shared with her husband, Bishop Alexander. All her life, she'd been groomed for the skillful organization and planning required for a residence this large—not that Bishop understood or appreciated her significant contribution to making their home comfortable. He was a very busy man, an important, influential man, and he couldn't be expected to care about such things. She knew that, in many ways, he considered her dispensable.

But she loved him anyway.

She loved the prestige he provided, the social circle, the authority.

He might not be the most charming man around, but he was an excellent provider and a respectable husband that society admired and that some even revered.

Her parents had raised her with advantages, but they

weren't powerful like Bishop. Marriage to him ensured that she kept a prestigious edge over others.

She happily basked in the cold shadow of his success.

What Bishop couldn't or wouldn't give her, she was resourceful enough to get on her own.

As Kathi looked around at the beautiful artwork on the walls and the fresh flowers in multiple vases, she nodded in satisfaction. Meticulous detailing ensured that nothing would ever mar her perfect existence.

Mentally listing her duties for the coming evening, Kathi considered the yoga class in an hour, then lunch with friends before she'd visit the salon in preparation for a dinner party with her husband's business contacts.

Everything revolved around those contacts. Over the years, Bishop's business investments grew more diversified, and even extended into political backing. She didn't understand all of his dealings, but she knew that he owned a chain of gun stores and several recreational properties. Business didn't interest her; she received a generous household allowance and personal account, and should anything ever happen to Bishop, she was a major beneficiary of his will. The house, the properties, would remain hers.

She was satisfied.

As she strode along the marble floors, Kathi's heels clicked rhythmically in a soothing cadence until she stepped into the master bedroom in search of her purse. That's when she spotted Bishop out on the veranda.

Despite the cool day and brisk wind, he wore no jacket. With his cell phone to his ear and tension in his shoulders, he leaned on the ornate iron railing and stared out at the grounds.

He spoke in a tone harsh with anger, and Kathi couldn't help but overhear him.

"Apparently she was missing, and I didn't know it." He paused, then added, "Well, of course it's a problem, because that crude Neanderthal felt free to accost me at a goddamned club!"

Kathi couldn't believe her ears. Someone had dared to confront Bishop? Out in the open? He didn't appear hurt, but all she could see was his back.

Concerned, she started to go to him, but hesitated when he blasted the caller with rage.

"How could I tell him anything that I didn't know?" Bishop ran a hand through his hair. "No, you can't ask around. I already told you, he *threatened* me if I said a word to anyone. If you go blabbing, then he'll damn well know I was talking, right?"

Stiffening, Kathy wondered who would dare to do such a thing. She didn't understand the complexity of Bishop's reach, but she knew her husband was a powerful man with many important friends.

And yet someone had the gall to encroach on their perfect existence? Unacceptable.

Bishop lost his control and shouted loud enough for the staff to hear. *"How the fuck should I know?"*

Appalled, Kathi stepped out to the veranda, too, admonishing him. "Bishop, remember yourself."

The look he sent her would have made most people quail. But Kathi cared more about appearances than his temper. She hadn't worked this hard to have his bad humor fracture their sterling reputation.

"Come inside to talk," she urged him. "I'll give you the privacy you need." She took his arm, but he jerked free of her hold and turned his back on her.

To her relief, he did lower his tone when he spoke

again to his caller. "I'm telling you, this goon knew a lot of my personal business, so I'm not taking any chances. He claims to have all kinds of reach, and given what he already knows, I believe him. All I want you to do is find out—discreetly—who he is and how he knows me. No, I don't have any suggestions on how you do it. That's what I pay you for!"

Kathi watched as her husband almost threw the phone. She didn't flinch, and in the end, he drew a calming breath, closed the cell and jammed it back into his pocket.

Inside, she was shaking, but outwardly she tried to give him what she knew he needed. "I apologize for blundering in on your private call."

His eyes burned with disdain. "There's never any god-damned privacy around here."

Kathi steadied herself with a deep breath. "We've discussed this, Bishop. Your library is off-limits to everyone except during the morning cleaning."

"I think it's bugged."

"Bugged?" She put a hand to her chest in shock. "Are you serious?"

Eyes narrowed and red, he paced past her, then back again. "I don't know. But I feel exposed in there."

She couldn't credit such a thing, but she would not take chances. "Shall I have it examined?"

His teeth sawed together, and he glared at her. "Do you have an answer for every fucking thing? Damn it, don't you ever get rattled?"

"Well, of course." She touched his arm, and, despite his coldness toward her, she felt the fine, masculine hair there, the warmth of his skin. He was a handsome, powerful man, and she protected what was hers. "But I want to be here for you always. It's my role to do whatever I can to help you—"

"Christ, woman," he shouted at her, jerking free of her touch yet again. "You fucking smother me."

She started to apologize again, but held back at the look he leveled on her. "Who is missing?"

He narrowed his eyes and almost as an accusation said, "Molly was taken."

Kathi backed up a step. "Taken? What do you mean?"

"You run the house," he told her. "You tell me."

Bewildered, she shook her head. "Your daughter doesn't live here. She's not under my jurisdiction, so I have no idea—"

"That was sarcasm, damn it."

"I see." His temper was ripe today, scorching her.

Not bothering to hide his disgust, he pushed past her. "But one would think you could keep up with your stepdaughters at the very least. If you had, then maybe I wouldn't have been taken off guard."

And with that, Bishop stormed through the bedroom and, Kathi knew, out of the house.

He hadn't said if Molly was okay or not, leaving her to wonder.

She took a moment to compose herself, but no more than a moment. Regardless of this unfortunate turn, she had duties for the day and she would never allow her own emotions to keep her from those responsibilities. Too many people depended on her. She would attend her yoga class as scheduled.

But first…first she had a phone call to make. And unlike her husband, she never did so without the privacy needed.

CHAPTER FOURTEEN

As MOLLY HURRIED UP the stairs, her thoughts churning over what Dare had said and his promise for the night, a fantastic change in her plot occurred to her. That's how her writing went—she got inspiration from everywhere, and Dare certainly inspired her muse in remarkable ways. So far, there was more sex in this book than in any of her others.

Her dad would abhor that, but she'd bet Kathi would appreciate the new scenes. Most of her readers seemed to enjoy a little steam now and then.

Since meeting Dare, she could understand why.

Closing the door to the stairs, Molly leaned back and grinned.

"Is that a look of satisfaction?"

She jumped at the intrusion. Somehow she'd forgotten all about Chris. "What? No. I mean…"

He laughed at her.

"You're terrible," she accused without any real insult. "Actually, I just worked out a plot problem, that's all."

"Mmm. Is that what they're calling it these days?"

She opened her mouth, but could think of nothing witty to say. "Where's my stuff?"

"I put the bags in the room you're using upstairs." His smile never wavered. "So, where's Dare?"

"Taking a shower. He said he'd be up in twenty minutes." That didn't leave her much time. She wanted to get the words down before Dare finished. "I, um…" She edged away. "I need to go write."

"Have at it." Chris saluted her and went back to unloading some groceries.

Forty minutes and six pages later, Molly saved her file and returned to the kitchen. Chris was at the computer, but looked up to smile at her as she entered. "You done?"

She nodded. "For now."

Dare stood at the stove, cracking eggs into a bowl. They shared a look. "Chris said you were writing."

"My muse takes some wild jumps, and good plot twists just occur to me. I like to get it on paper while the idea is fresh in my mind."

Chris sat back in his chair. "Am I old enough to hear the details?"

"Sorry, no." He was teasing again, but Molly answered with a writer's seriousness. "I never, ever talk about my stories while I'm writing them. It dilutes my creative energy."

"We can't have that." Chris laced his fingers behind his neck and stretched. "So, how long will it be before I can buy a copy?"

"A year, at least." It amazed Molly how comfortable she felt with them both already. She took a seat at the bar. "After I turn it in, which won't be for a while yet, it has to go through production. But when it's done, I'll give you an autographed copy if you want."

"Really?" Chris dropped his arms and leaned forward. "If you're serious, that'd be great."

"I owe you anyway, for driving into town for me today."

Dare poured his egg mixture onto a hot griddle. "You going to sign one to me, too?"

Why Dare's question made her blush, Molly couldn't say. She looked down at her hands. "If you want, I'd be happy to." The thought of Dare reading her both pleased and worried her. His opinion mattered, a lot.

"Molly?"

When she looked up at him, he said, "I'm going to pick up your other books, too."

"You don't need to do that."

He flashed her an intimate smile. "You've got me curious."

Aware of Chris watching them, Molly cleared her throat. "What I meant is that I have my own stash of author copies, so you don't need to buy them. When I get back to my apartment, I can package some up and mail them to you."

Dare sent her a look. "I'll have brunch ready in a few minutes."

All she'd had was the cold cereal earlier, and the crepes smelled delicious. "Thanks."

Then Dare said, "We're heading up to your apartment today, but no need to mail the books back. We're only going for a short stay."

A short stay. Molly stared at Dare in disbelief. She had assumed they'd go up and back. She needed to see her sister and check her messages, but she didn't want to stay there, where she'd been grabbed off the street, knowing that whoever had arranged for her to be taken was still out there somewhere, maybe just waiting for another chance at her.

"I can wait," Chris said. He asked Dare, "Do you want me to forward your calls and emails to you?"

"Just the important ones. Everything else will wait. Trace will know to call the cell."

At a loss, Molly rose out of her chair. She felt like running away.

Dare glanced at her, then said softly, "I met your father yesterday."

Her breath strangled in her chest. "You did *what?*"

"I tracked him down at a club in Kentucky. He was there to play golf with some business associates."

She couldn't believe this. What had her father said to Dare? Oh, God, she could only imagine, and shame burned her.

Folding his arms over his chest, Dare leaned against the counter and stared at her. "When we get to your place tonight, you'll call him and set up a dinner with the rest of the family for as soon as possible. I need to meet all of them."

Molly shook her head, blindsided and dumbfounded by his audacity.

Concerned, Chris turned his chair to face her. "Molly?"

She ignored him, giving all her attention to Dare. "I don't believe you." Her voice was raspy and faint, and that irritated her even more. She spoke up, adding strength to her words. "Don't you think you should consult with me about these major decisions?"

His brow went up.

Hurt clenched her heart, and she moved toward him with anger. "Especially when I'm the one paying for this!"

"It was off the clock," Dare told her, and he watched her so closely that she felt exposed.

"No, absolutely not." She pointed at him. "I'm paying you for *everything*. We agreed."

He said nothing.

His silence drew a harsh contrast to her raised voice,

making her feel foolish. "Damn it, Dare, you can't just spring these things on me!"

He remained calm. "Do you object to seeing your family?"

"Well…" She wanted to see her sister, and she knew that sooner or later she'd have to see her dad and Kathi again. "No."

He slanted a look at Chris and said again, "We'll be staying at her place for a few days."

"Ooookay," Chris said, emphasizing the tension in the room. "Do I need to pack your suit?"

"No, but something nicer than jeans, okay?"

"Got it."

Molly still stood there, so Dare gave Chris a telling look, and he said, "Yeah, I'll just… Yeah." He deserted the computer and left the room.

Dare watched Molly a second more, then carried a plate over to her. He set it on the bar and turned to face her. "You okay?"

"I'm—"

"Fine." He sighed in clear frustration. "Why did I bother asking?"

"I *am* fine." But she felt compelled to admit, "It's a subjective term, Dare. Compared to a few days ago, I'm better than fine."

"Got it." He pulled her into his arms, and despite her annoyance at him, it felt so good that Molly wanted to stay there, just like that.

But of course if she did, she wouldn't be able to write, or reassure her sister, or direct her agent on negotiations.

Life continued, and she wanted to move along with it, not hide forever.

With Dare's scent filling her head and his warm embrace around her, she whispered, "You want to know how

I really feel?" She didn't wait for him to answer. "I'm achy all over, especially in my shoulders and neck, but it's not too bad, considering. Mostly I'm uncertain, and I'm still scared. I'm anxious to get my life back to normal, but then I think about what was normal and how naïve I was, and I don't know if I really want that or not."

His fingers threaded into her hair, kneading her skull, caressing her. "I won't let anything happen to you."

Molly could tell that he meant it, but what if it proved impossible to find the one responsible? She couldn't expect Dare to put his life on hold for her.

He was the most capable man she knew, more capable than she could ever have imagined, but he wasn't invincible. What if he got hurt trying to protect her?

She pushed back from him a little. "Maybe I should just go to the police."

A gentle tug on her hair turned her face up to his. "You know that's not the answer."

Did she? True, the police would never have looked for her in Tijuana. But if she took extra precautions now to ensure no one else could get to her, then maybe they could—

Dare bent down and kissed her. It was a hard kiss, surprising Molly. She started to pull away, but he lifted her right off her feet and continued to take her mouth until she softened, until she warmed and reciprocated.

Positioning her to sit at the edge of the bar, he stepped between her legs. With his hands braced at either side of her hips, he leaned down to her. "You will not go to the police."

He looked harsh and possessive. And a little turned-on. It excited her.

"My dad…"

"Was a total prick. You know him, so you can imagine

how he reacted without me laying out the details for you. But if you want them, I'll share every word on our drive into Ohio. For now, though, I want your agreement that you won't veer off the plan."

Molly put her hand to his jaw. So many awful possibilities came to her, all of them centering around Dare's safety. "I don't want you to get hurt because of me."

"Christ, woman."

"You're not Superman, Dare, and you're not a psychic. Even if you could dodge bullets, you can't know about conspiracies or ambushes—"

"From your father, you mean?"

He sounded scornful, discounting the danger. "Or from whoever is after me." The number of threats out there left her shaken.

"You need to have a little faith." Scooping one big hand against her backside, he dragged her forward, hard against him. "Do exactly as I say and we'll both be okay. Understand?"

Her legs were around him, leaving her flush against his hard abdomen. His hand on her bottom kept flexing, feeling her, keeping her close.

Molly nodded. "Okay."

His expression heated. Slowly, he bent to kiss her again, softer this time. Against her cheek, he breathed, "Soon as we're done eating, we'll hit the road."

"Okay." She tipped her head back.

He put a gentle love bite to her throat. "And tonight…"

Molly's heart pounded. "Tonight?"

He touched his tongue to her ear, and whispered, "I'm going to be inside you, and I can't fucking wait."

In the next instant, he lifted her off the counter and onto a stool. Before she could catch her breath, Chris peered back in. He looked from Dare to Molly, and seeing them separated, walked on in.

"Glad you two worked that out, because I'm hungry again."

Through a haze, Molly watched Dare. He acted like nothing had happened, like he hadn't just made that provocative promise to her. He poured a glass of milk and set it before her, then sat down to eat while he and Chris talked.

In more ways than one, she was out of her league.

She picked up her fork with a shaking hand, and as she dipped her crepe in the dollop of whipped cream, she let out a pent-up breath.

Dare had managed to balance her apprehension about going home with an urgency to get there. Even knowing that he couldn't feel the same as she did, she wanted to cherish every second with him.

She believed that he'd protect her from threats. It was up to Molly to protect her heart.

AT CLOSE TO SIX THAT evening, Dare pulled down the street to Molly's apartment building.

He could feel her nervousness growing, but there was no help for it. On the drive, he'd told her about meeting her father, leaving out some of what Bishop had said. Not that it mattered. Molly knew her father, and, as Dare had suspected, she filled in the blanks on her own.

Because she didn't socialize in her father's circles, she hadn't met many of his business cronies. She knew nothing of Warwick or Sagan. Dare told her about the connections because she needed to know. If it turned out that her father was responsible in some way, better that she had the facts early on.

"I just thought of something." Molly kept one hand

clamped on the seat, the other on the dash as she stared out the windshield, looking everywhere as if she expected the same goons to show up and make another play for her.

"Relax, Molly. It's going to be okay."

"I know." She remained alert. "But how are we going to get in? I don't have any keys with me. I left my purse in the apartment and…" With a groan, she turned her wide-eyed gaze on Dare. "I didn't even have my door locked, because I thought I'd be going right back in. I didn't remember that until now."

"Then it's probably still unlocked." Either way, Dare wasn't concerned about it. He could pick a lock in no time at all, and would, if it proved necessary. "Stop worrying."

"You keep saying that." She returned her attention to the area.

Through mirrored, aviator sunglasses, Dare glanced at her and saw her unease. He reached over and put a hand on her slim thigh. "Try trusting me a little, will you?"

"This has nothing to do with trust."

It had everything to do with trust, but he could feel her trembling, so he let that go for now. "Where do you want me to park?"

She swallowed. "Across the street. If no one stole it, my car should still be over there."

It didn't surprise him that Molly had thought ahead. If someone wanted her absence to look uneventful, taking her car would have shored up that ruse. Folks would assume she'd left for a trip.

Dare turned where she indicated into a small parking lot. As Molly had claimed, there were floodlights mounted on poles to keep the area lit at night. He'd also noted some older people sitting on their porches, to take advantage of the warmer day. The area was a mix of stately, single-family homes and homes converted into apartments.

Typical of older structures, the buildings had a lot of character and structural details. The area was clean and well maintained and, as she'd said, quiet.

Hard to believe that no one had noticed her being snatched.

With relief, she said, "There it is." She pointed to a sporty little Mazda Miata in cherry red.

Huh. So her captors weren't concerned with appearances. "Cute car."

"Cute?" Pretending offense, she glared at him. "That was my gift to myself from my last contract."

"Personal reward, huh?" Glad to see her less focused on the danger, Dare said, "I like it." It was a little small for him to fit comfortably into, but he could see Molly behind the wheel. "It suits you."

After parking next to her car, he stored the sunglasses above the visor and turned to her. He hadn't known her long, but already he could pick up on her moods. He wished he could somehow make this easier for her.

And maybe he could. Looking at her mouth, at the way she worried her bottom lip, he reached for her. "Come here."

Surprise overtook the worry as he tugged her toward him. "Dare?"

Holding her face in his hands, he took her mouth in a kiss that started slow but quickly turned into a deep, soft distraction.

When she relaxed against him, he eased her back into her seat. Soothing her bottom lip with his thumb, he whispered, "Ready?"

Those beautiful, dark eyes of hers refocused and slowly filled with accusation. "You did that on purpose."

"Yeah." He bent forward and kissed her again, light and quick. "Just reminding you that you're not alone. I'm here, and there's no way in hell I'd let anyone hurt you."

"You are so cocky." She smiled when she said it, making it sound like a compliment instead of an insult. "I guess I'm as ready as I'll ever be." She turned and opened her door.

As she walked around the hood toward him, Dare took a minute to look over her car. Molly thought he was admiring it, but really he wanted to make sure that it hadn't been tampered with. He'd have someone give it a more thorough going-over before she drove it again, but for now, it seemed fine.

Constantly scanning the area, Dare retrieved his duffel bag and a small suitcase for Molly's clothes. His hand at her back, they started across the street to the building where she lived. Her next-door neighbors, sitting on their porches, made obvious note of the bags and Dare's presence.

"I thought you said no one paid any attention around here."

"All day long, you don't see a soul, especially in the colder months. But I guess it was warm enough today to entice some folks out."

He nodded to an older couple who stared at him, but said in an aside to Molly, "I take it you don't bring many guys around?"

Molly refused to look up at anyone. "Just Adrian, but not even him for a while."

She went in through the unlocked front door that let them into a foyer of sorts. Beyond them were two doors on either side of the building, presumably for apartments. On the right wall were four mailboxes.

Molly went to the stairs at the left. "I'm upstairs."

Dare kept her ahead of him, but only by a few steps. Something didn't feel right to him. He'd always been a gut-instinct type, and right now, his instincts were kicking hard.

There were two more units at the top of the stairs, one to the left and one to the right.

When Molly headed to the door on the right, Dare stopped her. "Let me go in first."

Catching on to his concern, Molly froze. "You think something is wrong?"

"I don't know." He kept his tone low as he opened a compartment in his duffel and withdrew his Glock.

Staring at the weapon, Molly pressed back to the wall. *"What are you doing?"*

Keeping his gaze on the door, Dare set the bags beside her. "Wait right here. Don't move. If you see anyone, call out to me. Otherwise, be quiet." He stepped away.

Her hand snagged his arm in a desperate hold. "Dare?"

Sparing her a quick glance, he asked, "What?"

"You're scaring me."

"Not now, Molly." This wasn't the time to soothe her, or to explain. At the door, he listened but didn't hear anything. The knob turned and the unlocked door opened with an ominous squeak typical to old homes. Even with the room in shadows, Dare could see the evidence of a search.

"Shit."

"What?" she asked in a harsh whisper. "What is it?"

Dare spared her a warning glance that silenced her

again, and then he slipped into the apartment. Someone had trashed her place.

Dare took it all in with a fast glance: furniture over-turned, drawers ransacked, papers scattered. Books everywhere. Damn, but the woman had a lot of books.

She was not going to be happy.

Trusting her to stay where he'd left her, Dare ventured farther inside. Whoever had searched her place had left the kitchen lights on, but the drapes closed. Without making a sound, Dare went through each room. He found most of them in total disarray, but empty of intruders. Stepping over toppled furniture, clothes, books and garbage, Dare went back for Molly.

He found her standing in the open doorway, her face pinched and her eyes burning with anger.

"Damn it." While stowing the gun at the small of his back, Dare strode over to her. "I told you to stay put."

Her slim shoulders were weighed down by their heavy bags, with one hanging from each hand. Molly didn't seem to notice as she stared around at her destroyed living room. "Who would do this?"

"Neither of us knows, and that's why you damn well should have waited like you were told." He took the bags from her and set them inside, then caught her arm and pulled her in, too. He closed and locked the door, caught her shoulders and pinned her to the wall.

She stared up at him without fear, her dark eyes huge—and, damn it, wounded.

But he couldn't let her slide on this. Her safety depended on her following his every order to the letter.

Dare gripped her shoulders. "Here's how this is going to work." She felt so small and delicate in his hold that he had to struggle not to hug her close. "From now on, you're going to do exactly what I tell you to do, how I tell you to do it. Do you understand me?"

She looked beyond him to the living room. Dare gently shook her. "This is important, Molly."

"I know." She sounded numb. "I guess I should have expected this. But the idea of someone going through my personal things…"

For now, Dare gave up. Later, he'd again go over the importance of her following his instructions. "It's mostly just dumped, not broken." He righted the chair closest to them and replaced the cushion. "We can straighten it up."

Her tongue slicked out over dry lips. "I didn't know you'd brought the gun."

Damn, but he wanted her. When he had her climaxing under him, she wouldn't worry about her rummaged apartment or his weapon. "I don't go anywhere without it."

"I should have remembered that." Her gaze went to his hands, then back to his face. "If you'd found someone in here, would you have shot him?"

"What do you think?"

After a second of thought, she said, "Only if you had to." She shuddered. "But I'm glad you had it, just in case."

She was glad? So why, then, did she look so rattled?

Molly picked up a floral throw pillow from the floor. "As much as I hate to ask this, should we call the police?"

He hadn't yet decided. "Why don't you look around and see if anything is missing?"

As she did that, she removed her corduroy jacket and the colorful scarf and dropped them over the back of the couch, which was the only piece of furniture that hadn't been turned or taken apart.

Arms crossed, she studied the room—and suddenly her eyes widened. "My manuscript."

Forgoing concern for her shelves, broken pictures and a dumped plant, Molly launched over and around the mess to race into her bedroom.

Dare followed right behind her.

At a large desk, she drew up short and groaned.

The keyboard hung off the front of the desk, still connected by the cord. Papers were strewn everywhere, and scattered clothes half covered the area.

But the large flat-screen monitor appeared unbroken and all the cords seemed intact.

She picked up some papers, saying, "My contracts are all mixed up now." She set the papers aside and turned full circle to see the room.

Dare did his own scrutiny, but for different reasons. Now that he knew there weren't any intruders still lurking about, he realized that Molly's regular wardrobe included a lot of provocative stuff. Panties in every color were mixed with camisoles and lacy bras. Draped over the open closet door was a skimpy red dress, and at the foot of the bed, a silky purple blouse lay bunched up with skinny jeans.

Huh. Somehow, he hadn't pictured her like this. He'd figured her more for a T-shirt and sneakers kind of woman. Basic. Unadorned. Earthy.

And she could be.

But he liked the new image in his head a lot.

In his quick surveillance of the place, he hadn't failed to notice the claw-footed tub in her bathroom, or the black-and-white tile, brightened with red towels and dishes of potpourri.

There was a decidedly sensual side to Ms. Molly Alexander. "You surprise me."

"What?" She followed his gaze to a floral demi-bra. With a gasp, she snatched it up and hid it behind her back. "You thought I did all my shopping at discount department stores?"

He sort of had. "You're adaptable."

Her chin came up. "Yeah, so?"

It amused him that she sounded so defensive. "It's an admirable quality, Molly, that's all. Sort of sexy, even."

"Yeah, right." Huffing, she threw the bra toward the bed and went to her knees in front of the desk. "Not like anyone sees me in any of that stuff anyway."

He would. Soon.

He watched as she moved a lot of stuff out of her way to search beneath the desk.

"What are you looking for?"

"My flash drive. It was in the computer, because I was working on the book when I…" She went still, shook her head. "I was writing before I took a break and went outside. It should be here. I was going to mesh the papers I'd written at your place into the pages I already have."

Would someone have reason to steal her work? Dare took a bundle of clothes from her and put them on the chair. "Did you keep a backup?"

"The flash drive is my backup." She pushed aside a box, and a broken dry-erase board.

Dare cursed low—and Molly said, "Found it!"

Amazed, he watched as she lifted the flash drive from a narrow space on the floor between her chair and the desk. She closed her fist around it and let out a long breath.

Sorting out his thoughts, Dare turned to scrutinize the

rest of her bedroom. "Involving the police will hinder what I can find out."

Now that she'd found her work, she seemed calmer. "Why?"

"Because I'd be their first suspect."

CHAPTER FIFTEEN

MOLLY STARED AT HIM, aghast. "What are you talking about? Why would anyone suspect *you?*"

"I'm the least-known person in this equation. And it'll only make the police suspicious if they start digging into my history, because they won't find much."

"They won't?"

"I've made a point to always cover my tracks." The last thing he needed was a public profile. "It goes with the security of the job. But cops don't like that. They see any concealment as a guilty verdict."

Molly accepted that without question, but the authorities wouldn't. And he didn't want them sidetracked investigating him, instead of getting to the real instigators.

Dare put his hands on his hips and looked at her full-size bed. The bedding was displaced, her clothes dumped, but otherwise the room seemed okay. "Another problem is that the police have an uncanny knack for forewarning every real suspect. It's the way they investigate."

Molly pushed up from the floor. "What do you mean?" She stowed the memory device in her pocket and began picking up clothes.

"They're upfront about everything. They have rules to follow, legal procedures to adhere to." Someone might have gone through her things in an effort to discover her whereabouts. Had Bishop Alexander put someone up to that task? It seemed possible. "But I don't."

"I hadn't thought of that."

"The easiest way to catch people is to take them off guard. Whoever kidnapped you is a pro with connections. If they were involved in this—" he looked at a dumped dresser drawer "—they wouldn't leave behind evidence."

"Since my door wasn't locked, anyone could have come in."

Dare considered that. "Where do you keep your keys?"

"In the kitchen on a utility cabinet. I always leave my purse in there, too." She started that way and Dare followed. The kitchen wasn't in as bad shape as the bedroom. Her purse had been dumped on the table, and two drawers were emptied of paper and pens.

Molly looked around but didn't find the keys anywhere. "They're gone."

"Anyone else have keys to your place?"

"My sister, and the landlord."

Dare opened a few cabinets that held food and dishes, and drawers filled with silverware, pot holders and dishcloths. They were undisturbed.

That told him a lot. "Whoever went through here was looking for something specific. He wasn't just trashing the place."

Frowning, Molly went back into the living room and looked around, and then back into her bedroom. Dare could tell she was studying the carnage, trying to make sense of it.

She stared at her desk, rearranged some of the displaced papers. After a minute, she said, "Whoever was here went through my printed notes, and he left my computer on."

Dare frowned. "Put the drive in the computer and see if your work is okay."

"I was working on my book before I went outside and got grabbed. That's the last file I had opened up."

Standing over her, he waited as Molly organized her desk, replacing the keyboard and the mouse. She hadn't yet put the flash drive back in before the movement brought the sleeping monitor flickering back to life. Rather than Molly's current manuscript showing, her iCal popped up.

"That's my calendar." She stared at the screen. "It's one of the programs I use most often, but I hadn't put anything new in there for a while."

"You didn't have it open?"

She shook her head. "Not for…I don't know, a few days at least."

So, whoever had broken in had been searching her appointments. "Someone found it."

"Seems so."

Reaching around her for the mouse, Dare minimized the calendar on the screen, and behind it they found an Evite—an emailed invitation—that Molly had added to her calendar. Dare straightened and put his hands on her shoulders.

As Molly read the reminder, her shoulders tensed. "I was supposed to attend a book signing yesterday." She twisted to see Dare. "I don't have a current book release, but this was a special occasion to honor a local bookseller who's retiring."

Dare had no idea what to say to her.

She turned back to the screen. "Thank God I wasn't the only author scheduled to be there. But I can't imagine what everyone thought when I just didn't show up."

"I can't imagine what your intruder thought, because I'm betting he was at the signing, looking for you."

She stiffened. "That's why the last Evite was still up on the screen."

He rubbed her shoulders. "Whoever was here was looking for a clue to your whereabouts, but he didn't have anything else to go on."

"God," she groaned. Elbow propped on the desk, she put her forehead in her hand. "I've probably missed a ton of promotional stuff."

"Let's don't worry about that right now, okay?" Dare noticed that Molly's other hand, resting on the desktop, was fisted, giving away her anger at being violated yet again. She understood the seriousness of this invasion and how determined *someone* was to find her again.

But true to her nature, she kept it together, reacting in a calm, sensible way that helped rather than hindered.

He urged her from the chair. "Let me."

She vacated the seat without argument. "What are you going to do?"

"Just take a quick look to see when our guy was here, and any other places he might've gone on the computer."

"You can do that?"

"I have some tech savvy, yeah." Actually he had a lot more than the average person, but he didn't consider himself a pro. "Trace is the real computer guy, but since you have a Mac, some things are pretty easy to find. Hopefully you haven't changed your settings to delete your history each time the computer is used."

"I didn't. I wouldn't even know how to do that."

Her lack of knowledge amazed Dare. "You work on this computer."

Shrugging, she dismissed that little fact. "I email, surf

the Net for research and write. But believe me, no one would accuse me of being a computer geek."

Eventually, Dare decided, he'd give her a basic education on how her computer worked and what it could do. Right now it just didn't matter. "If we know everything that the guy looked at, we'll have a better idea about what he wanted."

"He wanted to know my schedule."

"Yeah, but why?" Thinking aloud, Dare said, "He couldn't have thought to snatch you out of a book signing, right? There would be other people, and the bookstore manager. So what was his plan?"

Wrapping her arms around herself, she shuddered. "You really think he wanted to kidnap me again?"

"Right now, I don't know what to think." It could be that Bishop was searching for her to get a handle on things and keep her kidnapping out of the news. But why trash her place?

Dare's attention went from her to a tiny scrap of lace and silk showing from a bundle of clothes on the floor near the desk. He reached for the panties, but Molly beat him to it.

"Not funny, Dare." She tossed them toward her bed. "I *hate* it that anyone touched my stuff. I ought to just burn everything and start over."

"Hey." Dare pulled her down to his lap. "It's going to be okay. I promise." Somehow he'd make it true.

Rather than debate that, Molly put a hand to his jaw and leaned forward to kiss him. She kept it brief, and still he felt burned. "It helps so much that you're here with me. Thank you."

Dare brought her back for a hotter, deeper kiss. It was a little more satisfying, but he didn't let it get out of hand. "There's no place I'd rather be."

A crooked grin tipped her soft lips. "Yeah, it's a laugh a minute around me."

"Molly," he admonished. "Don't do that. Don't minimize the situation. I'm glad that I'm with you. Hell, there's no way I wouldn't be."

As if she didn't quite believe him, she lowered her gaze. "I know you miss Tai and Sargie."

"True, but they adore Chris. He takes good care of them, and that includes playing with them and cuddling them." Dare leaned down to catch her gaze. "Until recently, I was gone more than I was home."

"And now your schedule is finally freed up, and here I am, dragging you away from home again."

It was too soon for him to tell her how she mattered to him, too soon for him to even feel that way. "No one drags me anywhere, Molly." He tipped up her chin. "I'm here because I want to be."

For several seconds, they stared at each other—until Molly masked her reaction of disbelief with a long sigh.

Gazing around at her bedroom, she said, "While you snoop, is it okay if I start putting some of this stuff away?"

For now, Dare gave up on convincing her of his free participation. In the end, when he refused payment, she'd know the truth. "I don't see why not."

She left his lap. "The sooner I get everything back to normal, the sooner it'll feel like home to me again."

Damn, but he admired her. Not only didn't she fall apart, she sought ways to cope.

And that kiss… That Molly had taken the lead really turned him on. But she was right—they needed to get her life back on track. After he gathered all the clues available to him and they put her apartment back to rights, he'd have the rest of the night alone with her.

Somehow, he'd wait until then.

DARE MADE HIMSELF turn back to the computer. While Molly collected the dumped clothes into a hamper to launder, Dare searched through her computer. He looked at all activity from the day of her abduction until today.

Oddly enough, the day after Molly was taken, someone had accessed her writing files. It infuriated him to know that while she'd been held in a hovel in Tijuana, some bastard had read through her book.

There'd been no activity on her computer after that—until recently. Eyes burning, Dare looked at the dates for when several programs had been opened—including her calendar and her internet.

The day after she was taken, and then again after he'd spoken with Bishop, someone had gotten on her computer.

Sitting back in the chair, he considered the possibilities. Why the long wait between visits? And why *now?*

Would the same person visit twice, searching through different programs? A pro would know how risky it was to return, but then a pro would have found what he looked for on the first visit.

And if it wasn't the same person? Had Bishop ignored Dare's warning and sent someone of his own to investigate, maybe to check on his daughter's welfare?

Or to cover his tracks?

Dare was mulling over possibilities while also listening to Molly move about the apartment. She'd tidied the bedroom, which was mostly dumped clothes, and was now in the living room. Though she remained in the apartment, and not that far from him, Dare didn't like it that he couldn't see her. Until the people responsible for hurting her were found, he wanted to keep a very close watch on her.

He was just about to check the internet links when she

reappeared in the doorway. She'd removed her sweater, and her boots and socks. Barefoot, blouse untucked and the hem of her jeans dragging the floor, she stared at him.

One look at her face and Dare was out of the chair. "What is it?"

She took a shuddering breath. "A…note." She gestured behind her with a shaking hand. "Left for me by the phone table."

Grim, Dare put an arm around her. "Show me."

She walked to a small, overturned table against the wall that separated her kitchen and living room. "This is where I keep my landline, where my cell phone charges and where I put my mail, my change and…everything."

A dozen letters, several packages and boxes were dumped around the floor. "You've got a load of stuff there."

"I was gone for a while, remember?"

"So, who brought the mail in?"

Her hand to her forehead, expression bleak, she pointed a stiff finger at a lone pad of paper resting atop the answering machine. "Whoever left that, I guess."

Dare stepped over the broken landline phone to the answering machine that lay on the floor. It was unplugged, possibly broken, too, but he'd check on that in a minute.

Molly stuck close to him. "I use the landline for business calls, like with my editor and agent, or phone interviews, that sort of thing. Family almost always calls the cell. Whoever left that note knew I'd try to check my business messages, right? That's why he specifically left it there. He didn't want it to get lost in the rest of this mess."

"Probably." Written in large block letters with bold red

marker was a message that Dare read aloud: *"Still feel so forgiving?"*

He realized that Molly shook with anger, not fear. She'd curled her hands tight, clenched her jaw and her dark eyes were burning bright.

"I take it you have an idea what that means?"

"Got a good guess, yeah."

She looked ready to combust, so Dare said, "Let's see if the answering machine still works, okay?"

Nodding, Molly went to her knees and reconnected the cord to the machine and then plugged it into the wall. There were some calls from her sister, inquiring after her. Her agent, her editor, left urgent calls requesting her attention. The local bookstore sounded pleasant but confused about her absence.

Then another call from Natalie. She said that she'd gotten the email, but she wanted specifics. "Why won't you call me, damn it? I don't get it. This is nuts. If you're off having fun, that's fine. I'm thrilled for you. But you can take one minute to talk, so…call me."

Smothering in guilt, Molly groaned. "Natalie must be frantic."

"Yeah, but what was that about an email?"

"I don't know."

"Come on." Dare tugged her to her feet and together they went back to her computer. He checked the history and found her online email program had been accessed. "Mind if I take a look?"

"It's not like I have a lot to hide at this point." She gestured at the computer. "Have at it."

Dare pulled up the email program and looked for received emails, but saw none. Then he looked at the sent emails, and again, nothing.

Molly frowned. "Check the trash."

"I am." He opened the folder for discarded mail. "Bingo." There were three messages from her sister, one of them saying she was heading off for spring break and wanted to talk to Molly first.

"Spring break?" Dare asked.

"She's a teacher." Molly leaned over his shoulder and frowned at the monitor. "There's an email from me, but I wasn't here to send it."

Dare opened the deleted post and together they read the succinct message. "I'll be gone for a while. Off having some fun for a change. I'll get in touch when I can. Love, Molly."

Very slowly, she straightened. "It was only sent to Natalie, and it doesn't sound at all like me."

"Which is why your sister was worried."

She let out a breath. "Whoever sent that knew that Natalie was the only person who would notice my absence. I mean, my agent and editor, too, but they wouldn't panic if my family didn't, and Natalie's the only family who would."

"So it's someone who knows you." Dare had figured that much all along. He stood and pulled her into his arms. Holding her felt right—and despite the circumstances, it stirred him, because he knew tonight was the night.

Before he did something stupid, he set her away from him. "I told you this wouldn't be easy."

She nodded. "I need to talk to Natalie."

Molly's cell phone had been in her purse, which was now missing, and her landline looked as if someone had stepped on it.

Dare pulled his cell out of his pocket. "Go ahead and call her." Talking to her sister would give her something to think about besides the mess and the note.

"What should I say?"

He shrugged. "Tell her something came up but that you can't go into it over the phone. Ask her to come over." Meeting her sister in person would let him control things and afford him the opportunity to gauge her reaction to Molly's tale. Not that he had any real reason to suspect her sister; she was the only one who'd noted Molly's absence, as far as he could tell. But it was too soon for him to rule out anyone or anything.

Molly put in the call, but after a few seconds she covered the phone. "No answer."

"Don't leave a message. That'll just confuse things." Dare took the phone from her and closed it. "You can call her again later."

Regret had Molly biting her lips, but she accepted his decision. "If she's still on spring break, she could be away from her phone."

Keeping his hands off her wasn't an option. It seemed the more he touched her, the more he needed to. He craved the feel of her skin, the scent of her hair, her warmth and gentleness. It drew him like nothing ever had.

Trying to keep it casual with an arm around her waist, Dare led her from the bedroom. But even that affected him. He could feel her resilient flesh beneath the material of her top, the narrowness of her waist and how she fit so nicely into his side.

"What do we do now?" Molly asked.

"I want to hear about that note, but you're pushing it today. The long trip was enough, but then to find this mess… You need to eat something, drink—"

"Dare, I'm okay," she complained with a short laugh. "And I'm not hungry."

He stopped with her in the kitchen. Smoothing back her hair, he studied her face. She looked pale, stressed and beautiful. "All right." He couldn't keep smothering her.

She was too independent for that. "I'm not really hungry, either. But we might as well sit down to talk."

She looked around at the remaining mess. "I still have so much to do."

"We'll get to it." He cleared a chair and a spot on the table, then urged her to sit. "Take a few breaths, honey."

She did a double take at the endearment. "I really am okay, you know."

"I never doubted it." Her inner strength never ceased to amaze him. She took one blow after another, but always rallied. It was that, as much as anything, that set her apart. "Just humor me."

After ensuring that the carafe wasn't broken, Dare started the coffee prep. He'd noticed where she kept things earlier when he'd checked the kitchen. "While I get this ready, why don't you explain the gist of that note?"

She put her head in her hands. Voice muffled, she said, "It has to do with a book. The one that was so criticized." She raised her face. "You remember what you read in the most scathing comments?"

Dare thought for a second. As he measured coffee into the basket, he recalled the dominant complaint. "You redeemed a character, right?"

Molly nodded. "In the beginning, he did some pretty awful things, mostly out of misguided emotion. He'd had a rough life, and because of that his outlook on certain things was skewed."

"What kind of awful things?"

"He was a thief, a liar. Those sorts of things. He stole cars, credit cards. Definitely crossed the line. But while he was capable of it, he never really hurt anyone physically. Later in the book he realized his mistakes, tried to atone and the lead characters forgave him."

The idea of forgiveness intrigued Dare—maybe

because he, himself, wasn't a very forgiving person. Cross him, and he never forgot, and he sure as hell stopped trusting. "Some readers felt duped."

She gave one short nod. "I guess everyone doesn't buy into second chances the way that I do." As if she had a growing headache, Molly rubbed her temples. "I wouldn't even make the connection, but one reader in particular sent me plenty of emails detailing different, sort-of-threatening scenarios about what it would take to push me past the point of forgiveness. She would always end the setup by asking if I'd still be forgiving if *that* happened to *me*."

"The hell you say." Dare took the seat beside her. "You didn't tell me any of this."

She dismissed that with a look. "It was bad enough that you saw those reviews. And honestly, until now, I really didn't think that much of it. Over the years, I've gotten plenty of scathing letters from readers. It's part and parcel with the job."

"Give me an example."

Keeping her attention on the tabletop, she thought back. "I once had this secondary character who was a father."

Dare could feel her tension with the topic, and he hated it—but he needed details.

"After the character's wife died, he emotionally bailed on his kids. He wasn't there for them at all, didn't see them through the tough times or encourage them."

Had she drawn comparisons with her own father? From what she'd told him, he'd sure as hell neglected his daughters, especially when they needed him most: after their mother had died.

Molly folded her hands together. "He supported them financially, but that was it. I didn't paint him as a total jerk, but neither was his self-absorbed pity written off as acceptable."

"And?"

"A male reader was so outraged by my lack of understanding for what the character had gone through, he threatened my life." Irritation growing, she added, "As if there's ever any excuse for not taking care of your kids."

"No, there's not." Cautious of her mood, Dare asked, "How'd he threaten you?"

"He wrote me a bunch of letters—twenty or more. All of them were angry, some more insane than the others, but his overall theme was that I needed to be shown what it was to feel real loss before I judged anyone else on their own reactions." She made a rude sound. "I didn't tell him that I had lost my mother, so I knew what it felt like to lose a loved one."

"Good." To Dare's mind, it would never be smart to share too much of her private life with her readers. "Anything come of his threats?"

She waved it off. "Not really. I shared the letters with the local police, and they contacted a forensics team. There was some checking done. Other than telling me that the guy was back on his meds, they couldn't say much because it would have infringed on his rights."

Dare scowled. "Fucked-up logic, if you ask me."

"It doesn't matter. I never heard from him after that." Restless, she tapped her fingertips on the tabletop. "Then there was the guy who came to every local signing, and he'd buy the same book over and over again. I don't mean two or three copies, but like…dozens of them. I think in the end he must've owned forty or more copies of one title. It was downright creepy."

Deadpan, Dare said, "He must've really liked the book."

She rolled her eyes. "I finally told him that he had to stop. It was so awkward. For both of us."

"I can imagine." Dare took her hand. "How'd he react to that?"

"He got all flustered and stuff. I think he almost cried. But he didn't show up at any more signings, and as far as I know, he's never written me since then."

"As far as you know?"

"A lot of readers send anonymous letters. They don't sign a name or share an address." Her lips quirked. "Especially the angry ones."

"You say this stuff happens all the time?"

She lifted a shoulder in a halfhearted shrug. "I've gotten immune to it. I mean, I hate upsetting readers, but it's just part of the business. What one reader loves another hates." Her breath released in a sigh. "When that one reader kept telling me that no one would be that forgiving, I just ignored her at first."

"Her?" Dare cocked a brow. "Do you know that it was a woman?"

"Well…" Molly frowned. "Not really, no. Her letters have all been unsigned and unaddressed, too. It's just that most of my readers are women."

"But not all?"

She made a face at him. "Both of the readers I already told you about were guys."

"So let's don't make any assumptions, then." The coffee machine hissed to a finish, and Dare got up to find the mugs.

Molly went to a different cabinet to retrieve powdered creamer. "I don't even want to open my refrigerator. I'm afraid what I might find in there."

Struck by that, Dare looked at her, then went to the fridge.

"I was kidding."

"Might as well find out if we have anything growing." He opened the door, but it wasn't bad at all. "I think your lunchmeat is long gone, and I wouldn't touch the milk or creamer. But everything else should be okay." He closed the door again. "You keep a neat refrigerator. No leftovers."

"Thank God." She doctored her coffee and went back to the table. "Since it's just me, I don't cook much, which means there's seldom anything left to store."

Dare opened a few cabinets but didn't find any snacks.

Apologetic, Molly said, "I'd offer you a cookie or something, but I have no idea what I have anymore."

"Don't worry about it. We'll order in dinner and if necessary shop tomorrow."

Stirring her coffee with a spoon, Molly avoided eye contact. "How long will we be here?"

"Not sure yet." And he wasn't going to get trapped into trying to decide right now, either. "You know, unless you can think of someone that you've had a conflict with lately, your reasoning is as good as anything I can come up with."

"A conflict?"

Dare shrugged. "Maybe someone who you're angry at, who you *won't* forgive?"

Gazes locking, the same thought occurring to them both, they said in unison, "Adrian."

Why the hell hadn't he thought of that sooner? Would her ex have been dumb enough to trash her apartment? Could he have known that Molly was missing?

Could he have arranged her abduction?

Molly scoffed. "No way. I mean, I can't believe it. Not Adrian. He isn't the type to—"

A key sounded in the lock on the front door.

Stunned, they both stared in that direction.

Stumped, Molly asked, "Who—?"

"Quiet." Grabbing her, Dare dragged her down to the floor and behind the kitchen wall, turning off the lights as he went.

Molly's eyes widened when she noticed the gun already in his hand.

"This can't be happening," she whispered.

Dare pressed her back to the wall. "Stay. Put. And damn it, Molly, this time I mean it."

CHAPTER SIXTEEN

MOLLY SWALLOWED HARD as Dare slipped out of the room. Her heart thundered and her flushed skin felt too tight as she waited for a horrible conflict.

The door opened. Male chuckling. The rustle of people coming into the apartment. Female giggling and… smooching.

Her brows knit together. Something about that masculine laugh sounded familiar.

Dare would be so angry at her if she moved, but…she couldn't stop herself.

She peeked around the corner just in time to see Adrian practically fall into the apartment with a very pretty woman. They were all over each other.

In *her* apartment.

Furious, Molly pushed up to her feet almost at the same time that Dare stepped out from behind the couch, the gun aimed at the two intruders.

Oblivious to the danger, Adrian shut the door one-handed, then groaned and grabbed the woman's behind. Shadows enveloped them as they wrapped around each other, fondling, kissing, moving against the wall to grind a little, then stumbling free again.

Amplified by all she'd endured lately, rage boiled inside Molly, threatening to combust. But she stayed put.

She could see Dare's confusion in his stance. He didn't lower the gun, but he did flip on the light.

In an instant, the woman screeched and Adrian jerked around. They both went white.

"Let me guess," Dare said. "Adrian?"

Her idiot ex-fiancé stammered and slumped back to the wall, using it for support. The woman clung to him, horrified, uncertain.

They both looked lit. Drunk or high. Maybe both.

Molly cleared her throat. "Dare?"

Without looking back at her, he said, "Yeah?"

"It's safe enough for me, right?"

He didn't answer right away. "Just a second."

Adrian quailed in fear when Dare strode over to him. Dare held out his hand and said, "Keys."

Adrian handed them over with shaking alacrity.

After pocketing them, Dare frisked Adrian by roughly running his hands over his back, seat, legs and arms. It was unnecessary, Molly was sure, but she didn't stop Dare.

Finding nothing, Dare pushed her ex into a chair.

Molly stepped out of the kitchen. "What are you doing here, Adrian?"

Finally seeing her, Adrian shot to his feet. "Molly, thank God!"

Dare shoved him back in the chair so hard it almost overturned. *"Sit."*

Alarmed, Adrian looked toward her for help, and seeing her calm and collected helped him to calm down, too. As his panic receded, his surroundings sank in, and he noticed the state of the apartment. "Good God, Molly. What did you do?"

Dare said to him, "Just shut up." He turned to the woman, giving her a once-over.

Adrian's latest conquest wore very little, just a scanty, very tight black dress that showed a yard of cleavage and mile-high legs in open-toed heels. Tumbled bleach-blond hair and painted lips gave her the look of a starlet wannabe.

Dare moved toward her.

And Molly snapped, "Dare!"

He hesitated but didn't take his gaze off the woman. "What?"

Heat crawled up her neck. Talk about awkward.

But damn it, she didn't care. Molly filled her lungs with righteous umbrage. "I do *not* want your hands on her."

A heavy pause settled over the room. Dare slanted a fleeting look her way. "Because?"

Because… If he ran his hands over that overblown, on-display body, Molly would… Well, she didn't know what she'd do. Her jaw hurt from all the teeth-clenching she'd done lately. "I wouldn't like it."

He glanced toward her, and Molly saw the faintest sign of humor in his expression. "What she's wearing is so tight, I can't see how she'd be hiding a weapon anyway."

"Well…good." God, she felt ridiculous.

Dare held out a hand to the woman. "Give me your purse."

She handed it over.

Dare stepped away from them both. "Well, Molly?" He reached out a hand to her. "I'm just dying for an introduction."

Yeah, she could imagine. But it was sort of embarrassing for Dare to meet her creep of an ex under these circumstances.

Joining Dare in his stance before the intruders, Molly crossed her arms and tapped her foot. "What are you doing here, Adrian?"

He opened his mouth, glanced at the blonde and snapped it shut again.

Very blasé, Dare asked Molly, "Want me to beat it out of him?"

"I'm thinking about it," Molly said, and she prayed Dare was just joking.

Adrian couldn't make that assumption. "You haven't been here."

"It'd be hard for me not to notice where I have or haven't been, Adrian. What does that have to do with anything?"

He shook his head, keeping a watchful eye on Dare as if he expected him to attack at any minute.

Dare did make a rather imposing figure with his height, his muscle and that not-too-happy expression on his face. Not to mention the gun still in his hands.

For her part, the blonde stood there with her mouth shut tight.

Adrian licked his lips. "You sort of…disappeared."

"How do you know she wasn't here?" Dare asked.

"Her sister has been driving everyone insane, looking for her." And then to Molly, "But no one knew where you were, and when you didn't answer your calls, even on your cell, I thought maybe you had…abandoned the place."

"And you thought…what?" Molly couldn't fathom his reason for being in her apartment. "That you'd just move in?"

"No, of course not. I have my own place." He looked at the blonde, sat forward and appealed to Molly. "You know how private I am with my place."

"Private?"

"Yeah, I don't…" He glanced at the blonde again, and now she looked back, her brows starting to bunch together. "I like to keep my personal life freed up."

"You're not making any sense," Dare told him. "Just spit it out, will you?"

Showing some backbone, Adrian glared at him. "It's never good policy to take a one-night stand into your home. Everyone knows that."

The blonde said, "One-night stand?"

Molly's brain froze up at that awful thought. "You were coming here to have sex? In *my* apartment?" Her stomach recoiled and she yelled, *"In my bed?"*

With a shrug, Adrian said, "Yeah."

Molly launched herself at him, but Dare caught her with an arm around her waist. Adrian scrambled out of the chair and got behind it.

"You son of a bitch!"

Dare chuckled.

That infuriated Molly enough that she brought her elbow back hard into Dare's ribs. He stopped laughing but didn't loosen his hold on her.

"Settle down."

"I will, after I kill him."

Truly alarmed again, Adrian excused his behavior by saying, "I thought you were gone!"

"And you thought I'd never come back, you jackass? Is that it?" She redoubled her effort to get to him, which only caused Dare to lift her off her feet. "Are you the one responsible for this? Are you?"

"Easy," Dare cautioned.

His hold wasn't painful, but Molly knew she only looked foolish flailing around, trying to free herself when that wouldn't happen.

She couldn't really imagine Adrian orchestrating a kidnapping and transport over the border, but at the moment, she wanted it to be him. "Put me down," she told Dare.

He did, immediately. But he kept his arm around her and even gave her a warning squeeze.

Breathing hard, Molly said to Dare, "Do your thing, whatever it is, because I want him out of here, the sooner the better."

Dare released her and stepped in front of her to speak to Adrian. "You felt comfortable coming into her home, assuming she wouldn't be back to catch you at it. Why?"

"Molly never leaves without telling her sister. Since Natalie didn't know anything about it, I assumed she'd gone off to find herself or something. I called her cell but didn't get an answer." He shrugged. "If she was here, she would have picked up."

Dare crossed his arms. "How'd you get in?"

"The first night I dropped by, the door was unlocked."

Incredulous, Molly peered around Dare and repeated, "The *first* time?"

Dare moved to block her again. "Go on."

Uncertain, it took Adrian a few seconds to find his voice. "I found her keys in the kitchen, and, like any good friend, I locked her door."

"And kept the keys so you could get back in?"

"I…ah…"

"Look," the blonde suddenly said. "I have nothing to do with whatever's going on here. I only met the jerk tonight."

Adrian's mood went from scared to belligerent. "Shut up, Sally."

"You shut up!" Flouncing, she went to Adrian and poked him hard in the chest. "You're a miserable liar. You misrepresented yourself."

His lip curled. "Yeah, like you were all that discerning anyway?"

Fuming, Sally drew back and slapped him hard enough to unbalance him.

He stumbled, regained his balance and, with a feral growl, reached for Sally.

Before he could touch her, Dare caught his wrist. With only a simple shake of his head, Dare reined him in.

Satisfied, Sally gave her attention back to Molly. "So, can I have my purse? I'd like to get out of here."

Molly handed it over to her. "I'm sorry about this."

Dare gave her an incredulous look.

Molly ignored him. It wasn't Sally's fault that Adrian had duped her into a possible criminal act. "Do you need to call a cab?"

Sally put her nose in the air. "I have my cell phone with me."

Fretting, Molly said, "It's not really all that safe out front."

But the woman didn't agree. "It's not all that safe in here, either, so I'll take my chances." After another scathing look at Adrian, who smiled sickly in return, she headed for the door.

Dare stepped in front of her. She stopped short of plowing into his chest and, very slowly, put her head back to look up at him.

Dare didn't smile. "Are you a smart girl, Sally?"

She cast a quick glance at Molly, but Molly knew better than to interfere.

Seeing no help forthcoming, Sally stared up at Dare. "I like to think so."

"Good." Now Dare smiled, but it wasn't with humor.

In fact, to Molly, it looked outright threatening. Poor Sally. She could only imagine what the girl felt.

"You were never here, Sally. This never happened." Dare's eyes narrowed the smallest bit. "You got that?"

Her blond curls bobbed with her fast but uncertain nod. "Absolutely. I went straight from the club to home."

After a long, assessing look, Dare must have believed her, because he stepped out of her way and even opened the door for her.

Sulking, Adrian watched her leave. When the door shut, he let out a pent-up breath and turned back to Molly. "So." He tried to brazen it out. "What now?"

"Now you answer some questions." Dare's quiet tone did nothing to lessen the implied menace. "And unless I'm satisfied that your biggest transgression is trespassing, I just might take you apart."

"You're *threatening* me?"

Surely that was a redundant question, Molly thought. Adrian wasn't stupid.

"I'm explaining things to you," Dare said, "so there won't be any confusion."

"Well, your explanation doesn't help." A touch of panic raised the octave of Adrian's complaint. "I still don't have any idea what the hell is going on."

Molly took great pleasure in stepping around Dare and confronting Adrian close up. "You want to know why I wasn't here, Adrian?"

"Uh…yes? I suppose that's as good a start as any."

He didn't sound very sure of himself. But then, he never did. The stark differences between him and Dare were too many to count. Dare stood there, ready to do whatever was necessary to help her get her life straightened out. He had walked into danger for her without hesitation and without fear. All Adrian wanted was a quick escape from possible harm.

One man was a hero, the other a coward.

Shaking her head, Molly pondered aloud, "What did I ever see in you, Adrian?"

Dare snorted. "I was just wondering the same thing."

That insulted Adrian. "I'm a hell of a good catch!"

"No." Molly shook her head. "You were just…handy. A convenient companion. Handsome, yes. Educated. But now…now I can't believe that I was ever so dumb, or so desperate."

Dare frowned down at her. "You were desperate?"

She couldn't explain to Dare. Not here, not now. He was so independent, so capable and secure in his ability, he would never understand a woman's need to find the right man, to secure her future happiness, to have babies and a family and love everlasting.

Molly knew that she'd always wanted more than Adrian. Not better looking or richer, but someone with real honor, someone faithful and brave and…everything that was Dare.

But in thirty years, she hadn't met that person. She'd met others like Adrian. Some better-looking but not as settled. Some kinder but without means of support. She sighed.

Dare watched her, so she hedged by asking, "You don't think Adrian is handsome?"

Distaste narrowed his eyes. "Now you're just fucking with me."

The laugh surprised her; in the middle of so much turmoil, Dare could still do that for her.

Grinning, she said, "Now, Dare. He's not as tall as you, but he's tall enough." She pretended to examine Adrian. "He's not as muscular as you, either, but he takes care of himself."

Red-faced and outraged, Adrian said, "I go to the gym every damn day!"

"Blond hair," Molly continued, "green eyes, a nice

smile." Why she teased Dare, she didn't know. But with him looking so resentful over her past relationship, she couldn't seem to help herself. "And when Adrian wants, he can be pretty charismatic."

"Yeah, I bet." On to her, Dare took an aggrieved stance and flattened his mouth. "You finished now?"

She tried to hide her smile. It seemed a million years ago that she had settled for steady dating, good looks, intelligence and a pleasant personality. But now she knew something about her own strengths. Now she knew that she could get through just about anything.

Never again would a man of Adrian's ilk be good enough for her. She deserved it all.

She deserved… Dare.

"Yes." Now that she'd come to that conclusion, she felt more at peace than she had in a very long time. She patted Dare's chest. "I'm done."

The look he gave her was long and intimate. He took her hand in his own and kissed her knuckles before he turned back to Adrian.

Flummoxed, Molly stared at Dare's profile. She sensed there was some significance behind that tender kiss, but she wasn't sure of the meaning.

Dare brought her back around with a stark statement. "She was kidnapped."

"*What?*" Adrian looked from Molly to Dare and back again. His gaze sharpened on the lingering bruises visible on her face and arms. "Dear God."

Judging Adrian's reaction to that, Dare continued, saying, "Men grabbed her from right out front of this apartment."

He shook his head. "But *why?*"

As Dare took a step closer, Adrian backed up a step.

"They stuffed her into the back of a van, transported

her across the damn country and then took her over the border into Tijuana."

"Tijuana?"

The genuine, undiluted shock on Adrian's face convinced Molly one hundred percent that he had nothing to do with her kidnapping. He was a snake, but he wasn't a criminal of that caliber.

"When I found her," Dare told him, "she was chained to the wall of an airless hut, half-starved, drugged and abused."

Eyes bugging, Adrian struggled to lift his slackened jaw. "But that...that's not possible. Not here." He pointed at Molly. "Not *her.*"

Dare advanced again, and Adrian ended up with his back to the wall. "Why not her?"

"It doesn't make any sense, that's why. She's not a politician's daughter or a starlet or a wealthy heir." His eyes bugged again. "Aren't women taken across the border to sell as sex slaves or something?"

"More often than you'd like to think."

Clearly baffled that anyone would take Molly for that purpose, Adrian shook his head. "You said you found her there." His brows knit as he struggled to piece it all together. "What were you doing there? And what do you have to do with any of this?"

"I got her out of there." They were now almost chest to chest.

"But...how?"

"It's what I do."

In a sudden turnaround, Adrian's expression lightened and became shrewd. "Let me understand this. You rescue people...for compensation?"

Crossing his arms over his chest and looking down

his nose at Adrian, Dare said, "That's how it usually works."

"No fucking way!" Adrian shoved against Dare, but didn't budge him at all. "I see what this is now. You want me to pay her ransom, don't you?" Rage distorted his better sense, and he pointed past Dare to Molly. "She *dropped* me. Did she tell you that?"

"She mentioned it," Dare said, very deadpan.

"So I'm not responsible for her!"

"Not at all."

Adrian continued to fume. "I don't have that kind of money, and she knows it. If you thought to squeeze me for payment, well, then, you can damn well forget it."

A stillness filled the room as Dare expanded in fury, and Molly held her breath.

Too stupid to sense his own peril, Adrian added, "What happens to her now is no concern of mine."

CHAPTER SEVENTEEN

OH, GOD, THAT WAS LOW even for Adrian. Molly wanted to kill him. Again.

She charged forward, but stumbled to a halt when Dare's harsh, low voice sounded with the impact of an exploding bomb.

"You think, even for one fucking second, that I would take your goddamned money?"

Wow. Molly blinked at that lethal tone.

Smashing up against Adrian, Dare looked more enraged than Molly had ever seen him.

"You think I'd even let you be in her life?"

"I…" Intimidated, belatedly realizing his error, Adrian tried to appeal to Molly for help.

Still peeved, she silently mouthed the words *Fuck. You.*

Shocked, Adrian returned his attention to Dare. "That's fine," he soothed. He turned his face to the side, trying to escape Dare's deadly stare. "That…that's what I was saying. That I don't want to be in her life. I swear."

"Did you want out of it enough to coordinate this stunt?"

"*What?* No!" Alarmed, he smashed farther back against the wall. "I own a bar, that's all. Damn it, Molly, tell him that I'm not a kidnapper."

"I don't know," she hedged, examining a nail. "I didn't know you were the type to weasel into my apartment, either, but here you are." A thought occurred to her, and she looked up. "Did you have sex in my bed?"

"No!"

Unsatisfied, she narrowed her eyes. "But you would have?"

"Well...yeah. Probably."

Still not giving Adrian any room to breathe, Dare asked Molly, "What do you want me to do with him?"

Implicit in the question was that he'd pulverize Adrian if she wished it.

Just to make Adrian squirm, she pretended to think about it. But she wasn't a person who condoned unnecessary violence, and neither was Dare. Still, she appreciated his offer.

"You can let him go."

Dare didn't move. "You sure, honey?"

He called her honey again. It thrilled her, but this was no time for celebration. Molly cleared her throat and her thundering emotions. "Yes, of course. Come on, Dare, we both know that you don't hurt those smaller, weaker or *dumber* than you."

Dare stepped back, but he said, "For him, I'd make an exception."

Slumping against the wall, knees shaky, Adrian struggled to gather himself. "I'm sorry. I didn't mean... It's just that I don't have that kind of money...."

"You're broke, I know." Dare shook his head in disgust. "Now shut up."

"He's broke?"

It was almost comical, how quickly Adrian nodded agreement. "The business is struggling. Financially, I'm in over my head. I definitely don't have the kind of funds it'd take to set up a kidnapping this elaborate. I swear I don't."

Molly took a seat on the couch, not really surprised by that news. Adrian spent well out of his means—that was one reason he'd wanted *her* to buy him things. "When you first came here, Adrian, how did my apartment look?"

"Like it always looks." Keeping an eye on Dare, he inched over to a chair and dropped into it.

"It wasn't trashed like this?"

"No." He looked around again. "You didn't do it?"

So dense. "Now, why would I destroy my own apartment?"

"I have no idea." Shoulders slumping, he ran a hand through his blond hair. After a moment, his gaze lifted to Molly. Chagrined, he asked softly, "You're okay?"

His concern was too little, too late, to be anything but disingenuous. "I'll survive, yes."

He continued to search her face. "Why the hell did this happen?"

"That's what we're still trying to find out." She appreciated it that Dare stood beside her but didn't insist on taking the lead. As much as he openly disliked Adrian, he let her do the talking.

She knew that if she needed him to, he'd take over for her. But he trusted her to handle this, and that meant a lot. Molly leaned forward, her elbows on her knees, to give Adrian a direct look. "Until I know who set up this whole thing, I won't be safe."

That lifted his frown into high-browed surprise. "You mean it could happen again?" He glanced over at Dare. "That's why he's still with you?"

Molly wasn't sure how to answer that, but then, she didn't need to.

"Why I'm here is none of your damn business," Dare told him. "Just know that I *will* find the one responsible, so if you know anything, anything at all, you'd be smart to say so right now."

To placate Dare, Adrian held up both hands. "I think I've already proven that I value my own hide too much to lie." He smiled with self-mockery. "In all honesty, I wish I could help. Molly and I had our differences, but I never wanted to see her hurt." And then to Molly, "I hope you know that."

"You only wanted my money."

Annoyance distorted his concern, and he shot back, "You had more than enough to spend! But no, you were too tight-fisted for a measly gift."

Dare shifted, giving Adrian pause. He said quickly, "No offense intended."

Bearing no expression at all, Dare warned, "Don't insult her again."

Molly patted Dare's arm. In this, she didn't need his defense.

"Look," Adrian said, "all I know is that Natalie called me to ask where you were."

"Why would she call you?" That made no sense to Molly.

"Hell if I know. I told her that we weren't together anymore and she said she already knew that, but she'd gotten an odd email about an extended trip you were taking, and she hoped I could tell her something about it. She said she'd called Kathi, and Kathi didn't know where you were, either."

So Kathi had known she was missing? Dare said he'd talked to her father. Did that mean that Kathi hadn't mentioned it to him? Maybe because she thought nothing of it, but maybe…her dad had already known.

Was he capable of doing this to her? She was sad to have to admit to the truth: her father was capable of just about anything. She wasn't yet convinced that he'd done this, but neither would she rule out his involvement.

Molly sat back in the couch, thinking of all the odd angles. "So, since I was missing, you decided to just come to my apartment and pretend it was your own?"

Adrian had the good grace to show shame. "At first, I was only curious. It's not like you to take off without telling your sister." To Dare, he said, "They're really close."

Dare just bored holes in him with his dark stare.

Adrian looked away uneasily. "Anyway, I guess I pictured you making up the trip story for your sister, while you were here, wallowing in misery, maybe…missing me?" He tried a sickly, unsure smile. "I was sort of hoping that we might have a chance to get back together."

Putting a hand on Dare to restrain him—just in case—Molly gritted out, "Are you out of your mind?" Before he could answer, she held up a hand, silencing him. "If you were the last man on earth, I would embrace celibacy with gusto."

Adrian scowled at the insult.

And Dare emphasized, "Won't ever happen, so don't even think about it."

He accepted that as the warning Dare meant it to be. "Fine, but I figured if you were here and just not up to visiting with your sister, it couldn't hurt for me to try. When I came by, your landlord grabbed me because your mail had stacked up. I guess she didn't know we'd split, and she wanted me to bring it in."

"Other than telling Natalie, I didn't advertise our breakup." To Molly's mind, her personal life wasn't anyone's business.

"Right." Adrian continued to glance at Dare. "Anyway, she didn't think anything of me being here."

"Since you let yourself in, she must've assumed you still had a key."

Adrian shrugged. "Probably."

Dare spoke up. "Have you talked with Bishop?"

"Not since Molly and I split, no."

"Good. Don't."

"Do you know him?" He looked from Dare to Molly again, as if he wasn't sure who would answer him.

"I met him." Dare couldn't hide his distaste. "I told him exactly what I'm going to tell you."

Cautious now, Adrian said, "And that is?"

"Keep your mouth shut." Dare went to him and took him by the arm, pulled him to his feet and started him toward the door. "Don't mention this little meet and greet to anyone. Far as you know, Molly is still missing. You got that?"

"Yeah, sure." He looked back at Molly. "If there's some way I can help—"

Molly followed Dare. "You can stay away from my apartment for starters."

"Right." When Dare released him, he started to turn toward Molly.

Dare didn't give him the chance. He opened the door and shoved Adrian out to the hall.

"Wait! What do I tell her sister if she calls me again?"

"You have nothing to tell, right?"

The clear warning hit the mark. "Well…yeah, I know." Still Adrian waffled. "But—"

"Molly will be in touch with her sister and anyone else she wants to update. It's no concern of yours. Remember that." Dare shut the door in his face and then locked it.

Molly bit back a smile. "That was almost mean."

For long seconds, he stood there staring at her. This was a new look for him, one she hadn't seen before. He had that same intensity as when enraged, but she knew he wasn't truly angry over anything. The way he watched her made her feel...warm.

And aware. And...excited.

"Dare?"

"How do you feel, Molly?"

The gravelly tone to his low voice stroked along her nerve endings. The spark of heat in his blue eyes, and the slow rise and fall of his muscled chest, took the strength from her knees.

"I'm good."

"Not just fine?"

God, was he teasing her? Like a patient predator waiting to pounce, he kept his distance by the door.

Molly licked her bottom lip. "I..." She looked around at her still messy apartment, knowing it didn't matter. Everything else could wait. But she couldn't.

She turned back to Dare's probing gaze. After a deep breath, she said, "If you want the truth, I'm eaten up with wanting you."

He straightened his posture against the door. His shoulders flexed.

Voice rough and raw, he asked, "Are you sure, Molly?" And then, more harshly, "Tell me you're sure."

Seeing him like this, recognizing the lust, affected her, and she couldn't think of anything to say. Instead, she opened her arms to him.

A low curse, barely audible, left him. In the next instant he had his powerful arms around her. He pulled her up against his body, kissing her hard enough, hungrily enough, to tip her head back.

And Molly loved it.

DARE WAS NOT A MAN to lose control, but the things she made him feel... He wasn't used to being jealous, but, damn, he had been. Red-hot and enraged with jealousy, and for no other reason than that Molly had once cared for Adrian. Dare thought about taking the fool apart, and he would have, except that it hardly seemed fair. Her ex was pathetic.

What the hell had she ever seen in him?

And then seeing her so strong, so proud... It had damn near put him over the edge. Never before had he thought about the perfect female counterpart to him, but now he knew: Molly defined that woman.

He struggled to get it together, but she didn't help much. The taste of her, the way her fingertips dug into his shoulders with insistence, and how she lifted into him, pressing into his erection, made rational thought a far-fetched thing.

But he knew what she'd been through, the marks that she still carried and the memories that continued to haunt her. Never would he add to that. He'd sooner die.

"Molly." Dare opened his mouth on her throat, sucked on her soft, fragrant skin and lowered one hand to her ass. He loved the feel of that firm, plump flesh, kneading her, stroking. "We should slow down," he said against her throat, "I should slow down."

"No. Please don't." She grabbed his face and brought his mouth back to hers. "No more waiting, Dare."

"No." Hell, he couldn't wait. The need to consume her pushed him.

But he had to know.

Holding her shoulders, he put enough space between them to talk. "The bedroom is okay?"

She nodded, but then paused and asked, "What do you mean?"

"No…" Fuck, he hated this. "Your asshole boyfriend was here, and we both know he intended to use your bed, so…"

Her expression softened. "Forget Adrian. I don't think he did anything in there." She took Dare's hand and turned to lead him to the room.

He was so charmed by her urgency that he grinned. Lust and humor—who knew? He'd never experienced the combo before.

Molly's long, fast steps did amazing things to that delectable backside that he'd just been pawing, and he had to say, with heartfelt sincerity, "You have an incredible ass, Molly."

She smiled at him over her shoulder and tugged him into the room. "Thank you."

He stood in front of her, the bed right there, her need obvious. Damn, but his hands shook with the wealth of everything he felt. He'd known extreme lust, but he hadn't known this.

Smoothing her hair back, he bent to kiss her forehead, her cheek, her chin and finally her mouth. "I've thought of seeing you, all of you, a hundred times." He dropped his fingers to the top button of her blouse.

She kept her head down, watching his hands as he opened the blouse little by little. When he reached the button between her breasts, she sucked in a shuddering breath.

"Dare?"

He kissed her temple, slipped the last button free and opened the blouse. "Hmm?" Damn, she was sexy.

"I still have…marks."

"I know." He stroked the back of one finger over a bruise visible on her ribs. "I'd like to kill them all over again. But they're already gone, honey."

"It's not that. I just…they look awful."

He slipped the blouse off her shoulders and let it drop to the floor. "Nothing about you is awful." Bending, he kissed the angriest bruise left on her right shoulder. "And I won't let anyone ever hurt you again." To get her back where she needed to be, Dare kissed his way along her upper body, over her shoulders, her collarbone, her throat. Every so often, he gave her a gentle love bite and then soothed it with a soft openmouthed kiss and the stroke of his tongue.

Holding on to his forearms, Molly tipped her head back. His hands easily spanned the width of her narrow back. Holding her like that, he arched her up and closed his mouth over her left nipple through her bra.

Her vibrating groan tested his resolve, but he held on. Barely. While he teased her, he teased himself, too, by grinding his erection against her soft body.

She sucked in a breath. "Dare?" Her right hand left his forearm and went to his abdomen, then down along the fly of his jeans.

Through the denim she found and stroked him, making him nuts.

"That…" He went still, his stomach clenching. "That might not be a great idea." But God, he didn't stop her.

Calculating as only a woman could be, Molly whispered with pleasure, "You're even bigger than I imagined."

Fuck patience. "Tease." Dare opened her bra and pushed the cups down to expose her. Her heavy breasts, now freed of restraint, swayed with her every movement. Her nipples were soft pink in color, pulled tight.

Growling with impatience, Dare pried her hand off his dick so that he could remove the bra completely, and he could have sworn that he heard her laugh.

It didn't matter. She wouldn't be amused for long.

Going to his knees, he opened the snap on her jeans, slid down the zipper and tugged both the jeans and her panties to her knees.

"Dare." Sounding strangled, she braced her hands on his shoulders. "What are you—?"

Holding her backside in both hands, he pulled her close and pressed his face against her. He inhaled her scent and growled again. "I can't wait."

As he came back to his feet, she said something, but he wasn't sure what. Lifting her up and onto the bed, Dare stripped the clothes from her body.

Even though his gaze wanted to linger on her breasts and puckered nipples, her smooth belly and that neat triangle of dark pubic hair, he still saw the bruises. In stark contrast to her pale, soft skin, they were impossible to miss. They just didn't matter, not to how he felt about her, how much he wanted her.

As the marks healed, they turned muddied shades of yellow and green. But they *were* healing. Molly would be okay.

He didn't find the injuries ugly, as she did. If anything, they only served to remind him that when he'd carried her out of that place, he'd taken responsibility for her. She relied on him now.

She was his.

With one hand he touched the sleek silky skin of her upper thigh, while with the other he opened his jeans and eased the zipper down over his hard-on. He had to step back to get his shoes and socks off, and then he stripped off his shirt and tossed it aside.

Knees together in a modest—and enticing—pose, Molly rose up to her elbows to watch him.

He shucked off the jeans and straightened in front of

her. If she enjoyed looking at him half as much as he liked seeing her, he had no problem with that.

But the longer she looked, the more he wanted her. And she was taking her time, studying every inch of him.

"You've seen men before, Molly."

Slowly shaking her head to deny that, she whispered, "I've never seen a man like you."

What the hell did that mean? Given the way she held her bottom lip in her teeth, and how her gaze went all soft and heated, it wasn't a complaint. "I don't want to rush you, honey, but how long should I stand here?"

"It just occurred to me," she said, her gaze still on his cock. "I don't have anything. I mean, for protection."

That was her holdup? He didn't think so. "I'll take care of it."

Did she think, even for a second, that he wouldn't do the responsible thing? Or was she hesitating out of nervousness?

He retrieved a lone condom from his wallet; for now, it would do. But after that, he'd get the box from his duffel bag. To be sure, he asked her, "Anything else?"

Her gaze lifted to his, and she licked her lips. "Just… hurry up."

Smiling, Dare said, "Right." He should have known that she wasn't the type to hide her feelings. If she had second thoughts, she'd have told him so.

As he took precautions, she watched him with so much fascination that maintaining control wasn't easy. He wanted no secrets between them, no modesty or shyness. The light on her desk was enough, and he was relieved that she didn't ask him to turn it off.

Dare stretched out over her, and as her legs parted he settled against her with a feeling of rightness. He'd had sex; this was more.

While he again explored her lush breasts and taut nipples, he kissed her. She accepted his tongue, even sucked on it, making him nuts with lust. Her hands were all over him, from his back to his ass and thighs, and back up to his shoulders. She seemed every bit as urgent as him.

In minutes, they were both breathing hard and fast. Not moving proved impossible for him, especially with her so soft and giving beneath him, squirming each time he tugged on a nipple with his fingertips or nibbled on her earlobe.

When he first rolled his hips against her, she freed her mouth and moaned. Just as she had on the dock, she went hot and ready with blazing speed. Moving to the side of her, Dare slid his hand down along her body until it rested low on her belly.

"You are so small, and so sweet." He rubbed his cheek against her breast. "But not small here. God almighty, woman, you have a killer body."

Raising her hands over her head, her eyes closed, Molly clenched in anticipation. He loved looking at her, at the honest reactions on her face.

Watching her, he asked, "Are you wet, Molly?"

She nodded, then arched, trying to hurry him.

Teasing her was so hot, so sexy, that it slowed him down enough. He wanted to take his time and relish this. He didn't want to miss a single moan or sigh.

"Let me see," he whispered, and he cupped his hand over her.

Her fingers knotted in the sheet at either side of her head. She looked at him with dazed eyes and honest need. So beautiful. So real.

While he stroked over her, parting her, exploring her with just his fingertips, he bent and slowly sucked on one nipple. She twisted beneath him, breathing hard and fast.

With his teeth this time, Dare tugged on her nipple, and she cried out.

He chose that moment to relentlessly press two fingers into her, as deeply as he could.

The way her body clasped his fingers, the low sounds of raw pleasure she made, told him how she liked that. But it wasn't enough for him.

While he eased his fingers out, and then back into her, he kissed each nipple again, and then her ribs. When he trailed a path of damp kisses down her abdomen, she went still—maybe with expectation, maybe with uncertainty.

It didn't matter.

He dipped his tongue into her navel, making her squirm more, then over to her hipbone. A ticklish spot for her.

Liking that, he stored the knowledge away into his memory banks with plans to investigate it more later.

Right now, he wanted to taste her. He wanted to hear her cry out, feel her reaction, when he took her into his mouth, replaced his fingers with his tongue.

Already, her heady scent had ripened, sweet and rich. The strongest aphrodisiac for any man was a woman's arousal. For Dare, Molly's arousal amplified the effect tenfold because, in so many ways, she was special.

When she tangled her fingers in his hair, urgently holding on to him, he decided this had to be the biggest turn-on ever.

Nuzzling against her, her small cries filling his head, Dare licked over her turgid clitoris. She almost shot off the bed. Pleased with that reaction, he braced a forearm over her midsection to keep her still, teased with his tongue again—and then closed his mouth around her to gently suck.

The second he tasted her, he wanted to come.

Molly did, too.

Her deep rumbling groan said more than words could. She arched her back; her legs trembled. She moved against him, squeezing the fingers he kept deep inside her as her climax swelled, crested and wracked through her. The sounds she made were almost as good as the sweet taste of her.

Dare kept her there, at the peak, relishing every second of her, until she groaned and pressed back into the mattress.

Lifting his head, he looked up the length of her body to her face. Eyes closed, cheekbones damp, chest still heaving, she lay utterly limp. Slowly, he eased his fingers from her and then put them into his mouth. He closed his eyes, too, loving the intimacy, loving…

His heart damn near stopped.

He looked up at Molly again and found her watching him in sated amazement—and something more, something that unsettled him.

His whole body on fire, Dare rushed up over her. Pushed by turbulent emotion, he caught her face and kissed her hard. She gasped and then accepted his tongue again. The need to devour her pushed him. He reached down and, clasping a knee, spread her legs wide.

Still kissing her, unable to get enough to appease him, he situated himself. He could feel her, open, warm and wet, against the head of his cock, and it was enough to make him lock his teeth. He had to pause to get control.

No way in hell would he risk hurting her.

Leashing his tattered discipline, struggling to be gentle, he rocked into her. Small, tight and…perfect.

His head swam. Emotion mingled with carnality, leaving him blindsided. Molly wrapped around him, cocooning him in her scent and the feel of her. He savored the way she hugged him so tightly and the way she met his every thrust with the rise of her hips.

Dare put one hand beneath that delectable ass and lifted her even more so he could go deeper, so she'd take all of him.

In no time at all, it put her over the edge again. She freed her mouth to gasp and groan, her head back, her hair spread out around her.

Seeing her like that, feeling each contraction on his cock, did him in. "Look at me, Molly."

Lips parted, face flushed, she opened her eyes and shared everything with him. It was enough. Almost too much.

He drove into her, groaned, and at the last second took her mouth again as he gained his own volatile release.

Minutes later, Dare eased to his back beside her. Even as his heart still raced and his legs stayed shaky, his thoughts scrambled in an effort to sort out everything he felt. Dominant in those feelings was a need to cement his odd relationship with her.

He dropped a forearm over his eyes.

Hell, Molly still thought she'd be paying him for his protection. Did she also think that once he secured her safety, they'd be done? He snorted at that repugnant thought.

Molly stirred, turned to her side to cuddle against him and settled back into a deep sleep.

Looking down at her in amazement, Dare frowned… but when her breathing evened into a light snore, the frown turned into a grin. Apparently she didn't suffer the same confusion plaguing him. Given all she'd been through, he was glad.

He put his head back against the mattress and wondered what spell Molly Alexander had put on him. Because he sure as hell didn't feel like himself anymore.

CHAPTER EIGHTEEN

UNABLE TO SLEEP, Dare grew antsy. Taking care not to disturb Molly, he slipped out of the bed. Before he went into the bathroom he lifted the tangled covers over her. He'd left her crossways in the bed, her feet hanging over the side, but that didn't seem to interfere with her tiredness.

Seeing her like that, so peaceful, made his heart clutch anew. He noticed that her now-swollen lips were tipped up in a slight smile. God knew the woman didn't have much to smile about lately. Her innocence and optimism charmed him, burned him, brought out all his protective instincts and other less comfortable emotions that he barely recognized.

Turning away from the bed, Dare picked up his jeans and went into her bathroom. The space was small, but it didn't feel cramped. He disposed of the condom, washed up and pulled on his jeans. Curiosity got to him, and he opened her medicine cabinet. A few routine over-the-counter drugs sat with a prescription for birth-control pills. She'd missed two weeks' worth, of course, so condoms remained necessary. But the idea of being inside her without barriers...

He closed the cabinet and took a moment to clear his head. Inside a vanity drawer he found a few makeup items, a variety of hair brushes and combs, typical feminine hair adornments. The idea of Molly with a clip in her hair teased his senses and left him grinning for no reason at all.

Turning to the tub, he lifted the pastel-colored soap and breathed in the scent of hyacinth. He could imagine Molly soaking in that old-fashioned tub, covered in fragrant bubbles. But nothing smelled as good as her bare skin, her soft hair—and her excitement.

Damn it, he'd just taken her. She'd opened herself to him completely.

But it wasn't enough.

All he could think now was that he wanted more. A lot more. More hot sex, the full-body contact of her cuddling afterward, more talking and laughing and learning together…

Now what was he supposed to do?

MOLLY AWOKE TO AN empty bed. She reached out for Dare but felt nothing. Sitting up, she realized that the room was now dark with only a sliver of light coming from beneath the bedroom door.

She started to slide out from under the covers—and she heard it again. The noise that had awakened her: a key in the front door. *Again.*

Suddenly the light in the other room disappeared, leaving her in utter darkness.

What was Dare doing?

Heart in her throat, Molly slipped out of the bed and pulled a blanket around her. Padding barefoot, she went to the bedroom door, slowly turned the knob and opened it oh-so-quietly.

Her gaze scanned the dim living room. Enough moonlight filtered in the windows for her to see that Dare had been working. He was such a neat freak that the mess of her apartment must have made it impossible for him to sleep.

Or maybe, his lust appeased, he just hadn't been interested in staying that close to her.

That thought hurt, so she pushed it aside and instead concentrated on seeing the room. She noted that the overturned table had been righted and her mail neatly stacked.

She didn't see Dare.

Before she could worry too much about that, the front doorknob turned. As the door opened, it screeched in that familiar way.

Hushed voices came from the outer hallway, right outside the door, whispering, maybe even teasing.

Around niggling fear, Molly frowned in vague recognition. One voice almost sounded like—

The door swung open and there was a sudden rush. Her sister squealed, and a loud thump sounded, followed by a curse.

Hurrying out of the bedroom, Molly shouted, "Natalie!" She flipped on a light—and froze.

Sure enough, she'd recognized her sister's voice, even in a whisper. As if tossed there, Natalie sprawled in an easy chair, unhurt but stunned.

In the middle of the floor, Dare pinned down a man almost as big as him. He kept his gun barrel pressed hard against the stranger's jaw.

With the lights on, Natalie saw the gun and screamed. "Oh, my God! What are you doing? Who are you?"

Dare didn't take his gaze off his captive. With a nod of his head toward Molly, he said, "I'm with her."

As her sister and the man glanced at her, Molly gave a loose finger wave.

Dare nudged the man. "Who are *you?*"

His mouth flattened. Nodding his head toward Natalie, he said, "I'm with her."

Dare frowned.

Natalie scrambled from the chair in what Molly recognized as "attack mode."

"Wait." Molly had no idea what was going on, or who the man on the floor might be, but she wouldn't allow her sister to jump Dare.

She didn't want her sister to get hurt.

"Everyone, just chill a second, please."

"Easier said than done," the man beneath Dare quipped.

The stranger kept his palms, at either side of his head, open and nonthreatening. But something about the way he stared back at Dare made Molly uneasy.

Dare didn't move—which meant he didn't hurt the guy, but neither did he let him up.

Molly pulled the blanket tighter. "Dare, this is my sister, Natalie."

"Don't hurt him," Natalie warned. And then to Molly, "What's going on here?"

"Dare is, um, protecting me. Nothing to worry about. He's one of the good guys."

Disbelief flashed over Natalie's white face before she gathered her gumption. "Well, then, tell him to get off of Jett." She looked ready to launch herself at Dare if he made the wrong move, so Molly moved closer to her.

If she had to, she'd tackle her sister. But hopefully it wouldn't come to that, not with her naked beneath the blanket.

"Dare," Molly ventured. He looked to be in a killing mood. "Really, she *is* my sister, I promise."

"Sister, got it." Indecision plain, Dare eased back just a little but kept his gun on the man.

"Jett Sutter." The stranger lay there, not really discomfited by the attack. "I know. Sounds like *jet-setter*. My folks are regular comedians." He tilted his head to see Molly. Eyes so dark they looked black took her measure. His long, sinful lashes might have seemed effeminate on another man, but not on him. "I'm glad to see you're okay, Molly."

Molly blinked. "You know me?"

"Only from what Natalie has told me, which was all flattering but didn't include associates with guns."

His good humor left Molly gaping. He was a handsome man, and even flat on his back with a gun in his face he managed to appear competent.

"How do you know my sister?"

He looked Molly over in the blanket and cocked a brow. "Ask Natalie."

Natalie turned three shades of red. "Oh, Molly, there's so much we have to talk about." And then, as if she forgot the men, she wailed, "I was so worried about you. *Where the hell have you been?*"

Molly almost lost her blanket when Natalie jerked her into a tight bear hug. She wanted to soothe her sister, she really did. But with the men on the floor…the timing was definitely off.

"I'm okay, Natalie. Really." Over her sister's shoulder, Molly saw Dare eyeing Jett.

He said low, "You might want to stop looking at her like that."

The man actually grinned. "Right. Sorry. It's not lascivious, I swear. I was just noting the similarities between the two of them."

"Sure you were." Dare leaned into him a little more. "What are you two doing here?"

Jett put one hand behind his head, rested the other

on his chest and looked to be getting comfortable. "We just returned from a trip. I told Natalie that Molly was probably back by now. It's the middle of the night, so she didn't want to call, but she couldn't stand waiting until the morning to check on her. So…" He shrugged as if to excuse Natalie's misguided intention, and then, with caution, used the side of his hand to edge the gun away from his face. "She was going to peek in and make sure her sister was okay. That's all."

Dare didn't like that one bit. "You're shitting me. You two snuck in, and you were going to look at Molly in her bed—"

"I was only here to see to Natalie's safety. She'd have done all the peeking on her own."

With her hands on Molly's bare shoulders, Natalie pushed her back the length of her arms. "Do you have any idea how damned scared I've been for you?"

Molly sighed and again adjusted her blanket. If she lost it, she'd die on the spot. "I called you earlier, but you didn't answer."

Aghast, Natalie blinked as if ready to cry. "When?"

Since she didn't know what time it was, Molly couldn't answer. "As soon as Dare and I got back to the apartment. I don't know. Hours ago."

"Oh, God, Molly. I'm sorry. I…" She looked at Jett. "We… He…"

"We hooked up," Jett said with a smile. "Long past due. Anyway, your sister was focused on other things most recently, and she didn't remember to keep her phone charged." Now disregarding Dare's gun, he sat up, propped his forearms on his jean-covered knees and acted as if he hadn't just been assaulted. "The timing is off, but what the hell, right? We're getting married."

It was Molly's turn to gape. *"Married?"*

Natalie bobbed her head, and tears swam in her eyes. "I love him."

Jett smiled, too. "I hope you'll forgive her for missing your call. She really has been worried nonstop."

"Of course," Molly said, still trying to process the idea of her very independent sister planning to wed a man that Molly had never met.

"Where were you?" Natalie demanded.

"Kidnapped," Dare said, dropping that bombshell with great effect. "To Tijuana. By flesh smugglers."

Molly couldn't believe he'd just blurted it out like that.

Jett gave Dare a dirty look and pushed to his feet. Molly sensed that it wasn't what Dare said as much as how he said it that Jett took exception to. He reached Natalie just as the tears started tracking down her face. "Oh, Molly… *Tijuana?*" Natalie covered her mouth, and then, with even more feeling, *"Kidnapped?"*

"Calm down, Natalie." Molly couldn't think of anything else to say. "I'm okay."

"So she says, often." Dare didn't look at all happy with this turn of events. He closed the apartment door and locked it again.

"Who the hell are you?" Jett asked him. "Her bodyguard?"

Dare shrugged. "I'm the guy who got her out of Mexico."

Molly couldn't help but note how Jett kept a comforting arm around Natalie and how, for once, Natalie refrained from smothering her and instead leaned on Jett.

"She got an email from you," Jett said to Molly. "But she didn't really believe you'd written it."

"She hadn't," Dare told them.

"I knew it!" More tears came as Natalie understood the extent of the conspiracy.

Clasping her sister's shoulder, Molly tried to reassure her. "It was awful, I admit it. But I'm fine now, I swear."

"How can you say that?" Frowning, she touched Molly's face. "I see *bruises* on you." She turned a mean eye on Dare. "How did she get bruised?"

"Kidnappers are often careless that way."

Not appreciating Dare's sarcasm one bit, Molly scowled at him, but then forced a smile for Natalie. "Dare would never hurt me."

"No, I wouldn't."

"There, you see?" Molly smoothed her sister's wild hair. "He's the one who rescued me, and he's been keeping me safe since then."

"And he was protecting her still when we came in," Jett added. "That's what that tackle was all about." He glanced at Dare. "Right?"

"Of course," Molly said when Dare didn't.

Jett gave Natalie a small squeeze. "But even not knowing who we were, he didn't hurt you. I'm guessing because you're female, you got tossed into the soft chair instead of on the hard floor."

"Exactly," Molly said. "Dare doesn't hurt women."

"That's not entirely true, honey. A lot depends on the woman involved."

Damn him, did he have to antagonize them? Molly flashed him an evil look. "You're not helping."

Dare shrugged.

So he resented their intrusion—she got that. He didn't understand the closeness that she and Natalie shared. But she wanted her sister to know him as well as she did.

She wanted Natalie to like Dare and to understand everything he'd done for her.

Jett watched Dare with that piercing black gaze. "To be able to distinguish Natalie and me apart so quickly, you'd have to have special training."

"You could say that." Dare continued his visual analysis of Jett. "What do you know of it?"

Jett stared right back. "Enough, obviously."

The pissing contest was ludicrous. For heaven's sake, it was the middle of the night and they were all rattled. Holding the blanket together one-handed, Molly shoved her hair away from her face and let out a huff.

"Dare. Be *nice*."

Both Natalie and Jett looked at her like she was nuts for trying to dictate to him. Natalie whispered, "Is it wise to talk to a bodyguard that way?"

Molly rolled her eyes. "He's not really a bodyguard. Well, he is, I guess. But he's more than that, too."

"More?" Natalie asked. Jett just raised a brow.

Giving up, Molly looked at Dare for help. "I have no idea how to explain all this."

"I can see that." Finally Dare gave up his dark and broody mood. "If you don't want me to shoot either of them, then I guess we have a lot of talking to do." He stowed the gun at the small of his back.

"M.O.B. holster?" Jett asked.

Molly didn't understand until Dare explained to her. "Middle of the back." And then to Jett: "My gun stays with me."

If Natalie's eyes got any wider, they'd fall out of her head.

Dare wasn't wearing a shirt, so he couldn't pull it over the gun to hide it. Not that he seemed bothered by that.

"It's late, and Molly and I missed dinner."

Hearing him say that, knowing why they'd missed dinner, made a flush of heat go over her. Luckily her sister didn't notice; Dare held all her attention.

"After her ordeal, she's still getting her strength back, so she needs to eat. But she doesn't have a lot here in the way of groceries." Casting accusation on Molly, he added, "This place has piss-poor security, especially with windows that don't lock and that damned invitation they call a fire escape."

Because Dare currently looked more like a hired assassin than a domesticated man, Molly said, "Dare's really good in the kitchen." Then, being truthful, she added, "Actually, he's really good at everything."

"Everything?" Natalie asked, and she sounded strangled.

Jett coughed.

Dare's mouth lifted in the slightest of smiles. "Glad you think so." No one could misunderstand his look of intimacy.

Natalie did a double take. As she took in Dare's size and physique from head to toes, her lips parted.

Lacking subtlety, she turned to Molly to mouth, *Oh, my God.*

Jett frowned at her, then hauled her into his side.

Dare didn't miss any of it, but he chose not to say anything. "Maybe we can order up some pizza and colas to be delivered? That'd probably be easiest."

"No delivery this time of night." Jett gave it some thought. "There is a quickie-mart station around the corner that's open twenty-four hours. They'll throw a pizza in fresh for you."

"I've had it." Molly didn't realize how hungry she was until they started talking about food. "It's good."

Testing the waters, Jett said to Dare, "Don't worry. I'll stay here with the women while you go."

Dare did that strange thing where he looked bigger and stronger without really moving. "Not a chance." The quietness of his reply made it all the more lethal.

Jett's smile looked mean. "Still don't trust me, huh?"

"Hell, no."

Natalie shared a look with Molly. "He seriously doesn't trust Jett?"

Dare answered for her. "How long have you known him?"

When Natalie clammed up, Jett hugged her. "That sort of depends on your definition of *knowing*."

Through her teeth, Natalie said, "Don't you dare, Jett. I mean it."

Unsure what that was about, but sensing her sister's embarrassment, Molly intervened. "Dare, relax. If Natalie says he's fine, then he's fine."

Dare gave her a look. "When it comes to your safety, I say when it's fine, remember?"

Molly bit her lip. She had promised to trust him on this.

Jett stood only a few inches shorter than Dare, which still put him over six feet tall. Broad-shouldered and lean, he had that same capable aura that Dare had, but maybe without Dare's edge.

Insulted, he moved to stand right in front of Dare. "I'm not leaving Natalie here with you. Hell, for all I know, you could be the one who set up the kidnapping."

Before Molly could react to that, Dare muttered, "Hell." Resignation sharpened his expression, and he loosened his stance. "You're a cop?"

Surprised by the question, Jett hedged a little. "I used to be. Why?"

Rolling his eyes, Dare said to Molly, "Told you I'd be the first suspect."

"He did," Molly agreed, backing him up and hoping that put an end to the hostilities. "We didn't call the police immediately because Dare said he was the first one they'd look at, and their investigation might alert the real perpetrator."

"Happens sometimes," Jett agreed.

"You can trust me when I tell you that Dare is an amazing man. He's the only reason I'm here now, maybe the only reason I'm alive." Molly hoped to get things smoothed out quickly. Not only was she uncomfortable in her state of undress, but she hadn't seen her sister in what felt like forever. "If he hadn't already been in Mexico to—"

"Molly."

She bit her lip at Dare's quiet but firm interruption. Okay, so maybe he didn't want her to blab his private business, or that of his friends.

She cleared her throat. Omitting details, she said, "He was there on other business and just sort of decided to rescue me while he was at it."

That only whetted Jett's curiosity. "What kind of business did you have in Tijuana?"

"The kind that doesn't concern you." Dare didn't bother hiding his impatience. "So, if you're not still a cop, what are you doing now?"

Not nearly as closemouthed as Dare, Jett said, "Security work—domestic investigation, mostly."

"You're a private eye?"

"That's right." Jett extended a hand. "Feel free to check my background. I know how it is to be cautious."

"Yeah?" Still looking like he was made of stone, Dare ignored his proffered hand. "Why is that?"

"I'm ex-military, ex-FBI." He shrugged. "But old habits die hard, and I'm still the cautious type, too."

Dare didn't budge.

Making a face, Jett patted his right thigh. "Gunshot injury keeps me a little more grounded than I like, otherwise you wouldn't have taken me to the floor so easily." He grinned after saying it. "Need me to drop my jeans and prove it?"

Molly wanted to smack Dare for his bad manners. "Natalie would not trust a man who wasn't trustworthy."

"Ditto," Natalie agreed. She flapped a hand toward Dare. "If Molly says that he's okay, despite appearances to the contrary, then I believe her. My sister is an astute woman. I'll be safe with him."

"Fine. Acquit me of any intentional insult." Jett again held out his hand. "This has to start somewhere, so…?"

Dare eyed him up and down, and finally accepted Jett's handshake. "About that pizza?"

"Right." Jett glanced at his watch. "Assuming you aren't going to leave Molly's side—"

Dare's look answered better than words.

"—then I suppose I might as well run out for the eats. I should only be half an hour, tops. But save some of the story for me. I admit I'm curious as hell about all this."

Before he could go, Molly said, "Jett?"

Those dark eyes focused on her. "Hmm?"

"It's very nice to meet you."

Jett flashed the brightest smile she'd seen in quite some time. It worked wonders to counterbalance the ominous look of those dark eyes.

"You, too, Molly. I'm damned glad that you're back home, safe and sound." Then he went to Natalie, tucked her long, curly hair behind her ear, kissed her and said, "I won't be long."

"Be careful."

With another glance at Dare, he said, "For once I don't have to say the same to you. I have a feeling you're as safe as you can be right now."

The second he left, Natalie wrapped her arms around Molly in a tight, nearly choking embrace. "Thank God you're finally home."

Molly could feel her sister shaking. "I'm sorry you were worried." Over Natalie's shoulder, she met Dare's gaze. He watched her with heightened familiarity. She shivered.

In her ear, Natalie whispered, "I can't believe you're with him. What are you thinking?"

Insulted on Dare's behalf, Molly levered her back. "Why?"

"Look at him! He's…" When she caught Molly's frown, she let out a breath and tempered her wording. "Well, he's intimidating."

Proving he had great hearing, Dare said, "Not to Molly."

Natalie's eyes went round again.

Molly bit back a grin.

Dare smiled at her. Standing there like that, he *was* intimidating—to anyone who wanted to hurt her. He was also incredibly sexy.

Molly sighed. She wanted more. A lot more.

But now, at the most inauspicious time, her sister had shown up. Never before had she been sorry to see Natalie, but this time… Well, she would have preferred that she had the rest of the night alone with Dare to explore the new dimension to their relationship.

"Relax, Natalie." In a grand understatement, Molly said, "He's been very good to me."

"Are you two really…?" She glanced back at Dare,

who made no pretense of watching them intently, and spun back around. In a hushed undertone, she said, "Good grief, Molly. He doesn't scare you?"

"Of course not."

"But he's…"

"He's sweet," Molly insisted.

Dare snorted. "He's still listening."

Aggrieved, Natalie closed her eyes.

Molly hooked her sister's arm and dragged her farther across the room. "I'm so sorry that I couldn't call you, Nat." This was going to be difficult to explain. "The thing is, I don't know who had me kidnapped, or why."

"What do you mean?" Understanding dawned. "You think it wasn't a random thing? You were a specific target!"

"I'm afraid so." Unlike Molly's thick, heavy hair, Natalie's lighter hair grew in fluffy, corkscrew curls. Molly smoothed down a wild, wayward spiral. "You know how much I trust you."

"I should hope so."

Her sister never failed to back her up when necessary. "Well, as much as I trust you, I also know how you'll react in almost any situation. If I had told you that someone had set me up to be taken, that someone had deliberately wanted *me* gone, you'd have gone ballistic."

"Well, of course I would have. You're my sister!" She chewed over what Molly had told her, trying to sort it out. "*Who?* Who would do this to you?"

She wished she had a better answer. "I still have no idea, and that's what scares me the most."

Fear narrowed Natalie's eyes. "Until you know who did it, you can't keep it from happening again."

"That's about it."

Obliterating any pretense about their conversation

remaining private, Dare came over to them. "Molly feared that you'd go on a rampage trying to find out who wanted her hurt."

Whipping around to confront him, Natalie found him close and had to look way up. She stumbled back a step. "I can be reasonable."

"Can you?"

She opened her mouth, then closed it. After a few seconds, she sighed. "Well, maybe not. But you can't expect me to just…just *accept* this without getting angry."

Dare reached for Molly and tucked her into his side. "You can be as pissed off as you want. That's understandable. But I need you to stay out of it, and to trust me to find the one responsible."

Natalie frowned at him, at Molly, then back again. "Maybe it'd help if you told me what makes you so qualified for the job."

Dare searched her face. "All you need to know is that I'm not going to let anyone hurt your sister."

Confused, Natalie put her hands on her hips. "Why are you involved? Because you two are…" She waved a hand between them. "What? *Dating?*"

She made it sound like the most absurd idea ever. Trying to go for the easiest explanation, Molly said, "Dare's protecting me because I'm paying him for his assistance."

There was a heavy pause, and then Dare lifted her chin so that she had to look at him. With quiet authority, he stated, "No, honey, you're not."

CHAPTER NINETEEN

"But...*what?*" Flushing over this unexpected turn, Molly looked uneasily at her sister. "Of course I am. Dare, we agreed."

"You were insistent, and I didn't want to upset you."

Natalie chimed in with agreement. "She does like to pay her own way."

"Now, wait a minute." Molly jerked free of Dare's loose hold, and, in the process, she almost lost the blanket.

Saving her modesty, he caught it for her, but then used his hold on the blanket to haul her close. He kissed the end of her nose. "I won't take money from you."

She couldn't believe this. "Since when?" But she knew, of course.

Dare let out his breath and addressed her sister. "Natalie, you'll have to excuse us for a few minutes. Molly needs to get dressed before she flashes us both."

"Ah...sure."

Bemused by Dare's blasé attitude over this, Molly held her ground...but not for long. He was right; she did need to get dressed.

To her sister, she said firmly, "I will be right back."

Natalie dithered. "I, ah, could go with you."

"Not this time." Dare gave her a barely conciliatory smile as he started them both across the floor. "We weren't expecting you, and right now Molly and I have a few things to work out. I won't keep her long."

He left no room for argument, so Natalie directed a stern look on him before saying to Molly, "I'll be right here if you need me for anything."

Molly blinked at her. Natalie still thought that Dare might hurt her? He never would, but if he did, Natalie sure wouldn't be able to stop him.

Her sister meant well, and usually she was the most stubborn person Molly knew. But when it came to Dare, Natalie was well out of her league.

Over her shoulder, Molly said back to her sister, "Thanks, but I'll be fine, I promise."

Without regard to her sister's worry, Dare propelled her along into the bedroom. It was very rude, and didn't do much to put Natalie at ease. Stepping away from him, she went through the door on her own steam.

He shut it behind her, and Molly turned to demand an explanation.

Before she got a single word out, Dare's mouth covered hers.

Oh… Well, okay, then. Molly subsided and just went with the kiss.

As the tip of Dare's tongue prodded over the seam of her lips, her heart started thumping and her body hummed to life all over again. She opened for him to accept his deeper kiss.

Dare slanted his head for a better fit, and Molly wanted to melt on the spot.

It might only have been hours ago that he made love with her, but she felt fresh desire as an acute need.

Dare turned with her to brace her back against the door. He tilted in his hips, pressing the solid rise of his erection against her belly.

Every nerve ending buzzed to life until she clung to him, her sister temporarily forgotten.

She didn't realize that the blanket was gone until Dare stepped back to look at her. He held each corner of the blanket in his hands at either side of her shoulders. His gaze moved from her mouth to her breasts, and then slowly down her body.

His jaw worked.

"This is awkward," Molly said. She'd never been put on display like this before.

He shook his head. "Damn, but I need you again." He put damp, openmouthed kisses on her throat, her shoulder, and then he stepped away.

Molly couldn't believe he left her there, naked, while he still had his pants on. Breathing hard, feeling exposed, she considered making a grab for the blanket…but Dare stood on it.

His gaze went all over her like a hot stroke before stopping at the juncture of her legs. "You look good enough to eat." His gaze met hers. "Again."

"I…ah…" Molly shifted. Such outrageous sexual compliments were very new to her, and she had no idea how to respond. Feeling lame, she whispered, "Thank you."

Dare ran his hands lightly from her shoulders over her breasts, letting his palms drag over her now-puckered nipples. He lingered there just a second before sliding them down to her hips. He gave a low growl. "Turn around."

Voice going high and thin, Molly said, "What?"

Using his hold on her, Dare directed her around until she had her back to him.

Molly tried to control her breathing, but it wasn't easy. This was both embarrassing and highly erotic.

"God, baby, I do love this ass." With both hands, he cupped her cheeks, then stepped up close again to kiss the sensitive spot where her throat met her shoulder.

His attraction to her posterior thrilled her. "We can't… My sister is out there.…"

"I know." He took her wrists and lifted her arms above her head, and then pressed her palms flat to the door. "Just let me touch you for a minute."

Putting one foot between hers, he nudged her legs open. Molly widened her stance, all the while struggling with the conflict of need and her natural modesty.

Slipping his hands around to the front of her, then up to her breasts, he touched her. With her arms raised, her feet braced apart, everything he did seemed somehow more salacious.

Lifting each breast, Dare caressed her before teasing both nipples with his thumbs.

It was too much. "Dare…"

He closed his fingertips around her, lightly pinching, tugging insistently.

Molly dropped her head back as the sensation went straight from her breasts to her womb. She bit her lip to keep from moaning aloud, but the deep, throaty sound escaped anyway.

Dare hugged her, warm and soft, and then he stepped back. Slowly, Molly turned around to face him again—and what she saw astounded her.

Muscles clenched, nostrils flared and eyes burning, Dare watched her with such obvious yearning that her embarrassment disappeared. Never had she imagined him so out of control.

As he readjusted himself, his hands shook. He took another step away from her. Voice as rough as gravel, he said, "You'd better get dressed before I lose it."

Feeling a little powerful in this new situation, Molly smiled. "Let's talk about money first."

His jaw hardened. "Push me, and we'll be talking

about it on the bed, with me inside you and to hell with what your sister hears."

What a spoilsport. For most men that might have been a bluff, but she had a feeling Dare said what he meant, always. She'd already proven that she wouldn't stop him if he went that route, so maybe it'd be better if she didn't press her luck.

"Fine." She had enough explaining to do with Natalie without adding that to the details. From the pile of ransacked clothes, Molly dug out a T-shirt, panties and jeans.

It was a strange thing to have a man in her room, watching her every move with undivided attention. She felt brazen, but in an intriguing way; she rather liked how intently Dare watched her.

Once she was dressed, he relaxed a little and sat at the end of the bed.

"Come here." He pulled her onto his lap and shifted her to get comfortable. "Now. Let's talk."

In no way was Dare an average man, so Molly couldn't miss that definite rise beneath her bottom. "You still have an erection."

Not the least bit embarrassed, Dare gave a dismissive shrug. "I still want you." He kissed her forehead. "But we need to iron this out, and Jett will be back shortly, and I'm willing to bet your sister will only be patient for so long."

Molly tried not to squirm, but it wasn't easy. He'd gotten her aroused, and he still wore only jeans. Seeing his chest, even with the faded scars—or maybe because of them—counted as foreplay for her starved senses. She saw the battle signs as proof of all he'd done, all he could do, and the kind of man he was.

The kind who would keep her safe.

Over what looked like an old knife injury on his shoulder, she rested her hand. "You're a very perceptive man. It's true that Natalie is not known for her patience."

Dare smiled. "I like her, even if her timing sucks." Holding her chin, he brushed his thumb along her jaw. "She's different from you, but I also see similarities. It's there in the dark brown eyes and the shape of your mouth."

"And big boobs."

His smile twitched into a grin. "I guess I noticed that, too."

"Dare." Molly put her forehead to his. She wasn't sure how to say it, so she decided to simply spit it out. "Just because we slept together doesn't change anything."

"Wrong. For me it changes everything. And before we get into this too much, you might as well know that I'm firm on this. No way in hell will I take money from you."

Molly couldn't believe that he'd changed the rules on her without telling her. "That's not fair."

He half smiled. "I never told you I was fair." He smoothed a long hank of her hair, letting the back of his hand move over her breast. Voice dropping, he said, "But you'll learn to live with it."

Learn to live with it? Did he mean…long-term? Or was that just a figure of speech?

She didn't quite have the nerve to ask him yet. "I don't want to be indebted to you, at least not any more than I already am."

"There's no debt. I'm here because I want to be."

What could she say to that?

His thumb touched her bottom lip. "Relax and accept it, honey. My mind's made up. Actually, it was made up even before the sex, so don't feel guilty about that, okay?"

Emotion choked her. "Since meeting you, you've made me feel a lot of things. But not guilt. Not even when I kicked you in the nose."

He smiled. "Glad to hear it. So, what do you say we go check on your sister? I can almost picture her with her ear to the door."

Through the door, Natalie said, "Damn right. Now bring my sister back out here."

JETT RETURNED WITH the pizza soon after Molly finished sharing details with Natalie. The more Molly told her, the more distressed Natalie had gotten. She was literally sick with upset when Jett walked in. But as soon as she saw him, she hurried to mask her expression.

Similar to Molly, Natalie had a lot of pride. He liked that.

As he'd told Molly, he liked her. She was like Molly, but also different.

Natalie's honest reactions left Dare confident that, as Molly had insisted, her sister would never act to harm her.

That left only Jett for him to wonder about right now. Not that he really suspected Jett, but he refused to take any chances with Molly's safety.

With reluctance, Natalie had admitted that while she and Jett had known each other for close to a year, and had even shared a physical relationship, they'd only recently realized that they were in love.

The quick change in relationship could be construed as an attempt to ingratiate himself with Natalie's family— namely to get information about Molly.

It seemed more unlikely than otherwise, but still, Dare

was all set to get answers out of Jett when he opened the front door and let him in.

That is, until Jett strode in without a word, set the food on the table and, with admirable stealth, peered out the curtains to the street below.

"What's going on?" Natalie asked, alarmed. "What are you doing?"

Jett took in both women with calculated purpose. "I don't suppose you two would let the men talk in private for just a minute, would you?"

Dare snorted. He already knew what Molly would say before she started objecting.

He held up a hand to silence the women. Sadly, that didn't work. He supposed that he'd have to get used to Molly not following his every order, verbal or otherwise.

While the women continued protesting, Dare walked over to the window and did his own surveillance. He saw nothing.

Quietly, Jett said, "It's just out of view, opposite side of the street, less than a block up. But does an old white van mean anything to you?"

Molly gasped.

Dropping the curtain, Dare took in her expression with sharp-eyed concern. He said to Jett, "Rusted?"

"It's dark out, but I believe so." Jett looked grim. "I could see the driver and a passenger, but the back windows are painted."

Molly reached for a chair and dropped into it. Seeing her like this enraged Dare.

"I only really noticed them because the van is running, but they have the headlights off. They're watching the building."

Dare could barely credit that anyone would be that

dumb. If her father had sent someone after her again, he must be desperate.

Anxious to check it out for himself, he headed for the front door.

"Dare, wait!" Molly bolted from the seat to chase after him. "It…it couldn't be the same people as before."

No reason to worry her more. "Probably not." Dare gave a hard smile and opened the door. "Don't worry."

"Damn it, Dare!" Panicked, Molly charged after him. "Let's just call the police."

At the same time, Jett asked, "Need any help?"

Sighing with impatience, Dare said to Jett, "Yeah. Keep her in here. Got it?"

He looked very put out with the enormity of that task. "I'll try."

Trying wasn't good enough. "Just man up and do it." He gave Molly one stern frown and said in a tone that brooked no argument, "Stay put."

She folded her arms and glared right back at him. "I'm not stupid."

Meaning he was? But he saw the fear in her eyes and knew she was scared for him.

Fuck.

He went out the door anyway, saying to Jett, "Lock this behind me." Face pale, Molly stepped back, her lips rolled in, her body tensed. The door shut and Dare heard the lock click into place.

Guilt punched at his heart.

But for Christ's sake, he couldn't falter every time Molly bit her lips. He knew what he was doing, and if she trusted him at all, she wouldn't be worried.

It would have helped if he could put Molly from his mind, but that was like asking himself not to breathe.

Since the day he'd met her, she'd occupied his thoughts in a severely distracting way.

As he'd told her to do, he was learning to live with it. Now…he almost liked it. Having her at the forefront of his mind was becoming a comfortable thing.

He liked having her there.

Going down the steps two at a time, Dare ensured the hallways and foyer were empty. Given it was the middle of the night, not another soul was in sight.

Peeking out the front door, he saw the van at the corner, idling.

Waiting.

As Jett had said, the vehicle was in shadow, hidden from the streetlamp and the bright moon.

In a few hours, the sun would be up and people would be coming and going.

Were they hoping to catch Molly? Or maybe just to verify her presence in the apartment?

He needed to get closer. Maybe he could ID the men, or overhear something important.

Dare pulled back to think. If he went out through the front door, he'd be seen. Damn it, he should have investigated the entire building. He knew better than to go into a structure blind. But his concentration had been on Molly.

Mostly on getting her under him. Damn.

Dare glanced around the foyer. Almost every old building had a basement, so he searched for the right door—and found it. Luckily, it opened in silence. The dank basement with its concrete floors and walls smelled like mildew and held a thick chill.

He wasn't about to turn on lights, but the moon shining through a window guided him. Covered in webs and dead bugs, the rusted lock on the wobbly frame offered no real protection. The narrow window barely afforded enough room for him to hoist himself up and out. The casing scraped his spine, and his face met dry, brittle weeds outside.

He barely noticed.

Shooting to his feet, he circled the building and edged out along the side, using the shadows of the apartment building next door as concealment. Off in the distance, a dog barked. Cold wind rustled dry leaves and cut through his thin shirt.

Senses alert, Dare listened for any unnatural sound as he edged closer and closer to the street.

He detected the quiet rumbling of the van's motor and the hushed drone of conversation inside.

Certain words pricked his mind: *daughter* and *payment*. They were incriminating words that worked to ramp up his instinctive protectiveness.

Without making a sound, he edged closer until he could see the license plates on the van. He committed them to memory.

The ringing of a cell phone made the driver curse. He answered with a sharp "What?"

Silence, and then, "She's here. No, we didn't see her, but there are lights on inside." The driver waited, and then, "No one is going to see us. I know how to… Fine. Are you sure? Yeah, all right."

He disconnected the call with a curse, saying to his passenger, "We're done here for tonight." Then he put the van in gear.

The urge to go after them ripped through Dare. He could reach them before they picked up speed. He could drag the driver through the window and beat some answers out of him. If there were more than two of them…

Through his nose, he inhaled a long, deep breath.

The smart thing to do, the unemotional thing, would be to wait. If he got hurt, who would look after Molly? Who would protect her?

He had the plates. It'd be better to get hold of Trace and have him find out what he could about the owner of the van.

Putting his head back against a brick wall, Dare let out the breath and tried to ease the killing tension. The adrenaline dump left him humming with the need for violence.

He couldn't go back to Molly like this. The mention of the van had thrown her for a loop. She needed him calm and in control. She needed him to comfort her.

Somehow, he would manage that. But one word the driver said kept pounding in his brain: *daughter.*

For her own safety, he had to tell Molly that her father was likely the one who'd plotted against her, the one who'd wanted her hurt.

Dare still had to find out why. And until he did, Molly would never be satisfied.

Pissed off, more at himself than the situation, Dare re-entered the building by the front door. Hell, anyone could walk in and out of the place. And her apartment door wouldn't offer even a modicum of protection, not even to the dumbest criminal. And that damned fire escape...

Her apartment door opened right before Dare reached it. Jett stood there, a half-eaten piece of pizza in his free hand. "Didn't go after them, huh?"

He shook his head and pulled out his cell phone. From the corner of his eye, he saw Molly sitting on the couch. She curled in the corner, her knees up to her chest, her arms around herself, her shoulders hunched.

Beside her, Natalie hovered, no doubt offering comfort.

Dare punched in Trace's number as he went to Molly and sat down beside her. The couch dipped, and her hip rolled against his. He put his arm around her.

She remained rigid, but she'd get over it.

As soon as Trace answered, he said, "Sorry to wake you, but I need you to run some plates for me."

Looking suitably impressed over that, Jett went for another slice of pizza. The excitement of the night hadn't dented his appetite one bit—or else he was used to danger.

That'd make sense, because it wasn't the danger that affected Dare as much as Molly's reaction. If he wasn't so drawn to her, he'd have gone for the pizza, too.

There was the sound of Trace moving, probably hunting up a pen and paper, and then he said, "Go."

Dare gave him the number. "Soon as you know, let me know. And if you can connect the driver with anyone, it'd help."

"I'll see what I can do."

"Thanks."

Jett watched him. "Men of few words, huh?"

Ignoring Jett, Dare closed the phone and put it back in his pocket. That done, he caught Molly's chin and, ignoring her sister, turned her face up for a kiss.

From the beginning, that had been the easiest way to reach her, to take her out of her worry.

He meant it to just be a peck of affection, to thaw her a little. But her lips were firmed, and he could feel the tension vibrating through her, so he lingered, keeping his mouth on hers until she softened.

Smoothing her bottom lip with his thumb, he asked, "You okay?"

"Of course. Why wouldn't I be?"

Snippy. Dare gave a tight smile. "Good. Let's eat."

Her hands knotted his shirt. "I'm not hungry."

"Yeah, you are." He stood, caught her wrists and pulled her to her feet, too. "But you're also pissed. And scared. Not eating isn't going to help, though."

Her eyes reddened. Her bottom lip quivered.

Ah, hell. More softly, he said, "Everything is fine."

"What happened?"

"You heard me give the plates to Trace. He'll check them and we'll go from there."

"You…you didn't…"

"Chat with them? No." Fuck, he hated explaining himself. Especially with Natalie and Jett as a fascinated audience. "The driver got a call and left before I could decide what I wanted to do."

"Oh." Relief left her swaying on her feet. She averted her gaze.

"Molly."

"What?"

It wasn't like her to be detached. "We've got a long day ahead of us tomorrow, so it'd be better if you used the time we had for something other than sulking."

That got her attention.

She snapped her head around to glower at him. *"Sulking?"* She sounded mean. "Is *that* what you think?"

Dare narrowed his eyes. "I think Jett better stop his goddamned smiling."

Jett laughed and held up a hand. "Sorry."

He heard Natalie muttering to him, and then the two of them pretended not to listen.

Molly propped her hands on her hips. "Seriously, Dare?" She stomped two steps closer. "You *seriously* think that just because you ran outside after deranged kidnappers, I'd sulk?"

Reining in his temper, he closed his hands over her

shoulders and brought her closer. "I think you were worried about me, like I'm some damn grade-school boy without an ounce of sense or training. And you're starting to realize that your life is never going to be the same after this, and that'd fuck up anyone's day. And if that wasn't enough, you're wishing you were at least paying me, because then you'd feel like you had more control."

She gaped at him.

"Nailed it, didn't I?"

Her tongue slicked out over her bottom lip. "Pretty much…minus the insults."

Dare hooked his arms around her waist. "But it was insulting, because, Molly, I'm not going to get hurt, I will get your life back in order and paying me wouldn't really change anything. Something is going on between us, and money wouldn't blunt the effect of it at all."

"Maybe you're right." Her fingers played with the front of his shirt. She stared at his sternum. "What kind of something, though?"

Hell, he didn't know. And he sure as hell wasn't going to hash it out right now with people listening in. "We'll figure that out along the way." He kissed her forehead. "But it goes both ways, okay?" That was about as much of a promise as he could give her.

"I don't know." She let out a breath. "I hate it that you're in the line of danger trying to keep me safe."

"Funny, because, possessive as I am, I sure as hell wouldn't leave your security to any other man." He glanced at Jett. "Other than very short-term."

Jett saluted him with a canned cola. "Piece of cake. She's a reasonable woman, just like her sister."

"Glad to hear it." It did reassure him that Molly hadn't tried to do anything foolish, like follow him out.

When Molly stayed quiet, Natalie shoved her shoulder.

"For God's sake, Molly, men need reassurance, too, you know. Put him out of his misery already, will you?"

Jett laughed. "Seriously. From one guy to another, it is rather painful to watch."

Dare paid no attention to either of them. "Molly?"

She met his gaze. "Well, I'm possessive, too, and I can't help worrying when you run out blind to face off with people we already know are dangerous."

That was more like it. Dare turned her toward the table where the pizza waited. "Do you believe that insult, Jett?"

"Got ya where it hurt, didn't she?"

Natalie elbowed Jett. "What are you talking about? She didn't insult him."

Sprawling back in his chair, Jett said, "The hell she didn't. Insinuating that he can't handle himself against some thugs too damned stupid not to be noticed is a definite insult. Look at the man, Natalie. You can see that he knows what he's doing."

Dare accepted the accolade with a nod.

And then as an aside, Jett added, "And he took me down with almost no effort, a fact that still smarts. So you can see why I choose to think he's that good, rather than that I got taken so completely off guard."

"I'd say it was a little of both, but thanks all the same." Dare held out a chair for Molly. "If I'd wanted to get those bastards out of that truck, I could have, and I wouldn't have broken a sweat."

Natalie made a face. "Are all men so modest?"

Jett grinned. "Probably."

"But if I'd done that," Dare said, "there would have been a scuffle, maybe gunfire, and cops would be called. There'd not only be questions, but we'd be tipping our hand, and whoever is behind this would go to ground."

"Smart." Jett leaned forward, an arm on the table. "So, you're working with someone who can look up plates that easily?"

Dare put a slice of pizza on a plate and set it in front of Molly. "It's unfortunate that you're here, listening in, but you have to know that I'm not going to tell you jack shit."

"Fair enough." To Molly, he asked, "He's legal?"

Her gaze went from the massive slice of pizza to Jett. She opened her mouth, closed it again and shrugged. "Whatever he is, I'm glad, because I don't think anyone else would have found me in Mexico."

Dare grinned at her answer. "I operate outside the law when necessary, but usually with amnesty."

"Huh." Jett stared at Dare as he mulled that over. "Got a lot of pull?"

"Enough."

"This is all damned intriguing." He pulled Natalie into his lap. "When I asked you to marry me, I had no idea that your family would be so interesting."

Dare got his own plate ready. "If *interesting* is the best description you've got, I have a feeling you haven't met their father yet."

Natalie and Molly both winced.

Dare regretted his words. Regardless of her father's sins, Molly had feelings for the man. It was the way of nature.

For now, he'd withhold what he'd overheard from the driver of the Ford. She'd had enough confusion for one night. It'd be better to tell her away from the others, maybe right before she reunited with her father.

Facetiously, Jett said, "Ah, no, I haven't had the pleasure of meeting her folks. Something to look forward to?"

"If you have a strong constitution, you should be fine." Dare noticed that Jett hugged Natalie a little closer.

"That bad?" he asked.

"Stop trying to scare him off," Molly said to Dare. "You've only met my father once."

Once was enough, but Dare kept that thought to himself. Hedging the question he knew Natalie was about to ask, he brought up a new subject. "We can't stay here."

Slumping, Molly nodded. "I know."

Damn, but he hated seeing her life disturbed this way. She deserved her old life of naiveté, where bogeymen didn't exist. "Even if you didn't have creeps hanging around outside, this place isn't secure."

She didn't argue with him about it. "Where will we stay?"

"I have a guest room," Natalie offered.

Jett gave immediate objection to that idea. "Having her at your place would just put you both in the line of fire."

Cutting off Natalie's objection, Dare said, "He's right."

Molly touched her sister's hand. "The last thing I want is to put you in danger, too. This is all bad enough as it is."

Dare nudged the pizza toward Molly again. She needed to keep up her strength to get through the emotional shit-storm ahead.

He waited for her to take a bite before saying to Natalie, "When would be a good time to catch your father and stepmother both at home?"

Around her mouthful of food, Molly asked, "Why?"

"Because it's time that we paid them a visit. The sooner the better."

CHAPTER TWENTY

DARE WATCHED AS Molly all but deflated.

It couldn't have been more plain how she dreaded seeing her father. And no wonder. She was the smartest woman he'd ever met, so she probably already suspected her father's involvement.

Under the table, he clasped her thigh. When he got her alone, he'd comfort her in a hundred different ways. He only hoped that part of the comforting could be done in the nude, preferably on a soft bed.

Thinking that stirred him, so he had to push the erotic image aside. "I'd like to see both of them at the same time, if possible."

Oblivious to the undercurrent, Natalie shrugged. "Only time to catch them both at home is pretty early. Right after breakfast, Dad takes off to the gym, and Kathi takes off for one of her many scheduled things."

"Bishop goes to the gym every day?"

Molly smirked. "His personal appearance is real important to him."

"Kathi encourages him. She likes it that he stays in shape." Natalie wrinkled her nose. "The two of them are really big on image."

Molly slumped back in her chair. "Kathi means well, but she's forever telling us that we need to exercise more."

That insulted Jett. "The hell you say?"

Natalie added, "According to Kathi, we're too soft."

"We should tone up," Molly chimed in, saying, "because we jiggle."

Dare shared an incredulous look with Jett, before ruling out such nonsense. "I think it's safe to say that men enjoy women who are soft."

Getting a handful of Natalie's soft hip, Jett agreed. "Hell, yeah."

Laughing, Natalie moved his hand to her waist. "Don't worry. Molly and I don't take it to heart. We both learned long ago to just let the criticisms roll right off."

"Good." Jett cupped her neck and drew her face to his. "Because you can take my word for it—you're beautiful."

Molly watched them share a kiss, and she smiled at Dare. He could almost read her thoughts and see the wistfulness in her expression. She was happy for her sister, but did she want the same for herself?

When he didn't return her smile, she sighed and shook her head at him, as if he were a lost cause.

Was that how she saw him?

Rubbing the back of his neck didn't really ease his sudden tension. "What about your stepmother? You said she takes off in the morning, too? To do what?"

Molly picked a piece of pepperoni off her pizza. "Kathi stays involved in a lot of stuff. Tennis, swimming, aerobics and a whole slew of fundraisers and public projects. She stays busy, but she always sets things up around Dad's schedule."

Nodding, Natalie added, "Because God knows he doesn't try to accommodate her."

"Most times," Molly said, "he barely acknowledges her. I don't know why she puts up with him, if you want the truth."

"I wouldn't," Natalie said. "But for Kathi, I guess it's a trade-off. She likes the prestige of Dad's wealth. The fancy parties with the upper crust of society. The respect and…" She searched for the right word.

"Power," Molly supplied. "Dad has a certain level of authority, and they both know it."

Dare twisted to look at the clock on the kitchen wall. "How early are you talking?"

Following his gaze, Natalie, too, checked the clock. "You've probably got three and a half hours. They're always up by six and out of the house by seven-thirty. You can call on them anytime in between that and catch them at home. After that it's a guessing game. They both stay überbusy with stuff."

"Thanks." That would give him some time. He watched Molly take her pizza apart, eating the pepperoni ahead of the rest. She had feminine hands, despite the short nails. She licked pizza sauce off the tip of one finger, and everything in him clenched in need.

He wanted her again, bad. Soon as he got her sister and Jett out the door, he'd work that out.

With that end goal in mind, he sent a pointed look at Jett. "If you're done eating…"

"Dare." Sounding stern, Molly admonished him. "Don't be so rude."

"Not a problem." Jett stood, bringing Natalie to her feet with him. "We should get going anyway. And I'm sure you two have plans to make."

Natalie wavered. "I don't understand why you want to visit Dad and Kathi."

"You said it yourself." Jett put an arm around her. "Your dad has influence, so he probably has connections that'll assist their inquiries." Over Natalie's head, he gave one small negative shake at Dare.

Both Dare and Molly understood: Natalie didn't need to know that her father might be complicit in Molly's kidnapping. She was in love, looking toward a bright future. No reason to drop a black reality on her right now.

"I guess." The strain of exhaustion and worry showed on Natalie's face. "But I really hate to let you out of my sight. I'm so afraid you'll disappear on me again."

"I promise that I won't." Molly hugged her sister tight. "Go home and try to get some sleep now. I'm safe, and I'm going to stay safe."

As if she sensed how things would soon be changing, Natalie lingered in the hug. "We have so much to talk about."

"I know." Showing that inner strength that Dare admired so much, Molly smiled when Natalie finally released her. "I'll call you later, when I can." In a stage whisper meant to tease, she added, "I'm dying to hear all the details about your and Jett's whirlwind romance."

"Ditto," Natalie told her. She gave a pointed look at Dare. "I think your story is going to be far more riveting."

"Makes sense," Jett said. "She is a writer, after all."

Jett had the nonchalant air of a man who knew his ability, so wasn't threatened by much. Dare only hoped the attitude was warranted. "All joking aside, you two need to be careful. I don't think there's any direct threat to Natalie, but we know that the apartment was being watched, so someone could be keeping tabs on her, too. We can't assume otherwise."

"Never would." Jett kept Natalie close to his side and pulled out his wallet. He fished out a business card and handed it to Dare. "If anything happens, give me a call. I'll keep my phone on me." He met his gaze. "You want to share a number so I can return the favor?"

"Oh, yeah," Natalie said. "I want to be able to call Molly."

Molly shook her head. "My purse is missing, and my phone was in it."

"Not a problem. We'll get her another phone today, but until then…" Dare got a pen and paper from the table that had held the note. He jotted down his number and gave it to Jett. Depending on what happened tomorrow with Molly's father, they might be leaving straight from there to return to his home, and Molly wouldn't get a chance to see her sister again for a while.

The only way he'd be staying is if he busted her father right off and could call in the authorities to put an end to the threat.

Jett looked around the apartment. "You have this place locked down?"

"I rigged a few things. No one is going to get in without me knowing it."

Molly turned to him with surprise. "When did you do that?"

Not touching her was getting damned difficult. "While you were sleeping."

She tucked in her chin. "I'm usually a light sleeper, but I didn't hear you."

Which only showed how safe she felt with him, and how sated she'd been after her climax. "You were…really out." He couldn't hold back a sense of satisfaction.

"Oh." Color tinged her cheeks.

"That reminds me, I also stacked your mail over on the table. You have some stuff that looks important. I think from your publisher and maybe your agent."

Immediately she put down her napkin and went to the table to check it out. Natalie followed her.

Dare motioned for Jett to join him around the corner into the kitchen.

"Nice work. You knew she wouldn't ignore business."

"We needed a minute." Dare kept his voice low to keep from alerting the women. "Do you still have friends in the FBI?"

"'Course. How can I help?"

"For starters, keep Natalie pinned down. I didn't want to rattle Molly any more than she already is, but neither of them should be out and about on her own."

"Already made that decision." Jett ran a hand through his hair. "It's not going to be easy, though, especially when she gets back to teaching."

"Figure it out." Molly was his priority, but as her sister, Natalie got his concern through association.

"Yeah, I will." He considered things, but only for a moment. Then, with a shrug of resignation, he stated, "I'll either drive her or follow her. Don't worry about it."

With that settled, Dare said, "Molly's car."

"What about it?"

"It's been sitting out there in the lot the whole time she was gone, easy prey for tampering. No way in hell am I letting her in it until it's been checked. But it's not safe to leave it there, either."

Comprehension lifted Jett's chin. "Ah. You want me to get someone to check it over?"

"Off the grid." Dare made sure Jett understood the stipulations. "I don't want the FBI up my ass about this, getting in my way. So unless you know someone who owes you a favor—"

"I have a friend from ATF. Don't worry about it. I'll get it done right away, then let you know."

Perfect. "If it's clean, have it towed somewhere safe, will you?"

"To ensure it stays that way." He nodded. "Sure, no problem."

"Thanks." Dare clapped him on the shoulder. "I appreciate the help."

Molly stepped back into the kitchen, landed a look of suspicion on each man but chose to let it go. "I need to deposit some checks at the bank, and I have a contract to mail back at the post office."

"All right." Dare couldn't expect her to put her livelihood on hold. With him by her side, a few stops should be safe enough. "We can take care of that after we leave your father's."

She nodded but continued to study both men. "Everything okay?"

"I need your car keys." He didn't give her a chance to question that. "Jett will move it someplace safe until you're back here."

Dare could tell that she didn't buy that simplified version, but she went to a drawer in the kitchen and withdrew a spare key.

"Thanks." Jett took it from her and stuffed it into his pocket.

Natalie had followed Molly in. She put her hands together, stared up at Dare and the tearful smile came. She opened her arms and embraced him tight. "Thank you, Dare. I'm so glad to know that she's safe with you."

Relieved that Molly at least had her sister's support, Dare returned the hug with genuine affection. As Natalie stepped away from him, she turned her face and mouthed again to Molly, with even more exaggeration, *Oh, my God.*

Dare had no idea what her theatrics were about this time, but Molly nodded in dramatic agreement.

Shaking his head at the women, Jett said, "If there's any news, let us know."

"I will. Thanks."

Jett kissed Molly on the cheek and, finally, escorted Natalie out of the apartment.

The second they were alone, Dare's sexual desire sharpened. He went to the door and fastened the lock, then moved the chair to wedge it under the knob.

Seeing that, Molly's face tightened with dread. "You're sure those guys in the van are gone?"

"I watched them leave." Dare came over to her. "But either way, I'm not going to let anyone touch you. You have my word."

A sad smile flickered. "If anyone can make that promise, I believe you can."

He needed to change the subject to lighten her mood. "What was all that *oh-my-God* business from your sister?"

Genuine humor brightened her smile a touch more. Molly poked him in the side. "Your hard body impressed her, that's all."

How ridiculous. "Meaning Jett is a slouch, huh?"

Now she laughed. "No, of course not. You saw him."

Refusing to compliment another man's physicality, Dare just grunted.

Molly wasn't fooled. "You know he's a prime specimen, Dare Macintosh. Don't pretend otherwise." She turned to look out the window, watching her sister and Jett leave the lot. "It's just that you're so far beyond average buffness, not many guys could ever compare." She put a hand to the glass. "You're beyond anything, I think."

He knew his own ability, had always accepted it, but

her excessive praise made his ears hot. "You're being silly, Molly. I'm just a man."

"No." She shook her head, and Dare saw her shoulders slump a little. "You're exceptional in so many ways. Natalie was just acknowledging it to me."

Dare stood behind her, not touching her, but close enough to feel her heat and breathe in her scent. Keeping his hands off her challenged him. Even after her sister and Jett pulled out of the lot, she stood there.

"You okay, honey?"

She nodded. "Yeah, I am. It's just…" She gave up her supervision from the window. "When will I get to see her again?"

What she really wanted to know was when would her life be returned to normal. Sometimes being an honest man sucked. He would have liked to lie to her, to promise her a quick resolution. But lying to her would never sit right. "I don't know, baby. But I'm working on it."

Soft breath left her in a sigh. She closed her eyes, but only for a second of grief. When she opened them again, the melancholy had been replaced with acceptance. "I'm sorry."

"Don't do that."

"I don't mean to be a complainer. You're doing so much already. And I know it's going to work out eventually."

"You are far from a complainer, Molly." She was so damned accepting that it amazed him.

"I guess…being here, back at my apartment…" She waved a hand, at a loss for the right words. "I just see so many loose ends that I can't really tie up, not while I have to keep looking over my shoulder."

Her warmth drew him, so Dare trailed a knuckle along her jaw. "Will you tell your agent or publisher what happened?"

"God, no." With an emphatic shake of her head, she said, "The fewer people who know, the better I like it. If it comes out, then it does. I won't hide from it or be...be ashamed about it."

"You have no reason to be."

She agreed. "But this is one of those things that if I tell even a little of it, people will want to know more. They'll start digging for every ugly detail." Pride stiffened her spine. "It's private, and I have no interest in advertising it."

Dare got it. Many would pity her if they knew what she'd endured, and some would speculate on things that had not happened. Molly wasn't the type to accept wrong assumptions or excess compassion.

But she wasn't naive. She knew the truth would come out eventually. "I guess that's not the kind of publicity you want."

"Can you imagine?" She stepped up against him and wrapped her arms around him. "I already feel far too exposed without people talking about it."

The perfect fit of her in his arms stirred Dare more, but right now what she wanted, what she needed, was comfort, so he only held her.

Through the window he saw that the black night had faded to gray. Before long, the sun would rise.

Molly tipped her head back to see him. "I think I'll take a bath."

Disappointment knotted his guts, but no way in hell would he let her know that. "Okay." Exhaustion pulled at him, but he wouldn't sleep. Not yet. Not until he had her somewhere safe. "It'll do you good to relax a little. Go ahead, and I'll clean up the mess in here."

Both palms on his chest, Molly whispered, "I was sort of hoping that you'd join me."

That compelling offer blasted his tiredness into oblivion. "Yeah?"

An impish smile teased him. "I don't know, though. The tub isn't huge," she said. "And you're awfully... big."

He fought the grin trying to take over. "If we work on our positioning, I think we'll fit just fine." After one quick kiss, he turned her and planted a light swat on that tempting ass. "Go get things started while I put this mess away."

She sent an indulgent laugh over her shoulder. "Chris is right, you know. You are a neat freak."

The mention of Chris made him wonder how his girls were doing. It was too early to call, but he'd check in with them on the way to her father's home.

Dare watched Molly disappear around the corner, and a second later he heard the water running. Primed, he made short work of the empty cola cans and pizza box. After rinsing the few dishes they'd used, he put them into her dishwasher. Other, soured dishes, had been in there since her abduction, so he went ahead and ran a cycle.

Already he'd seen every inch of her place. But as he surveyed it again, he thought that it could benefit from a good cleaning; it showed the absence of use since she'd been gone. If they were staying, he'd help her with that. But he wanted Molly as far from this place as he could get her, the sooner the better.

After checking all the windows again, Dare went to find her in the bathroom.

She didn't hear him come in, and he lounged against the doorframe, content to watch her. Already naked, with her shoulder-length hair pinned atop her head, she tested the water filling the tub—and gave Dare one hell of a show.

Lust carried him forward until he had her within reach. From behind, he cupped his hand over her sex—and she jumped in startled surprise, jerking around to face him.

Face going hot, she said, "You are far too quiet for a big man."

Dare's attention went to her heavy breasts. He cupped one in each hand, but resolutely held himself in check. She wanted a bath, he'd give her a bath. And now that he'd already had her, he'd be able to explore her body as he wanted without losing control.

Releasing her, he moved to the tub and turned off the water. "Get in."

She bit her lips, already breathing fast. Dare waited, visually exploring her ripe body until she gave in. He held her hand as she climbed into the tub and eased down into the warm water. Steam rose around her. The water lapped at the bottom of her breasts.

Wearing only jeans, Dare knelt down on the outside of the tub. "Lean back."

"I thought you were going to get in with me."

"I will. After."

"After…what?"

"After you come for me again."

Her eyes rounded, and she started to protest. Dare leaned in and drew one nipple into his mouth. She inhaled sharply, tangling her fingers into his hair and holding him close.

Dipping his hand down into the water, Dare cupped her inner thigh and parted her legs. "Bend your knees, Molly." He helped her to lean back as he gave that instruction.

Uncertain, she reclined in the tub until most of her body was submerged. After parting her legs more, Dare lifted one foot up and to the outside of the tub, then growled at the sight of her. "Just like that."

"I..."

"Shh." He picked up the soap and built up a lather in his hands. "Let me enjoy you."

"Oh, God." She closed her eyes and half turned her face away from him.

Smiling, Dare used the slick suds to tease her breasts, concentrating on her pointed nipples. Sliding his fingers around them, slicking over them, tugging.

Molly groaned, but quickly stifled the sound.

When her legs started to tense and close, Dare stopped her. He caught the leg closest to him and held her still. "Relax, Molly." He could see her small clitoris, now distended, begging for attention. He wanted to taste her again, and he would. Soon. "You're beautiful."

"I'm not. I mean, I'm not ugly, I know that. I was just worried about the bruises before. But...I mean, I'm not fishing for compliments or anything. It's just that I'm not..."

Dare rinsed her breasts, removing all the slick soap, then again playing with her nipples, using the new friction to arouse her even more.

Beneath the water, her small hands curled into tight fists. The sleek muscles in her thighs tensed. She'd lost weight through her ordeal, and he wondered how she would look when fully recovered. Would she flesh out even more with another ten or twelve pounds?

Leaning over her, a hand on each thigh to ensure her legs stayed open, he blew on her nipples. They drew painfully tight, and he couldn't resist drawing on her again, tonguing her nipples, sucking. He could spend an hour doing just this, but given her wriggling and panting, Molly wouldn't last if he did.

She needed release. Now.

Dipping both hands into the water, Dare said, "Keep wide-open for me, baby, okay?"

A soft groan was her only reply. Dare opened her lips, pressed one finger into her, and encountered silky slickness. He eased back from the grip of her body and added a second finger.

Her back arched as he worked them into her, slid out and pushed in again. With his other hand, he played with her clitoris, softly circling with his thumb, gauging her every shuddering breath, each small contraction.

"Dare."

He looked up at her face, saw her eyes squeezed tight, her lips parted to accommodate her deep, fast breaths. He strained his jeans, she was so damn sexy.

And so real.

With a broken moan, she grabbed his wrist, holding him still with his fingers buried inside her. Water sloshed out of the tub as she curled forward—and came.

Damn, but he'd misjudged his own discipline. His earlier release meant nothing, not with her like this, so wild, so carnal.

Gasping, she oh-so-slowly settled back again, limp, her legs dropped open, her arms lax. Dare eased his fingers from her and felt her flinch with an aftershock of sensation.

Standing, he shucked off his jeans and boxers and, holding her shoulders forward, stepped into the tub behind her. With a sigh, she rested back against his chest.

He knew she was sensitive still, but he couldn't resist covering each breast with a hand. He kissed her temple and tried to ignore his raging hard-on.

"Dare?"

"Yeah?" He sounded hoarse even to his own ears.

"I've never…" She went silent, then struggled to sit

up, to turn and face him. She looked at his body, at his erection, and a shameless grin appeared, followed by an embarrassed laugh. "I feel like a…I don't know. A hussy?"

Dare grinned. "You're a healthy woman, thank God."

She shook her head. "You don't understand. If someone would have told me that I'd do…well, what we just did… I'd have died of embarrassment just thinking about it."

"Why?" He toyed with a damp tendril of hair that hung to her shoulder. Her dewy skin looked lustrous and smooth, the bruises almost gone. His stomach knotted with the need to taste her all over.

"Because it's not like me. I mean, I wasn't a virgin—"

Emphatic, Dare interrupted her to warn, "I don't want to hear about you with other men."

That gave her pause. Then she complained, "I wasn't going to give you details, for crying out loud."

Damn right, she wasn't. "How about I cut to the chase here?" He drew her down to him, chest to chest, and kissed her. With his hands on her ass, ready to explore again, he said, "You aren't used to being so uninhibited."

"I'm really not." She jumped when he pressed a finger into her from behind. "Dare."

Against her lips, he whispered, "Hmm?" She was even slicker now, a little swollen, and he wanted to hear her come again. As he teased in and out of her, he kissed her more deeply, loving the way her belly moved against his boner, how her cushiony breasts rubbed on his chest. "Scoot up."

"I don't know about this." But she arched her back, driving his fingers deeper.

"Scoot up, Molly. I want to suck on your nipples."

She whimpered, and her sex tightened around his fingers—but she finally did as he asked. Bracing her hands on his shoulders, she levered up—and Dare closed his mouth around her, sucking hard.

She let out a deep, vibrating moan, rocking against him, damn near pushing him toward release until she finally cried out, climaxing hard again.

On a sigh, she whispered, "Oh, my God," and tried to settle down against him.

Laughing, Dare caught her shoulders and sat up with her in the tub. "Baby, don't go to sleep on me."

"No, I won't." But her eyes were slumberous, her body utterly boneless.

Dare grabbed the soap and washed while looking at her. At half-mast, her lids looked heavy, her lashes long. The heat of the bath and her orgasms had left her skin rosy.

And he wanted her more than he'd ever wanted anything.

After he rinsed, he used the soap on her. Ignoring her disconcerted exclamations, he bathed every inch of her, lingering between her legs again until he knew he had to stop torturing himself or he'd lose it.

He stepped out of the tub to dry off, then helped her out, too.

Licking her lips, Molly stared down at his aching erection. She reached out a hand, saying, "I had wanted to spend a little more time on you."

Ah, hell. Feeling a nearly uncontrollable surge of lust, Dare caught her wrist just short of her touching him. "Not this time." He'd had her, but he hadn't gotten enough. Not yet.

He was beginning to think a lifetime wouldn't be time enough, not with this one particular woman.

CHAPTER TWENTY-ONE

MOLLY WATCHED AS Dare drained the tub and used the towel to dry it. She stood there, aching all over, nerve endings alive, and he was indulging his tick for orderliness.

He had such an amazing body that she couldn't look at him without wanting him. But it was so much more than that. Even with everything that had happened to her, he made her feel more independent, stronger and capable than she'd realized possible.

He also brought out her carnal nature, so easily encouraging her to a lack of modesty, a total indulgence into sexuality. It was amazing.

He was amazing.

If he didn't come to bed with her, right now, she'd probably attack him. Bare foot tapping the tile floor, she asked, "Does my messiness bother you?"

Folding the towel and hanging it over the shower bar, he looked at her—then all over her. "You should see the inside of Chris's place if you want to see messy. And I still love him."

Her mouth went dry over that *L* word. Never had she known a man so comfortable with stating affection, especially for a friend.

Molly cleared her throat. "Well, it's just that you're…" She gestured at his naked body. "I mean…" She gestured at her own. "All this could be done later, right?"

"You think I give a damn if your bathroom is

cluttered?" He glanced at her askance as he picked up their clothes. "I'm hanging on by a thread here. I was just buying some time to get myself under control." He strode past her into the bedroom.

"Oh." Molly hustled after him. "I guess I'm not used to guys—"

Dropping the clothes on the floor, he turned and put a finger to her lips. "Again, I don't want to hear about you with any other man." He took her shoulders and dragged her closer to him. "No one has ever made me feel so god-damned possessive."

She started to say "Oh" again, but he took the word from her in a deep, hot, *really* possessive kiss.

Her toes curled.

Without her realizing it, he freed her hair from the topknot, and it tumbled down to her shoulders.

He sank both hands into her hair. "I can't believe you were going to cut this."

His mouth grazed her throat, her jaw. "I can't believe it mattered to you."

"It does." He kissed her neck, then her ear.

"I couldn't believe you took the time to work the tangles out for me." In fact, that might have been the moment she started falling for him. The tenderness after so much brutality, the matter-of-fact way he'd handled her and her personal trauma, had devastated her senses. She hadn't been prepared. She still wasn't.

"I enjoyed it." Hooking a forearm under her derriere, he lifted her and turned with her to the bed.

It was insane, how easily he handled her, the ease with which he lifted her, carried her. His strength continued to amaze her; his care would forever impress her.

Settling into the cradle of her body, he lifted to one

elbow and looked down at her. With care, he smoothed back her hair, kissed her swollen lips.

Molly touched his face. Tears threatened.

"What's wrong?"

She shook her head. "The way you look at me makes me feel pretty."

Pressing a hand between their bodies, he touched her, and his cheekbones darkened with aroused color. "Pretty doesn't cover it."

"No?" She could barely speak as he pushed not one, not two, but three fingers into her. Breathless, she whispered, "Then what does?"

Stroking in, back out. In again, so deep… "Smokin'." His chest expanded. "Sexy as sin." His gaze was so intent, it affected her as strongly as his touch when he said, "Mine."

Startled, Molly stared at him. She didn't know what to say, how to interpret that. "Dare…?"

He moved away from her in a rush, going for a condom that he rolled on in record time. When he came back to her, he caught her hips and turned her to her stomach. "On your knees."

Even as she got to her knees, her thoughts scrambled—until his hands clasped her waist and he drove into her with one hard thrust.

After two climaxes, she was swollen and sensitive and oh-so-ready for him. She cried out with that initial entry, then cried out again as he began a hard, fast rhythm. It was so deep this way, she felt every inch of him.

"Arch your hips up," he told her in a rough command. She felt one hand on the small of her back, the other under her, first touching her nipples, then sliding down between her legs.

It was too much. "Dare…I can't."

"Yes, you can." Just as he'd done to her nipples, he caught her clitoris and held it with his fingertips. Each of his deep thrusts caused her to tug at his hold in a maddening stimulation.

When she groaned, he said, "Spread your knees out a little more, baby."

The pleasure drugged her until she couldn't think, could only feel. She felt heavy, so heavy that her arms didn't want to support her and they bent until she rested on her forearms.

Dare growled a low approval over that.

Another release began spiraling within her, drawing tighter and tighter. Her body throbbed, ripe and aching and in need.

Dare started pumping faster, and she knew he was close. His thighs were slapping hard against the back of hers. Heat poured off him, off her.

Tighter and tighter.

Her lungs burned. Her legs trembled.

Eyes clenched, Molly fisted her hands in the sheets to hang on—and the release hit her. She cried out loud, sobbing with the power of it, her body on fire.

Dare's savage groan filled her ears. He stroked deep, stiffened, and she knew he was coming, too. He'd held on, waited for her.

When he stilled, she literally collapsed flat on the bed. Dare landed over her and started to move, but she whispered, "Please. Not yet."

She could still feel him inside her, not as big now, but she didn't want to lose the sensation yet.

"Just for a minute," he whispered with a kiss to her ear, and he wrapped his arms around her, giving her his weight.

It felt heavenly. It felt safe.

It felt like love.

MOLLY FELT THE HANDS on her, pinching. Deliberately hurting. She couldn't see beyond her fear, but she cursed them, English curses that she knew they might not understand but gave her strength all the same.

One man reached for her breast and laughed at her panic. Instead, he struck her in the ribs. She lost her breath, gagging with the pain, falling to her knees, knowing they might kick her, knowing the ground held bugs and mud and worse. She struggled to stay upright, struggled, struggled...

Jerking awake with a start, Molly cried out—and immediately Dare came into the room.

"Hey. It's okay." The overhead light came on, blinding her. The bed dipped when he sat down beside her, when he pulled her into his arms.

Her throat felt too tight for her to swallow, burning with the need to cry. She was crying. She felt the tears hot on her cheeks and shame beat at her.

Angry at herself, at the bastards who'd done this to her, she tried to struggle away from Dare.

He tightened his hold. "Don't do that, Molly. I understand. I know. But don't push me away." He kissed her hair, closed those impossibly strong arms around her.

"I hate them." Her voice sounded high and broken, infuriating her more. Shaming her more.

"I do, too." Shifting, he pulled her onto his lap. "When I was younger, when I got that knife wound on my chest?"

That got her attention, and she nodded to let him know she was listening.

"I was so pissed off I was blind with it. Mostly at myself for not being able to stop it, but at the man who did it, too. It took me a few weeks to recover, especially after I got an infection."

Dare wore a shirt now, and she subtly tried to dry her eyes against the soft cotton.

He caught the sheet and lifted a corner of it to her. "Do you need a tissue?"

"No." She sounded strangled, as if those awful hands were around her throat again, threatening to kill her. She buried her face against Dare. Ignoring the rasp of her voice, the weakness, she asked, "What were you doing when you got stabbed?"

"This isn't to be repeated."

She nodded.

"A senator's son was being held hostage. I was hired to go get him. Me, specifically, because no one knew me yet. I was brand-new, tested but not yet tried, if you know what I mean."

His hands moved over her back, up and down, not in any way sexual but still possessive.

Molly gulped back a fresh wave of tears. "I don't."

"I'd been trained. Everyone knew what I could do in live-action tests, but I hadn't yet gone out in the field. This was my maiden run. And I almost fucked it up."

As the nightmare faded, she licked her dry lips. "But you didn't?"

"No, thank God. Not entirely. If I had, the kid would've died. Talk about nightmares…" He shook his head and squeezed her again. After a deep breath, he continued. "The boy, who was around twelve at the time, was being held in a compound in Arizona. The place was owned by a wealthy, supposedly law-abiding businessman. No one would have thought to look for the kid there. But I've always had good instincts, and I tracked him to that location."

"How?"

"You can almost always gauge a person by their

associations. If a man has enough ties with people of questionable character, then I label him questionable."

"Like my dad."

"Like your dad," he agreed.

Thinking about her father added to her angst. "How do you think you messed up?"

"I got too emotional." Disgust sounded in his tone. "Thoughts of that kid and how scared he had to be, wondering if he was hurt or even being hurt right then, riddled my discipline." The muscles of his face tightened, and his voice lowered. "Even knowing better, I went in too soon."

Concern for Dare dispelled the leftover fear of the nightmare. She looked up and saw his beautiful face, the clean-cut jaw, the straight nose and deep blue eyes. "What did you do?"

"I found the boy. They'd roughed him up some, deliberately terrified him, but he was being so damned mature, so strong... He didn't cry." Dare looked down at her, using his thumb to brush away a tear. "I would have understood if he had. His eyes were red, and his voice shook. I was so proud of him—just like I'm proud of you."

"You saved him?"

"Yeah, I got him out of there, though not before I had to tackle a guard." His mouth quirked. "The son of a bitch blindsided me, and he was going to cut my throat. But that scrawny little kid jumped on his back, wrapping around him like a spider monkey. It slowed him down and gave me the advantage I needed."

She knew, but still she asked, "To do what?"

Dare's eyes darkened. "I pulled that fucking knife out of my chest and gutted the bastard with it."

Dear Lord. "You could do that?"

"He didn't hit my heart or a lung, so yeah. It hurt like

hell, but it wasn't a death blow." He rubbed his ear. "The thing is, if the kid hadn't acted when he did, we both would have died, and that's inexcusable. It was a lesson about taking my time, studying everything before I make a move." He went silent for a second, then he let out a breath. "It was a lesson, too, about my own ability."

"Because you got him and yourself out of there."

He discounted his own heroism. "God, I bled like a stuck pig. Twice I almost passed out. Luckily my guys were waiting outside the perimeter of the place, because I'm not sure I'd have gotten much farther before dropping."

Tucking her head against his shoulder, Molly hugged him. "I'm so glad you made it."

"Yeah." He let her sit there for a while, not rushing her. "The thing is, that day plagued me for months. I couldn't close my eyes without thinking about all the possibilities, all the what-ifs and what-could-have-been scenarios. It's human nature to agonize over unsettling episodes."

"How did you finally get past it?"

"Time. And closure." He gave her a hug. "After I healed, I exposed everyone involved in that kidnapping, without putting the kid or his father out there for the media to pick apart. Knowing those bastards were punished helped me to put it behind me and move forward."

Would finding the one responsible for her abduction somehow rid the dregs of fear from her memory? God, she hoped so.

Molly would have liked to linger in Dare's embrace, but she knew they had to get moving. She tipped her head up to see Dare. "How long have you been awake?"

"I didn't go to sleep."

Now she felt doubly bad. She moved away from him and shoved her hair from her face. "I'm sorry I did."

"You needed your rest." Holding her chin, he bent and kissed her, lightly, easily. "You think you can get ready now? We don't want to miss your dad."

She'd like to miss him. The last person she wanted to see was her father. He could be abrasive at the best of times, and this… Well, he wasn't going to add to the festivities.

But the reality was that the confrontation had to happen.

"Sure." Realizing that she was naked while Dare was dressed, Molly blushed. "Could I have some privacy?"

He stared at her for a long time before his mouth curled into a grin. "All right." He got up from the bed. "I'd like you to pack a bag, too. Take whatever you think you'll need."

Not sure what to say to that, Molly looked around her room for inspiration and found none. "How long will I be gone?"

He gave her another lingering look. "Pack enough for a few weeks, and we'll see what happens." And with that, he left the room.

Molly took a few moments to catch her breath, but a peek at the clock told her she had to hustle if she wanted to pull it together in the right way. After washing, brushing her teeth and dressing in casual jeans, a red sweater and boots, she styled her hair and applied some makeup. Seeing herself in the mirror, she felt better, more like herself.

Then she remembered everything she'd done with Dare, and a flush of heat brightened her skin. She put her hands to her cheeks and fought back the giddiness. No, she wasn't like herself at all, at least not with Dare.

Not sexually.

With him, she always felt better than ever before—at everything.

Hurrying so that Dare wouldn't be waiting on her, she got out her briefcase first and stowed what she could of her manuscript, her flash drive, everything she thought she might need to continue working on her book. Remembering that both Chris and Dare had said they wanted to read her work, she found a few of the paperback copies in her closet and packed them, too. While in the closet, she found a replacement purse on the floor. Although she didn't have her wallet, she'd feel more complete with a purse on her arm. She loaded it with a few essentials like a comb, lip gloss, a small mirror, mints…anything she thought she might need. Later, after they went to the bank, she'd put money in there, too.

She did not like being dependent on Dare for everything. It was enough that he kept her safe without him paying her way, too.

Next, she dragged her suitcase out from under the bed and packed the toiletries she used most often. She spotted the birth-control pills, and decided to get back on them ASAP. Any woman who was sexually active couldn't be too careful. And she fully intended to stay sexually active with Dare.

After taking one, she packed the rest in her purse. Assuming she wouldn't need any dressier clothes, she folded in several pairs of jeans, sweaters and sweatshirts, underwear, bras, socks, another pair of shoes, her sneakers and two sets of pajamas.

It was as she was placing those in that Dare looked in on her. He frowned at the ice-blue, very cute PJs on top of her case. "You won't need those."

"They're pajamas," she told him, just in case he didn't realize.

He settled an incendiary gaze on her, studied her a moment with interest and moved closer. Distracted, he continued to look at her as he said, "We'll be sleeping together."

She had assumed as much, but was glad to have it verified all the same. "Chris—"

"Goes to his own place at night." He tipped his head, examining her features with a touch of confusion. "I'm the only one who will see you, and you don't have anything to hide from me." His gaze dipped to her breasts. "I like looking at you."

Pleasure expanded inside her. "It's still cold outside, especially in the evenings."

Now standing right in front of her, Dare touched his fingers to her cheek. "I'll keep you plenty warm enough."

Oh, boy, did she believe him on that. Around Dare, she spent most of her time overheated. "Still, there might come a point when you want your privacy—"

"No."

Just that, nothing more. But he sounded pretty sure about it. Molly tucked in her chin. "All the same, you might have to go off on business again—"

"I won't be leaving you."

Exasperated, she forged on without missing a beat. "Or I might want *my* privacy, so I think I'll bring them along. Just in case."

For the longest time he watched her, until a slight smile transformed his stern expression. "There's something so damn sexy about a take-charge woman."

The quick switch threw her; Dare had the strangest way of interpreting things.

He continued to look her over, her eyes, her cheeks, her mouth.

Discomfited by his probing stare, she finally said, *"What?"*

"Sorry." He shook his head. "Seeing you in makeup… It's surprising."

Fidgeting, Molly asked, "In a good way, I hope?"

"You look classy. Polished." He bent for a quick kiss. "I got used to seeing you barefaced, but you always look good, never doubt it."

Did that mean he preferred her without makeup? "Thank you."

"One thing." His gaze sharpened. "Did you spruce up for your father, or just because you wanted to?"

Molly laughed with disdain. "Oh, trust me, Dad wouldn't notice if I was bald and painted blue. But, yeah, Kathi can be critical. She's really into appearances. Being snatched off the street and taken across the country for torment is no excuse for not looking your best."

Dare turned away with disgust. "Kathi sounds like a real twit." Then he indicated her overflowing luggage. "You done with this?"

Glad that he hadn't mentioned how much she'd packed, Molly nodded. She didn't want Dare to think she was moving in or taking advantage of his hospitality. But like most women, she liked to be prepared. "Yes, thank you."

"I'm not your stepmother."

She snorted. "An indisputable fact."

"I just meant that you don't have to be all proper with me." He closed the lid and lifted the heavy case off the bed without any effort at all. "You want to get your stuff together for the bank and the post office? I'd like to carry everything to my SUV in one trip."

Likely because he wanted to be at her side every

second. Molly had been with him enough to understand how seriously he took his intent to keep her safe.

"Sure." She went into the kitchen to get a plastic grocery bag. She couldn't help but notice that Dare had been busy. He'd found one of her big green plastic garbage bags and filled it with old food from the fridge and the empty pizza boxes and cola cans.

Usually she recycled, but she couldn't see making an issue of it now. That he'd done so much work in her kitchen amused her and at the same time made her feel like a slug. Hands on her hips, she told him, "You cleaned."

"I like to keep busy." He helped her store her packages into the bag, and she gathered up the checks she needed to deposit. "You have your account numbers?"

"I know them. But I do need to cancel my credit cards."

She could see him making a mental list when he said, "We have a lot to take care of today."

"If we go to the bank before the post office, I can get some money." And maybe on the drive back to his place, they could stop for her to buy an actual wallet to keep the money in. But she'd broach that possibility later.

At the mention of money, Dare started to say something, then wisely changed his mind. "If that's what you want."

The long-suffering way he said that gave her pause. "I'm perfectly capable of paying my own way, you know. If I somehow made you think otherwise—"

"No, it's not that. I know you're financially independent." He nodded toward her bookcase—which he'd also straightened. "That's quite an impressive showing."

The bookcase held not only the books she liked to read, but many of her own in various formats. "I grabbed a few copies for you and Chris, with no obligation that you'll have to read them."

"Thank you." He used the side of his hand to tip up her face. "Anyone can see that you're a successful woman. It's just that I don't want you to have to worry about financial stuff right now."

"I'll feel better having my own money with me."

He rubbed a hand over his mouth, considered what she'd said and then gave in with a nod. "Yeah, I know I'd feel the same." He cupped the back of her neck and kissed her. "Anything else?"

The way he constantly kissed her and touched her was like a balm to her abused spirit. And it gave her hope that her affection was returned.

"Molly?"

She shook off the warmth of his attention. "Is it all right if I call my agent and editor, too?" She'd always been conscientious about her work, and wondering what they both thought plagued her. "I really need to get in touch with them. I'm sure they're confused as to why I just disappeared."

"How about after we leave your dad's?"

"That'll work. It's too early right now anyway." With all the arrangements made, Dare gathered up everything they had to take out. Molly turned off the lights, and they left the apartment.

WITH EACH PASSING mile, Molly's dread grew until finally they pulled into her father's estate. Anxiety kept her chewing her lip, until Dare squeezed her thigh.

"Relax, will you?"

It amazed her that he paid almost no attention to her father's obvious wealth. But then, she didn't, either. For her, the massive estate represented only sadness.

To her, Dare's home was far more magnificent—and was about half the size of her father's.

She'd grown up knowing what material things meant to her dad and how skewed his priorities were. Bishop Alexander would do just about anything to maintain his wealth.

Dare wasn't like that at all. He was a man of substance, a man who had amassed wealth, but not at the expense of others. Just the opposite.

"When Adrian first saw this," she said, indicating the vast European-style home ahead of them down the long drive, "I swear he almost drooled."

Dare took off his mirrored sunglasses and leaned forward to look out the windshield as he slowed. But it wasn't with awe.

"The security is lacking. Anyone who can afford a home that size should have a gated and monitored entry."

Molly shrugged. "There are sensors around the grounds. But deer come through here, along with a lot of other wildlife, and they were forever setting off alarms. Dad gave up years ago and hired people to keep an eye on the place instead of technology."

"He keeps guards on staff?"

"You could call them that. Natalie and I always called them sentries." She grinned. "There's always one around back, one around front, in rotating shifts." She wrinkled her nose. "They act really cold, and they're good at mean-mugging everyone. No smiling or chitchat. I don't like them much."

"What about your stepmother? She likes them?"

"Kathi is fine with anything Dad wants. Her biggest goal in life is to keep him happy." As they neared the house, she saw the front guard step out and talk into a walkie-talkie–type device. "So ostentatious."

"How many rooms does the place have?"

Seeing Dare in analytical mode always impressed her. He didn't ask out of mere curiosity, but rather to get a sense of the layout. "Six bedrooms, seven and a half baths."

"What else?"

"Hmm." She thought about it for a second, trying to think what might be important to Dare. "Five sitting rooms. Five garage bays. A library and a gallery. Kitchen and breakfast room, of course, and a covered, outdoor salon."

"Master bedroom upstairs or down? Is the basement finished?"

"There's a master up and down, but unless they've changed it, Dad and Kathi's bedroom is on the main floor. They have a wine cellar downstairs, and Dad has a work area, like with tools and stuff, that he seldom uses. Not much else."

The guard had come down the stairs to await Dare. He didn't look happy.

Come to that, Dare didn't, either.

"Do you know him?"

"I've seen him before. I think his name is George Wallace, but I'm not certain," Molly whispered. "It's been a while since I visited."

Dare got out and, ignoring the armed man, came around to Molly's door. He helped her out and then locked his car with the click of a remote.

The man came to stand in front of them, deliberately blocking them. "Are you expected?"

Molly started to step in front of Dare, but he stopped her. "George?"

The guard's expression went flinty. "Do I know you?"

"Tell Bishop I'm here. And you might want to tell him that I'm coming in—" he stared into the man's eyes "—one way or another. How much ruckus is caused is up to him."

Keeping his stony expression, George asked, "And you are?"

Dare gave that eerie, mean smile of his. "He'll know."

The sentry looked beyond Dare to Molly. "You're one of the daughters?"

Dare answered for her. "She's none of your damned business."

Green eyes narrowing, the man back-stepped a few feet away and put in a call. A light breeze ruffled his dark hair; he wore a stark white dress shirt and tie, with his belt holster exposed. Though he spoke too softly for Molly to hear, she had a gut feeling that nothing got by Dare.

After a minute, the man stowed his phone and approached again. "You can go up to the front door. Someone will let you in."

Unnerved by all the tension and more than ready to escape it, Molly started forward. Again Dare stopped her. He and the man did more staring, and although no words were exchanged, the guard must have understood, because after one laconic nod, he preceded Dare to the front door, rang the bell and then stepped to the side, where Dare could still see him.

Under her breath, Molly asked, "You didn't trust him?"

"At my back? Hell, no."

A young Hispanic girl in a pale blue uniform answered

the door and gestured them into the cavernous two-story foyer. As the girl moved away again, Dare made note of every door around them. Had he packed his gun? His knife? She peeked at the small of his back and saw that now-familiar bulge beneath his shirt.

Strangely, knowing he was armed made her more at ease.

He caught her gaze and easily interpreted her thoughts, because he told her, "With a weapon or without, no one is going to hurt you as long as you're with me. You have my promise on that."

He spoke with so much confidence, Molly believed him. He would protect her from physical harm. Sadly, with her father, it was more the verbal abuse that she dreaded, and there'd be nothing Dare could do about that.

CHAPTER TWENTY-TWO

HER FATHER WASN'T the one to greet them. Kathi came around the corner, heels clicking on the floor, her face full of smiles. Her chin-length, wavy brown hair danced around her face in a precise style that somehow managed to look casual. She wore dark designer jeans, pointy-toed ankle boots and a cozy cashmere sweater.

"Molly! I must have missed your call. I'm afraid I wasn't expecting you."

The mild rebuke didn't faze Molly; she was used to it, whether she'd made an appointment to see her father or not. "There wasn't time to call."

Kathi embraced her, kissed the air near her cheek and then held her back. "My, my, my." She touched Molly's hair. "It looks like you haven't seen the inside of a salon in forever."

"It has been a while."

Kathi smiled and, as if she knew nothing of the kidnapping, said, "I know how you are. You start writing, and you forget everything else. Have you lost weight? That's good, I suppose, but not if you've done it improperly."

Acutely aware of Dare beside her, Molly wanted to groan. "A few pounds, yes." Being starved often had that effect.

Did Kathi truly not know of her kidnapping? It wouldn't be beyond her father not to share that news. But somehow,

Molly thought she knew, and that made her inane chatter all the more annoying.

"You have the darkest shadows under your eyes, too." Appearing concerned, Kathi studied her face. "Aren't you getting enough sleep?"

"I sleep fine." *Now.* Since crawling into Dare's bed, she'd found it easy to relax and catch up on her sleep. "Those are bruises."

Kathi looked more closely, and she tsked. "Oh, dear. What have you done to yourself? You always were accident-prone. I've told you that yoga would give you added grace if only you'd—"

Feeling the flush in her face, she cut off Kathi's ridiculous banter and gestured toward Dare. "Kathi, this is Dare Macintosh. Dare, my stepmother, Kathi Berry-Alexander."

Having paid no attention to Dare until he was formally acknowledged by Molly, Kathi looked up at him. Fingers splayed over her throat, she whispered, "Oh, my."

Dare said nothing.

Kathi held out a delicate, well-manicured hand. "Mr. Macintosh, how very nice to meet you. You're a friend of Molly's?"

Dare didn't miss a beat. He held Kathi's hand for the briefest of greetings that barely passed for polite and said only, "Mrs. Alexander."

"Berry-Alexander." Nonplussed by his lack of a response to her direct and social question, Kathi fiddled with the end of her hair. "Yes, well...I'm sorry that we're ill prepared for guests. I was just finishing breakfast and was on my way out the door. We're breaking ground on a new youth community building today."

And that explained the jeans, Molly thought. Not that

anyone would mistake Kathi's clothing as appropriate for dirt-digging.

"We won't hold you up." As if Molly weren't with him, Dare said, "I'm here to see Bishop."

Kathi's strained smile wouldn't have fooled anyone. "I'm so sorry." She looked to Molly. "Of course he'd like to see you, you know that. It's been forever since you visited." She let out a breath and looked back to Dare. "But I'm afraid my husband is rushed, as well. He has an important business meeting this morning."

Molly wanted to groan. She needed this—whatever it was—over with.

"Tell him I'm here." Dare stared down at Kathi. "He'll make time for me."

"Oh." Kathi pursed her mouth. "He's acquainted with you?"

Dare waited, again not answering. His blatant disregard for her nosiness left Molly desperate to fill in the silence, but she fought off the urge.

Kathi put her hands together. She tried, but she didn't have the same lethal qualities that Dare possessed. "Yes," Kathi finally murmured. "Let me ask him what he'd like to do."

She turned and, in regal fashion, exited the room.

Molly didn't realize she was holding her breath until Dare put a hand between her shoulder blades.

"Breathe, honey."

She inhaled with a gasp. "Oh, my God, that was painfully awkward."

Dare just shrugged. "If you thought so, then gird yourself, because I hear Bishop approaching, and given the weight of his stomping footsteps, it's about to get worse."

Now that Dare said it, she noticed the difference in her

father's usual metered approach, too. He came around the corner, but he wasn't alone. He had one of the guards, and Kathi, with him.

For only a second his concerned gaze roamed over Molly, taking her in from head to toes. Something tightened in his face—concern for a daughter who had survived a kidnapping and severe treatment at the hands of goons? Molly just didn't know. Often her father had been cold, but then, she'd never had her life threatened before.

Seeing that she was whole, Bishop quickly focused all his attention on Dare, a more deserving adversary.

Resentment brought the words to Molly's mouth. "Hello, Father."

All three of them glanced her way. Together, they made a potent triumvirate of animosity.

Dare laughed over their united front. "Should I consider this your idea of backup?"

The guard didn't like that. His left eye twitched, and he made a point of showing his gun.

Softly, Dare taunted, "Try it." Without breaking eye contact, he said, "I guarantee Bishop will get the first bullet."

Kathi made sounds of alarm, her hand at her throat, her gaze going everywhere.

Bishop didn't move.

Finally, the guard disengaged from his challenge. It was an amazing thing for Molly to see, but then, she'd known all along that Dare had that intimidating effect on people.

Expression severe, her father started to speak, and Dare silenced him with a look.

"You want this aired, Bishop, fine by me. Let's open the windows and make sure the whole staff hears. But I had assumed you'd want some privacy—given your over-riding concern for keeping things quiet."

Impotent with rage, face distorted with displeasure, Bishop dismissed the guard with a raise of his hand.

The guard hesitated. "Should I stay inside, sir?"

He shook his head, and in a bid for privacy, said, "Take the rest of the day off."

It was clear that the guard wanted to argue, but didn't dare.

As he started away, Kathi frowned, moved with him and spoke quietly before returning to stand at her husband's side.

Bishop's gaze shifted to Molly again. "You're back."

"Yes."

He hesitated, struggling with himself, but finally asked, "Unharmed?"

Kathi hugged his arm. "She's well, Bishop, as you can see."

Annoyance showing, her father continued to watch her. "She can speak for herself."

"Yes," Molly said. "Thanks to Dare, I'm okay."

He nodded. To Molly, he almost looked relieved.

But now that the guard was out of range, he said low, "I can't believe you came here, Molly. What were you thinking?"

Dare spoke up. "I brought her."

Bishop looked at them both with disdain, but again gave his attention to Molly. "Do you have no shame?"

Molly did what she'd always done when faced with her father's loathing. She squared her shoulders and donned an air of nonchalance. "I have no reason to be ashamed."

"That's not…" He inhaled deeply, looked away and

then back again. "You'll bring a scandal down on all of us."

Molly curled her lip. "And that's what matters most to you, right?"

"What the hell are you saying?" Freeing himself from Kathi's hold, Bishop took a step toward her. Before she could blink, Dare was in front of her. He didn't draw a gun, but he did take out his phone.

"You want to be an ass, Bishop, fine. I'm sure the FBI will be interested in investigating Molly's abduction into Mexico and your probable role in it all."

Kathi reacted theatrically. *"Mexico?"*

Bishop cursed as he pulled her back, signaling that he wanted her silence.

"No." Inside his fancy suit, her father bunched and shifted and, knowing him as she did, probably worked up a sweat. "No, goddamn it, I do not want the law involved in this. *Not* because I have any involvement, but because—"

"It's bad publicity. Yeah, I get it." Dare shut his phone, and took a step forward to tower over her father. "Insult her again, give her so much as a dirty look, and I'll make the call with the sole purpose of ruining you. Understand me?"

"How dare you?" Kathi whispered, sounding truly enraged. "You can't—"

"Fine." Bishop inched back from Dare's quiet, controlled anger. To Kathi, he ordered, "Get some coffee. Bring it to the library."

Kathi touched his arm. "Bishop, I don't know about this. I don't know about him." She looked at Dare so no one would misunderstand.

"I'll be fine." He shrugged off her hand and stormed

ahead, saying to Dare, "Come on then. Let's get this over with."

Dare slipped an arm around Molly. Near her ear, he asked quietly, "You holding on okay?"

She nodded with ill humor. "Typical day with my dad." But she knew this wasn't typical at all. Her father didn't love her. He'd never loved her. For him, she was an inconvenience that he'd been saddled with, a daughter that forever disappointed him.

But now she had to accept that he might have had her kidnapped rather than continue to suffer her.

Her heart didn't break, because long ago her heart had accepted that her father would never care. But she did feel shame—bone-deep shame for Dare to see how little she mattered to him.

They stepped into the large mahogany library. It smelled of lemons and leather and books. Lots and lots of books. As a child, Molly had been forbidden entrance to this room, which had of course made it all the more desirable.

Her love of storytelling had begun while disobeying her father and raiding his most cherished room.

Dare's hand found hers. He laced his fingers through her own, gave her a gentle squeeze. She glanced up at him, and there was so much warmth in his gaze, so much acceptance and, oddly, admiration.

And then, right there in front of her father, Dare bent to kiss her. Molly knew what he did, and why: he wanted her father to understand, without a single doubt, that for Dare she was a priority.

How her father would take that news was left to be seen.

DARE SAT BACK ON the leather couch, his legs stretched out and relaxed, one arm on the back of the couch behind

Molly. He hated putting her through this, but already he'd learned a lot.

Kathi wasn't what he'd expected. Other than her damn mouth that could cut with sugary sweetness, she seemed soft and comfortable, not at all the rigid, uptight, perfectly coifed woman he'd expected.

Didn't mean she wasn't a bitch. She was.

And it didn't mean he'd cut Bishop any slack, even though his wife wasn't the trophy Dare had assumed she would be.

But maybe if he'd already misjudged Kathi, he'd made other misjudgments, as well. He'd have to think about that and strive to keep an open mind.

On everything, and everyone.

Bishop had taken refuge behind a massive desk where he held his peace while Kathi poured fragrant, gourmet coffee into china cups resting on saucers.

Both he and Molly declined the drink. Not that Dare would have let her consume anything offered by these people. They weren't beyond poisoning.

The device on his key chain buzzed, and Dare lifted it out. After a glance at it, he said to Bishop, "Instruct your men to stay out of my car."

Bishop harrumphed. "I don't know what you're talking about."

"Then you're dumber than I assumed." Dare held up the device for him to see. "Someone is trying to get into the back of my SUV. If it's not under your order, then I'm free to kill the bastard for his daring." He made to rise.

Nearly choking on his anger, Bishop waved Dare back to his seat and then spoke quietly to Kathi.

She nodded and left the room.

Dare noticed that Kathi hadn't blinked an eye over

his statement that he might kill. Was she used to such things?

From Bishop and his cohorts?

Disbelief brought Molly forward on her seat. "Dad, really? You had someone break into Dare's car? And don't play innocent. Nothing happens here without your consent."

Lacking remorse, Bishop shrugged. "I'm sure your *guardian* understands caution."

Molly wasn't appeased. "I understand an invasion of privacy!"

Dare put a hand on her thigh—something that Bishop didn't miss—and Molly subsided.

That Bishop now understood the intimacy of their involvement suited Dare. He wanted her father to know that in every way, Dare had a stake in keeping her safe. Unless he really was an idiot, Bishop would understand that an emotionally involved man would be far more lethal than someone only interested in financial remuneration.

"I understand precaution, too, Bishop. There's no way in hell you're going to catch me off guard, so you might as well give it a rest." Dare watched him closely as he sipped his coffee. "But then, you didn't get the message the last time we spoke, did you?"

Kathi reentered the room and went to sit in an ornate armchair at the side of her husband's desk. Like a well-trained lapdog, she looked prepared to wait in silence until her husband needed something from her.

Bishop set his cup aside with a clatter. "What are you talking about?"

"You had Molly's apartment ransacked. Tell me, what were you looking for?"

"The hell I did!"

"You tossed the place." In his peripheral vision, Dare

saw Kathi look down at her hands. Interesting. He didn't want to look at her directly, but even indirectly he saw that she knew...something.

Was it guilt over her husband's involvement? Had Bishop actually told her of what he planned? Had he involved her?

Furious, Bishop leaned forward. "I did nothing of the kind."

"It wasn't destruction meant as a threat. You wanted something. Tell me what you were looking for."

His fist slammed down on the desk, causing Kathi to jump. "I'm telling you that I didn't go anywhere near her damned apartment."

Conversely, Dare kept his tone mild. "Maybe not personally. But you sent someone."

"I didn't!" Emphatic and insulted, he braced both hands on the desk and rose to his feet. "Yes, I told a private investigator that's assisted me in the past about your...visit. But I didn't send anyone to Molly's apartment."

"I told you not to speak of it to anyone."

"You had my daughter!" Bishop shouted. "You told me she'd been kidnapped. I had a right to find out what I could about you."

Dare almost believed him. His reactions were honest umbrage, not subterfuge.

The idea of him trying to dig into his past made Dare smile. "Came up blank, didn't you?"

Bishop switched tactics and appealed to Molly. "What do you really know about this man? Have you checked into his past? Do you know what he's done, what he's capable of doing? How safe do you think you are while under his control?"

"He doesn't control me. I'm with him because it's the safest place for me to be right now."

That struck Dare. Was safety her only reason for being with him? No, he didn't believe that—but it sounded viable to tell her father.

"He's had his hands all over you!" Bishop accused. "He's sleeping with you for your money, and you're desperate enough—"

"Bishop." The softly spoken reminder cut through Bishop's raised voice. Dare wanted a reason to take the bastard apart.

But he'd prefer that it not be in front of Molly.

Panting, her father retrenched, taking his seat in a formal display that left Kathi twitching beside him.

Lower, he mumbled, "He's after *my* money, Molly. Can't you see that?"

Molly shook her head. "You're painting him with your own attributes, Dad. Dare isn't like that. And in fact, he's wealthy in his own right. He doesn't need your money, and he won't take mine." Sounding sour, she added, "I've tried to pay him, and he won't let me."

Kathi licked her lips and joined the fray. "Molly, honey, you haven't shown the best judgment in the past. Adrian is a perfect example."

Molly turned on Kathi with disbelief. "But you and Dad *wanted* me to marry Adrian! Have you forgotten that?"

"He was the only prospect, and you were already involved with him. And at least he had some breeding." She glanced at Dare and cleared her throat. "Perhaps if you had taken our advice just that one time, we wouldn't be here now, dealing with this new...*situation* of yours."

"She's right," Bishop said. "You refused Adrian's attention and then went and got yourself kidnapped and God knows what else."

"I can't believe this." Molly shot to her feet before

Dare could get hold of her. She charged toward her father, finger pointed. "He was a user! Adrian only supported my career once he saw I was making good money. You're right—he probably wanted your money, too. The poor fool didn't realize that you'd disowned Natalie and me ages ago."

"You aren't disowned," Kathi quietly said with a disapproving frown. "You know your father only wanted to ensure that you reached your own potential rather than relying on his accomplishments for your happiness. He wanted you to be independent. He is a wonderful father."

Good God, Dare thought. Did the twit really believe that nonsense?

Molly snorted. And then to her dad, she said, "For the record, I didn't *get* myself kidnapped. Someone else arranged that for me."

"Whoever took you must have had a reason." Kathi moved to put a supporting hand on Bishop's shoulder. "And now you want poor Bishop to bail you out of this predicament."

"Ha!" Molly's scorn cracked like a whip in the quiet library. "Fat chance, Kathi, because I would never take anything from him."

Bishop held up a hand to quiet any rebuttal from Kathi. "Then what are you doing here?" He joined the women on their feet. "If he's not after some sort of payoff, what do the two of you want?"

Dare looked from one person to the next, and he sighed. "So, we're to do this standing, huh?" He shook his head and rose from the couch.

Withdrawing two photos, Dare went to the desk and laid them down, then slid them around for Bishop to see. "You're friends with Ed Warwick and Mark Sagan."

Confused, Bishop shook his head. "Friends? No. We're associates. We've done business together on occasion. What of it? They're reputable men."

"Sagan is a white separatist."

"Nonsense." Genuinely perturbed, Bishop huffed—and stared at those photos. "You can't prove that."

"Wanna bet?" Dare pointed to the other photo. "Warwick was busted on sliding illegal immigrants through the system to get them ready to vote for a senator that *you* backed, likely in exchange for favors."

Through his teeth, Bishop said, "Warwick was cleared of that."

"Not even close. He was never prosecuted, no, but not because he was innocent. Your good buddy Sagan took care of the evidence. A dead body has a way of spooking anyone else who might want to testify against his client."

"That man died in a hit-and-run!"

Ah, so Bishop knew of all that. Of course he did. Dare shook his head in loathing. "Sagan has plenty of muscle to go around. He staged that hit-and-run, and you know it." Dare shoved the photos closer to Bishop. "The people hoping to emigrate here were cheated of a chance at a better life because of Warwick's bullshit. They were all sent home with their papers revoked. Warwick and Sagan have hurt more people than you and I can count."

Mulling that over, Bishop shook his head. "It's not like that. They've shared inside tips on property. A restaurant, a hotel... That's all."

"Properties that you bought under market value?"

He shrugged. "They were good deals for me, and they've proven lucrative. I stay in touch with many different people for just such business advantages." Sounding more subdued, he again insisted, "All of them are *only* associates."

Dare wasn't buying it, not for a second. "Lie to yourself if you want, but you can't fob that story off on me." He pointed a finger at the photos where Bishop and Kathi were socializing with the men, well outside of business. "A man who lies with dogs always ends up with fleas."

Chin up, Bishop skewered Dare with a hate-filled look. "So I'm guilty by association?"

"Damn right. What's really telling, though," Dare continued, "is that your friendship with those fucks gives you opportunity."

Appearing ill, Kathi sank back into her seat.

Showing uncharacteristic discomposure, Bishop demanded, "Opportunity for *what?*"

Dare drew Molly closer to him. "To have your daughter kidnapped and smuggled into Tijuana."

With visible effort, Bishop drew himself together. "Why the hell would I want to do that? She's my *daughter.*"

Face paling, Kathi looked between the two men. "It's incomprehensible that Bishop would do such a thing." She glared at Molly. "I can't credit this. You little fool. You would dare to accuse your father?"

Dare said, "*I'm* accusing him."

"Then you go too far." Angry color tinged her cheeks and made her eyes glassy. "Bishop is a highly respected businessman, an icon in society! He is above reproach."

"Yeah, right." Dare didn't bother hiding his contempt. "He's a social climber who enjoys leisure time with the bottom-feeders as long as they have something of interest to give to him."

Kathi stiffened. "You make him sound like a...an opportunist!"

"Dead-on." And then, tiring of the game, Dare said,

"Face up to the real life, will you? Your husband spends his time with a white separatist who sports a laundry list of criminal activity, not the least of which is murder. Sagan is the worst kind of phony. He's festering on the inside, then acts like he can hide it beneath the suits and ties he always wears."

No doubt hoping to disprove Dare's claim, Kathi shook her head. "That's not true. Mark doesn't always wear a suit. Sometimes he plays tennis, and he swims—"

In wide-eyed incredulity, Bishop swung around to stare at Kathi. "Shut up."

Breathing hard, Kathi frowned at him.

"I mean it." He looked at her as if she had two heads, as if he'd never really seen her before. Finally he turned back to Dare. "Enough of this nonsense. I know nothing about what you're saying. I wouldn't even know how to get such a thing done."

"Bullshit. With Sagan's muscle and Warwick's contacts in Mexico, you have everything you need."

Bishop didn't blink. "I would never risk the scandal of having my daughter kidnapped to some godforsaken place."

"No." Kathi put her hands on Bishop's shoulders. "He wouldn't. He doesn't even approve of her writing."

"I heard. And I figured that might be the motive." Dare stared at Bishop. "With the movie deal in the works, her name is really going to be out there. Folks will be making the connection, and soon you'll be known less for your own accomplishments and more as Molly Alexander's father."

Bishop narrowed his gaze on Molly. "It's absurd, all of it. You, at least, have to realize that."

Trembling, Kathi curled her lips in an unbecoming smile. "Speaking of your work, Molly, I presume you haven't had much opportunity for writing lately, have you?"

Molly sent a tight smile right back at her. "Actually, I've written quite a bit. Dare has a computer that he lets me use. At present, I'm only a little behind schedule."

Dumbfounded, Kathi lost her smile. "After your... ordeal, you still took time to write?"

Molly shrugged. "Writing has always been my entertainment, and my escape." She gave her father a defiant look. "It's always been my way of coping with the uglier things in life."

With a critical sneer, Kathi looked her over. "Then you obviously weren't hurt all that badly, were you?"

"Bad enough," Molly told her, and she never faltered from holding Kathi's gaze. "But I wasn't about to let those creeps, or anyone else, ruin me." She sniffed, and said as if it made perfect sense, "I do have a deadline, you know."

Dare wanted to intercede, but it seemed important to let this little exchange play out, so he kept silent. He had a feeling that before now, Molly had never really told her father or stepmother how she felt about their mistreatment of her.

Fidgeting with the sleeve of her sweater, Kathi asked, "What about your...controversy?"

"What controversy do you mean?"

Dare gave Molly points for pricking Kathi's already crumbling façade. The older woman barely held herself together. She looked like she wanted to sob, or perhaps fly at Molly for bodily harm—all in defense of her asshole husband.

Interesting.

Dare stayed alert. The verbal abuse was difficult

enough. No way in hell would he let either of these monsters lay a finger on Molly.

Before anything more could be said, Kathi noticed Bishop giving her the oddest look, and she drew in a long, deep breath. "Forgive me. Bishop prefers that I not speak of her books in his presence. In the middle of all the turmoil, I forgot myself."

Bishop worked his jaw. "Exactly. This is hardly the time for chatting about her outrageous career choice." In clear recrimination, he watched Kathi a moment longer before turning back to Dare. "I say again, I would never get involved in such a thing."

"Stick with that story if you want. My goal now is to keep Molly and Natalie safe, whatever it takes."

Kathi made a rude sound. "Why ever would Natalie be in any danger?"

"Why wouldn't she be?"

Kathi waved a hand at Molly. "You said whoever took her wanted Molly."

"No, I didn't." Softly, Dare told her, "We don't yet know why she was taken. If it wasn't Bishop, then the threat could be to any or all of you. But I promise I'm going to get to the bottom of it, no matter what it takes."

"Fine." She dismissed his warning as unimportant. "As long as you accept that Bishop wasn't involved."

She wanted verification that her husband was in the clear. She wouldn't get it from Dare.

Molly stayed rigid beside him; for her sake, he needed to end this and soon. "I think my next course of action is to go to the law. This wasn't done by one person. Whoever arranged it had help. Once the story breaks, someone will talk." He leveled a look on Bishop. "Someone always does. And then we'll know the truth."

Putting his head in his hands, Bishop whispered, "I'll be ridiculed, ruined…"

"A little useless gossip is all you care about, right?" Dare tugged Molly into his side. She was too silent, and it worried him. But when he looked at her, she appeared more thoughtful than hurt. "The fact that Molly was taken doesn't even factor in?"

Sighing, Bishop lifted his head and looked up at his daughter. A flicker of genuine emotion showed. "I can still see the bruising," he said quietly. And then, "You'll be okay?"

"Yes." Molly positioned her chin as she always did when on the defensive. "Thanks to Dare, I'm fine now."

"She was damn near dead when I found her," Dare said. "Drugged. Tortured. Dehydrated and starved."

Molly gave him a sideways glance at how he played up her mistreatment. She *had* been tortured, but probably not in the way her father and Kathi now assumed.

"Molested?" Kathi asked.

Molly shook her head. "Don't sound so broken up over it, Kathi. They spared me that humiliation."

Her sarcasm was wasted. "Well, I would assume…that is, if you were truly treated so badly, why would they not have raped you?"

"Goddamn it, Kathi! *Shut up.*"

Startled by Bishop's rebuke, she was quick to say, "I'm glad you weren't subjected to that."

Sitting back in his seat, Bishop ran both hands through his hair. He took a steadying breath, and locked gazes with Molly. "You might not believe me, but I'm truly sorry for what you've suffered, and you need to know that I had nothing to do with it."

Molly said nothing.

"If you go public, no one will believe that you weren't

used sexually. You realize that, I'm sure." Bishop shook his head. "Your life will be under a microscope, Molly. Not only will you damage me, but your sister's livelihood as a teacher could be at stake, and you'll ruin yourself, as well."

"Natalie only wants what is best for me," Molly told him.

Dare admired her aplomb under fire. "And, you know, I think it'd work as publicity for Molly's novels." No way in hell would Dare let that happen, but Bishop couldn't know that. His opinion of Dare was not favorable.

And that suited Dare's purpose just fine.

"Think about it," Dare said. "Every newspaper and magazine out there will be talking about her and, by association, her books. Her sales are already through the roof with the movie deal, but this would bring a real focus to her and her work."

Incredulity widened Kathi's eyes. "Monster," she whispered with venom. "You would destroy my husband and all he's worked for to *promote* her?"

Dare lifted a shoulder in negligent disregard. Molly, God bless her, held her own council. "It'd be a by-product of finding the truth, but what the hell? All publicity is good publicity. Isn't that what they say?"

"I can't stop you," Bishop announced, and when Kathi started to protest, he warned, "That's enough from you."

She subsided.

Coming around the desk to face Molly, Bishop studied her. "I've always credited you with being a smart girl."

She gave him a *yeah, right* look.

"No, I don't approve of what you write, but you've made it a profitable enterprise. You knew what you wanted, and you stuck to it, worked at it, and you've gained your own success. Unlike many young people—"

"Dad, I'm thirty years old. Not a child."

His expression softened in sadness. "To someone pushing sixty, thirty is still young, believe me. My point is that you've avoided the pitfalls of drugs, alcohol or lack of initiative. I think you could have done more, something truly worthwhile with your talent—".

"Entertaining others is worthwhile," she insisted. "Not everything in life has to be a lesson."

Bishop let out a long-suffering sigh. "Debating it now is futile. What I'm attempting to say is that I want you to think long and hard about this. Don't make yourself a matter of public gossip just to hurt me."

Indulgent, more understanding than Dare could believe, Molly huffed a small breath. "Oh, Dad, don't you see? Not everything is about you. This happened to me, and I need to know who wanted me hurt, and why."

Bishop didn't touch her, not to embrace her in comfort, not to exert his paternal will and not to vent his anger. To Dare, the two feet between them felt like miles.

He was willing to bet it felt even wider to Molly, a chasm that would never be bridged. Even as a child, she'd learned to live with that emotional distance.

Bishop nodded his acceptance of her decision and looked at Dare. "When do you plan to go public?"

"Soon." Remaining noncommittal, Dare scooped up the photos of Mark Sagan and Ed Warwick and tapped them against his thigh. "First I think I'll get in touch with your buddies, maybe squeeze them a little."

"Your many connections, I suppose?"

"I have ways of getting to the truth, yes. Both men have a jaded history that they'll want to protect. If you're a party to this, they'll eventually let something slip. You know that, right?"

Bishop gestured in resignation. "Do your worst. There's nothing they can tell you about me, because I have never engaged in kidnapping, and I never would."

For once, Kathi held silent. She kept her gaze on her hands, and Dare almost felt sorry for her. *Almost.*

"I'm taking Molly back to my home with me."

"Where?" Bishop asked.

"Kentucky. A good four hours from here—well out of your reach."

Bishop gave a slow nod of compliance. "She'll be safe with you?"

"A hell of a lot safer than she ever was without me."

"Then I suppose that's for the best."

After a timid glance at Bishop, Kathi interrupted. "What about your contracts, Molly? The movie negotiations, your agent, your editor…" She dampened dry lips. "You could stay with us, here. You'd be safe, and then you could finish conducting your business."

Again Bishop looked at her as if she'd lost her mind.

"Not happening," Dare said before Molly or her father could respond. "She goes where I go."

"You could both stay, then."

"No. I have dogs at home that need my attention."

Bishop said, "Dogs?" while Kathi blinked at him in clear confusion.

"My girls," Dare said, knowing how they probably felt about pets that were, in all the important ways, a part of his family. "I don't like to leave them for long."

"You jest," Kathi said. "You're putting *animals* above Molly's safety?"

Molly put a hand on his arm. He understood, and let her handle it her way.

"Since most everything is done on computers, I can conduct my business dealings wherever I'm at. Dare's home is a very calming place. I'll be able to work on my deadline, and as soon as I let my agent and my editor know how to reach me, I'll be able to catch up on the legal end of things. There's no reason for Dare not to be with his dogs."

Bishop was impatient. "Can't they already contact you on your cell?"

"My phone, along with my purse, went missing after I was…taken." She steadied herself. "Dare has agreed to stop long enough for me to pick up a new cell today. If you want, I can call and give you the number after I know it."

Kathi nodded. "Your father and I would appreciate that, thank you."

Personally, Dare didn't give a shit what they'd appreciate. He saw no reason to give them the means to torment her further, but he'd leave that decision up to Molly.

"Time for us to go." Dare put his arm around Molly and started from the room.

Before he got far, Bishop said, "Wait."

Dare looked back at him. Indecision held Bishop in stony silence for several beats until his face pinched in reluctant decision. "I need a moment to speak with you. Alone."

Dare didn't trust him. "Molly stays with me."

Kathi had already hooked an arm around her. "She'll be fine with me. We'll wait just outside the room."

"No."

Bishop chewed over alternatives, and settled on saying to Kathi, "Step out, leave the goddamned door open and stay in view." And then to Dare, "Good enough?"

Not really, but Molly said to him, "I'll be fine, Dare. I promise."

Kathi rolled her eyes. "For heaven's sake. She's safe with her family."

Yeah, right. From what he'd seen, her family was worse than a hated enemy.

Dare pointed at Molly. "Stay where I can see you."

She smiled agreement.

Bishop moved to the farthest end of the room and waited for Dare to join him. Molly stepped out into the hall with Kathi. Dare heard her remark on a new painting and knew she was talking with Kathi to keep her stepmother from eavesdropping on whatever Bishop wanted to say to him.

So damn smart. And cunning. She put up with more shit than any woman ever should, and somehow, against all odds, she remained kind and open and honest. In and out of bed.

Dare accepted that he was fast falling in love with her. And little by little, the idea grew on him.

CHAPTER TWENTY-THREE

MOLLY WAITED FOR Dare to tell her what her father had wanted.

He didn't.

She knew he had his own way of doing things, a way proven effective. But it hurt her to be shut out, enough so that she didn't want to have to ask. For the longest time, they rode in strained silence.

But Molly knew she had to direct him to her bank, so she was the first to speak. She kept it curt and to the point. Dare had to know that she was annoyed.

And still he didn't volunteer the information.

At the bank, with Dare frowning at her, Molly deposited her checks, keeping a thousand dollars in cash. The bundle of money created a nice wad within a zippered compartment in her purse. While at the bank she also cancelled her two credit cards.

Next she directed Dare to the post office, where she found yet another pile of mail waiting for her in her post-office box.

"You don't have all your mail delivered to your apartment?"

Molly shook her head as she flipped through a dozen or more envelopes. "Not from readers, no." She glanced up at him. "It's safer to keep my residence private. I'm sure the majority of readers are lovely people, but reactions to fictional work can be very subjective. Why take a chance?"

"Agreed."

She paused over one letter in particular. There was no return address. She stuck it back into the pile for now. The post office wasn't busy yet, so she was able to finish in a short time. Dare was quick to get her back out to his SUV, and all the while he looked around as if expecting someone to jump out at them.

His gaze went past the car dealership across the street—and then snapped back for a suspended moment before casually looking away again.

Trying to be discreet, Molly peeked up, hoping to see what Dare had seen. All she noticed was nice, shiny new automobiles and a few well-kept used cars.

They were still in the parking lot, so Molly asked, "Do we need to leave quickly?"

He looked at her curiously. "No, why?"

So he wasn't going to tell her whatever he'd seen across the street, either? She rolled her eyes and handed him the letter.

"What is it?"

"From my most critical reader."

Brows lifted, he opened the envelope and read the scrawling text with a judicious eye. "Interesting."

"Repetitive," she countered.

"You didn't read it yet."

Shrugging, she again looked across the street—and noticed a shadow in the front driver's seat of a black car. "It's always the same thing from that reader," she said without really thinking. All her attention focused on that shadow.

Were they being followed? Was there any immediate danger involved?

Uneasiness raced up her spine.

"Let's go."

"Just a minute." He turned over the envelope to check the front.

"There's no return address." There never was. And she really wanted to go.

Still Dare studied it. Without a word he folded the envelope, put it in his pocket and finally started the SUV.

Molly hooked her seat belt. Striving for some sense of normalcy, resenting the return intrusion of fear, she turned to Dare. "Is there a reason you're keeping my mail?"

"There's always a reason for the things I do." He checked behind him, then backed out of the lot and steered into traffic. "Any other stops?"

Oh, she could play this game if that was what he wanted to do. "I wouldn't mind stopping somewhere to buy a wallet. Maybe if we get the phone at a mall, I could find a wallet then."

"No malls. But you're a quick shopper, so I'm sure we can work it out." He pulled out his cell and put in a call. While it rang, he said, "Let's get into Kentucky first, though. I'll feel better about it then."

"That's fine. As long as I get to call my editor and agent before it's too late." Molly didn't know who he had on the phone, but she went silent when she knew the call had been answered.

"How are my girls?" Dare asked first.

Ah, so he'd called Chris. While she continually peeked out the side-view mirror, watching for that black car, she half listened to Dare. He caught up with Chris and told him that they'd be back before dark. It'd be a relief to settle into Dare's home with him again. She felt calmer there, less expectant.

But Kathi was right; that could be a problem.

While Dare and her father had talked in the library, Kathi had used the time to whisper warnings to her, all in the name of stepmotherly concern. But she had made one very valid point.

As the one who had rescued her, Dare held responsibility for her continued well-being. But when would his sense of obligation end? As long as she remained in his home, would there ever come a point when he would be comfortable in ending their relationship? How, Kathi had asked, could Molly ever know Dare's true feelings as long as he was saddled with the task of caring for her?

Molly glanced over at Dare and noticed him watching the rearview mirror. Her stomach knotted.

"No, I'll take care of that once I'm home," Dare said into the phone. He listened again for a few minutes and then said, "Thanks. Call Trace back for me. Ask him if he and Alani want to meet for dinner tonight. Yeah. Tell him anywhere along I-75, from Cincinnati down, would work. He can pick the place, but get back to me soon on what he has to say." He nodded. "Appreciate it. Tell my girls I'll be home soon." Dare ended the call.

She couldn't keep the frown at bay. He'd made dinner plans for them without conferring with her. She had no say in his decision.

And why should she? She reminded herself that she was a guest of Dare's hospitality; of course he had to maintain a regular schedule, and he couldn't do that by completely putting his life on hold for her.

Dare held out his phone to her. "If you want to make any calls right now, you can use my phone."

She thought about it and decided she wanted to get it out of the way. "Thanks." Right now, any routine normalcy, like talking business, would be welcome.

She called her agent first. As it worked out, once she'd

explained to her that she'd been "caught in circumstances beyond my control, which left me incapable of calling," her agent was very understanding and offered to get hold of the editor for her. She also had several things she needed to fax to Molly for immediate signatures.

Molly checked with Dare, got his fax number and shared it with her agent. Using the excuse of being under the gun on time, Molly promised to talk more when she could, and she told her agent that she'd explain in more detail when she was able.

After she handed the phone back to Dare, he asked, "Everything okay?"

Molly nodded. In the beginning, she'd been so excited about the movie, so flattered and so proud. Now, it seemed almost insignificant in the scheme of things. Her priorities had shifted in a big way.

"She was far more understanding than I thought she'd be."

"No big questions?"

"No, thank God. She just said that she hopes I'm okay and to let her know if she can do anything."

Dare grinned. "You're making her a lot of money."

Molly shrugged. "Sure. But she's also a very nice, warm woman with loads of good business sense."

While she had Dare talking, Molly decided to venture into her concerns. "Will Natalie truly be all right?"

"I don't think anyone wants to bother her, but even if they did, Jett's going to keep an eye on her. He won't leave her alone, except for when she's at school." He put a warm hand on her thigh. "Try not to worry, okay?"

Resting her head back against the seat, Molly wondered how she could *not* worry. Especially when she again saw Dare look in the rearview mirror.

Still with a hand on her thigh, Dare asked, "What are you thinking?"

It wasn't like her to play games, so she gave him an honest answer. "I was going over conversational pieces."

"Like?"

"Mark Sagan in, and out of, a suit." She swiveled her head to look at Dare. "It was strange how my stepmother said that, don't you think? Almost as if she knows him more intimately than we first thought."

Dare chewed his upper lip, glanced at her, then back to the road. "You picked up on that, huh?"

He had to be kidding. "Didn't you?"

"Yeah." He shifted in his seat, put both hands on the steering wheel. "Yeah, I did."

"Dare?"

His mouth flattened.

"Oh, for crying out loud." She'd had enough of his macho posturing. "I'm not that fragile, you know. I won't break."

"You've been through a hell of a lot. That business with your father and his nutty wife…" He shook his head. "Damn, Molly, that was painful for me to watch. I can only imagine how it is for you to live it."

He'd been distracted in his concern for her? Okay, she could forgive that—as long as it ended right now. "That's the one good thing to come out of all this. I realize now that I have very real endurance. If what happened to me had happened to someone else I know, I'd expect her to be falling apart. And I'd understand if she did. But…" She shook her head. "I really am going to be okay. I know it, and I can't tell you what that feels like, but it's…good."

"It's empowering." Voice low, expression intimate, Dare said, "Your strength is undeniable."

Such a smooth talker. Somehow Dare made a comment on her fortitude sound like a very sexy compliment. "Then we agree that I'm not the type to crumple into an emotional mess. So, out with it." She half turned to face him, as far as the seat belt would allow. "Does your silence have to do with that car following us?"

Surprise flashed in his gaze before he masked it.

Molly rolled her eyes. "I'm not a complete dummy, either."

"I'm aware of your many qualities, honey, you don't have to keep reminding me." He checked the rearview mirror again. "I would say that car likely means that we're on the right track."

"You think Dad sent people to follow us?"

Dare hedged. "I'm still mulling things over."

Narrowing her eyes, Molly said, "Mull them over out loud. It'll help bring clarity."

His gaze clashed with hers for a heartbeat, and then he looked away with a grin. "You really are getting back to normal, aren't you?"

Her neck went stiff. "Meaning what?"

Now the grin turned into a laugh. "Nothing insulting, I swear. You were just so damned polite and reserved at first, it made me nuts." He glanced at her again, all over her. "I like this new..." He thought about it, then shrugged. "Confidence. But more than that, really. You're self-assured, poised, assertive." He held out his hand, and when she took it, he lifted her palm for a kiss. "I'm glad that you're getting back some of your own."

Molly gave him a stern and direct stare. "I think this is your way to avoid telling me what my dad wanted with you."

"Wrong." He let her go to return his hand to the wheel

again. "Your dad asked for a little time before I break the big story. That's all."

"But you aren't planning to break a story anyway."

"We know that. He doesn't."

"What was his reasoning?" A horrible thought occurred to her. "Did he offer you something in exchange for your silence?" She wouldn't put that past her dad. Public humiliation would be hell on earth for him.

"He did." Dare took an exit off the more rural streets and onto the I-75 highway. "He offered to hand over the one responsible."

Her stomach lurched, and pain squeezed around her heart. Damn it, she'd thought herself immune to her father's vitriolic machinations.

Apparently not.

Trying to hide her reaction, Molly nodded. "So he does know who's responsible?"

"Not exactly, no. But he has a few ideas, and in an effort to exonerate himself, he's going to do a little checking on his end. At this point, I don't think his snooping around will hurt anything, so I told him to go ahead. Later in the week, I'll call him to find out how it's going."

"He really believes that you would throw the story out there for the media?"

"I was convincing, wasn't I?"

"Not to me, but then I know you better than he does." Molly wasn't at all sure that she really wanted to know, but neither did she want to hide her head in the sand. "So who does Dad suspect?"

"He wouldn't say." Dare worked his hands on the wheel. "But I believed him that he has an idea or two. And you know…" He thought about it, glanced at her and away, then admitted softly, "I'm rethinking him as the one responsible."

It felt like a weight had been lifted from her, with just that possibility. "Really?"

"Something didn't fit. I don't know. I'm sure your father is a slick liar."

"He's a shark, in business and out."

Dare nodded. "But he seemed genuinely insulted to be accused of having you hurt."

Ridiculous hope sprang to life. She knew her father would never love her, but apathy would be easier to bear than deep hatred.

With tentative caution, Molly admitted, "To me, too."

Dare slanted a measuring look her way. "You didn't say anything."

She looked down at her hands. "I guess my trust in you outweighs my need for my father's affection." When Dare's silence wore on her, she looked up to see a very thoughtful frown on his handsome face. "I didn't want to obviate your instincts with my own, likely jaded, perspective."

"Actually," he told her, "I trust your instincts, too, so always feel free to tell me what you're feeling."

"Do you mean that?"

His frown darkened more. "Of course I do."

"All right." She took a breath. "Then why are you keeping me in the dark?"

That accusation didn't sit well. "I tell you everything you need to know."

Now, that hurt. "So, I'm on a need-to-know basis?"

"No. Don't twist my words."

"You're the one who said it." Her throat felt thick. It was insane that something so small could hurt her feelings on the heels of everything else she'd been through.

Dare made a visible show of striving for patience. After

another glance in the rearview mirror, he took an exit toward a newer strip mall.

He said nothing, so she didn't, either. But she hated the tension between them.

After he parked, he watched the mirrors, waiting, and when the black car didn't show, he turned off the SUV, released his seat belt and reached for her.

Molly stiffened in surprise. "What—"

Holding her shoulders, Dare pulled her over the console and kissed her. This was no friendly peck. His lips worked over hers until she parted them. Then his tongue stroked in. The kiss was hot and deep, and oh-so-stirring.

Molly came up for air and straight-armed him. "If that's your way of shutting me up—"

He laughed and kissed her again, this time for a tickling, teasing smooch. "That was my way of making myself feel better." He smoothed his thumb over her cheek. "From the very beginning I've been irresistibly drawn to you. If you're near enough, I'm going to want to touch and kiss you for no reason other than that I like it."

Oh. Grudgingly, she said, "I like kissing you, too."

"I know you do." Smiling, he dropped his hands and stared out the windshield while he gathered his thoughts. "I always work alone, Molly. Other than Trace, there's never been anyone that I confided in to help me sort out details when I was on a case. When I'm not sure about things, I don't want to alarm you, or give you false hope."

She could understand that. "But nothing is ever really concrete, is it?"

"I can usually narrow things down to some pretty damn good guesses."

His lack of modesty amused her. "I know. And I understand why at first, you tried to…shield me."

"It hasn't been that long yet." He turned his head to give her a long look of consideration. "Yeah, you're more relaxed every day, but it's there, Molly. I see it in your eyes still. The fact that someone is following us—"

"Still?" She twisted around to peer out each window, and saw no one.

"You see? You're jumpy as hell about it, when there's no reason. Do you honestly think I'd stop here if there was any danger to you?"

Venturing the right reply, she said, "No?"

"So much confidence in me." He shook his head. "No, I wouldn't. We're being followed, but not aggressively. Whoever is on my tail is a pro and probably just wants to know where I'm going with you. Hell, it could be your dad just keeping up with you out of concern."

She snorted.

"Yeah, I doubt that, too. But it's possible."

"Want me to call him and tell him to back off? If he knows we're on to him—"

"No."

"Because…?"

"It might not be him, and I don't want to tip off anyone."

Molly let out a sigh, and insisted on the truth. "So, what's the most likely scenario?"

After gauging her interest, Dare shrugged. "I'd say it's probably someone who wants to know where I'm taking you in the hopes of getting to you again."

Oh, God. She bit her lip. Hard. Then nodded. "Okay, so I assume that you have a plan?"

"Yeah." Blue eyes glittering, Dare said, "To kill anyone who tries to touch you."

"Oh." Rubbing her forehead didn't relieve the sudden

pressure there. "You know, maybe if it's possible *not* to kill anyone—"

"And that's why I don't tell you everything." He opened his door and circled around to her side. When she stepped out, he held her face to kiss her again, this time with measured gentleness. "It's not on you, Molly. You have no reason for guilt over anything or anyone. Understand?"

She nodded. In reality, she didn't blame herself. But the idea of someone dying just because he followed her father's orders...

Growling in exasperation, Dare put his arm around her and started her forward. He kept his gaze straight ahead when he said, "If it's at all possible to safely detain without killing, then I will."

He made it sound like the grandest concession. Odd that she had to fight a smile over something so serious. "Thank you, Dare."

Drily, he said, "Don't mention it." He opened the door to a wireless store, and they went inside to pick out a phone. While Molly perused the selections, Dare got a call and stepped over by the door to talk. Molly used the time to make her purchase, paying for the phone in cash before Dare could give her more frowning looks over it. It was the oddest thing, how he objected to her spending her own money.

In some ways, he was the most old-fashioned man she'd ever met. In other ways, he was by far the most advanced. In every way, he was unique.

The small shop also had a supply of cell-phone covers with matching wallets, so she was able to kill two birds with one stone. With her bagged purchases in hand, she went over to Dare just in time to hear the tail end of his plans with Trace.

Dare closed his phone and put it away. "All done?"

Nodding, Molly told him, "I got a wallet here, too, so I don't need to stop anywhere else."

He scanned the parking lot before opening the door and leading her out. "You getting hungry? We'll meet Trace and Alani right before we get to my place, so not for three hours or so, depending on traffic. We can grab something before then if you want."

"Are you hungry?" Big as he was, Dare probably needed to refuel often.

"Getting there." He looked around the area and spotted a bakery a few doors down. "How does a bagel sound?"

"Not as good as a few donuts."

Grinning, he conceded that and together they picked out a bag of mixed donuts with large coffees. "Anything else?" Dare asked her.

Thinking of the long ride ahead, she said, "I'll take a juice, too." And at the last minute she snagged kettle chips and added them to the purchases.

When Dare made a point of not saying anything, she elbowed him. "It's awful, I know. But I eat when I'm stressed."

As he paid the cashier, he said, "I don't want you to be stressed."

"Tough." She hooked her arm through his, and they headed back for the SUV. "I know I'm safe with you, Dare, I really do. It's just that I hate the necessity for you to have to protect me."

"Molly—"

Knowing he didn't understand, she cut him off. "I wish I was just safe, without any qualifiers, you know? Like I used to be."

"I understand." He opened her door and then handed her their goodies. "It's unfortunate, but now you know that no one is ever truly secure. There are dangers out there, always, and sometimes you can't avoid them. It's a hell of a lesson." He kissed her and then shut the door.

Is that how Dare felt? Is that how he'd always felt? Did he live his life forever on guard against peril? What a terrible way to live, always waiting for something to happen.

When he got behind the wheel, she said, "Dare?" And when he looked at her, she stretched over the console so that she could initiate the kiss this time. Smiling, she told him, "I like this kissing business, too."

He didn't smile back. Instead, he put one big hand around her neck and drew her forward for a deeper, firmer kiss that left her coiled with need.

While Molly tried to regroup, he reached around her to fasten her seat belt, then prepped his coffee and put it in the cup holder.

Molly licked her lips. "Wow."

"Yeah." Since she didn't do it herself, he fixed her coffee, too. "We have some powerful chemistry going on between us." He put the SUV in gear. "Now, how about a donut?"

He really could rattle her thoughts. She put a donut in a napkin and started to hand it to him. "You really don't think my dad is the one behind this?"

Though she'd asked that totally out of context, Dare knew exactly what she meant. "I think we shouldn't jump to any conclusions at all."

That nonanswer had her withholding the donut before he could get it. "Dare?"

The grin flickered before he grew serious again. "I'm leaning away from him as the instigator." He took the donut. "By tonight, I should be able to give you a more definitive answer. How's that?"

She supposed it would have to do. And if he had a straight answer tonight, if he discovered the one who'd orchestrated it all…then what?

Molly took one more look in the mirror, but didn't see anyone.

"He's still there," Dare told her. "But he's not going to be a problem. Relax, eat your donut and trust me."

CHAPTER TWENTY-FOUR

FEW PEOPLE WERE inside the restaurant when they got there. Dare had chosen it because he knew the owners, it had decent home-cooked food and it was right off the highway.

He spotted Trace and Alani, already inside and seated at a back, more private, table. With just a look from Dare, Trace understood that he'd set this up for a reason well beyond socializing.

Dare and Molly headed toward them.

As usual, Dare made note of how Molly was different from other women. At five feet six inches, Alani was close to the same height as Molly, but Alani had a more willowy build. With her long pale hair and golden eyes, she always looked a little ethereal to Dare. Like a whimsical creature of the night. Those who knew Alani always treated her gently, which was one reason the kidnapping had devastated Trace so badly.

Dare knew that Alani was beautiful, but for him, he saw her as a little sister, without a single ounce of sexual magnetism.

Molly, on the other hand, was so intrinsically sexy that Dare didn't understand how she'd stayed single so long. There was real substance to her, not in weight or height, but in attitude, in her bearing and her determination.

Trace stayed behind his sister as they rose to greet Dare and Molly.

After a nod at Trace, Dare said, "Alani." He pulled her into an affectionate, one-arm embrace while keeping a hold on Molly. "It's good to see you again."

"You too, Dare." Distracted with curiosity, she peeked past him to Molly.

Dare put a hand to the small of Molly's back. "Molly, I don't know if you remember Alani or not, but—"

"Of course I do."

With her bottom lip caught in her teeth, her eyelashes fluttering, Alani showed her nervousness.

Molly was just the opposite. She stepped right up to Alani and took her hands. "How are you, Alani?"

Alani nodded. "I'm fine."

Laughing, Molly looked over her shoulder at Dare. "Don't let him hear you say that. He has an objection to sugarcoating things." After giving her a long, sympathetic perusal, Molly drew her into her arms. "You were so brave, Alani. I had hoped that we'd get to meet again. I'm so glad to see you looking so well."

Alani put her face in Molly's shoulder and clung to her.

Trace lifted a brow.

So softly that no one else could hear, Molly spoke to Alani, which earned her a tighter hug and a shuddering nod.

Dare drew his friend aside. "Let's let them talk a moment in private."

Reaching back with one hand, Molly shooed them away, then urged Alani to sit down while still staying close to her, holding her hands, talking to her.

They both heard Alani give a short, watery laugh, and then saw her nod at whatever Molly had said.

"Damn. I didn't expect that." Trace watched his sister

with growing concern. "She was fine a few minutes ago."

Alani was only twenty-two, and she'd always been very protected. Not that Molly had led a worldly lifestyle herself, but again, there was that difference in backbone. Molly's home life had made her tough, whereas Alani's had done just the opposite. "If you say so."

Trace rubbed the back of his neck. "Yeah, it's bullshit. She's holding it together, but she's still shaken."

"Who wouldn't be?" While watching Molly with Alani, Dare pulled Trace back a few steps more, toward an empty corner. "I'm being followed. Black Charger, newer model. I don't want you to risk Alani, but—"

"No problem." Trace folded his arms. "How many in the car?"

"Molly only saw one, but I've picked up three."

Trace gave him a blank look. "You told her about the tail?"

Shaking his head, Dare explained, "She spotted it herself." And damned if it didn't make him proud to admit that.

"No shit?" Looking back toward Molly with new appreciation, Trace whistled low. "That's bound to make things more difficult for you."

"I don't know. She's pretty levelheaded about it all." Then Dare grinned. "But she did ask that I try to refrain from killing anyone."

Shaking his head, Trace said with a laugh, "Women."

Even now, Dare couldn't keep his eyes off her. "Actually, I think for me it's just this one particular woman."

"You're serious?"

Definitely serious. "I don't have it all figured out yet, but I'm not about to let her go."

They shared a look over that, and Trace gave Dare a commiserating pat on the shoulder. "Don't worry about your tail. I'll keep an eye on things. If anything goes down, I'll be on it."

"Appreciate it."

"No." Trace drew in a deep, emotional breath. "The appreciation is all mine. Alani might be struggling, but thanks to you, she *is* going to be okay."

"I'm glad." Seeing that the women were ready for them now, Dare asked Trace, "What will you tell her? About following me home, I mean."

"The truth."

That shocked Dare. Trace had protected Alani from the edgier aspects of his career for most of her life. "She's ready for that?"

"I think so. She says she wants to know everything, all of it, because being sheltered left her ill-prepared for what..." He stopped, tightened his fists. After a second he cleared his throat, and still the words came out raspy with emotion. "For what happened."

Dare felt for him. It seemed Trace was having as hard a time as Alani.

"You've done right by her, Trace." As they headed back to the table, Dare added, "Beating yourself up is only going to add to her guilt."

"She said the same." He shook off the tension and forced a smile as they reached the women. Without missing a beat, he picked up the conversation on careers.

"Alani is an incredible interior designer," Trace bragged, "but Dare didn't let her do his place."

Dare pulled out the chair next to Molly. "You both know that I'm particular."

"And no one knows you like you. I know." Alani rolled

her eyes and said to Molly, "But Dare does have great taste, so I can't fault him."

"Agreed. His house is incredible—inside and out."

That gave Alani pause.

Dare said, "She's staying with me."

"Oh." Alani tried not to react to that, but she still ended up grinning at Dare and saying slyly, "I didn't realize."

Molly wasn't put off by her humor. "Once I get my life back in order, I think I'll buy a house of my own."

Dare sat back. "Since when?"

"My apartment… Well, it's obviously not secure enough, so I can't see me going back there to stay." And then to Alani, "If you have the time when I'm ready to buy, I could use some professional help, I'm sure. Maybe we can work together."

"Oh, I'd love that!" Alani gave her a business card, and for a few minutes they discussed Molly's preferences and style.

Dare couldn't believe that Molly was thinking along those lines. Where the hell did she think she'd be moving to? Was she just biding her time until it was safe to leave him?

Yes, he knew that eventually they'd have to work out the relationship kinks. But the idea of her moving away… No, he didn't like that idea at all.

Trace flagged the waitress. "I don't know about the rest of you, but I'm starved."

"Judging by Dare's black mood, he's hungry, too," Alani teased.

Molly looked over at him, and concern colored her expression. "Dare? What's wrong?"

Knowing he was scowling, but not about to explain why, Dare tried to lighten up. "Not a thing." He picked up a menu, even though he knew it by heart.

After they'd all ordered, he reached for Molly's hand and spoke to his friends. "Did Molly tell you that she's a writer?"

"She did!" Alani nodded. "Romantic suspense. It's exciting, isn't it?"

"No kidding?" Trace asked about her work, and Molly patiently answered his questions. Lacking subtlety, Trace said, "I wouldn't wish it on anyone, but this could almost be research for you."

Molly looked struck by that observation. "I hadn't…I mean, it didn't occur to me…"

Alani took sympathy on her. "Danger and romance probably mix better on paper than in real life."

The danger part, yeah. He wished like hell he could have spared Molly. But the romance? How did Molly feel about that? No way could it be worth what she'd gone through, but if it hadn't been for her abduction, he wouldn't have met her.

Molly didn't quite look at Dare when she said, "The dose of reality has been an eye-opener, that's for sure."

Dare hoped he didn't end up in a book, but then, he trusted Molly to have discretion.

For the rest of the meal they all socialized like everyday, ordinary people, as opposed to women who'd been abducted and men lethal enough to maneuver outside the law.

Considering the circumstances, it actually turned into a relaxing social time. Dare enjoyed watching Molly interact with Trace and Alani. Trace was smoother than him, but still managed to intimidate most people.

Not Molly.

She kept steering the conversation away from her writing and back to others, asking questions that weren't intrusive or insensitive, but came from genuine interest.

Trace smiled at her a lot—and so did Alani. Yes, she still seemed fragile, but with Molly, Alani related on a deeper level.

For her part, Molly didn't treat Alani with kid gloves the way so many others did. She treated her as an equal, and Alani responded to it.

When they were ready to leave the restaurant, Molly again embraced Alani. "I would love it if you stayed in touch." Lower, she said, "And if you ever need to talk, know that I'm always available."

Alani gave a tremulous smile. "I wish I was as strong as you."

That made Molly laugh. "Trust me, if you'd seen me going to Dare because of a silly nightmare, or because I couldn't bear to be alone with my thoughts, you'd know I wasn't that strong at all." She squeezed Alani's hand. "We each have to deal however we can. I'm so lucky that Dare was there for me, and you have a brother who loves you. I hope every woman who was there has someone as caring to help her through this now."

"Me, too." Alani stepped over next to Trace. "Let's get together again soon."

Trace hugged her. "We'll see them again soon enough."

They were back on the road, radio playing, when Molly said, "Did you ask Trace to follow us home?"

Dare gave her a double take. Would she always surprise him like this? She couldn't have overheard him talking with Trace; she'd been focused on Alani at the time. And no way in hell would she spot Trace. He was far too good for that.

Skirting a direct answer, Dare said, "Why do you ask?"

"I don't know. There was just something in his expression when we said goodbye."

She was so damned intuitive. "Yeah, he's back there."

"Just in case?"

"That's right." The days were getting longer, but already the skies had darkened. It wasn't the season so much as the weather. Clouds rolled in, leaving everything gray and downcast. "I'm not worried about the highway. But we have to take a lot of side roads to get to my house, and that could leave us vulnerable."

Molly reached over and put her hand on his thigh. "Before you say it, I won't worry. But if you notice anything happening, would you please tell me? I prefer to know what's going on and I promise I won't get in the way or panic."

"You want to be prepared."

She nodded. "I don't ever again want to be taken so completely by surprise."

"All right."

She put her head back and closed her eyes, but left her hand on him. Briefly, Dare covered it with his own.

It felt good to be going home.

It felt even better to have Molly with him.

THOUGHTS IN TURMOIL, Bishop sought privacy to make his call. No, he didn't trust the library. But his bedroom no longer felt secure, either. Not for this.

Unsure where to go to avoid the prying eyes and ears of servants and his doting wife, he headed out to one of the garage bays. Head down and guts tight, he went behind the building, uncaring of the landscape he trampled or if he ruined his shoes.

For a while now, he'd had awful, unthinkable, unacceptable suspicions, but as yet they hadn't been confirmed. Now…now he felt more positive than ever. Though he was due to meet with his discreet investigator for an update in a few days' time, he no longer wanted to wait.

The second the call was answered, Bishop said, "Do you have anything for me?"

A pause sounded on the other end. "Bishop?"

Though no one could see him, he slashed his hand through the air in a sign of impatience. "Who else would it be?"

"I thought we were going to meet in person."

"I can't wait. Now, do you have anything to tell me or not?"

"As a matter of fact, I do." In a quieter tone, the investigator said, "You were right. I'm sorry."

Feeling sick, Bishop closed his eyes—and smelled his wife's perfume. He spun around, and there she was, her gaze on him, searching, caring. She approached cautiously, unsure of the situation.

He was used to her deference, and before now, it had only mildly annoyed him.

"Bishop?" she said, sounding small and afraid. "What are you doing out here?"

Had she followed him? Breathing hard, filled with revulsion, Bishop held the phone down to his side. "It was you, wasn't it?"

She summoned a small, placating smile. "What was me? Who are you talking to?"

He wanted to tell her that it didn't concern her. But it did. It concerned her in a very big way. "You've been cheating on me, Kathi."

Alarmed, her head shaking, she fell back two steps. "What are you talking about?"

Lifting the phone out toward her, Bishop shouted, "I

have a man following you, damn it. I know. I knew even before I hired him."

"But…how?"

God, did she really consider him such a fool? Well, no more. "You think a man can't tell when his wife is fucking someone else?" He moved closer to her. "You honestly believe I'm that obtuse?"

She shook her head. "It's not like that." And then, beseeching, "I did it for us. For *you*."

Incredulous, Bishop stared at her.

Exasperated, she explained, "To protect your reputation."

Was she insane? "Having a whore for a wife is supposed to *help* me?"

"I'm not a whore! How could you say such a thing?"

Bishop just stared at her. "You disgust me."

"Don't you see?" Kathi reached out, almost touching him, but he stepped away. "She would have ruined everything."

Sickness crawled in his guts. He closed the phone, belatedly preserving his privacy.

Already knowing what she'd say, but praying he was wrong, he asked, "Who?"

"Molly."

Dear God. So it was her.

Energized by his apparent interest, Kathi surged forward, trying to get hold of him, but again he stepped back. If she touched him, he'd kill her.

"What did you do, Kathi?"

"You heard Dare. They're going to make her book into a movie. Don't you understand? You haven't read her, Bishop, or you'd know that I had to do something to protect you, and me, from being tainted by her popularity. Her stories are…depraved, just as you've always said.

The characters are entertaining, yes, but they're without moral standards. I tried to tell her, but she's ignored my letters."

Sweat gathered on the back of his neck, his temples. "What letters? What are you saying?"

Kathi looked off, talking as much to herself as to Bishop. "She refused to change anything, and now it's going to be a movie and all the world will know. They'll find out that she's your daughter, and they'll know what type of person she is, what type of daughter *you* raised."

She was insane. Trying to make sense of everything, Bishop asked, "You…ransacked Molly's apartment?"

"I had to. Somehow that horrid man got her out of Mexico. I didn't know where she was, or what she was doing."

Christ almighty. "You had Molly kidnapped?" His daughter could have died…because of his wife. Repercussions slammed through his brain; he couldn't bear it. "But…*how?*"

"Oh, that part was easy." She half laughed. "Mark knows all kinds of people. He easily arranged everything." Going smug, she added, "For me."

So, Dare was right. She had involved Sagan and in the process left them both exposed to unthinkable consequences.

He looked around, expecting thugs to jump out of the bushes at any moment. "Do you know what you've done?"

She twittered a laugh. "Don't worry. Mark thinks we have something special, but he doesn't understand that I did it for *you*." As if sharing a confidence, she leaned forward to whisper, "George is going to kill him for me. After he's taken care of everything else."

Her twisted logic left Bishop floundering. She spoke of killing with the same detachment she gave to housekeeping duties. She actually appeared proud of her cunning, as if she'd helped him to handle a tricky business deal.

Suddenly what she'd said presented a new horror. *After he's taken care of everything else.* Heart thundering, Bishop grabbed her shoulder and slammed her up against the brick facing of the garage bay. His fist twisted in her finely made top. "Where is George now?"

"Bishop," she complained, trying to wriggle free, fussing at the damage he did to her clothing.

"Where is he?"

Her bottom lip came out in a pout. "He's gone after Molly and Dare, of course. You heard what Dare said. He wants to destroy you. But I'm not about to let that happen. Thanks to you, I have everything I ever wanted, everything that's important to me, and no one is going to rob me of it." She put her arms around him and laid her head on his shoulder. "I love our life together too much to ever risk it."

Arms at his sides, strangled by loathing, Bishop accepted the truth; everything he'd worked so hard for would be destroyed. And though indirectly, he had no one to blame but himself.

He couldn't cover up something this monumental. That she'd whored around on him, playing him for the fool, was bad enough. But to be complicit in the rest…

Once the news broke, he'd be pitied by some, scorned by the rest.

But it beat the hell out of dying.

Determined, he shoved Kathi back an arm's length away but retained a bruising hold on her upper arm. It shamed him to know that, for even a second, Kathi had thought he'd go along with his daughter's murder.

Deciding on a course of damage control, he started across the lawn toward the house.

"Bishop?" Kathi resisted him with each step.

Calmly, to keep her off guard, Bishop said, "Come with me now."

"Oh. Yes, of course." She drew a breath and stopped fighting him. "What are we going to do next?"

At the front of the house, he found the other guard standing there, dark sunglasses in place, but with an alert stance.

Bishop stopped in front of him and shoved Kathi forward. "Were you fucking her, too?"

"No!" Kathi reached out for him, but he kept her away. "Bishop," she pleaded, "don't be like this."

Startled, the guard went very still. "Too?"

"George," he said.

The guard pushed his sunglasses to the top of his head; he didn't so much as look at Kathi. "No, sir."

The relief was overwhelming. "Do you value your job, then?"

Without hesitation, he affirmed, "Yes, sir. Very much."

"Then restrain her." He pushed Kathi forward, and the guard automatically caught both of her arms. Lifting his phone to punch in a number, Bishop said, "The police will be here soon enough."

"No!" Kathi fought with a decided lack of class or refinement.

Bishop turned away from her, but he couldn't tune out the awful noise. And he couldn't tune out the grinding guilt.

CHRIS DIDN'T LIKE IT when the alarm system glitched, shutting off and back on. Twice. It reset itself as it was programmed to do, but still he stewed. Had the weather affected things? It wouldn't be the first time the weather had tripped something. It was all electrical, but on a backup system, too.

Going to the porch outside, Chris looked down the hill to the lake.

Though colder winds buffeted him and he could smell the impending rain in the air, it wasn't all that bad yet. Beyond the lake, to the north behind the hills, he saw black clouds rolling in and bringing with them brilliant bursts of lightning.

Both dogs nervously circled his legs, almost tripping him. Sargie whined, and Tai put her ears back. Noisy weather sometimes spooked them, but this was odd behavior, especially since the thunder hadn't yet reached them.

He crouched down to talk to them. "What's the matter, Tai? There's no noise yet. Dare will probably be home before the rain gets here, so you don't need to worry." She crowded in close to him, making her worry clear.

Sargie, always the jealous sort, wormed in front of Tai to soak up his attention, too. She whined in anxiety.

Laughing, Chris dropped to his ass and let the dogs crawl over him. To help put them at ease, he tussled with them a little, played and petted. In mere minutes, the skies darkened enough that the security lights flickered on.

Sargie turned and started a furious barking. She looked toward Chris's house, but Chris saw nothing amiss.

"What's the matter, sweetie? Did a leaf spook you? Is there a frog deserving of your wrath?" Often, when Dare was away, the dogs spooked easily. "Doesn't say much about your trust of my abilities, does it?"

The lake grew turbulent, rushing up to the shore to

splash over rocks and plants before ebbing out again. Fish jumped. Birds circled, swooping low.

He loved nature. He loved his place here.

If Molly became a permanent fixture, would it change anything for him? He liked her. Dare more than liked her.

Damn it, he didn't want to be a third wheel...

The sound of a car sent the dogs bounding away and around the house in barking excitement. Chris was quick to follow. It had to be Dare, because no one else could get past the gates.

But when he saw Dare leaving the car, he knew something was wrong. The look on Dare's face said it all.

Molly, bless her, didn't appear to notice. She took her time greeting the dogs and laughing at their enthusiastic welcome.

Quietly, Chris said, "What is it?"

"The gate was tampered with."

"Shit. How so?"

"Looked like someone tried to pry open the control box. The plants on the ground around it were trampled."

Chris chewed his bottom lip as he thought. "Everything flickered twice, but came right back on."

"Yeah." Dare looked around, then got knocked back a step when Sargie jumped up to greet him. Because Molly was watching, Dare laughed and let Sargie snuffle around his face before dropping down again, racing off and back from Molly to Dare. She even included Chris in her gusto, though he'd been with her the whole time.

Tai came over and leaned on Dare until she'd had her fill of gentle attention.

Molly looked up at the sky. "It's going to be a storm."

"Storms on the lake are something to see," Dare told her.

Tai grabbed her attention by turning and presenting her butt for Molly to scratch. Chris laughed. "On her back just above her tail is her favorite spot."

Dutifully, Molly bent down to scratch.

Turning his back on Molly, Dare asked, "Everything secure inside?"

"I was in there until just a few minutes ago. No one could have gotten in."

"What about your place?"

Damn. "The dogs were barking..." He shook his head. "But you know how they get spooked when you're not around, and then with the storm... I didn't see anything or anyone."

"I don't want to take any chances." Concentrated in the way he got while working, Dare searched the immediate grounds. "Take Molly inside while I look around."

"Not a good idea." Chris stopped him. "If something comes up, you should be with her. If someone has intruded, she's the one they want."

Dare looked downright lethal over that possibility.

"Go get her settled," Chris said. "I'll check out my place, lock it up and come right back."

He knew Dare didn't like that plan, but Molly joined them, and, given that she was the priority right now, he gave in. "Finish up and then come back to the house, ASAP."

Molly frowned over the curt order, so Chris was quick to say, "I'll give you a full report on the dogs in just a few minutes. Coffee is ready to go—all you have to do is switch it on."

"Thanks." Dare gathered Molly close into his side. "Come on. Let's get in before it starts to rain."

"What about our stuff?"

"My job," Chris said, walking backward a few steps. At the side of the house, he turned. Damn it, now Dare had him feeling anxious when he doubted there was reason to be. "I'll be right back."

Because he jogged off, Sargie decided to follow him. Usually she'd be glued to Dare's side, but she thought Chris was playing, and honestly, he didn't mind the company. "Come on, girl. We'll get this over with before we get soaked."

Telling himself that everything was fine, Chris went down the lighted path to his front door. Tall budding trees, swaying in the wind, surrounded the perimeter of his smaller home.

Sargie found a stick, tossed it and then chased it down again.

Though the dog was no longer concerned, Chris felt an eerie sense of uneasiness edge up his spine. He looked at the curtains on his front windows. He was almost certain that he'd left them open, but now they were closed.

His jaw locked. With Sargie right at his side, he opened the front door, deliberately making noise. Stealth was Dare's thing; he'd prefer to confront any intruders head-on—or better yet, give them the chance to hightail it out of there without any confrontation at all.

A flip of the wall switch showed that the combined living room, kitchen and dining room was empty.

Now.

But footprints on his carpet meant that someone had been inside. They came from the hallway leading to his back bedroom. Crushed leaves, dirt, mulch—all the things around the outside of his windows at the back of his small house.

Chris stared down the hall toward the bedroom, took one step in that direction—and smelled the smoke.

"Oh, shit." He stepped back to the front door to yell for Dare and found him already coming down the slope.

Dare had the Glock in his hand, and he looked really, really pissed.

"GET OUT OF THERE," Dare shouted to Chris. Tai followed on his heels, but Dare knew he wouldn't be able to dissuade her from following. After Trace's call, it was all he could do to give strict orders to Molly before going after Chris.

Trace told him that the car he'd followed was missing a few people, and when he questioned—aka forced answers from—the lone man left behind, he was told they were setting up a distraction at the smaller house so that they could grab the woman.

The type of distraction is what really shook Dare.

Furious, Chris looked back at his place, undecided, Dare knew, on whether to try to put out the fire or to do as Dare instructed. He still stood in the doorframe.

Dare cursed. "Move, damn it, it's a—" His words were swallowed by a loud blast.

Flames shot out of the shattered windows, and Chris hurtled face-first out the door and onto the ground.

"No." Running now, Dare reached Chris just as he rolled over onto his back with a groan.

Dare had to push Tai away from Chris; she was as worried as Dare was. Kneeling over Chris, Dare saw the rising lump on his forehead where he'd landed against a rock. He took Chris's shoulder and demanded a response. "Say something, damn it."

Chris coughed.

Thank God.

If Chris had been any farther in the house when the blast happened, he probably would have been killed. But they had little time for rejoicing right now.

Dare leaned over him. "Anything broken?"

"No." Chris shook his head, but stilled that movement real fast, wincing as he raised a hand to his head. "Jesus, what was that?"

"Fucking bomb. If you're sure you're okay, I need to get you clear in case anything else goes off."

"Yeah, I'm okay." He started to struggle upright.

"Let me." Dare hoisted him to his feet, but Chris's legs wobbled. He was hurt, and it scared Dare so damn bad he had to clench his jaw to keep from howling. He locked an arm around Chris, turned—and found Molly standing there, her hands twisting together, her expression ashen.

Red-hot rage hammered inside Dare. She was supposed to be locked inside, safe.

Before he could speak, she did.

"They're in the house, Dare." Her pale lips trembled. "A window broke and the alarm went off, but someone shut it down.…" She panted, gulped air, and whispered, "I heard them. I…I couldn't stay in there with them." She covered her mouth as she looked at Chris. "Oh, my God, is he okay?"

A hand pressed to his head, his nose bleeding, Chris nodded. "Yeah." In a smoky rasp, he asked, "Did Sargie come out?"

Molly's eyes widened, and just that easily, her own fear evaporated. She looked beyond Chris, gasped and took off running. "I'll get her!"

Dare went blank with panic. *"No!"*

But Molly didn't listen. Christ, if anything else blew…

Never in his life had he been so divided. Done with delays of any kind, Dare lifted Chris half over his shoulder, making him moan and curse, then moved him several yards away. He eased him down to the ground against the base of a large oak tree and told Tai in the sternest voice she'd probably ever heard from him, *"Stay."*

Ears flattened, she plopped down beside Chris with a heartbroken whimper. Even as hurt as he might be, Chris locked a hand in Tai's collar, and Dare knew that short of passing out, Chris wouldn't let her go.

It had taken him mere seconds to settle Chris, but in that time, Molly could be caught in another explosion.

Blood rushing hot, Dare rose to go after her—and she came tripping out the front door of the house, leading Sargie.

Relief nearly disabled him.

Dare shoved the gun into his waistband and reached them in a few long strides.

Sargie was panting, eyes wide, as much in panic as from the smoke that now colored her beautiful fur. Molly had tears tracking her cheeks.

But neither of them appeared to be injured.

Dare grabbed them both and practically dragged them up to Chris.

"She was cowered down, scared, behind the door," Molly babbled. "I think the door is what kept her safe. She came right to me, though. She's going to be okay, isn't she, Dare?"

"She'll be fine."

"And Chris?" On her knees, Molly jerked around to Chris and smoothed his hair away from the blood on his forehead. "Oh, God, Chris, you could have been killed."

Dare's eyes burned. After all his fucking assurances,

all his confident promises, Molly could have been killed, too—but he couldn't think about that right now.

She'd saved his dog.

He closed his eyes, overwhelmed and out of control. But that just made him relive the moment when she'd rushed into Chris's house, when he'd realized what he'd lose if anything happened to her.

He had to get it together.

After a deep breath, Dare said softly, but with iron demand, "Be quiet now."

Molly looked at him, but he didn't meet her gaze. She would unravel him if he did. He couldn't soothe her yet, couldn't crush her close or tell her...

He sawed his teeth together and cleared his mind.

Under cover, he passed the gun to Chris and closed his hand around it to ensure he had a good hold. "Okay?"

Chris took a breath. "Yeah. Got it."

But Chris didn't look good. He probably had a damned concussion—or worse. Dare's heart twisted...

"I'm up for it, Dare. Just go."

Molly's mouth opened twice before she gasped, "Go *where?* What are you talking about?"

Dare couldn't seem to make himself move. If this all went wrong, if the intruders spotted Chris with that gun, they'd shoot him dead. Fuck. *Fuck, fuck, fuck.* He filled his lungs, and tasted smoke. "You know I love you, Chris."

Chris focused pain-filled eyes on him. "God, man, not now. I'll live, I swear." And then, grudgingly, he muttered, "But yeah, love you, too."

That exchange only worked to further incite Molly's fear. She grabbed Dare's arm. "What are you doing? We need to get out of here."

He peeled her hand away and guided it to Sargie's

collar. "Keep the dogs here for me. Do not let them go." He couldn't look at her; if he saw her expressive eyes, he'd falter. "Remember, there are two of them."

He had to speak louder to be heard over the crackling of wood, the hissing as the fire consumed Chris's home. Smoke billowed into the air and the flames licked the sky, sending an eerie orange glow to dance over everything in the immediate area.

He'd told Molly that he would keep the story quiet, but how could he do that now? He hadn't counted on the crazy fucks blowing up Chris's house. Even if the security system wasn't set to alert the authorities, the fire would draw them.

Dare turned to gaze up at his own home just as two men stepped out. Black hoods covered their heads and faces. Seeing them kicked him into automatic pilot.

He knew what to do, and he'd do it.

Narrowing his concentration, Dare watched their bodies, how they moved, how they held themselves. He recognized George Wallace, the guard from Bishop Alexander's home. The man had a distinctive stance and telling body language.

The other man he hadn't yet met, but he knew his type and what he wanted, what he was capable of.

Each of the men held guns.

Without taking his attention off of them, Dare said to Molly, "Stay here with Chris. Do. Not. Move."

He could feel Molly watching him, but she said not a word.

Sensing danger, both dogs went berserk. Molly hugged Sargie, restrained Tai, and tried to shush them.

With a groan, Chris repositioned himself, turning to get a good view but keeping mostly concealed behind the trees. "I got this, Dare. No worries."

Nodding, Dare stood and stepped out into the open. He composed himself as he went up to the men. All the emotion had to be put aside. Rage, worry... He couldn't think about that right now.

Deliberately, he went cold and hard. One step at a time, not racing but not hesitant, either, he closed the distance between himself and the two men who were now his targets.

They had broken into his home, had tried to kill his best friend and had possibly injured his dogs.

They were men who wanted to harm his woman.

Dare flexed his neck, his knuckles. The side of his mouth lifted in a deadly smile. He was ready.

Hell, he was more than ready.

George stepped forward. "That's far enough."

Dare stopped, his stance casual, unconcerned. "Where's the third guy, George?"

His body quickened with surprise. "What are you talking about?"

"You thought I didn't know? I recognized you right off." Dare shook his head. "You are so fucking dead," he told him and started walking again.

George lifted the gun higher. "Stop, goddamn it!"

Dare stopped, but only to say, "What do you want with her?"

Feeling in control again, George laughed. "It's just a game. No one's going to kill her."

"So you're playing with her? Why?"

George shrugged. "More like detaining her."

"In Mexico?"

"Out of sight, out of mind."

Knowing Molly was probably listening, but seeing no help for it, Dare nodded. "I see. So it is Kathi, huh?"

Both men went still.

Idiots. Bishop had suspected his wife after her ridiculous scene in the library. No, he hadn't named her, but Dare had suspected her, too. Knowing Bishop likely had his own agenda, Dare hadn't ruled out other possibilities.

But then he'd seen that most recent hateful letter from the post office. No return address, but the postmark showed it was mailed from within the same town.

"Fess up now," Dare told them, "and I'll let you go." To give the lie credence, he showed his teeth in a semblance of a smile. "Otherwise, I turn you over to the feds."

"Bullshit." Though it was falling apart around him, George tried to bluster his way through. "You can't do anything."

"You know better than to believe that."

He aimed the gun at Dare's chest. "No one wants the woman killed. But you, you're plenty fucking expendable."

Dare's expression didn't change. "You're already too late, you know."

The man with George got antsy, taking his attention back and forth between George and Dare. "What's he talking about?"

"Shut up," George told his accomplice. He took a step off the porch toward Dare. "He doesn't mean anything."

"That's not precisely true. The minute you fucked with my security, a report went out. Cops will be here any minute. On top of that, I knew all along that you were following me. When I stopped at that restaurant? That was just to give my friend a chance to follow *you*." Dare looked beyond them and, as if he saw someone, said, "Right on time."

The second man jerked around to face the new

threat—and Chris shot him in the back of his shoulder. The impact of the bullet propelled him forward and into the back wall. He sank down to the ground.

George looked over at his buddy for only a second, and Dare charged him. George jerked up in time to get off a single shot, but the bullet only grazed Dare's arm.

No way in hell would that slow him down.

As if they'd timed it, the skies opened up in a torrential downpour. Dare tackled the guard, and they both went down hard onto the porch. George's head gave a satisfying thud against the concrete. The gun skittered out of his limp hand.

Another shot sounded, and Dare glanced over to see Chris standing there, soaked to the skin, the rain mingling with the blood to trail down his face. Though he wavered on his feet, he held the gun secure in both hands.

He'd shot the other man again to ensure he wouldn't be a threat, just as Dare had always instructed him to do.

Using his elbow, Dare struck George in the jaw and felt the tension in his body slacken. Grabbing him by the shirtfront, he hauled him up to punch him hard, once, twice.

He wanted to kill the son of a bitch. The *need* to kill clawed inside him.

But he had promised Molly. And she needed the whole truth, every word of it. He couldn't get that from a dead man.

With an effort, Dare pulled back.

George was utterly limp.

With his twisted sense of humor, Chris asked, "You done?"

"No." Dare grabbed the hood and yanked it off of

George's bloodied and battered face. His nose was broken, his jaw already turning purple. "I'm just getting started."

CHAPTER TWENTY-FIVE

DARE PUSHED TO HIS FEET and looked at Chris. "You sure you're okay?"

"Yeah." He curled his lip. "But it's not like I'd complain about a bump on the head or this freezing rain, not with you standing there all macho, a damn bullet in your arm."

"Shit, I forgot about that." Dare realized then that his arm was half numb, half aching. "It was just a graze, I think."

Chris rolled his eyes—and almost fell over.

Dare looked around for Molly. Frozen, drenched, she stood several yards away—right where he'd told her to stay—with a hand latched onto the collar of each dog.

God love her. "Molly, come here."

Even from the distance he could see her hard swallow. She started slogging forward through the downpour, half dragged along by the dogs.

"You can let them go."

George stirred, regaining Dare's attention. "There's a third man with Trace, but just in case, don't let down your guard." Dare picked up George's gun, kicked the other man's gun out of reach, and then checked them both for any other weapons.

At the mention of a third man, Chris started scanning the area.

The dogs were subdued, upset, watchful. They crept forward, ears and heads down, body language showing their fear. They wanted Dare's attention and couldn't understand the circumstances.

Dare took a moment to reassure them both. "Good girl," he told Sargie. He stroked Tai's wet fur. "It's okay, baby."

Hugging herself, her eye makeup trailing down her face, Molly stood cold and silent, just out of his reach.

He started to go to her, but to do what? This was far from over, and now the whole world would know what had happened to her.

Would she be able to forgive him for underestimating the situation?

Trace came around the side of the house with another man in tow. The fellow's face was bloody, one eye swollen shut, his hands bound behind him.

"He was the lookout in the car," Trace said without much inflection. "He's the one who told me about the bomb." He pushed the guy to the ground to sit. "So. Everyone okay?"

It took a lot to rile Trace when on the job.

"Yeah, we're all fine." Dare felt freezing rain trickling down his back. As Molly had said, *fine* was a subjective term. "Where's Alani?"

"Inside." Trace glanced at Chris, whistled, and said, "You look like hell. Maybe you should join her."

Gladly, Chris handed the gun over to Trace and turned to Molly, gesturing to her. "Come on, hon." He gave Dare a mean look. "Let's go get dried off."

She blinked hard and fast, swallowed again.

Dare wanted to reach out to her, but he couldn't touch her. Not yet. To Chris he said, "Yeah, take her inside."

"I was already doing that, damn it."

Chris was pissed at him and not trying to hide it. But then, Chris didn't understand just how emotionally involved Dare was this time.

Molly unglued her feet from the mud and stomped up to Dare. Her bottom lip trembled, she made a fist, and then she thumped him in the chest.

Unsure what that was about, Dare caught her hand and held her still. "Go inside, Molly. Change your clothes. I'll be in soon."

She just stood there, looking equal parts furious and frightened. She shook her head and said, "Dare..."

Chris wrapped an arm around her. "Shh. Come on, now. He knows what he's doing."

"All this," she whispered, her voice breaking. "All this because of *me*."

Chris glared at Dare again.

Knowing he'd have to say something to her, Dare said, "That's nonsense. Now go in."

Trace lifted a brow. "Real smooth, Dare. I can feel the love from over here."

George groaned, and half sat up.

Molly pushed away from Chris, saying, "I'll go in, but you should help him."

"Why would I help him? He took part in burning down my house."

She slugged Chris, too, but not as hard as she'd hit Dare. "Not him, you idiot. *Dare*."

Chris grinned, and it was a lopsided, ridiculous-looking thing considering the damage to his head. "Believe me, Dare doesn't need any help with that trash. Now, come on. Alani is inside, and I know she'd like the company."

"Go on," Dare said to his girls. They, too, were soaked—but thanks to Molly, they were both alive and well. "Go with Chris."

Chris called the dogs to him, and Molly, almost by rote, caught Sargie's collar.

Dare said to Chris, "Call Henrietta. See if you can get her out here, the sooner the better."

"I'll tell her you'll pay double," Chris said. And then to Molly, "Henrietta is the vet, and her business hours are over for the day. But when I throw around Dare's money, business hours mean nothing."

Molly put an arm around Chris to help steady him. Sargie almost pulled her off her feet, and Tai, after one look back, caught up to Chris. They made a wide berth around the downed men and went in through the kitchen.

The strangest thing happened to Dare. He watched them all until they were out of sight, and he felt…whole. Complete in a way he never had before.

He had three men on the ground in front of him, one of them maybe dead, and still, it was the best feeling ever.

Trace looked at his arm. "Let's wrap this up. You and Chris could both use a little medical attention."

"Right." With Molly out of sight, Dare grinned at the man Trace had contributed. "I have some questions first."

"Fuck yo—"

Dare's boot hit him in the ribs, and he doubled over, wheezing in pain.

George surged to his feet and tried to throw a punch, but Dare grabbed his hand and squeezed—and felt a few fingers break. George bellowed, and Dare was quick to wrap an arm around his mouth. "Shut up. You're going to frighten her more, and I don't want that to happen. Do you understand me?"

His face contorted in pain, George nodded.

"Good." Dare let him go and helped him to sit back down. "Now, you can answer my questions, or I can break more bones. Up to you—and believe me, I'm fine either way."

Out of the corner of his eye, he saw Trace step to the side, his phone to his ear. His friend would call this in, but before anyone arrived, Dare would know everything. After that, the law could have them all.

ONCE THEY WERE inside the house, Molly went for several towels. She found Alani sitting stiff and frightened in the living room, and rather than coddle her, she said, "Come on. I could use your help."

Alani jumped to her feet. "What's happening?"

"Dare and Trace have the men...subdued. It's fine." After they gathered up several thick towels, she led Alani to the foyer, where Chris and the dogs waited. "Help me dry them."

Alani took her arm. "I'll handle the dogs. You should go change."

Molly looked down at herself and winced. The cold had seeped into her bones, and she wondered if she'd ever be warm again.

"Go on," Chris told her.

"Let me help you change first." She put her arm around him again. "Dare's clothes will fit you."

Chris tried to object, but she didn't let him. He held it together, but anyone could see that the knock to the head had hurt him badly.

In Dare's bathroom, she stripped off Chris's shirt and gave him a crewneck sweatshirt to wear.

His black hair was plastered to his head, in some places stuck with blood. His blue eyes looked vague. And still he teased, saying, "Touch my shorts and we're going to have a problem."

"Modesty?" Molly asked, pretending everything was normal, instead of chaotic and insane.

"No one has changed my pants for me since I was

five." He leaned against the sink. "Go on and get yourself changed. I can do it."

Molly nodded. "Tell me before you come out, because I'm going to change, too."

"I won't peek if you don't."

She found a half grin over that, but honestly, she was so cold and scared, and so devastated, that she felt anesthetized.

She'd just finished pulling on one of Dare's big flannel shirts and a pair of the shorts he'd bought her in San Diego when the dogs came running in. Alani had done a good job at drying them, but Sargie's eyes were still too red and her fur showed signs of smoke.

Molly's composure almost cracked. "Poor baby," she whispered and went down to her knees to hug the dogs again.

Chris asked, "You dressed?"

Alani answered for her. "Come on out."

Now with them all relatively warm and dry, Chris sat on the bed and used the phone to call the vet. It amazed Molly how he teased with Henrietta and coerced her into a house call without really telling her anything that had happened.

When he hung up, Molly said, "Shouldn't we call the police?"

"The security alarm does that automatically. But if they get here too soon, the bastards will call their lawyers and Dare won't be able to get the info he wants." Eyes closed, he dropped back on the bed. "Let Dare find out what's going on while he still has the opportunity."

Sargie leaped up onto the bed to snuffle around Chris's face until he gave up and sat forward again. Molly started to say more when they all heard the sirens.

"Shit. That sounds like the fire department. Someone

must have seen the smoke." Looking steadier by the minute, Chris pushed off the bed. "I have to tell Dare that his time is cut short."

Dare stepped into the bedroom doorframe. "No need."

Molly shrank back. Dare…didn't look like Dare. There was a vibrating tension about him, a set to his mouth and harshness in his gaze that was more dominant than anything she'd ever seen. He'd wrapped his shirt around his injured arm, leaving him in a soaked T-shirt and sodden jeans.

He looked rugged, capable.

Deadly.

And he'd shut her out.

She felt like a stranger to him. It ripped up her heart to think of how hurt he and his friend had been, all because of her.

Alani didn't seem to notice Dare's dominant manner. She went over to him and hugged him tight, totally at ease with him in this strange mood. "Where's Trace?"

"Keeping watch on our goons." He kissed her forehead. "Why don't you and Chris go start some coffee? We could all use it."

Alani looked back at Molly and, with understanding, nodded her consent.

The dogs bounded off the bed and went to him. Dare knelt down to give them the attention they so badly needed from him. His gentle tone, filled with sympathy, went a long way toward calming the dogs.

Molly needed attention, too, but…she didn't want to force herself on him.

The fretting was awful, unbearable, so she asked in a whisper, "Did you kill anyone?"

"The one Chris shot might not make it." He looked up,

considering her for only a moment before adding, "And don't you dare feel bad about that."

She bit her lip. "Okay."

Grudgingly, or so it seemed, Dare said, "The other two should be fine."

Her chest hurt. "You're okay?"

"Yeah." His gaze was direct, intense. "You?"

"I'm fine." Sliding off the bed, she went over to him. He stayed down on one knee with Sargie squeezed up against his chest and Tai lolling on her back to get her belly rubbed.

With him looking down at the dogs, talking softly to them, Molly could see the nape of his neck, the breadth of his shoulders and the muscles in his back. She put a hand in his wet hair—and her knees almost gave out. Trying to make her voice strong, she asked, "You were shot?"

"Bullet grazed my arm. It's nothing."

Still smoothing his wet hair, she sank down beside him. She wanted to grab him, kiss him all over and beg him to...what? She just didn't know. Everything felt so uncertain now.

Already, blood soaked through the shirt wrapped around his "nothing" injury. "You need to go to the hospital."

He turned his face so that her hand was on his jaw. "Trace called paramedics for the guy Chris shot." His gaze locked on to hers again and held her captive. "They'll be here any minute."

I love you. She wanted to say it so badly, but this wasn't the time. They'd soon be overrun with cops and other emergency personnel. He needed medical care, as did Chris. The dogs were still frightened.

There were a thousand reasons not to burden him with

her emotional excesses. But oh, God, it was hard keeping herself in check.

"Thank you, Molly."

Drawing in a shuddering breath, Molly whispered, "For what?"

He rubbed Sargie's ear, pulled the dog close to kiss her head, hug her into his chest. "You saved her."

His voice sounded strained, thick. "You would have done it. But with Chris hurt…"

His chest expanded. "When I saw you go into the house…" Breathing hard, he squeezed his eyes shut, and his voice went harsh. "I've never been so fucking terrified."

He sounded angry, sending regret to churn with the rest of her overwhelming emotion. "I'm sorry."

"Don't." His eyes flinched. "You have no reason to apologize. Hell, I should be apologizing."

She shook her head, not understanding him.

He looked back to Tai. "I scared you."

"No."

The look he gave her said *liar*. And that hurt.

Defensive, Molly shrugged. "Okay, you did. Just a little. But not like…not like I was afraid for me. I would never, ever fear you that way."

"Then how?"

"You were like a…a machine." She put both hands to his face, holding him, wanting him to know the truth. "You somehow took the love you have for Chris, and you turned it on those men. Not in an emotional way, but it was so…cold."

"Methodical," he corrected.

"Yes." She licked dry lips. "That you could…refocus like that, that's what scared me."

"It's necessary for the job I do."

But that type of power meant he could shut out anyone and anything. How could he ever really care for a woman if he could so easily turn his emotions on and off?

Scowling, he said, "If I hadn't—"

She nodded. "I know." She even managed an uncertain smile as reassurance that she *did* understand. "I'm so very glad that you're okay."

Disregarding the injury to his arm, he reached for her, hugging her so tightly that it took her breath.

"Dare?"

In a flat tone, he told her, "It's over."

She froze.

"It was your stepmother, honey. All of it. Some twisted, sick idea of protecting Bishop from your growing popularity."

"Kathi?" She shouldn't have been surprised, but… A strange relief overtook her. "So it wasn't Dad?"

Dare smoothed back her hair, cupped her jaw. "George's cell phone rang a little bit ago. It was Bishop. He got a full confession from Kathi."

Her thoughts went blank. "Dad called?"

"Yeah. He said that the cops are at his house right now." Dare rubbed her shoulder. "He wanted to warn you, honey, and calling George's phone was the only way he knew to maybe reach us."

Molly struggled to assimilate all that. "You don't look surprised."

"No."

And then she remembered. "I heard what you said to George. You knew it was Kathi, didn't you?"

"After talking with them, I thought she was probably involved. Bishop apparently thought so, too. That's why he said he wanted to check into things."

Dare explained to her about the postmark, the way

Kathi spoke so familiarly of Mark Sagan, and how protective she was of Bishop.

"What I didn't know, George gladly filled in."

"Gladly, huh?"

He shrugged. "I'm sorry, Molly. Kathi wanted to make you understand her idea of morality, that you protect what you have, or you lose it. No room for mistakes, no room for human error."

Thinking aloud, she whispered, "The character that I redeemed…"

"In Kathi's mind, there is no redemption. There's only the perfect appearance." His thumb brushed the corner of her mouth. "I guess she figured if you were going to find fame, it had to be with her moral code, with characters she approved of."

"I wonder if she ever really enjoyed my work, or if she just read it to keep tabs on me." It made sense, because the minute her popularity really bloomed, Kathi took action against her.

Dare bent to put a soft kiss on her lips. "According to George, she never intended to kill you. She just wanted to throw off the movie deal. Once the opportunity was lost, she was going to have you released."

A rush of anger shot through Molly. "I might not have survived that long!"

As if that thought hurt him, Dare briefly closed his eyes.

Refusing to dwell on her stepmother's deviousness, Molly let her thoughts skip ahead to other details. "She and George…?"

"They were having an affair. But George wasn't the only one. Kathi was sleeping with Sagan, too."

"So you were right about that." It amazed Molly, how

much Dare had figured out, how he'd put the puzzle pieces together.

"That's how Kathi arranged everything. When George found out, he had this sick need to prove himself to her."

Not being a dummy, Molly guessed, "By killing Sagan?"

"His death would take care of any evidence against Kathi, and remove Sagan as a threat to her or to Bishop. But George was in way over his head. If I hadn't busted him now…"

"Sagan would have had him murdered."

"That's about it." Footsteps sounded in the hallway, and Dare stood, bringing Molly up with him.

"Kathi never would have left Dad for a hired guard."

"George was okay with carrying on an affair. He said she was worth it." Dare's mouth twisted. "But he was also financially compensated."

"So money was a better motive than love."

"She paid him with her own allowance, which I gather is substantial."

"It is." Kathi had often bragged about the extravagances Bishop lavished on her. He wanted his wife to wear the best of everything, drive the best…be the best. The irony gave her no satisfaction. "I guess Dad was devastated?"

Dare scowled. "A little numb."

"I understand that."

"Thing is," Dare said, "at least now he'll be alive. If for no other reason than to clean up loose ends, Sagan would have killed him after he got rid of Kathi and George."

"Dear God." Abhorrence left her feeling sick. "So much scheming."

"All of it centered around your stepmother." Dare lifted

her chin. "I don't get it. She's attractive enough, but she's nothing special, so why these men were so anxious to win her over—"

"Under the circumstances, you hardly saw the best of her. Most of the time, she's a charming hostess." For as long as Molly could remember, she'd enjoyed her stepmother's company more than her father's.

"I saw the real her. That's what everyone should see." He kissed her, and that felt so good, so real and honest, that Molly didn't want it to ever end.

Sliding his hand into her wet hair, Dare ignored the uniformed officer now standing there watching. "Outside earlier…I'm sorry if I hurt your feelings."

"You had a lot on your mind." She touched his jaw. "I'm sorry that I punched you."

Half smiling, Dare put his forehead to hers. "I couldn't look at you, honey. I knew you were scared, and as much as I needed to separate from everything that had just happened, and how I felt about it, I knew I couldn't, not if I saw how those bastards had affected you." He kissed her again, harder this time.

The officer cleared her throat.

"Give us a minute," Dare said.

Annoyed, she hesitated, then gave one sharp nod. "Make it fast."

Dare gathered Molly closer. "You need to understand something."

Her heart started thundering, and her breath felt trapped in her lungs.

"It isn't just Chris that I love, or my dogs. Christ, Molly, I could have faced off with ten men to keep you safe, because I love you, too."

Her knees felt weak again. She clutched at him, hopeful, dumbfounded. Elated. "You…?"

Dare smiled. "I love you like I didn't know I could love anyone." His eyes glistened, but only for a second. He looked down, took a few breaths, then met her gaze again. "I never thought it was possible, but you fit in here, Molly Alexander. In my life, my home and with my friends. Chris loves you, my girls love you."

He hesitated, frustrated, and glanced over at the cop. With a roll of her eyes she moved out of sight.

Dare held Molly's face in trembling hands. "Now that you've been here, nothing would ever be the same if you left."

"Are you…? Do you mean…?" She couldn't pull together a complete thought. So much had happened, but she knew how she felt, had known for a long time.

But she didn't want to jump the gun and do or say anything to make Dare's life more difficult.

"Stay with me, Molly."

Well, that was pretty clear. *"Dare."* God, she loved him. "Are you sure? No, wait." She put a finger over his mouth. "You're hurt, and you've been through hell tonight. You might not know—"

"I know."

She shook her head. "I mean, you've felt responsible for me for so long—"

"Hell, honey, I feel responsible for almost everyone. That's not going to change."

"You do?"

That gorgeous mouth of his curled into a sexy smile. "Everyone smaller, older, weaker, younger—"

Molly couldn't help but laugh. "And that covers about everyone."

He shrugged. "Trust me, what I feel for you is different. I'd love for us to be responsible for each other, but it's more than that. Hell, I don't know what to call it, because

I never felt it before now. But it's as real as it gets, and it won't change."

"I've never felt this before, either." Molly forced herself to think it through, instead of leaping with open arms. "Dare, you need to be sure."

His brows knit together. "Are you sure?"

She didn't care about protecting her heart or her pride. "I love you."

He let out a breath. "It's going to be a rough road ahead." He trailed his thumb over her cheek, along the line of her jaw, down her throat. "I haven't protected you well at all. That damned bomb is going to cause a stir. The law, both local and federal, is going to be all over this. There'll be a massive investigation, most of it centered on your stepmother and father. I'll pull some strings and keep you out of most of it—"

"Dare, no." She let out a breath, and smiled. "None of that matters to me."

"No?"

She shook her head. "Dad might care, but he and I have so little in common."

Filled with sincerity, Dare glanced at where the officer had been, and then lowered his voice. "I can spin this to protect him, too, if that's what you want."

"No." She put her arms around him. He had enough responsibility in his life; her father could fend for himself. "All I really want is you."

On a groan, he lifted her off her feet. "God, baby, you've got me."

The officer cleared her throat, and Dare released Molly to stand on her own again. "Are you okay to do this?"

Molly couldn't help but smile again. After everything else she'd been through, facing the police would be a piece of cake.

Just to tease him, she said, "I'm fine."

Dare rolled his eyes, but he smiled, too. "Come on, then. Let's get this over with."

MOLLY WORE HER cutest pajamas, the ones Dare hadn't wanted her to bring, when she went into the kitchen early in the morning and found Chris sprawled in a chair, more disheveled than not. Dare was at the stove cooking breakfast, and the dogs jumped up to greet her.

She petted each one, went to Chris to kiss him on the ear and then went to Dare to wrap her arms around him from behind.

He looked over his shoulder at her. "Morning, beautiful."

She gave him a squeeze, then went to pour some coffee. "Chris, you look more out of sorts than usual. Everything okay?"

Dare gave her a look. "All the decision-making on his new place is keeping him awake at night."

"Alani is a slave driver," Chris complained. "I just want the house done, but she keeps saying it has to be done right."

"Now, Chris," Molly teased. "You're hurting my feelings. Am I really so difficult to be around?"

He sat upright. "I didn't mean that."

"Are you sure?" For a couple of months now, Chris had been living in the main house with them while his home was rebuilt. "I know I'm an interloper—"

Both men protested so strongly that Sargie barked. Molly started out by snickering, but ended up laughing out loud.

Chris gave her a dirty look. "Not funny." And then to Dare, "She has a twisted sense of humor." He swilled some coffee and added, "I like it."

"Dare, don't forget that we're meeting Natalie and Jett for dinner tomorrow." They were needed back in town yet again. Her stepmother had been arrested, along with Mark

Sagan and Ed Warwick, but amazingly enough, her father hadn't been implicated in any wrongdoing. He was still bitter about how it had all turned out, the intrusion into his life and his business affairs. But he cooperated with the investigation and out of necessity spoke with Molly more often now than before her abduction. The scandal hadn't affected him too much, business-wise. There'd been gossip, of course, and long looks from some of his so-called friends. But all in all, he'd been business as usual, throwing himself into his work and his social life.

For her part, Molly stayed too busy with her writing, the exciting progress on the movie and loving Dare to worry overly about her father's affections.

"Let's pick out a ring while we're there, okay?" Dare put pancakes in front of her. "I like that little jewelry shop near where Jett works."

So much joy filled Molly, she thought she might burst. "All right." She reached for Chris's hand. "Want to come along?"

"Sorry. I'd love to, but the contractor will be here in an hour." He lifted her hand for a kiss to her knuckles. "Pick out something outrageous, okay?" He winked at her.

Chris did enjoy spending Dare's money.

"She can pick out whatever she wants." Dare put pancakes in front of Chris, too.

Once Chris had his house back and the legalities were all settled, she and Dare would marry. She was happy to wait and do it right. As long as she got to do it all with Dare, nothing else mattered.

Life had challenged her. Life had brought out her strengths.

Life had given her love—and knowing how it had all turned out, she wouldn't change a thing.

* * * * *